A QUEEN'S GLORY

KRISTIE M. HARRIS

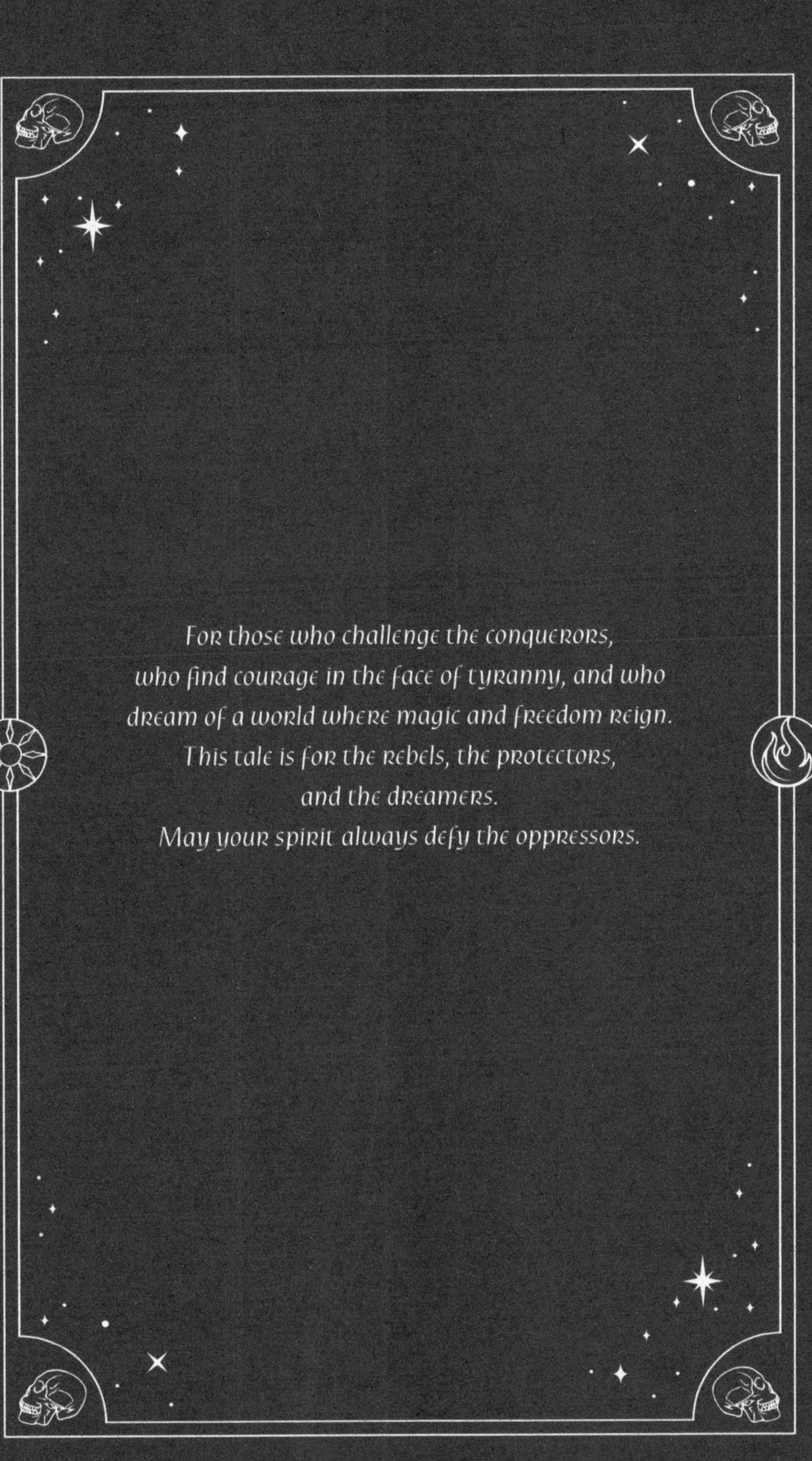

For those who challenge the CONQUERORS,
who find courage in the face of tyranny, and who
dream of a world where magic and freedom reign.
This tale is for the rebels, the protectors,
and the dreamers.
May your spirit always defy the oppressors.

EMODOREA
UNCHARTED LAND
TIMELESS FIELDS
TRETARA RANGE
NORTHERN MORTAL REALM
WINHELM
MA DESSA'S TRIBE
OSTERIA
THE WANDERING RIVER
NAVASSA
ZADEA'S PASS
NONNELLE
FOREST OF BRIELLE
THAMES
ORABELLE BAY
ALANAH'S HUT
ERIKAH'S COVEN
WITCH'S KEEP
SKY KINGDOM OF NONNELLE
THORNWELL
SOUTHERN MORTAL REALM
THE BLUE SANDS

CHAPTER ONE

Thornwell, Southern Mortal Realm

+ REID +

REID ABSENTLY FLICKED the small metal tin open and closed, each time letting his finger brush against the few cigarettes he kept inside, careful not to crease them. He lurked in the alley beside the pub, leaning against a damp, mould-covered wall. With his shaggy brown hair, face covered in filth and grime and a scratchy, pathetic excuse for a beard; it would still be a few more weeks before they'd let him in the front door.

Oscar, barely old enough himself, was due to give Reid the signal for his half-baked plan. Of course, none of Oscar's plans ever worked in their favour. Reid gently pulled out one of the cigarettes and popped it in his mouth. He closed his eyes and leaned his head back against the wall. Reid wasn't sure they'd pull this plan off, but they had to try. There was no way they would ever be out of debt to Gillian if they didn't start bringing in more goods. Nevertheless, he couldn't shake the feeling that Oscar was about to get them in more trouble than it was worth.

The boys had watched for a few weeks leading up to today, figuring out which patrons came back often, which ones weren't as drunk as they seemed, which ones would have the best haul, and what alleyway had the least view from the street. Well, at least that was what Reid had been doing. Oscar, on the other hand, had been more interested in the ladies who tended the bar. He repeatedly lost focus when they came outside for their short breaks.

It was worse when the mistresses from upstairs would leave after their night shift; they'd parade around inside waiting for their pay from the barkeep in their too-tight corsets and torn-up pantyhose. Oscar would stand there gawking at them like a scocin caught in a snakyte web, or at least what Reid assumed that would look like, since he had never been far enough west to see a snakyte before.

Reid was sweating; it had to be almost noon with how hot it had become. He wiped his brow, grime smearing across it, as he dared to sneak a peek through the window. Oscar had insisted that he should head inside first to help pick their target. He was meant to pop the window near Reid open enough for him to hear what was happening inside. But judging from how high the sun had risen, that was hours ago. There were only so many times he could risk peeking into the window before someone saw him. He was sure his companion had most likely gotten drunk or found his way upstairs to gawk at the women. The latter would never end well for him if they found out he was underage, or worse – that he had no money for them.

Though, with Oscar's looks, Reid wouldn't be surprised if a few of them enjoyed the change in company, considering what most of their visitors looked like. He'd heard enough from passing girls to know that Oscar was deemed to be attractive. Rarely did he overhear anything about himself. Which was probably for the best, since if he was too busy worrying about girls, Gillian would most likely make sure Reid didn't make it to his eighteenth birthday.

He slunk back against the dirty wall, water from the puddle at his feet seeping through his hole-ridden boots. He played with the golden feather that was woven into a piece of his matted hair. It was something he'd had since he was a kid. Reid's aunt had given it to him at some point when she was telling him stories of the great eagles that used to roam the Western World. Regardless, for one reason or another, it gave him peace of mind when he touched it.

He would have to leave soon; he didn't want to risk the guards seeing him here. They didn't care about street rats like him, so long as they kept themselves out of trouble. The first time he'd been caught stealing food from the markets, when he was six, the guards had taken pity on him and let him go. The second time, he was ten; he'd sneaked into a stable to sleep for the night. By his mistake, it had been the stable of a lord in the Inner Ring whose daughter had found him and called for them. He'd never known that a baker could be a lord, but he'd also never thought to venture into the Inner Ring before. He could still see her mousy face as she turned her nose up at his stench when they dragged him past her. He wasn't sure how long they left him in the cell for, only that Gillian had shown up at some point and paid the guards to let him go – Reid had been working the streets for him ever since. It almost seemed like the debt just kept growing, especially since O had come into Gillian's care not long after. He rolled his eyes at the thought.

Footsteps brought him back to reality and he scrambled up against the wall as the door was blasted open with more force than necessary. A bleary-eyed Oscar appeared in the alley, blinking his golden-brown eyes against the harsh sunlight. The stench of alcohol emanated from him as he stretched his arms over his head and yawned before turning to give Reid a lopsided smile.

'Sorry, chap, forgot you was out 'ere,' his thick Northern accent near-incomprehensible when mixed with the drunken slur.

'I've been sitting in this stinking alleyway for hours waiting for your sorry ass,' Reid hissed at him. 'How did you even get the coin to pay for drinks?'

Oscar opened his mouth to reply just as a loud shriek rang out from the upper floor. Instead, he winked at Reid and took off down the alley away from the street, stumbling as he ran.

'He left me a pile of coppers!' A woman screeched at the barkeep before the door swung open again.

Reid ducked out of the way to avoid it.

'You!' The woman pointed at him. 'I bet the blonde piece of shit was your mate!' She stepped into the alley, making way for the bartender, who followed with a pipe in his hand.

'Look, I didn't do anything.' Reid held his hands up in defence, scowling as Oscar's blonde curls disappeared over the wall at the end. His only way out was toward the street. The walls were too thick with grime for him to get a decent grip to climb. Typical Oscar, always leaving him in the lurch. If he weren't his only friend, he would rat him out to the guards, or worse, Gillian.

He turned from the mistress and her boss and sprinted toward the street. Curses flew at him as the man followed him down the alleyway, the woman returning inside, no doubt to send another lackey to meet him out the front. Finally, he reached the street, stopping only momentarily to decide which route to take. Left would take him in the direction he needed to go, but that meant passing the tavern entrance; right would mean avoiding an unnecessary confrontation but would take him past the guards' lunchtime patrol route.

Right on cue, a burly man with a bat stepped out of the front door, deciding his direction for him. He hurtled down the street to his right, both men now in pursuit.

Damn Oscar and his ideas, he thought as he dodged past people on the sidewalk. A horse-drawn carriage just barely avoided hitting him as he crossed the street, the driver shaking his fist at him and swearing over the clatter of hooves. With the two men still close behind him, all he could do was wave backward over his shoulder in apology. Taking a hard left, he bounded down a narrow street that would lead him to the city's inner edge, right where the guards would be. He glanced back over his shoulder, hoping that the men would realise where they were and slow down.

Reid never came into this part of the city unless it was to accompany Gillian, and then he would be dressed to the nines to ensure he didn't stand out. It was occupied by the wealthier inhabitants of Thornwell, those who considered themselves important enough to live close to the palace. The guards ensured that any who passed through without proper permission never wanted to return – or couldn't.

Sure enough, as he stepped off the discoloured stone street and onto the clean, light-coloured pavement, the two men behind him slowed, the one with the bat drawing a line across the ground, daring Reid to come back. He gave them a cocky smile and disappeared down the road, keeping as close to the shadows as he could. Gillian would skin him alive if he got caught by the guards here; that was if he paid to have him released first. Another debt that Reid didn't need.

He tucked his hands into his pockets and kept his head down as he passed a small group of young women, daring to shop this close to the slums. A pretty brunette risked a glance in his direction before grabbing her friend's elbow to steer her away; the others quickly followed suit. He caught a glimpse of his reflection in a shop window. He couldn't blame them for avoiding him. His hair badly needed to be cut, his face was covered with god knows what, his clothes were far too small for him, and he most definitely smelled worse than the rear end of a horse. He was sure he heard one of them give a slight squeal of fear. At least she would have something to gossip about at her next dinner party.

Ahead, two guards came into view, their backs to him. Without a second thought, he opened the shop door and ducked inside just as the guards turned his way. The bell jingled as he closed it quickly behind him. He leaned against the door and closed his eyes. He was safe, for now at least.

'Can I help you, young man?' Reid's eyes shot open. An elderly gentleman sat at the back of the store, a pipe hanging from his lips. Reid touched his empty pant pockets.

'Sorry, sir, I must have left my coins at home today.' He stooped as he peered out the lower window, watching the soldiers. 'I won't be here but a moment.'

'I have some marvellous wooden carvings.' The old man held up a small statue. 'This one is Kasin, the God of Protection.' He held it out for Reid to take. Reid took one last look out the window and moved toward where the old man sat.

'I really can't afford to buy it from you.' Gillian would most likely take double from his next haul to prove a point of him missing this week's payment.

'I didn't ask for your money, son,' he said. 'It seems to me that having Kasin in your pocket could come in handy at a time like this.'

'Please, don't tell the guards I'm hiding in here. I won't touch anything, I swear.' Reid held his hands up in defence.

'Dear boy, I meant the mere fact that there is a war brewing in our midst,' the old man chuckled. 'I'm too old to bother with the nonsense of the king's guards.'

Reid knew he was talking about the witches. Gillian was one of the only merchants to continue to trade with the clans in the Forest of Brielle. He sent Reid to the edge of Thornwell at least once a month into the camps that dwelled just inside the forest line to sell the goods he pickpocketed. Occasionally, he was even sent with human organs to trade – both fresh and grave robbed – for potions and tonics Gillian could sell to Inner Ring residents. Reid hated it. Small villages filled with women who looked deceivingly young despite their possible thousand years of age. During his last fleeting visit, he had heard talk of Queen Isadora's plans for the witch clans. Apparently, this new queen wanted to rule every realm, not just her own.

He shuddered at the thought, remembering the few who had tried to entice him into their beds with promises of spells and potions to make him live longer or to be wealthy. He had sold his items as quickly as he could before high-tailing it back to the city, avoiding their glances as he went. It would do him no good to get in bed with a witch, regardless of the possibilities.

'Take it,' the old man said, setting the figure on the counter. 'There is a door in the back that leads onto a street in the Outer Ring.'

Reid stared at the man for a moment, then nodded his thanks. He pocketed the carving of Kasin and headed to the back door as suggested. Reid was unsure why the man had helped him, especially when he had every right to turn him over to the authorities. Reid silently thanked the small god in his pocket as he left the little shop, recalling the shopkeeper's words as he made his way through the filthy streets to Gillian's.

Maybe now was the perfect time to have a god in his pocket.

CHAPTER TWO

Thornwell, Southern Mortal Realm

+ REID +

OSCAR AND REID both sat opposite Gillian's desk in the study. Oscar's face was covered in purple bruises, a mirror to Reid's that hadn't had time to darken yet. Assuming Gillian would be mad when they got back was an understatement. He was furious. One of the pub patrons had recognised Oscar as Gillian's lackey and had tracked him down. Gillian had paid the man off for his silence, and then taken it out on Oscar's face until he fessed up. Reid had received the same treatment when he returned an hour later.

'How stupid do you have to be?' Gillian slammed his hands down on the table. 'You have one job! Bring me goods to fence and don't get caught while doing it.'

'That's two jobs,' Oscar replied.

Reid hid his smirk at O's reply as Gillian threw the closest thing to hand – a bottle of rich, amber ale – at the blonde's head.

'I didn't ask for your smart-arse answers!' It just barely missed O as he ducked. The bottle smashed against the wall behind them, cheap whisky running down the wall. 'That's coming from your pay, Oscar.'

Reid kept his wood carving and the short trip to the inner circle secret, even from Oscar, as Gillian grilled them about how they must follow protocol. It would do more harm than good for him to know that Reid had been close to getting caught by the guards, especially with how strict they were with protecting the royals. The threat from the witches was more than enough for everyone to worry about without fear of the Outer Ring moving into the city.

'The two of you had better up your game if you want to continue living in this house after you turn eighteen.' Gillian sat down behind the desk, pulling out a cloth for his hands. 'I will not have freeloaders under my roof.'

Oscar and Reid nodded their understanding as they watched their master clean their blood from his skin. Gillian's knuckles had split in spots; he winced as he dabbed alcohol on them. Reid could still feel them against his cheek as he stood to take the beating Gillian had dished out. He didn't dare touch his face – he wouldn't give Gillian the satisfaction of knowing how much pain he was truly in.

'Triple fees will be taken from your next haul.' Gillian reached into his drawer and pulled out a notebook. His hand shook slightly as he wrote down a few numbers.

'Triple!' Oscar stood from his chair and threw his hands on the table. 'We only missed one week!'

Gillian moved faster than Reid thought possible as he backhanded Oscar across the face, knocking him back into his chair. His clotted lip split open, blood flowing down his already stained chin. Reid hid his wince as his friend spat blood into his lap.

'I will not tolerate your insolence,' Gillian said before sitting back down in his chair across from them. He ran his hands around the back of his stiff neck in annoyance. 'Are we clear that, from now on, you stick to what I've taught you and not these ridiculous plans that you seem to come up with?' He eyed Oscar until the boy yielded and hung his head. 'Now, you both have chores that need doing and I have to head out for the evening. I'm leaving you both in charge of the younger boys until I get back. Don't mess up this time.'

'This'—Reid gestured at his face after they'd cleaned up from the small dinner of bread and something he assumed was potato soup—'is all on you, O.'

Oscar rolled his eyes at Reid as he laid on his makeshift bed of straw and rags. 'I didn't see you coming up with anything better.'

'The normal routine would have been fine!' Reid threw his hands up as he leaned against the window. 'It would have been better than copping this.' His face had clotted, but the swelling hadn't gone down, and if Gillian saw them stealing ice from the box, they were sure to get another beating.

'Yes,' Oscar replied dramatically, 'because working our arses off all day pickpocketing around the outer edge of the city is going to get us out of debt to Gillian.'

Of course, he was right. There was little point in trying to steal from people who lived in the city's outer part. They were as underprivileged, if not more so, than the boys were themselves. A few weeks were left – at most – before people started to move toward the inner population, searching for food and shelter. A life thrust upon them by the wealthier folk of Thornwell, sanctioned by a king who probably didn't deserve the throne. Unlike their sister city, Winhelm, which resided in the Northern Mortal Realm, Thornwell's more affluent occupants had pushed the lesser townspeople to the town's outer edge.

To make matters worse, the inner-city lords and ladies refused to spend their money on the outer edge, forcing them into even worse circumstances. The king still bought from the farmers; he didn't have any other choice. To compensate, he raised the taxes they were meant to pay, which meant most were handing over their crops for free.

'They're boxing us out, you know,' Oscar said as he watched Reid staring at the window. Reid raised an eyebrow at the boy who was now lying with both eyes closed on the cold floor, his hands behind his head in a way that seemed far too relaxed for Reid's liking.

'Marlo was saying that the king has builders working day and night without rest to get it built.' Oscar grinned slightly as he referred to the girl he sometimes saw of a night. The daughter of one of the lords in town had a thing for crossing to their side. Reid knew it would end badly for Oscar if she was ever caught slumming with them here.

He leaned his head against the cold glass of the window. Sure enough, where the invisible line ran that separated their two factions, a stone wall was taking shape. How had he not realised what was happening? Sure, he'd taken note of the work being done and the wall going up, but the idea of completely splitting the two factions? He shook his head in despair.

The recent increase in guards and patrols suddenly made sense; they were preparing for a surge of people trying to enter the Inner Ring before the Outer Ring was cut off. The wall stretched around the rest of the city already; the only part left to build was their western side.

'Maybe it's for the best,' Reid mused as he plopped down on his dirty makeshift bed, piled with old sheets and clothes. 'You should stop seeing Marlo before it's finished. I doubt she'll be breaking out of her city to come to see you.'

Oscar chuckled to himself, muttering something about not being able to help that the girls found him irresistible, before rolling over to sleep. Reid waited until Oscar's quiet breathing turned to the familiar, heavy, grunting sounds that reminded him of the pig pens outside the markets, before pulling the little god from his pocket.

'Kasin, the God of Protection', that's what the man in the shop had told him earlier. Reid had only heard stories from afar of the gods and goddesses that created their world. Vaguely, he could remember his aunt telling him things when he was little. Many did not pay tribute anymore to the divine beings that had supposedly once walked amongst their world. It wasn't that they didn't believe in them, it was more that the miracles and blessings that were once abundant had vanished from the lands, and the people saw little reason for devotion to absent deities. His aunt had been devout, especially to Dagmar. He was sure she had only prayed to the Goddess of Life because she was the wife of Krah, the God of Death and the Afterlife. Perhaps his aunt thought it would keep them both alive if she pleased Dagmar ... she died not long after Reid's fifth birthday.

So much for that plan, he thought to himself.

Reid ran his finger over the polished wood, examining the fine details that had been carved into the little god's face. He wasn't overly confident that the carving's gentle-looking face was what the protector honestly looked like, but it was oddly satisfying to think such a being would watch over him. Somewhere in the back of Reid's mind, a fleeting word glided ghostlike through the murky waters of his thoughts, its presence acknowledged only in the faintest ripples of awareness. *Always.*

He thought over his plan for tomorrow, how he would offer to take some more goods to trade with the witches for Gillian – without Oscar's help this time. As much as he dreaded going anywhere near the god-awful beings that roamed the Forest of Brielle, it was the best plan he had if he wanted to pay off his now-extended debt with Gillian. If he went alone, he would get the full commission and not have to split it with Oscar. Plus, without O in the way to slow him down, he could be in and out well before midnight when they became their real demons.

There were a few witches that Reid knew by name. Those were the ones he preferred to trade with, the ones that didn't make him feel like he was a meal on two legs. Erikah was usually the first Reid sought out when he entered the camp closest to Thornwell. The first time he met her, when he travelled in with Gillian, she had terrified him. She had long, sandy blonde hair that she wore tied in two flat braids hanging down either side, and her face was peppered with a small number of freckles, starting on her nose and fading as they spread across her high cheekbones. She was different to most of the other witches, who wore tattoos or scars instead of the pretty freckles. Such a human feature on something so ... inhuman.

How she'd dealt with Gillian had been unsettling to witness. Taking a sample of his blood as part of the trade. She didn't ask him, merely walked over and sliced her long talon-like nails across his wrist before dripping the blood into her crystal jar. She had only smiled at Reid when Gillian introduced him as the new merchant for her coven. Reid remembered how her self-sharpened teeth had gleamed in the moonlight that filtered through the trees, and his skin prickled again at the thought.

It was different now. After over a year of trading with Erikah, he'd become cautiously comfortable around the witch. He'd probably go as far as to say they had a friendship of sorts, or at least a mutual understanding of one another. The other witches, however, he'd never let his guard down around. Not with what he had witnessed among their hearths. It helped that Erikah was their leader; most witches left him to his business with little interference.

Reid shuddered as he rolled over, facing away from the window. Tomorrow. He would speak with Gillian about going to see the witches tomorrow. With one hand still tucked inside his jacket pocket with the carving, he let his mind slip into darkness.

CHAPTER THREE

Witch's Keep, Forest of Brielle

✦ ELSBETH ✦

ELSBETH STOOD WITH her sister as their Queen sauntered into the room. This morning there would be a meeting with an emissary sent by Queen Nerophine to discuss whether the sirens would fight with the witches – or against them. With the talk circulating about the impending war, the kingdoms that bordered their forest had ceased communicating with them. Merchants from the eastern ocean stopped visiting to sell their seafood; they even risked the Tretara Range, a longer and more perilous journey, to avoid passing through the witch realm. The fae who often came down to share in the immortal festivities, such as the summer solstice a few moons ago, had not returned.

Elsbeth dared a glance out the window toward the northwest, where The Timeless Fields lay. It had been two moons since she had seen Raynor, the handsome Fae Prince she had dared to love in secret. Norella, Elsbeth's twin sister, nudged her just enough to force Elsbeth's gaze from the window and back to their Queen. Norella was one of the few who knew about her affair with Raynor – she disapproved.

Isadora Mallum, High Queen of the witches, slowed as she neared the base of the dais. Her long, fiery red hair was neatly braided, hanging over her shoulder and stopping just below her hips. The witches and servants remained bowed even after she had passed them, without Isadora so much as glancing their way. Elsbeth and Norella acknowledged her with low bows of their own, staying in that position until she seated herself on her throne. The throne which would have rightfully been one of theirs, had their mother lived.

Three skulls for the three seers that Isadora had slain in place of her sister's bloodline upon seizing the throne. They hung right above her crown, as if they looked down over the court itself and watched. A vengeful act she had taken upon herself to complete after she had defeated the previous queen, Elsbeth and Norella's mother. It was customary for the new Queen to assert her power in these ways; they were told to be thankful it had been the seers and not themselves. Most new queens would have destroyed their predecessor's coven to ensure there would not be backlash for losing their matron.

Isadora flicked her eyes toward Norella, a silent summoning. Elsbeth kept her eyes ahead, hiding the disdain she felt as Norella knelt before the throne. Perhaps she should be grateful that her mother never had to decide between her twin daughters. They would never have the chance to truly hate one another as Isadora had hated Hesta.

'You will stay for the meeting, along with Zala and Imogen.' Elsbeth stiffened at the words. She was still not accustomed to being separated from her twin, let alone to have two lower sentinels permitted to stay for political meetings while she was shuffled out like a child, as if she wasn't the daughter of a deceased queen and the current Queen's niece.

Brielle, help me see patience, she prayed as the Queen continued speaking to Norella.

Elsbeth looked up at Norella, who had stood and was returning from the throne. Her face turned hard as she brushed off Elsbeth's questioning eyes. Norella would never question the Queen's decision, ever loyal to the Crown, no matter who sat under it. It was a strategic move on the Queen's behalf to keep the twins separate, not that there would ever be a chance they would unite to revolt against her. Elsbeth sometimes even thought her twin would go as far as killing her, should the Queen ask it. It disgusted her that her own blood acted this way. Although, considering what she had witnessed her aunt do to her mother to gain the crown, nothing surprised her much anymore.

A breeze blew softly under the closed doors that led out of the throne room. Norella snarled softly as she breathed in the scent. The sweet smell of blood, wind, and a touch of fear filled Elsbeth's nose. Her eyes glazed over from the pure instinct to hunt; it had been a few days since she had tasted fresh blood. Zala and Imogen, younger witches barely three hundred years old, moved from their position against the wall and came to flank the other side of the dais and bared their sharpened teeth at the door. Elsbeth often forgot they came from the forest's southern edge, where the covens commonly filed their teeth into sharp points. A wild and barely controllable coven that an old friend oversaw, Isadora had recruited them after the last blood moon, placing them directly under Norella's charge.

Elsbeth looked to their Queen and took the blatant stare as a sign that she was no longer required in the room. She bit her tongue to hide the words she wanted to say to her aunt. Words that would probably see her deemed a traitor to the Crown. She nodded to Norella before giving a quick, almost disrespectful bow to the Queen and headed down the carpet toward the doors. Her pace was almost too fast for the servants as they raced to pull the heavy doors open for her. She didn't wait, slipping between them as soon as the opening allowed.

The siren stood on the other side; Elsbeth watched a glimmer of dread spark in the bird-woman's eyes and ripple through her feathers as she beheld Elsbeth standing before her. She looked at her feet as Elsbeth strode past her without so much as a glance in her direction. Fear wafted down the hallway after her, making Elsbeth smile slightly at the thought. At least someone showed her the respect she deserved.

Elsbeth didn't hide her annoyance as she descended the steps from the throne room tower and out into the morning sunlight. Her long, blonde hair braided neatly out of the way, as her mother had always worn hers. She looked again toward the kingdom where her prince dwelled. Her hands ran over her stomach, absently feeling for what may be there. Two moons since she had seen him, and almost the same time since she had her last bleed. A tiny seed of joy filled her as she considered the possibility, followed shortly after by terror and concern. She needed to speak with Alanah, urgently.

Her face settled to her usual calm as a group of witches passed by her, only a few acknowledging her presence. The change happened the moment her mother lost to Isadora. Queen Hesta had ruled over the witch covens for over five-hundred years, becoming Queen shortly before having the twins. The only set of twins that had been born in millennia within the covens. Isadora had defeated her in one-on-one combat. A challenge made by Isadora for the right to be called Queen, as per witch law. Elsbeth was almost sure Isadora had used some form of trickery to best her mother. Hesta had been one of the most powerful witches the coven had seen since Queen Brielle – aside from Isadora, apparently.

Since Hesta's death, few acknowledged Elsbeth or Norella as heir in any way. Isadora kept Norella close to her side as her Second, and all but shunned Elsbeth. Fearful of the new Queen, most of the covens had followed suit, save a few of her coven members. Alanah remained one of the latter. Admittedly, Elsbeth was partly grateful that she was left alone. It meant that it was easier for her to hide her relationship with the Fae Prince – no one seemed to notice too much when she skipped a court meeting or two. Isadora also made it her prerogative to send Elsbeth away on many meaningless tasks, which meant she got to be by herself. She enjoyed the time alone, away from the keep.

Covered in vines and moss, the thatched roof of the healer's home was barely visible to anyone who didn't know it was there. It was there long before Alanah had been born, and would likely remain long after she was gone. Its stone walls were chipped and marred, some falling away. Someone had begun to fill in cracks with caked mud bricks as a temporary replacement. Elsbeth was sure it wasn't Alanah; the witch never concerned herself with such things. Nevertheless, she found comfort in the sight of the rundown hut. Memories played on the edge of her mind, of her and Norella playing there when they were young. She smiled as she continued toward the path.

Smoke was rising slowly from the chimney, swept away quickly on a phantom breeze. Alanah was one of the few witches that lived this close to the castle, save for the Queen's coven. She was the head healer; it was her duty to be accessible to everyone, but to be near enough at all times to aid the Queen should she need it. Often, Alanah would travel to the other camps to train their healers or drop off newly found medicines. She'd tried to convince Elsbeth to become her apprentice when her affinity to water had come about, but the young witch had been more interested in harnessing her powers for war than for healing. She'd been eighteen at the time. It was centuries ago, even if it only felt like yesterday. Elsbeth took a deep breath and walked down the stone steps that led to the shack's crooked door.

CHAPTER FOUR

Witch's Keep, Forest of Brielle

+ ISADORA +

ISADORA'S MAGIC SURGED within her, her eyes glowing like embers, a perfect mirror to her hair and her affinity for the fire element. She sat on her throne of bones and glared down at the creature before her. The demon within her smiled at the smell emanating from the emissary; Isadora hungered for the fear she created amongst those lesser than she.

'What is Nerophine's answer?' Isadora hissed at the siren; her long nails tapped the armrest on her chair. The sound echoed through the near-empty throne room. She was bored. Nerophine herself should have made the journey to meet with her, not this commoner.

The siren quivered as she answered. 'My Queen has decided that her armies shall not join you in this war. She does not wish to join either side in the war.'

Isadora rolled her eyes at the response. 'Nerophine is an idiot to think that your kind can avoid what is to come.' She picked up the chalice that was sitting beside her and took a sip, watching the siren over the rim as she did. Warm, red liquid ran down her chin, forming a small pool in the hollow of her throat. The blood was thick and warm – it was a shame to spill any, but she loved watching them squirm in front of her.

'It is her wish to keep our kingdom neutral, at peace with all others for as long as possible,' the siren replied, ruffling her wings.

A harsh cackle escaped Isadora as she slammed the cup down onto the table, liquid splashing out as she did. All these so-called rulers, scared of confrontation. They didn't want to fight her, but they would not bow to her either, it seemed.

'She wishes to avoid confrontation, such a poor excuse for a queen,' she said, looking out the window toward where the Sky Kingdom of Nonnelle sat. 'Nerophine is a fool to not join with me. My victory is inevitable.'

'Then perhaps,' Norella said boldly, 'we do not need Nerophine or her siren legion.'

'Perhaps not,' Isadora mused. 'Though I don't wish for them to join my enemy, either.'

The legion of sky warriors that Queen Nerophine could potentially be harbouring might be detrimental to who eventually won the war. Despite how confident Isadora was of her success, no one knew how many resided in the Sky Kingdom.

'My Queen is no fool. She is doing what is best for our people.' The fleeting moment of bravery from the emissary was short-lived as Isadora stood from her throne and walked down the dais' cold stone stairs. Her heels clicked with each step, the noise echoing through the quiet chamber.

'What is your name?' Her voice was like silk as she stopped in front of the creature.

'Tallon,' the siren replied, unable to meet the witch's gaze.

'You would do well, Tallon,' Isadora purred, 'to not speak out of turn when you are in my court.'

Tallon dipped her head in acknowledgement, her hair falling around her face, 'I meant no disrespect, Your Majesty.'

'Oh, but I'm sure you did,' Isadora went on walking around her, assessing her. Maybe an inch or so shorter than Isadora, she was pretty. With shoulder-length, white-blonde hair, with pink and purple feathers woven neatly through it – not as beautiful as her Queen Nerophine was said to be, but enough to warrant looking at. She could easily be mistaken for a human if it weren't for the two large wings – currently tucked neatly into her sides out of the way – or the large, bird-like legs that caused her to tilt forward slightly more than a human.

Feathers traversed from where her hair stopped, out across her shoulders to join to the wings. They were a golden-brown, mixed with the same pink and purples that were in her hair. From her waist down she resembled an enormous eagle, with thick legs covered with the same tawny feathers of her wings branching out into a colourful tail. Instead of feet, she had strong, sharp talons designed for hunting and killing. Tallon wore only her silver armour, moulded perfectly to fit her chest. She held a matching helmet in her left hand. Her bow and quiver of arrows had been taken from her upon arrival.

A flawless aerial legion for wiping out enemies, the only force the witches might encounter that could diminish their numbers. Isadora herself had a few hundred witches that could fly, but they would be nothing compared to the numbers that Nerophine could have hidden away in the vast Sky Kingdom.

'If Nerophine refuses to aid my campaign, I have no choice but to take action against the sirens of Nonnelle.' She ran a polished nail over Tallon's collarbone as she circled back around. The siren shuddered at the witch's touch. Her hand twitched at her side, brushing air where she no doubt usually had a sword. Isadora's lip lifted slightly, a hint of a smile lingering as the siren's eyes widened in fear before they fluttered closed, a sigh of defeat slipping from her lips. The keen eyes of a siren missed nothing, Isadora knew she could sense the weight of every witch's gaze boring down on her. The Witch Queen knew her sentinels would not have allowed the siren to land a single blow on her, no matter how fast Tallon could move. But still …

'You're a brave one, aren't you?' Isadora mused as she contemplated what her next move was going to be. She knew that if she acted out against Nerophine and her Sky Kingdom, they would join with the fae and humans to ensure retribution. If the pathetic mortals could get their act together quick enough to form a rebellion with the other races, that was.

+ TALLON +

Tallon's instincts screamed at her that the longer she stayed in this place, the more precarious the situation became.

She tried to keep the desperation from her voice as she asked, 'Do you have a message you wish for me to convey back to Queen Nerophine?'

The Witch Queen tapped her chin in thought as she stepped away from Tallon, her heels clicking on the stone floor. Tallon's feathers bristled as Isadora turned and walked toward the balcony, her servants rushing to throw the doors open before her. Sunlight poured through the doors, and the Queen paused, seeming to relish it for but a moment, before she stepped through.

From inside, Tallon saw her look, not towards the Sky Kingdom in the west, as she had earlier, but toward the east, where the Ocean Kingdom lay. She stood there for a few moments before turning, almost triumphantly, to face Tallon and the others. A wicked smirk spread across the Queen's face as she strolled back into the room, and Tallon's stomach clenched with dread.

'You may tell Nerophine that I have taken pity upon her sky people,' she said as she climbed the stairs once more. 'If she does not wish to choose a side, then I shall choose for her.'

'Your Majesty?' Tallon's face scrunched in confusion.

'You may tell your *Queen*'—she spoke the word as if it were nothing more than a joke— 'that I will give your people three days to surrender and join my army.'

'She has already said no.' Tallon shook as she took a step back away from the Witch Queen. Her feathers prickled as her animal instinct urged her to run.

'I am giving her another chance,' Isadora replied. 'Be gone, before I change my mind and send her a different kind of order.'

'I will convey the message and send word with her answer.' Tallon turned, eager to leave and head back to Nonnelle. She was almost to the door – almost to her freedom – when the Queen's voice split the air again, like lightning in a clear sky.

'Wait.'

Tallon's claws snicked in the stone, she stopped so abruptly, her wings twitching as she turned cautiously on the spot.

'I've had a change of heart.'

'What are you doing?' Tallon screamed as Isadora made a quick hand motion and two witches seized her, their hands frozen vices, and forced her to the ground. Each grabbed a wing and spread them out wide. Tallon kicked and thrashed, but no matter how she tried, she was pinned in place. The two witches seemed unfazed by her attempts to free herself.

'Wait! This was a peaceful meeting!' Her voice turned to a high-pitched screech of pure outrage and pain as they slammed their knives through her wings and into the stone beneath.

Isadora inclined her head to the blue-eyed, stone faced witch who had stayed beside her throne throughout the meeting. Tallon froze, her mouth working in fear and disbelief as the witch removed a long, serrated blade from her side as she walked toward her, the silver metal glowed in the morning sun. She stood over Tallon, blocking Isadora from view. There was no remorse in her face, just business-like determination as, without hesitation, she started at the top and began hacking away.

Tallon writhed and screamed in pain as one wing was cut free, kicking with her feet and gouging into the floor with her talons.

'Imogen, hold her down,' the witch with the blade demanded as Tallon tried to break free from her. Sharp pain ricocheted through her as a knee pressed down on her open wound, stopping any chance of escape as the witch began removing the second wing.

Tallon went limp on the floor, strangely weightless as pain roared through her body. Her beautiful feathers were scattered around her, mixing with the green, thick blood. Her wings were a gory mess amongst which she lay, curled like a newborn babe. Rage bubbled inside her, but her strength failed her, her body now separate from her will as it remained lifeless on the ground. Tallon met the blade-witch's eyes as she stood over her still, wiping the cloth meticulously into each serration of her knife. Tallon met the witch's icy blue eyes and sent a near silent prayer to Thora through teeth gritted in pain.

✦ NORELLA ✦

Norella watched in silence as Zala and Imogen took the giant wings and placed them at the foot of the dais, an offering for their Queen.

'Norella,' Isadora said, 'you have done well, daughter.'

Norella stiffened at the term, a strange look coming over the witch's face. *Daughter* ... the term sent a wave of emotions spiralling through her mind as she toyed with the idea of it. No one but her mother had referred to her by that name before – was this how Elsbeth felt when she was with Alanah?

Both shame and pride washed over as she relished in the title bestowed upon her by her mother's killer, by her Queen. She did little but nod in acknowledgement before returning to the right-hand side of the throne.

The siren still lay on the ground, her body convulsing in uneven movements. Imogen and Zala moved at Isadora's command and dragged her to her feet. A cry of pain escaped her, and Norella watched as fresh green blood oozed from her wounds.

'Why?' The pain was visible as the singular word slipped from her panting lips.

'You didn't think I would let you just fly off and warn your so-called Queen so easily, did you?' Isadora smiled, her voice empty of emotion as she continued. 'You are the first of your kind to have their fate chosen for them. I'm sorry to say that yours was more brutal compared to what the others will endure, but Nerophine has to know I'm serious.'

Isadora motioned for the witches to take the siren to the balcony.

'You see that sparkling blue mass to the east?' Isadora spoke as though she addressed a naive child. Norella could almost feel the contempt that rolled off the Queen's tongue as she went on. 'Well, that is the kingdom of Orabelle. As I'm sure you know, the people of Orabelle are much like your sky people, only water-dwelling.'

Almost all of Emodorea knew what kind of creatures lived beneath the glimmering surface of Orabelle Bay. A race considered sisters to the sirens, separated by an age-old feud between two ancient beings. *Sisters* that the sirens wanted nothing to do with, regardless of Typhonis and Thora being siblings. Norella had heard stories that the sirens' royal bloodline – blood this siren apparently shared – stemmed from the original siren and her sister, who chose the sea. A sister who was shamed and forsaken for her choice, along with those that decided to go with her.

Norella watched as the Witch Queen raised her hands above her head to form a diamond shape, absorbing the sun's powers. She turned to angle herself toward the siren and the Sky Kingdom, far beyond. A beacon of light shot from her palms and impaled the siren, causing her body to arch forward violently before lifting off the ground. The light travelled from where the magnificent wings had been severed, through the clouds, toward the Sky Kingdom in a sharp beam. The siren began trembling as the Queen began to chant in a language that had been all but burned into Norella's mind since infancy. The heat from the sun that coursed through both siren and witch grew brighter and brighter as Isadora's chanting quickened. Imogen and Zala joined their voices to the mix, their words not as fluent as the Queen's, but they seemed to add to the curse's strength nonetheless. Norella, not daring to cross the threshold to the balcony without the Queen's permission, could feel the magic ebbing through the pulsating light. It burned white as it arced through the siren, a tether to her people in Nonnelle, to their Queen Nerophine. The siren's eyes rolled back in her head. She screamed in pain once more, as though the heat became unbearable.

Slowly, the chanting ceased. Isadora lowered her hands, and the light faded into nothing. She rolled her shoulders and Norella could almost see the power as it left Isadora's body when she whispered a prayer of thanks to Katinka, the Sun Goddess, for lending her the strength of the sun.

'What have you done?' The siren whimpered as she looked down at her legs. No longer did she have the feathered, muscular legs like the great eagles. Now they were weak, bare-skinned human legs. A shiver coursed over her as the cold breeze caressed her naked skin.

'Hmm,' Isadora mused as she took in the sight of the siren's transformed body. 'I suppose my curse didn't take hold the way I intended it to.'

'My legs ...' The siren brushed a trembling hand over her thigh. Her legs wobbled, threatening to buckle, as Imogen and Zala's iron grip held her in place. 'Wh-what have you done?'

With a voice as cold and sharp as a blade of ice, the Queen's decree pulled the siren's attention away from her transformed body.

'I will not have the sky legions of Nonnelle as a threat to my winning this war. You may tell Nerophine that the sirens that soar in the skies above Emodorea will soon vanish like mist in the sun. Since you will not fight with me, I will see to it that you cannot join with my enemies.'

Norella's head snapped up at Isadora's words. Had she actually declared that her curse would be the end of the siren race? Taking over the seven realms was one thing, but to erase an entire kingdom of people was another.

'I'd say you have a fortnight, maybe a little more, if you're lucky, to make it to Orabelle Bay before you change completely.'

'What do you mean?' The siren whispered. She sunk to the floor, her hands bracing her upper body on the stone.

'If you all wish to remain so neutral in the war, then you can do so with your pathetic sisters, who stay hidden in their Ocean Kingdom.' The Queen gestured over her shoulder to the east.

'Mermaids ...' Norella muttered in disgust. The siren glanced up at her in horror.

'You've taken our wings and cursed us with tails ...'

Isadora smiled, her white teeth gleaming in the sunlight as she turned to Zala and Imogen. 'Show her out, will you?'

CHAPTER FIVE

Alanah's Hut, Forest of Brielle

+ ELSBETH +

THE DOOR SWUNG OPEN before Elsbeth even raised her hand to knock, and a young girl stood before her. Witches, though not immortal, lived incredibly long lives, ageing very slowly. Most died before they ever actually showed greying hair or wrinkles. This girl could be sixteen or three hundred and sixteen. Elsbeth couldn't tell anymore, nor did she really care to.

'Well, don't just stand there, Athena. Let the woman inside, would you?' Alanah's sharp voice came from somewhere at the back of the cabin, amidst the shelves full of different herbs, vials, and artefacts. Stepping to the side sheepishly, she gestured for Elsbeth to enter. The door closed with a soft click behind Elsbeth as she took herself to the table. The girl disappeared back to the kitchen without another word, though Elsbeth was sure she was alert to everything that was happening.

'What brings you here this early, child?' Alanah came out from the shadows, arms laden with various jars and vials. Elsbeth moved to help her but was brushed off as Alanah plunked everything onto the kitchen bench. The old healer's shelves were lined with jars of preserved animal parts, dried herbs that gave off a pungent aroma, and vials of mysterious, glowing liquids. Strange bones, twisted roots, and feathers from exotic birds hung from the ceiling, swaying gently with every soft breeze that crept through the gaps in the walls of the old cottage. A cauldron bubbled in the corner, emitting a thick, greenish smoke that filled the room with an eerie tinge. She never knew what Alanah was concocting with her various creepy items, but whatever it was, there was a reason Alanah was the best healer amongst them.

'I was out for the morning, figured it had been a while since I'd seen you.' Elsbeth's eyes darted toward Athena, who had started to clean the dishes from the cluttered sink. Elsbeth hesitated; she wasn't willing to divulge her real reason for visiting in front of a witch she didn't know, nor that she hadn't been wanted in the castle. She didn't need the humiliation of admitting she wasn't involved in political matters anymore, even if Alanah trusted Athena enough to take her on as an apprentice.

'You never just visit, my dear.' Alanah clanked the two fire rocks together a few times, swearing to herself, before a spark sprung from them. She hurried to add a few logs into the stove as the fire began to eat the dry kindling.

Elsbeth shrugged her shoulders as she sat in the rickety old chair, fiddling with a shard of wood that had come loose from the old table. Knowing her luck, she would likely end up with a splinter to go with the rest of the mess she was possibly creating for herself.

'What are you making?' Elsbeth looked over all the items the witch had gathered in front of her. 'A potion for someone?'

Alanah laughed as she picked up her teapot. 'Heavens no, child, I thought a nice cup of tea might calm your nerves a bit. Chamomile and honey?' she asked and held up the jar of sickly sweet golden nectar. 'It's fresh from the hive this morning.' She cracked the lid, letting the sweet smell fill the room.

Elsbeth nodded; it had been ages since she had tasted some of Alanah's honey. The healer raised her own hybrid bees. Somehow, they produced an addictive honey that Alanah often used for her potions and the odd tea now and again. No one really knew what species she crossed them with, but Elsbeth had her suspicions from when Alanah had gone west hundreds of years ago.

Elsbeth cleared a space across from her, so Alanah could join her at the table with the two cups. Her eyes flicked to the young girl, still cleaning, and back to Alanah, who seemed to get the idea. She reached for the pot and quietly asked Athena to retrieve something from the woods for her. The girl grabbed her satchel and nodded at Elsbeth before she left through the back door. She didn't seem at all phased by Alanah asking her to leave.

'She's a good girl,' Alanah mused as she poured the hot liquid into the cups. 'Now, why have you truly come to see me?'

Elsbeth thought for a moment, stirring her cup slowly, watching the leaves twirl around. She struggled with the words that were forming in her mind as she reached for the honey. *Baby. Pregnant.*

'I've missed two bleeds.' She looked straight into Alanah's eyes, so much like her mother's. They had been distant cousins, though Alanah was far older than Hesta. Alanah was Graciella's Second while she had been queen. When Graciella passed the crown to Hesta, Alanah happily stepped aside to allow a new Second to be chosen, relinquishing the title and taking up the role of head healer instead. She laid a warm hand on Elsbeth's cold one. Even when Hesta had been alive, Alanah had taken to mothering Elsbeth. She had had no children of her own in her long life, by choice or by chance she had never said, and Elsbeth had never questioned. Either way, Elsbeth was glad the witch was still around.

'The Fae Prince, then?' Alanah took a sip of her tea. 'What's his name again? Roland? Rayland?'

'Raynor,' Elsbeth dropped her head into her hands. 'I haven't had contact from him since the summer solstice.'

'Ah, so the timing would be accurate then, just over two moons since you saw him last.' Alanah looked at the roof, adding up days in her head as she spoke. 'Is this something you want?' Alanah's face changed to concern. Their kind struggled to fall pregnant, for a witch to rid herself of the babe was considered sacrilege. But Elsbeth knew what Alanah was thinking. Her being pregnant was one thing, but with a half-witch, half-fae child ...

'I love him ... yes, I'd want to keep it,' Elsbeth said, breaking the silence between them. 'I have to leave and find Raynor. I have to escape the forest, Brielle save me if Isadora finds out.'

'You need to calm yourself, child,' Alanah patted her hand. 'Sip your tea, the chamomile will help.'

'I don't know what to do,' Elsbeth confessed. 'There are too many things to consider.'

'I doubt his kind would accept you to live amongst them, they might allow the odd encounter here and there to go unnoticed, but they despise us witches,' Alanah mused. 'They call us abominations of nature – the elders think that each of us has a demon inside.'

'Well, they're not exactly wrong.' Elsbeth gave a half-hearted laugh. 'I mean, look at our Queen.'

'Isadora would do anything to remain unchallenged,' Alanah's face was stern. 'A half-breed between the two races isn't unseen. But the power that a child of your bloodline and the fae royal bloodline might wield ...' Alanah didn't need to finish her sentence. Elsbeth knew what Isadora would do. To her and her unborn child.

'Well,' Alanah slid her chair back. 'First things first, let's confirm whether you're indeed with child or not.'

She downed the dregs of her tea and walked to the shelves in the back. Elsbeth could hear her digging around, moving jars of plants and herbs. A loud crash echoed through the room, followed by a series of curses from the old witch.

'Are you alright?' Elsbeth called, turning to look over her shoulder. 'Do you want some help?'

'No,' Alanah called out. 'I'm fine. Just doing some reorganising!'

Arms laden with two vessels of what seemed to be plant seeds and a pail, Alanah gestured for Elsbeth to follow her outside.

'I have some wheat seeds and some barley seeds,' she said as she tipped a handful of each into the bucket before handing it to Elsbeth. 'In a few days, if either of the seeds sprout, then you're pregnant.'

Elsbeth sighed as she accepted the bucket. It was such an old way of doing things. Elsbeth would have thought Alanah would have a spell or something that would tell her sooner than two or three days, not just urinating on some seeds. It must have been her hesitation looking into the bucket that made Alanah speak again.

'My dear, there are spells I could use, but they would require the full moon to do so and that, as you know, is at least two weeks away.'

Elsbeth nodded her understanding and headed into the thick of the forest. She felt silly as she looked around to check that Athena wasn't still wandering around. She was almost finished when a scream pierced the silence. Hurriedly fixing her leather pants, she headed back to the hut's small garden, where Alanah was staring up at the castle balcony.

'I don't suppose the emissary told her what she wanted to hear,' Elsbeth broke the silence that followed, not caring to hide the spite in her tone. 'Can't say I blame the sirens for wanting to stay out of our grounders' politics.'

'Mind your tongue, child, you know she has ears everywhere. I dare say even the trees are on her side,' Alanah chided.

Silence followed for a while before a faint movement was seen from the balcony. The two witches stood too far away to tell what was happening, so they waited.

A few seconds later, the hum of magic surrounded them. The skin on the back of Elsbeth's neck prickled where her witch mark was etched into her skin, a sign that was given to all newborns to signify their power. A glowing light shot through the sky over their heads, straight across the land to the west. It held for a few moments, glowing its brightest before fading away as if it were never there. Alanah turned away, muttering to herself before disappearing into her house with Elsbeth's bucket, leaving the other witch alone in the small garden.

Elsbeth wasn't sure how long she stood there, contemplating what she had just witnessed. Athena brought her back to reality as she entered through the garden gate. She was carrying a basket of wildflowers, along with other herbs Elsbeth knew grew deep in the forest. With the sun now high in the sky, Elsbeth could see the light blonde streaks that shone through the girl's brunette hair. An oddness Elsbeth wasn't used to seeing amongst the witches. She wondered who she descended from. The two witches exchanged small smiles before Athena headed into the cabin and Elsbeth finally moved to head back to the castle.

Chapter Six

Nonnelle, Sky Kingdom of Nonnelle

+ NEROPHINE +

THE LIGHT WAS BLINDING as it surrounded Nonnelle, and the kingdom went silent as it was encased in a dome of white. Queen Nerophine's guards instinctively stepped between her and the source from which the light came.

'Tallon,' Nerophine muttered, pushing past her guards. 'Thora save her.'

Others around her muttered similar prayers for themselves and the Queen's cousin, who was sent to speak with the Witch Queen. The council had deemed it too risky to send their leader, and Tallon was the only other option; sending a lower born would be considered an insult. No, the Queen's cousin had been the only answer to the argument that had continued for well over a week. Tallon had eagerly offered herself to go, to prove her worth as Second, much to Nerophine's dismay. The Queen had known Isadora would not accept the sirens' neutrality in the issues the world below was having.

The light from Brielle Forest merely grew brighter and sharper as they waited to see what would happen, unable to do anything. If it was coming from the witches, Nerophine knew it was going to be wicked. A wave of power washed over them and the Sky Kingdom trembled as the dome covering their city shattered, dousing them all in the blinding, white light. The silence broke as the sirens began screaming. Nerophine wished she could tell them to not be afraid, that their goddess would protect them, but even she could no longer feel the presence of their beloved divinity, Thora.

Millennia ago, when the world was born, the divine beings had walked amongst the creatures of Emodorea. They offered blessings to their devoted followers in the form of many different things. Sirennea, first of the sirens, asked Thora, the Goddess of the Air, to bless her people with a kingdom in the sky. Thora, grateful to Sirennea for her devotion, lifted the kingdom from the ground. The goddess enchanted it to float high above, untouchable by any who could not fly. Half of the women who followed Sirennea and her sister, Merlian, decided to go with Sirennea to this new kingdom in the sky. Thora gifted them with bodies similar to the great eagles that roamed higher than any grounders knew.

Nerophine glanced around her as she listened to the prayers that were coming from her subjects. Perhaps it was too late for the sirens to ask their once beloved Thora for help. Although the royal bloodline still worshipped the deities, many of the sirens forgot their daily prayers and offerings after living long lives of bliss. Settled far away from the rest of Emodorea, very few sirens had met any of the ground dwellers. Of course, select sirens were chosen to mingle with other races on the land below. When a siren was chosen by the council, they had the chance to seek a male from the ground.

However, the rules with babies were harsh and upheld by years of tradition. A male had yet to be born that held the pure siren gene, even the females that were birthed rarely did. Most were a mix of the two races and shared more similarities with the male parent, meaning they were not accepted in the Sky Kingdom. Thus, the siren race was dwindling in numbers.

'My Queen,' one of her sentinels said warily as the light surrounding them faded away, leaving the sky people clutching each other as they waited for their Queen to speak.

Nerophine looked out over her people as they crowded the courtyard. An array of beautiful colours, from the deepest violet to the brightest orange, filled her vision. Whatever that light had been, it hadn't yet left any physical damage, but she could tell her people were shaken from the experience. A murmur ran through the crowd as they waited impatiently for their Queen to direct them.

'Please, stay calm,' Nerophine's voice washed over the sirens, all now looking toward her as she drew their attention away from the East. 'I'm sure that Tallon will return soon and inform us of what has happened. Until then, if anyone needs anything, they need only ask. The palace doors are always open.'

It wasn't much, but support was all she could offer her people until she had more information. She nodded to her guards to lead her back to the castle; she needed to discuss what had just happened with the council. She also needed to send an escort to find Tallon, who she prayed was on her way back home.

'I'm sorry, my Queen, but sending an escort of that size to retrieve Lady Tallon is just not reasonable right now.' Joryn, the captain of Nonnelle's forces, was seated across from her. The grief-stricken look in her eyes showed Nerophine that she didn't like the decision any more than the Queen herself.

'Then send a small elite team to find my cousin,' Nerophine begged. She was never the kind of queen that ordered her subjects around. She wanted them to make their own choices in hopes that they would create a better world than the other kingdoms.

'I can possibly spare two from my private guard – more than that without knowing what is happening down there is too high a risk,' Joryn replied. She folded her hands in front of her, the signs of battle visible in the many scars marring her knuckles. Battles that they no longer had to fight, thanks to Nerophine's ideologies.

'Then send them, at once.' Nerophine paced back and forth in front of the table. The other council members shared worried looks; Nerophine on edge was something they weren't used to seeing.

It was a day's flight to get from Nonnelle to the witch's keep, in the middle of Brielle Forest. If Tallon had left before that light struck, she should meet the escort about halfway back. The word *if* floated around in Nerophine's mind. She knew she shouldn't have sent her cousin, at least not alone. Nerophine had wanted to send an escort, but the Witch Queen was already offended that she refused to attend in person. Tallon had said it was better and faster if she went alone, that it showed a sign of trust between the sirens and the witches – a trust that Nerophine did not have.

'This light,' Galia said, 'needs to be investigated. We need to know what it means for our people.'

Galia, with her greying hair, was one of the oldest in the council, possibly close to five hundred years old with the witch blood that flowed through her veins, diluted as it may be. She often offered some wiser insights regarding the people of Nonnelle. Today, though, Nerophine was sure it was fear in the old siren's eyes.

'You fear that it was a bad sign from the witches?' Nerophine asked.

'I fear that this new queen is nothing like the previous ones we have dealt with. I fear that not joining a side in this war is not something she will have taken lightly.'

'Even if we decided to join a side, it would not be hers.' Nerophine stopped pacing and placed her hands on the back of her chair. 'I was not going to send my cousin to convey that we will be fighting against the witches.'

'Isadora has been Queen little over a century, and just look at the destruction and terror she has already caused, not only among her witches, but among all of Emodorea.' Joryn offered. 'It might have taken the witches the better part of that time to accept her reign, but now they are undoubtedly loyal.'

They were right – Isadora had turned Emodorea upside down with her threats of war. The sirens had been secluded from the world for so long, Nerophine wasn't sure they would even have connections to the other realms. They were self-sustained in their Sky Kingdom; the only option Nerophine and the council had when Isadora sent word for a meeting was to decline being involved in the war at all. She wasn't even sure if the other kingdoms had spoken against Isadora, or joined her.

The land kingdoms had no choice if the Witch Queen decided to show up on their doorstep; only the fae had any chance of defending themselves. The Sky Kingdom was impenetrable; even if the few witches who could fly – or Isadora's shape-shifting demons – made it to Nonnelle, Nerophine's aerial legions would obliterate them, no matter how few they had left. There just weren't enough sirens to face the witches alone on the ground.

Nerophine sighed as she placed her head on her hands and stretched her back out. It had been a long meeting after the events of this morning, a morning that had started with such a beautiful sunrise over the eastern ocean.

'There isn't much we can do until Tallon returns.' Concern for her cousin flickered across her face as she sent another silent prayer, this time to Kasin, to protect her. 'In the meantime, let's keep the palace doors open. I want to know if anything changes in our kingdom. If that light was from Isadora, I also fear that it was not a good sign.'

'Should we send word to the other kingdoms, perhaps?' Joryn asked.

'I wouldn't even know who was ruling the other lands. I'm sure the Ashshade's are still ruling the fae, but as for the humans ...' Nerophine sighed as she wandered to the open window. 'Let's just focus on getting my cousin home.'

Nerophine had heard the curses Isadora set on people who went against her wishes. It wasn't something she wished to witness in her life, nor was it something she wanted her people to endure. Even so, she couldn't shake the feeling that she had just caused Isadora to curse them to Krah.

CHAPTER SEVEN

Alanah's Hut, Forest of Brielle

+ TALLON +

TALLON, BLOODIED AND BROKEN, had crawled as far as she could in her strange new body before she ran out of strength and gave up, dragging herself under the partial cover of the shrubs lining the forest path. Footsteps roused her from the fitful doze she had fallen into and she looked up at a blonde witch staring down at her. The mid-afternoon sun was at the witch's back, casting shadows over her face – the face of the witch that had taken her wings from her.

A tremor of terror ran through Tallon as the hard-faced woman decided what she was going to do, because she knew there wasn't an ounce of strength in her left to fight back. Tallon opened her mouth to tell her if she had come back to kill her, to get on with it, but the witch spoke first.

'Well, you're a bit of a mess, aren't you?' She crossed her arms as she squatted down beside Tallon to examine her further. Tallon's arms were covered in thick, green blood, and caked with dirt; they were likely infected.

Tallon trembled, attempting to slide away from her further into the shrub, as if that would help protect her. Her legs had withered from their once muscly, eagle-like design; now they were weak, human legs, limp on the ground before her. The witch's brow was creased with concern as she rose to her feet and scanned around her before turning back to smile down at Tallon, crossing her arms once more.

Tallon's mind grappled in confusion, the warm smile on the face of the blade-witch so out of place.

'Pathetic little thing, whatever you are,' the witch scoffed with an amused shake of her head. 'I really should leave you here.'

+ ELSBETH +

Elsbeth wasn't really sure what it was she had found. The creature at her feet was a matted mess of blood and dirt. Had it not been for the brightly coloured feathers woven through her hair, she might not have noticed her at all. Hidden away as she was in the bushes lining the path that laced its way through the dense forest to Alanah's cottage, she may as well have been invisible.

Elsbeth's thoughts trailed off as her hand absently slid to her stomach, the scared girl on the ground still trying to get away from her – still fighting even though she was all but dead. The last thing Elsbeth needed right now was more drama in her life. Wasn't it enough that Brielle possibly blessed her with a baby, but for the goddess to now cast this creature into her path? She sighed. If it was the goddess's will, then who was she to argue?

'Brielle save me,' Elsbeth whispered as she bent down to grasp the girl under the arms. Hauling the mess of a girl to her feet, she practically dragged her back the way she had come – all the while scanning the forest for the watching eyes of those who would report back to Isadora.

When they reached Alanah's cottage, she didn't knock this time, didn't wait for Athena to open the door or for Alanah to invite her inside. After leaving what seemed like only moments ago after burdening Alanah with one problem, here she was returning with a potentially worse one. Elsbeth didn't want to give the healer the chance to turn her away – not that Alanah ever would. She turned the handle and pushed the door open with slightly too much force.

'Elsbeth,' Alanah demanded as she jolted to her feet from the kitchen table. 'What in Brielle's name ... who ...'

Before she could finish, Elsbeth pulled the bloodied body onto the workbench beside the kitchen. Athena moved without instruction, closing and locking the front door before drawing the curtains at the window closed. She moved to stand beside the table that the girl lay upon, instinctively reaching out to feel her brow.

'She has a fever,' Athena told no one in particular as she reached for a damp cloth.

'I'm sorry, Alanah,' Elsbeth apologised. 'Truly I am, but this girl was in my path on the way back to the castle. Almost as though Brielle herself placed her there.'

Alanah shook her head, muttering something about her being just like her mother, before walking over to examine the semi-conscious being.

The girl's eyes flitted back and forth, fear swirling in their depths as the trio moved around above her. Every so often, Elsbeth would see her frail, blood covered body tremor as small whimpers escaped her.

'Nerophine,' she whispered, her eyes rolling back in her head.

Alanah put down the damp towel Athena had handed over to her. Her brow scrunched as she thought about the name the girl had murmured.

'What is it? Why did you stop?' Elsbeth asked as she re-dipped her towel into freshwater, the green blood settling on the top like oil. Athena took the bowl and refilled it in the kitchen, while keeping one eye on Alanah for further instructions.

'She's a siren,' Alanah muttered before continuing her work. 'Or at least she used to be.'

'But she doesn't have wings,' Athena observed as she wandered back to the table with a clean bowl of water for Elsbeth. Elsbeth wiped more grime from the girl's face before taking a closer look and breathing in her scent.

'She's the emissary that the Sky Kingdom sent.' Elsbeth's eyes widened as she vaguely recalled passing her at the doorway, remembering that she didn't give the siren the time of day. 'She smells the same, but she looks ... different.'

'It seems she's had her wings removed – and not in a pleasant way, mind you,' Alanah commented as she straightened one of the girl's arms out.

'Why would Isadora do such a thing?' Athena looked horrified, proving to Elsbeth that she was indeed very young for a witch.

'If we help her, Elsbeth, and this is Isadora's doing, you know it will be considered going against our Queen,' Alanah warned. However, even as the healer spoke, she was already moving to grab herbs and other items one would assume to have healing properties.

'I'm more concerned about what that light meant earlier,' Elsbeth said. 'If it had to do with this siren losing her wings, then Isadora has truly declared war.' Her face drained of colour as she weighed the consequences, whether she should help this creature or not. She'd be considered a traitor to the witches – a traitor to her sisters. 'This means that we witches are at war with Emodorea.'

'Well,' Alanah said as she returned to the table and asked Athena to begin grinding some herbs, 'perhaps the good we do here will help peace fall over Emodorea once again.'

Athena passed the powder from the herbs back to Alanah, who looked to Elsbeth for confirmation before beginning. She merely nodded and followed the healer's instructions to hold the emissary down. Alanah mixed the powder with some water, watching as it turned milky–white.

'It will keep her sedated for a few hours while we work,' Alanah told them after she poured every last drop down the siren's throat. The girl had no strength to fight it and simply swallowed what she was given.

The healer and her apprentice worked tirelessly, with Elsbeth offering whatever assistance she could before stepping aside to prepare dinner for them instead. By the time they had finished wrapping the last of the wounds, Elsbeth had dinner on the table. A soft blanket was placed over the still sleeping siren before the two fell into their chairs to join Elsbeth, exhausted from their efforts.

'Thank you,' Elsbeth offered, not just to Alanah, but to Athena also, as she dished the pheasant and potato onto the plates in front of them. 'I know I've put you in a terrible position by helping her.'

Alanah held up a hand, stopping her. 'Don't be silly, child. I served your mother before Isadora and, to be fair, I had hopes that yourself or your sister would be the next to take the crown.'

Athena gave a curt nod of agreement as she filled her mouth with the juicy bird. Alanah had undoubtedly chosen her prodigy well. 'She'll be out for a few more hours. I've given her a little more of the sedation herb and something for the pain also, but she will be weak for a while once she wakes up.'

Elsbeth nodded her thanks again as she took up the spare chair at the table. As the witches finished the food and Athena moved to clear the table,

Elsbeth was still in deep thought about what she should do next. She had no idea what her plan was after tonight. It would be a few more days before Alanah's test confirmed if she was carrying Raynor's child. She needed to speak with him, to let him know that he would be a father, even if he decided against partnering with a witch.

'You should head back to your chamber.' Alanah came to stand beside where Elsbeth was watching her tea go cold. 'If you stay here, it might be reported to Isadora.'

Elsbeth didn't have the energy to argue with her. She glanced back at the broken siren lying on the workbench. She had known Isadora was ruthless, but harming an emissary on a peaceful visit was generally unheard of. The other realms would not take it lightly. Elsbeth doubted any would bother sending a response to Isadora's demands now.

'She'll be fine. Athena will tend to her until you return in the morning,' Alanah offered as she read the concern on Elsbeth's face.

'I'll be here at dawn, I promise.' She stood from the table and made her way to the door. With one last glance over her shoulder at the bench and a quick nod to Athena, she disappeared outside into the night.

+ ATHENA +

'Why do you suppose she did it?' Athena asked as Alanah locked the door behind Elsbeth.

'It's not our place to make assumptions about what the Queen does or doesn't do,' Alanah replied.

'I don't like it,' Athena said as she watched over the siren. 'The poor thing. To have her wings stripped away … I can't imagine the pain.'

'It will be more than physical pain she feels when she wakes up. Not only has Isadora sliced off her wings, but I'll bet that light earlier was her cursing this creature and the others in Nonnelle, too. Only something as powerful as a curse would alter the appearance.'

'What are you talking about?' asked Athena as she brushed a few strands of the blonde hair away from the other girl's face.

'Sirens,' Alanah replied, 'usually have the lower half of a bird, not a human.'

'Why would she curse them to be humans?' Athena was horrified at the idea. She pulled the blanket up a little higher on the siren, tucking the sides in gently.

Alanah shrugged her shoulders in response. 'Assumptions often lead us astray and cloud our judgement with shadows. We will have our answer soon enough, I'm sure.'

CHAPTER EIGHT

Alanah's Hut, Forest of Brielle

+ TALLON +

TALLON WOKE ON a cold stone bench, in what seemed to be a very dimly lit cabin. It was either night, or very early morning, she wasn't entirely sure. Everything was quiet around the house. The warmth from a small hearth floated toward her as she slowly sat up, the blanket falling from her shoulders as she did. Everything ached as she moved, but the worst pain was in her heart as Tallon slowly remembered what had happened.

She needed to warn Nerophine about the curse, beg her forgiveness for failing their people by allowing the Witch Queen to cast this atrocity upon them. She knew Nerophine would never hold it against her; it wasn't Tallon's fault. Isadora was a demon that had crawled out of the depths of Wynlara, and Tallon cursed Krah himself for letting the woman roam freely amongst the land of the living.

She slid her legs over the side of the table and rested her groggy head in her hands. Tallon wasn't sure how long she had been asleep, or knocked out by whatever she'd been given, but her head was pounding as it began to wear off. Her tongue slipped over her teeth and gums as she tried to swallow any amount of saliva she could muster to get rid of the god-awful taste.

Her eyes skimmed over the room, resting upon a small figure curled on an old lounge in the corner, and her heart stopped as the girl's eyes flicked open, glowing slightly red in the dark.

Standing in a fluid motion, the witch's long brown hair fell over her face as she straightened her skirts before moving toward where Tallon sat. Whether it was from lack of energy or the anger boiling up inside her, the siren didn't move as the gap closed between them.

'Here,' she said to Tallon as she handed her a cup, almost too quiet to hear, 'your throat will be sore from the herb milk you drank.'

Tallon hesitated before taking the cup from her delicate hands. She barely had enough strength to hold it, and her hands shook as she gently lifted it to her nose and sniffed.

'It's just water,' the witch said as she went to the kitchen, 'Are you hungry?'

Tallon took a small sip of the water as she examined the girl before her. The cold water stung as it ran down her dry throat. She gulped down more before responding. The witch stood in the kitchen and quickly braided her hair out of the way before gathering some food from the cold box.

'Who are you?'

'My name's Athena,' the witch said as she placed some cheese and meat on the bench before her and began cutting it up.

'You're a witch,' Tallon stated as she glanced around the room again, trying to take in her possible exit options. Not that she thought she could get very far in her current condition.

'I am,' Athena replied as she placed the tray of prepared food before her.

Tallon eyed the food before taking a piece of uncooked meat from the tray and eating it. She didn't remember when her last meal was, and had barely stopped to rest on her flight from Nonnelle. Her stomach grumbled as she reached for more food that the witch offered her.

'What is your name?' Athena asked as she pulled a chair up beside the siren.

'Tallon,' she replied. 'There were more of you. I remember someone carrying me here. Why did you help me?'

'We helped you because Elsbeth didn't agree with what happened to you,' another voice said from the back of the cabin. She walked forward into the light of the kitchen, placing the book she was carrying down on an empty bench.

'Elsbeth?' Tallon asked as she looked the older witch over from head to toe. Her strawberry-blonde hair was in a neat bun on top of her head, like she hadn't been to bed yet despite the late – or early – hour.

'Yes, she is the one who brought you here – and I am Alanah. Elsbeth will be back in the morning to check on you,' Alanah replied and crossed her arms. 'In the meantime, may I suggest moving to the spare cot in the back and getting some more sleep before morning?'

'I need to get back to Nonnelle. I must tell Queen Nerophine what has happened ... the curse ...' Tallon was cut off by Alanah holding up a stern hand while shaking her head.

'That can wait 'til the sun comes up and Elsbeth is back,' she said to the siren. 'In case you have forgotten, you cannot fly.'

Tallon's heart sank as she reached over her shoulder, feeling the raised trail of the wounds and sharp edges of her damaged feathers. She wouldn't fly, probably ever again. Even if the curse was ever to be broken, Tallon would not regain her wings.

'Please,' Athena said as she stood from her chair and held out her hand. 'I can help you to the back.'

Tallon knew she should hate all witches, but as she traced where her wings once were she could also feel where the wounds that might have killed her had been meticulously cleaned and stitched together, thanks to these two witches. So, Tallon accepted the young witch's help as they hobbled past where Alanah was standing toward the room at the back of the cottage. The small bed was lined with a clean sheet, the blanket folded at the foot, prepared and ready for someone to sleep in.

'This is your room?' Tallon asked as she breathed in the scent that covered the room. The same smell came from the girl who stood beside her.

'Yes, but it's okay. I will need to be awake in a few hours to start my morning chores,' Athena offered as she helped Tallon take a seat on the bed. 'Besides, sleeping on the bench or lounge isn't good in your condition. You need proper rest.'

'Thank you,' Tallon said as Athena walked back to the door. The witch gave a slight nod to the siren as she slipped outside the room and disappeared. Tallon could hear the faint whisper of the two witches as she lay down and drifted back to sleep.

CHAPTER NINE

Thornwell, Southern Mortal Realm

+ REID +

Reid sank into the worn leather lounge, the early morning light filtering through the grime-smeared windows. His fingers picked at the peeling armrest. Reid could still smell the faint scent of herbs and smoke that clung to his clothes, a reminder of the previous night's events. When Reid had arrived, Erikah was waiting for him at the edge of the clearing as if she had known he was coming. Gillian must have tipped them off; he had always told Reid that the witches didn't take too well to unexpected guests in their camp. Even still, the entire camp seemed to be more restless and lively than his previous visits. Erikah warned him to make his visit short – it was as if even she was on edge around her own coven.

He didn't quite understand what he had learned during his visit to the witches' camp. He felt as though the trees had been whispering to him as he had approached, the air thick with the scent of damp earth and a tinge of something unfamiliar to him. Erikah's cryptic warnings and flits of scattered information about something stirring in the forest's heart, at the Witch Queen's keep, left him more confused than most visits.

Reid didn't know much about the forest, or witch politics, only what he overheard amongst the covens he traded with, or from listening to Gillian when he had his secret meetings. Meetings that appeared to be hidden from everyone – except the two boys, who had often eavesdropped through the vent that went down to Gillian's private cellar for as long as they could remember.

He was hesitant to discuss his findings with Oscar, as the other boy didn't seem to care about the goings-on around them anymore. That, and he would probably blab to Gillian if he thought it meant he would be in his good graces for doing so.

The ramblings from the different witches swirled through his head. War, curses, rebellions, it was all such a mess. It was no wonder the wall was being put up around the Inner Ring of the city; the higher born seemed to be preparing for a war against the witches. The wall wouldn't stop them, not really. The witches would break it down quickly with their magic – or with their demons, whichever got here first.

Reid's hand closed in his pocket around the little wooden figure he had so quickly become accustomed to having there. He thought it was silly, but lately, he often found himself strangely reassured during moments of worry or danger, as if an unseen presence was guiding him through the darkness. It was a subtle feeling, almost like a whisper at the edge of his consciousness, offering comfort and direction when he needed it most.

A blonde figure joined him on the lounge, breaking his concentration and bringing him back to reality. The noise was louder than he remembered; all the younger boys were goofing off. A few had gotten into Gillian's stash of gin and were becoming very drunk. He'd lost count of how many times he had told them to settle down, he'd have to intervene soon before one of them hurt themselves.

Gillian was another problem entirely. Reid thumbed his cigarette tin. He'd have to barter for more soon, he was down the last three. Gillian hadn't returned since the day before Reid had gone to the witches. It wasn't odd for him to disappear for a few days at a time, but he always let Reid or Oscar know he wouldn't be back for a while. He also would have taken his alcohol or locked it in his cellar where they couldn't get to it.

'The wall is almost finished,' Oscar said, breaking the little bubble of silence they sat in. He was still dirty that Reid had gone to the witches alone. 'Marlo says maybe a day or so more before it's complete, then they lock the gates.'

Reid nodded. 'So, that's it then, they're cutting us off completely.'

'Seems like it.' A flat response. Reid expected as much. It had been relatively awkward between the two since he got back. Reid hadn't told Oscar where he was going; he had just left early the previous afternoon to make sure that he got to the coven just after dusk. It was the only time the witches would undeniably be around to trade. He wasn't entirely sure what they did during the daytime, but he was certain he didn't want to find out.

'How long are you gonna be mad at me for?' Reid asked while he looked at his only friend.

'Who says I'm mad?' Oscar replied as he put his hands behind his head.

'Oh, come on, you've been raggin' on me since I got back.' Reid half turned in his seat to face the other boy.

'You went without me. Without even telling me where you were going.' Oscar eyed Reid warily before continuing. 'I just thought we were better friends than that.'

'I went to trade with the witches.' Oscar cringed as Reid explained himself. 'You never like visiting them. Besides, they were so on edge because of everything that's happening lately ... I'm just glad I was able to leave in one piece.'

The witches took a particular liking to Oscar on the few occasions they had made trips into the forest together. Reid wasn't sure what it was that had them so interested in his friend. Perhaps it was the fae-like features Oscar had; the slightly pointed ears, the fine-boned cheeks. Then again, it could have been the mere fact that he was a little too eager to indulge when he first entered the camp full of seemingly young women. Either way, Oscar had been off-put after the third or fourth visit when two younger coven members had nearly bled him dry. Had it not been for Erikah intervening, neither boy may have made it back to Thornwell.

'You still could have told me where you were going. I know you didn't want to share the payment – I just thought we were past lying to each other.' Oscar said, suddenly very interested in his feet.

'A fat lot of good it did me anyway,' Reid replied. 'Gillian hasn't been back to take his fee.'

'To be honest, I don't think he's coming back,' Oscar said and sat up straighter on the lounge.

Reid's only response was to raise his eyebrow and wait for his friend to continue.

'He didn't lock his study, so I went to have a look at what was in there, and everything is gone. Well, everything important, anyway. Books and clothes were thrown everywhere, like he had been searching for something in a hurry, which we both know isn't like Gillian.'

'Do you think he's left to head inside the wall before they close us out for good?' Reid asked, again fiddling with his wooden god.

'Marlo says that once the wall is finished, no one will be able to get in or out without the King's permission.' Oscar smiled to himself. 'She asked if we could run away together, her and me.'

'You're not actually considering it?' Reid replied. 'I mean, if Gillian has somehow cheated his way inside the wall, why on earth would Marlo want to risk being locked out?'

'Love makes girls do dumb things.' Oscar grinned again. 'I half-considered it – taking her and heading south.'

It wasn't a complete surprise to Reid that Oscar would consider running away with a lord's daughter. As much as O was a lady's man throughout the Outer Ring, his one constant had always been Marlo. She took preference over the other girls who seemed to throw themselves at him.

'Why south?' Reid asked as he stared ahead to where a pair of younger boys were fighting over the last of the bread.

'The Blue Sands is meant to be nice this time of year. Plus, it's said to be the furthest away from the witches.' Oscar stood from the lounge, the old fabric going slack at the lack of weight. 'If the witches launch a war against the other realms, it will be chaos. We're all humans here, we never see the fae or witches coming to our town, we don't have alliances with the sirens, and no one hears of the mermaids.' His nonchalant manner slipped as he said, 'This wall they're building won't stop demons from slaughtering us all when we have no allies to call.'

Reid considered for a moment just how right Oscar was. As much as he acted like he didn't care about Thornwell or its politics, it seemed he had been listening in a little too well to Gillian's meetings.

'I've heard some things too,' Reid said slowly, watching for Oscar's reaction. He could have sworn he saw Oscar's pointy ears twitch at the tempting piece of information. Reid didn't know when it happened, but Oscar seemed older suddenly, as if he was invested in what was happening around them and not just girls and drinking. Maybe it wouldn't do any harm to tell Oscar what he overheard in the witch camp.

'It seems their new queen has declared war against any who won't kneel before her. She wants to rule Emodorea as a whole, not just her witches. I overheard some witches bragging last night. From what they were saying, I don't think the sirens would be of much use to us anyway.' Reid briefly explained that the sirens had declined Isadora's offer for an alliance between the two races, and that Isadora was so angry that she cursed them to the oceans.

Oscar was quiet for a moment as he considered what Reid had told him, as if summing up what this meant for his plans, his chances of possibly leaving with Marlo. They would need to go soon if that was the case. King Oswald of Thornwell would not kneel before anyone. Building the wall was a statement to the rest of Emodorea that he would not submit, stupid as it was for a mortal king to go up against possibly the most powerful witch since Brielle. At least that was what the witches raved about in the forest.

'Last night after you left, when Gillian was leaving, I overheard him talking in his study,' Oscar said. 'I'm not sure who he was talking to, but they were mentioning a bright light that some travellers had seen earlier that day to the west, toward Nonnelle.'

'I wonder if that's the curse the witches were talking about in the forest,' Reid offered.

'I'm going to search in his study.' Oscar began walking toward the door, gently pushing the two squabbling boys out of the way. Reid followed him, stopping only to tear the piece of bread in half, giving each boy a bit before continuing down the hall. The house had seen better days – it was no wonder why Gillian had up and left without caring about what happened to his property.

The two boys stopped at the base of the staircase, before the doors to Gillian's private study. Below the house, in what was presumably an old food storage room, was where he held some of his most secret meetings.

The doors were closed; Oscar had made sure to keep them shut in case any of the younger boys decided to have a closer look. He had hoped that they would assume it was locked like always and not bother trying to open them.

'What exactly are you looking for?' Reid asked Oscar as he shoved his shoulder against the heavy doors, forcing one of them open enough to slip inside. Reid glanced up the stairs to make sure they weren't being watched before heading inside and closing the door behind him.

'Money, or things I can sell,' he answered as he began pulling books off the shelves beside them. 'We'll need money if we want to travel south. To travel anywhere, really.'

'What about the other boys?' Reid asked, 'What are we meant to do with them?'

'We,' Oscar turned to face him, 'aren't meant to do anything with them. They're not our responsibility.'

Oscar had always felt that way toward the other boys, that they were all just a nuisance to him. He had told Reid that if Gillian got rid of them, they could live a lot better. Gillian wouldn't have to take as much from them to feed everyone. Reid had pointed out that Gillian's income would severely decline if he had fewer pickpockets working for him. They would be doing triple the work for the same earnings they got now, which wasn't much.

'We can't just leave them – they'll die,' Reid replied sternly, crossing his arms.

'If you want to stay and care for them, so be it, but I am not going to risk my own life to stay here and watch over a bunch of street rats.' Oscar pocketed the few pieces of coppers he had found and looked his friend in the eye. Reid could see that Oscar was silently asking him to not stay, to leave with them, or by himself, but not to stay here.

Reid was the one to break eye contact first. He flicked his cigarette packet open and closed, thumbing the top of one in the process. He wouldn't leave, not without knowing the kids were going to be looked after; and with the wall being put up, he very much doubted that the dozen or so boys upstairs would survive without him.

'Suit yourself,' Oscar said roughly as he finished up his pillaging by grabbing the half-full bottle of amber liquid from a shelf next to him. 'I'm going to meet Marlo tonight and tell her we're leaving tomorrow, before they lock us out.'

Reid nodded, standing alone in the study as his only friend opened the door and left. He knew there would be no point trying to talk him out of it. If Oscar made his mind up about something, that was the end of the discussion, he wouldn't be swayed. The wood in his pocket warmed, Reid took it as a sign that he had made the right decision to stay and protect the boys, even if it did mean signing his own death warrant.

Reid stood by the roadside on the southern side of the city. In front of him, packed and ready to go, was the only person he'd called a friend for as long as he could remember, and a very petite, somehow familiar, pretty brunette. Reid couldn't shake the feeling that he had seen her somewhere before. Marlo had agreed to leave with Oscar; she had sneaked out last night to be here this morning. By sunrise, the pair would be a few hours from Thornwell and on their way to The Blue Sands. The couple didn't know what would be waiting for them at The Blue Sands, but were eager to head away from whatever the witches would bring to Thornwell.

'Are you sure you won't come with us?' Oscar asked one more time. He had spent most of the night trying to convince Reid to go with them. Marlo, however, seemed slightly annoyed at the idea of a third wheel. She showed her annoyance at Oscar's question by rolling her eyes.

'No,' Reid replied, glancing at Marlo, the supposedly sweet daughter of a lord. 'No, I have to stay and watch the boys, or at least try to organise moving them south as well.'

Oscar nodded. 'Well, this might be goodbye then.'

'We'll see each other again,' Reid said, hiding the small amount of pain that built inside him as he spoke those words. They both knew the chances of seeing each other again were very slim. Even if Reid survived whatever was to come, he would have to make it to The Blue Sands. He prayed the pair made it safely.

'Maybe we will,' Oscar agreed, holding out his hand. They had spent the better part of eight years together, and it was all ending so suddenly. Yesterday afternoon, chatting in Gillian's study before Oscar headed off to meet Marlo – who, in turn, decided right then was the best time to leave her home and her family without a word to anyone – to today saying their final goodbyes. Such little organisation or planning before the pair rushed off ... well, it worried Reid.

'We need to go.' Hushed but stern words from Marlo, who was standing with her arms crossed looking down her nose at Reid. With a brief shake of hands, Oscar bid farewell to Reid as he and Marlo turned and left Thornwell. It would take them well over a week to travel by foot, so long as they didn't get lost in the dunes on the way. Reid had never ventured outside the city, save for the forest, and he wasn't sure that Oscar had either, considering he was from the Northern Mortal Realm. The north, where it was snowy and had more dark days than light, was very different from the south's dry, barren desert. Spanning the treacherous expanse between Thornwell and The Blue Sands, colossal dunes rose like silent behemoths. Golden crests, tinted blue from the vast open sky, the lure of the horizon as deceptive as a siren's call, meant many travellers met their fate in the shifting embrace of the arid giants.

Oscar turned and waved to him one last time before disappearing over a dune, and Reid prayed his friend wouldn't be another one lost to the whispers of the wind. Reid stood watching the desert for a few more moments before turning and heading back toward Gillian's. He needed to develop a plan, and fast, before they were all locked out of the inner city.

CHAPTER TEN

Thornwell, Southern Mortal Realm

+ REID +

THE IDEA OF LEAVING the boys at Madame Jessamine's wasn't one that Reid liked. He was, however, out of ideas as he made his way through the marketplace. He'd thought to stop and ask one of the farmers closer to the forest, but he knew they would never agree to take on one, let alone all the boys. They were struggling as it was, another mouth to feed would potentially end them. Madame Jessamine might not have a use for boys so much as if they were girls, but she might be able to offer them shelter. They could clean, run errands, and perhaps she might take a liking to them if they brought her pretty trinkets every now and again. Reid turned left and headed past the dismal looking fruit stalls and toward one of the fancier buildings in the Outer Ring.

His fingers curled around the worn rope, fibres fraying under his desperate grip. With two sharp pulls, the brass bell above clanged, its echo slicing through the murmurs of the crowd. Cheeks aflame, he felt the weight of the onlookers' scornful eyes, their silent judgement as palpable as the midday sun. The door flew open a few moments later – just like Madame Jessamine to not keep her guests waiting. The young girl who opened the door couldn't have been much older than thirteen.

'Please come in, sir.' She curtsied awkwardly while Reid tried to shuffle past her into the dimly lit parlour. 'What service can I offer you today?'

'Ugh.' Reid stilled as the girl eyed him expectantly. 'No, I just wish to speak with Madame Jessamine.'

'Madame doesn't take new clientele anymore,' the girl offered with a tilt of her head. 'Perhaps there's another lady that would tickle your fancy?'

'No, sorry, you misunderstand.' Reid held his hands up. 'I work for Gillian, he's a close friend of hers. I need to speak with her urgently if you could—'

'Please, wait here.' The girl cut him off, gesturing to the plump, velvet armchair behind him before she disappeared up the spiral staircase.

Reid stood for a moment, watching her all too young figure sashay her way up the last few stairs before he took a seat on the edge of the chair. It was softer than anything he had felt before, even softer than the silk shirt Gillian had given him to wear to the Inner Ring when they went. He was busy running his hand over the deep crimson armrest when a familiar voice interrupted his thoughts.

'When Tati said one of Gillian's boys had come to see me, I had hoped it was that fair-haired fellow. What was his name again?' Madame Jessamine stopped on the bottom step, thinking for a moment, her fingers toying with the lace of her dress.

'Oscar,' Reid supplied. 'Madame.'

'Ah, yes, I do wish he would have taken my offer the last time we spoke.' Madame Jessamine positioned herself in the matching chair across from Reid. 'Such a shame. So, why has Gillian sent you to see me?'

'He hasn't, Madame,' Reid's fingers raked through his hair. 'I haven't seen him in a few days.'

'Well, whatever would you need to speak to me about?' Madame Jessamine raised an eyebrow. 'We have no business together.'

'No, Madame, we don't. But you see, Gillian left a handful of boys—'

'If Gillian did not send you for business purposes, then we have nothing to discuss.' Madame Jessamine cut him off as she stood, straightening her skirts in the process. 'Tati, see him out, will you?'

'Please, Madame.' Reid's voice broke through the silence as he rose swiftly, his hand reaching out to clasp her arm. She spun, recoiling from his touch as though scorched by invisible flames. 'I have a group of young boys. They need shelter, what with Gillian having left us.'

'What would you have me do about it?' Madame Jessamine turned on him. 'What use do I have for little boys?'

'They could clean,' Reid offered. 'You could send them on errands, they could perhaps put their skills to use the way Gillian had them do.'

'With the wall going up, I doubt I'll be able to maintain my girls much longer, let alone boys.' Madame Jessamine confessed, her gaze drifting towards the looming barrier. For a heartbeat, her steely facade melted, revealing a glimpse of the struggle within. But as quickly as it came, it vanished, her eyes crystallising into frosty resolve. 'I cannot help you.'

Before Reid could argue, she disappeared through the two doors that led to the entertainment area. Tati gently touched his arm, a knowing look on her face.

'You could try the orphanage,' Tati offered before she closed the door. He stood on the steps for a moment, wondering if it was worth the risk to try again. No doubt Madame Jessamine would just become angered if he persisted with the request. His hands found solace in the depths of his pockets as he meandered through the bustling market. The scent of ripe fruit and the clink of coins tugged at his resolve. With each step, the urge to lift a loaf or a shiny apple grew, fuelled by the stall owners' lax gazes, more fixed on the passersby than on guarding their wares.

There was no way the orphanage would take on Gillian's boys, not with the closing of the wall. Madame Jessamine had said it herself – the people of the Outer Ring were already struggling. Add the loss of business from the Inner Ring, and it wouldn't be long before people started fighting and killing each other to survive. He would have to think of something else. Maybe he could convince the boys to head south, follow Oscar and Marlo. It would be the safer option, that was certain. Though, there was an ominous feeling in the air as Reid walked up the street to Gillian's that things were going to get much, much worse.

CHAPTER ELEVEN

Witch's Keep, The Forest of Brielle

+ ISADORA +

IT HAD BEEN FOUR days since Isadora had cursed the Sky Kingdom to be bound to their sister nation of the sea. Four days and she had heard nothing from Nerophine, nor any other ruler. She had sent word to both the Northern and Southern Mortal Realms, all but ordering them to kneel before her. Neither had replied. Her witches that returned from The Timeless Fields said the fae had openly refused the command. The fae were her only genuine concern if it was to come to a war, and they were the only real threat now that the sirens had been dealt with.

She sat in her room before her mirror, contemplating her next move. Frowning, she curled her hand into a fist until her sharp nails pierced the skin of her palm, then slammed it down on the marble vanity, her black blood splattering around it. Years of planning were being wasted because mere humans would not fall at her feet willingly.

'Anika!' She bellowed to her servant waiting outside her door. The door creaked open slightly, enough that she could hear her Queen, but not enough to see her. 'Send for Norella.'

'As you wish, my Queen.' The reply was quiet and timid. Anika wasn't someone the Queen would typically have around, but her family had served the witches for thousands of years. Anika's ancestor was one of the first servants who had tended to Isadora when she had come of age. She stared into the mirror as she remembered the first time she had met Lacey, the first one who had seemed to give a damn more about her than her half-sister, Hesta.

†

'You need to work on your concentration, Isadora,' Graciella chastised from across the room as she watched her daughters summon their magic. Isadora and her sister had been practising for hours. Yet, much to Isadora's dismay, only Hesta's magic had flourished, earning her older sister praise from their mother while she was merely criticised and lectured.

Isadora collapsed onto her knees in exhaustion. She looked over to where her sister was idly toying with her latest creations from sand and rock. Her sister, unlike her, used the earth as her element to draw power from. It was clear that Brielle favoured her when she was blessing the unborn babies with their abilities.

In front of Hesta, the pile of rock and sand swirled in a small circle. She had not only been able to summon power from the earth for spells but had also been able to bend it to her will; few witches were able to do that. Graciella smiled brightly at Hesta as she circled the floor, inspecting her handy work. Her eyes met Isadora's as she glanced up.

Hesta must have sensed their mother's attention shift, because she also looked over at Isadora for a second before returning to her work. Isadora dropped her eyes to the floor, annoyed at her sister, her mother – but mostly herself. Hesta never even seemed to try, her power just came out of her – as naturally as breathing. It wasn't fair that she had struggled for the past fifteen months trying to master her element. Trying to summon the flames from the embers in her stomach to her fingertips was like trying to coax water from a stone. No matter how hard she concentrated, no matter how fervently she willed it, the magic remained elusive, a distant echo she couldn't quite grasp. Each failed attempt left her feeling more hollow, as if the embers that made her whole were fading away, slipping further from her reach.

'Isadora, you need so much more practice.' Graciella stopped to stand before her, while she remained kneeling on the ground. The Queen looked heavenly today. The morning sunlight streamed through the castle's stained-glass windows, and the hues of red gave her white-blonde hair a tinge of pink. All Isadora could see was an older version of Hesta, as everyone seemed to, looking down upon her.

Isadora's arm shot out, a sharp gesture toward Hesta that cut through the air like a blade. 'Hesta is ten years older than I am, of course she has mastered her powers already!' Her voice crackled with vexation, each word a spark igniting the space between them.

'By your age, Hesta was already well ahead of where you are.' Her mother spoke down to her, the disappointment in her voice barely concealed.

To the side, Hesta stopped what she was doing, her sand and rocks falling quietly back to the floor.

'Perhaps, Mother,' she offered as she strolled over to them, ever the graceful Princess, 'Isadora's sun magic is harder to learn than my simple earth magic.'

Graciella smiled at Hesta before returning her cold stare to her younger daughter. 'You are my daughter, Isadora, there is a high expectation of you to be powerful. Much more powerful than the other witches.' She continued walking around the room as she spoke. 'What do you think would happen if the rest of the covens discovered that one of my heirs was weak?'

Isadora kept quiet; she knew it wasn't a question that her mother wanted her to answer. If she was weak, the other covens might try to take the crown from their family. The title of 'Queen' – which had been in their family since the great Brielle had passed it to her Second after the gods decided she deserved a place amongst them – would be bestowed on another bloodline.

'Do you want a lesser born to be able to take the crown from you?' her mother chided.

'No, Mother. Please, I just need more time, more practice,' Isadora pleaded, something she unquestionably hated doing.

'Lacey!' Her mother called to the door.

A petite, brunette human walked forward from where she was standing near the doorway with the others. She held her head high for a servant, especially one that was amongst royalty and power. She bowed low as she came within speaking distance of the Queen and her daughters.

'You will attend Isadora from now on. You will do whatever you can to assist her in her royal duties, find her whatever books she needs, and help her to train with her powers. Your bloodline is hers,' Graciella said. 'But you will still always answer to your Queen first.'

'Mother, please, I don't need a handmaid.' Isadora looked upon the human with disgust. She hated mortals, almost as much as she hated her mother right now.

'It seems to me that you need to be watched a lot more closely than I thought. I will be getting daily reports from Lacey about your activities.'

Lacey nodded her understanding before holding out her hand to help Isadora from the ground. She ignored the help and hauled herself to her feet before storming from the room, acknowledging no one on her way out.

Lacey followed behind her silently, as if she wasn't there at all. Isadora had to check a few times to see if she was still following her and, when it was clear Lacey was still there, she would mumble under her breath about a disgusting smell following her. Of course, it was a lie. Lacey seemed to have an entirely different smell about her than the other humans around. Something a little more ... enticing than the typical smell of fear she got from the others.

'Is there anything I can get for you?' Lacey asked politely as she closed the door behind her. She had followed Isadora to her room, as she had been instructed by the Queen.

'No, I'm done with training for today, it has given me a headache.' Isadora flopped backward onto her bed. She would be eighteen soon; most witches had complete control of their powers by her age. Hesta had mastered hers at fifteen, one of the youngest witches to ever even get her gifts that early. After all, it was rumoured that her father was born of witch blood, as rare as they were. Isadora wasn't sure who her father was, probably some human her mother had been fraternising with, which would explain her lack of power.

'Some tea or food then?' Lacey offered, supposedly she wasn't going away.

She must have taken Isadora's lack of reply as a no because she continued to talk. About trivial things mostly, the weather, the winter solstice that would be upon them in the next month. Isadora had laid there half-listening before her eyes jerked open as Lacey gave a slight squeal upon noticing Isadora's hand.

Isadora herself hadn't noticed that her palm was bleeding where her nails had dug into the skin in her frustration earlier. Three gashes were openly weeping as she stretched her hand out to inspect it. Lacey was there within a second, rags in one hand and ointment of some sort in the other.

Isadora watched in awe as Lacey tended to her hand. This girl, not much older than she was, who was clearly not scared of what she was, sat beside her on her bed and gently mended her wounds. Something inside Isadora shifted as she watched the soft hands move over and under as they wrapped a rag around it, tying it in a little bow on the top.

Lacey looked up when she was finished and gave Isadora a genuine smile, something she wasn't used to receiving.

†

Isadora wiped away the tear that was rolling down her cheek, annoyed at herself for letting a memory like that slip its way into her head. She didn't have time to start feeling sentimental about this sort of thing. In the end, Lacey had left her, just like everyone else eventually had. Hesta had all but turned against her once she was named heir. The other witches only saw her as second to Hesta, no longer equal. She had been all but useless to them, despite being more powerful than her elder sister.

'My Queen.' Norella knocked on the door before pushing it open. She could see so much of herself in Norella and so much of Hesta in the other one. There had once been a time when she thought she could love the twins, despite their mother. They just happened to be another thing that the covens cared for more than herself.

'I want you to gather your coven and head north to Winhelm.' Isadora stood from her chair and wandered to her window. 'I want you to offer King Artor one chance to surrender.'

'If he doesn't?' Norella asked.

'Burn it to the ground.' Isadora's eyes were almost glowing red as she turned to face Norella. 'Leave nothing and no one.'

CHAPTER TWELVE

Eastern Borderlands, Sky Kingdom of Nonnelle

+ TALLON +

'I told you it was too soon for you to be making such a journey,' Athena said to Tallon sternly. The pair were into their third day already of walking, and it was starting to wear on Tallon's wounds.

'It's at least another two-day walk to the base of Nonnelle.' Tallon's breaths came in ragged gasps as she slumped against the cool, unyielding surface of a nearby rock. Each inhale was a struggle, each exhale a surrender of the fatigue that gripped her body. 'We've already spent three days since she cursed us travelling, they won't have enough time to fly to the sea if we don't hurry.'

It had taken them two long, slow days to make it from Isadora's keep to the edge of the forest, where they were then met with vast green plains that stretched on as far as either could see. They would be out in the open from here on, save the few odd trees and rocks here and there. The fields stretched north to join The Timeless Fields and south to become the dunes of The Blue Sands.

'I was sent with you to make sure your wounds don't fester and if you keep going like this without rest ...' Athena's voice trailed off and she gave Tallon a meaningful look as she handed her the water flask.

'I know, but my people ...' Tallon looked toward her home in the west as she lifted the flask to her lips, the cool water cascading down her parched throat. Tallon knew Nerophine's worry would be etching deeper lines in the Queen's proud face with each passing moment, and her anticipation to return was tinged with unease. The air itself seemed to hold the weight of her decision to journey unaccompanied, a choice made for the swiftness solitude could grant. Now, the unforeseen and perilous consequences were hers alone to bring word back to her people.

She had been ready to leave the moment Elsbeth had arrived at dawn yesterday morning, had already spoken with Alanah and Athena about some supplies. She had sat and listened to Elsbeth's story, learning the witch that had maimed her was Elsbeth's twin sister, Norella. Elsbeth had explained to Tallon briefly about how internally she was at odds with the changes that had occurred since Isadora's ascension to the throne.

Tallon had asked for Elsbeth to come with her, as a way to escape and as thanks for saving her life. Elsbeth had refused, swapping glances with Alanah before asking Athena to accompany Tallon home instead. Uncertainty shrouded their every thought, with no clear path on how to stop Isadora. Yet, Elsbeth had insisted that Tallon had to make it home safely, that the sirens needed to reach the ocean's sanctuary. For, if the transformation overtook them – tails unfurling, gills blossoming – away from the sea … well, their existence on the parched earth would be short-lived.

As long as they still had their wings, Tallon planned to get them to fly east, following one of the rivers that led to the bay. At least if they didn't make it the whole way, they'd have a better chance of surviving if they were in the river.

Athena placed a hand on her shoulder, just above where her wings would have been.

'It's okay, we'll make it in time, I promise.' Athena's voice was firm with confidence. Tallon smiled at her, thankful that she wasn't making this trip alone. They'd have until sunset to get as far as they could before they would need to find somewhere to set up for the night, preferably somewhere out of the open.

'Come on then.' Tallon pushed off the rock and slung her water satchel over her back again.

+ ATHENA +

As the sun climbed higher, its fiery gaze bore down on the pair. Tallon pressed on, her protests growing with each halt Athena demanded. Every few hours, like clockwork, she would coax Tallon to pause their relentless march, insisting that it was for Tallon's own good that she rested and had her wounds cleaned and redressed if they needed it. Yet, it was the weight of her words, heavy with unspoken truths, that seemed to anchor Tallon's restless soul.

'If death claims you before we reach Nonnelle,' Athena was blunt as she wiped yet another layer of grime from the siren's back, 'then your people will suffer a worse fate than you.'

Athena's gaze swept across the landscape, drinking in every nuance of the world around them. Beside her, Tallon moved with a confident stride, her every step sure and unerring, as if an invisible thread pulled her towards their unseen destination. Athena, however, felt adrift, her sense of direction unravelling like thread from a spool. For her, this was all new territory. She had felt a thrilling pulse of discovery quicken her heartbeat this morning when they broke the tree line. It was a landscape so starkly different from the cloistered forest she had lived in, where the dense canopy held whispered secrets. Here, the world was an open book, its pages blank and waiting for her footsteps to write their story. Even though they walked in a reasonably straight line, she wasn't entirely sure that she could find her way back to the Forest of Brielle alone. Tallon was yet to say whether she would be accompanied or not.

They were less than halfway when the sun began setting on the horizon in front of them, covering the green fields around them in an orange hue. As Athena declared it was time to stop for the night, a silence settled between them, thick with unspoken fears. She watched as a shadow passed over Tallon's face, the corners of her eyes creasing with a sorrow too profound for words. Her shoulders slumped ever so slightly, a silent surrender to the encroaching night that whispered of their delayed arrival. There was a heaviness in her gaze, one that spoke volumes of the journey's toll and the weight of consequences yet to come. It was a look that needed no translation, a testament to an inevitable reality.

'There's no way I can get to them and give them enough time to get to the sea.' Tallon's head hung in her hands as the pair sat between some boulders they had come across. Athena stoked the small fire that separated them. It was big enough for them to cook their food and give them warmth, but small enough to remain unnoticed.

'It'll be alright,' Athena offered. 'Perhaps the curse will take longer to reach them than Isadora thinks.'

'A fortnight was all she gave us.' Tallon looked lost as she stared at Athena through the fire. 'It's easily a two-day flight without rest to get to the Eastern ocean – that's if they haven't already started the transformation.'

'Curses can be a fickle thing,' Athena said as she handed Tallon a cup of warm tea. 'No one is ever actually sure what the outcome will be when they chant them. I mean, one can hope that it ends up how they want, but there is always a chance that it won't be exactly as they wish.'

'If only I had accepted my Queen's offer to take an escort with me, they at least could have flown home to warn everyone.' Tallon sipped her tea – chamomile. Athena was trying to settle her nerves.

'They most likely would have suffered the same fate you have, or worse.' Athena drained her cup. 'Do you want me to look at your wounds for you before we go to sleep?'

Tallon opened her mouth to reply but stopped, twitching her head slightly, so the feathers in her hair caught the firelight. Athena was about to ask her what was wrong when a thunderous noise surrounded them. Tallon jumped to her feet, wincing at the pain as her movements pulled on her healing skin.

'What in Brielle is that noise?' Athena asked, covering her ears as she moved to stand beside Tallon.

'That,' Tallon said, her face alight, 'is the sound of home.'

Tallon rushed from their small spot between the boulders and into the open field that surrounded them; Athena followed suit just as two muscular sirens landed before them.

Athena had never seen a siren before, save Tallon, of course. She marvelled at their wings before they folded in at their sides, the feathers settling along their shoulders and arms. Athena couldn't imagine seeing Tallon with the same solid legs and huge claws that these two had, let alone with golden brown feathers and colourful tails.

'Cilla, Peita,' Tallon cried as she rushed toward them, the pair barely able to kneel before she collided with the first one.

'Lady Tallon,' the first one said as Tallon released her. 'Your wings …' her voice trailed off as she inspected the rest of Tallon's body.

'Queen Nerophine sent us after you didn't return yesterday as expected, we feared the worst,' the other said in a much sterner voice than the first one.

'Cilla.' Tallon moved toward the second, stopping short of hugging her as well. 'Is my cousin alright?'

'There has been a little unrest amongst our people after the light two days ago, but otherwise fine,' Cilla replied. She placed a fist over her heart before adding, 'my Lady.'

'My Lady?' Athena stepped out from the shadow of the boulders into the moonlight.

Both of the sirens moved to step in front of Tallon as they sized up the potential threat before them. Athena stepped back slightly, looking to Tallon for help.

'Peita.' Tallon put her hand on the first's arm as she was about to pull her sword from her waist. 'She's fine, this is Athena. She helped save me.'

'Save you?' Peita asked Tallon questioningly.

'Now's not the time to tell it,' Tallon said to both of them. 'I need you to take us to Nonnelle.'

'You intend for us to take the witch as well?' Cilla all but spat the word at Tallon.

'Yes, both of us.' Tallon stood tall, despite the two sirens being taller than her with their eagle-like legs.

'Outsiders, especially witches, are not welcome in Nonnelle,' Cilla replied. 'Nerophine will not be happy.'

'Queen Nerophine,' Peita corrected, 'will be happy that her cousin is alive, and I'm sure she will appreciate anything that this *woman* has done to help.'

Tallon gave Peita a thankful glance as she nodded at Athena to follow her back to their small fire.

'Are you sure you need me to come?' Athena asked as they doused the fire and packed away the few bits of food they had out.

'Of course, you will be able to offer counsel on the subject of your Queen,' Tallon said. 'Besides, I like your company.'

Athena's cheeks reddened slightly at the compliment; she had never really had anyone *want* to spend time with her since moving from the bay to the forest. She had her coven, sure, but that was more of a birthright than anything – they didn't choose her.

'I'm not carrying the witch,' Cilla declared as the pair came back with their things, her silver eyes glaring at Athena from under long black lashes.

'Her name is Athena,' Tallon asserted. 'Peita, would you mind carrying her? I don't trust Cilla – she would probably drop her.'

'Yes, my Lady,' Peita replied as she held out a hand to Athena.

Hesitantly, Athena took the offered hand and stepped toward the siren. She looked to where Cilla had wrapped her arms around Tallon's waist and was about to launch into the sky.

'You'll be fine,' was all Peita offered before launching into the air herself.

The wind rushed past Athena, a fierce companion that tangled her hair in wild abandon. It lashed against her skin, a cool, insistent force that heralded their climb towards the heavens. With each surge upward, the air grew thinner, a subtle shift that whispered of their proximity to the realm above. Her eyes stayed scrunched shut as they propelled forward through the night sky. She listened to the heavy beat of Peita's wings, almost in time with Cilla's, who flew a few metres to the side of them.

'You can open your eyes.' Peita laughed. 'I thought you witches were used to flying on your brooms.'

'We aren't all able to fly.' Athena swallowed a laugh as she cracked one eye open, then the other. The world below dwindled, a tapestry of colours and shapes blurring into the distance, as they pierced the veil of clouds.

'Well, I remember my grandmother telling me stories of the covens of witches that flew through the skies when she was a child,' Peita said fondly.

'That must have been centuries ago,' Athena said, feeling her stomach lurch as a space in the clouds appeared and she realised just how far up they were. 'Less and less of us are being born with the ability.'

'Must be to do with the diluting blood,' Peita said. 'Our kind is much the same.'

She told Athena that Peita, Tallon, and a few others remained the only ones born in their generation that had ended up with the appearance of pure sirens. The others had all taken on the father's traits and had been cast out by the sirens. It was something that Peita hated the idea of, but then she was one of the few who thought that way about their lifestyle. Athena listened with interest.

They soared through the night's embrace, the stars their silent companions, until the first whispers of dawn began to chase away the darkness. Behind them, in the east, a crescendo of light burst forth, spilling over the edges of the world in a symphony of colour. As the light flooded past them, it set the world ablaze with life; the crystal-covered castles that floated on the horizon caught the sun's fiery kiss, igniting into a spectacle of sparkling brilliance. The castles shimmered, reflecting the dawn's radiance, and for a moment, it seemed as though they were not merely structures of stone and crystal, but living things, pulsing with the heartbeat of the new day. Even from this distance, Athena could tell that the Sky Kingdom was a beautiful place. It was no wonder they kept outsiders away. The kingdom sat alone on this side of the continent, floating high enough that Athena doubted you would even see it from the ground.

To the left, all she could see was golden dunes and desert for miles; to the right, the empty fields gave way to darker green pastures and snow-capped mountains. The fae lands lay in that direction, to the northwest of her home in Brielle Forest. As Peita began their descent into Nonnelle, Athena prayed to Brielle that the Queen would welcome her as Tallon had, especially after hearing what Queen Isadora had done.

CHAPTER THIRTEEN

Nonnelle, The Sky Kingdom of Nonnelle

+ TALLON +

NEROPHINE STORMED THROUGH the castle, Tallon close behind, her wounds aching as she tried to keep up.

'She's a witch!' Nerophine practically screeched.

'Yes, but she helped *save* me,' Tallon countered as the pair turned down another hallway, further from the room where Athena had been locked. They had arrived the day before, and since then, Tallon had been trying to prove that Athena could be trusted, explaining that the young witch had helped heal her, that she'd probably be dead if not for Athena's help.

Tallon swallowed, phantom pains tracing the path of her still-raw scars.

She knew that Nerophine would disregard her pleas that Athena was an ally the moment she saw the scars. She'd seen the decision forming in her cousin's mind, and desperation had clawed at Tallon as she tried to argue against the Queen's decision. But Athena's feet had barely touched the surface of Nonnelle before the Siren Queen had ordered the guards to arrest the witch. Tallon had spent every moment since pleading with Nerophine, her words falling on deaf ears.

Thankfully, Athena had been placed in one of the castle's spare rooms under constant supervision from the guards and not in one of the dungeons. As a peaceful race, the sirens hadn't made use of their dungeons for aeons, and Tallon was now glad that they had fallen into somewhat of a ruin and were deemed unusable.

Nerophine stopped before the door to the council room and sighed as she turned to face Tallon. Her face was etched with worry, the lines as pronounced as the scars now marring Tallon's once smooth, flawless skin. There was no doubt in Tallon's mind that Nerophine had been filled with dread the entirety of her absence. But her heartache would have been tenfold had Athena and the older witches not ensured Tallon's return.

'Nerophine,' Tallon seized the moment to voice her concerns again, 'I know there's a lot happening, but Athena hasn't wronged us. She helped me – healed me.'

Nerophine's gaze was steely, her voice unwavering. 'I cannot be concerned with this right now. I need to ready our people to move.'

Tallon felt a knot tighten in her stomach. Late last night, when not imploring Nerophine to reconsider her actions, she had shared the dire news about the curse with the council. By her calculations, they only had a few days to reach the ocean. The council had debated late into the night about the best course of action to take. Nerophine had suggested they head south toward The Blue Sands, to avoid the heavily mermaid-populated area to the east, but some council members argued it was too risky. There was no water between Nonnelle and The Blue Sands; if they transformed suddenly, they would all be at risk of dying. After much back and forth bickering, they had decided it was best to head east, following The Wandering River until it met the sea.

Tallon shivered, remembering how – even though she had sat to the side, remaining quiet unless spoken to – she had felt the weight of the many curious eyes that roamed over her now human form. Her heart pounded with anxiety at the thought.

'I understand that, but keeping her locked up isn't the answer. She can help us.' Tallon was annoyed – and tired – and she let it show as Nerophine opened the door to the room and the two entered.

'How can she help us?' Nerophine asked as she moved inside and to the window to view the preparations taking place outside.

'She can help ensure that we have a safe passage through Brielle Forest,' Tallon hobbled over to the window beside her. 'We can't very well go around it, we don't have the time.'

'I just ...'

Tallon watched and waited as Nerophine struggled to find the right words.

'I just can't trust any of them after what they have done to you.'

Nerophine's fingers were gentle against Tallon's cheek as she sighed, clearly frustrated at the situation.

Tallon stared up at her cousin. For the first time since they were children, she was shorter than Nerophine. Without her strong siren legs and wings, Tallon felt so small and fragile. She shivered again. Soon, they would all look as she did.

Nerophine removed her hand from Tallon's cheek and turned back toward the window.

'We leave at dawn.' Tallon stared at the ground as Nerophine spoke. 'We will fly as far as we can before we lose our wings ... then have to walk the rest of the way.'

Tallon waited in silence, unsure of what else she could say to sway her cousin's mind.

'In the meantime, I will think over what we will do with your witch friend.'

Tallon nodded. She knew it was the best answer she would get, and so left her Queen to watch the guards outside organising their supplies and headed back inside. She needed to see Athena, to let her know that she was trying to get Nerophine to understand.

+ ᴀᴛʜᴇɴᴀ +

Athena sat alone in the spacious room the sirens had escorted her to not long after their small party landed at the outpost. When she first laid eyes on the glittering castle of Nonnelle, she had assumed they would all land in a courtyard or something. But Peita and Cilla had veered left and aimed for a high tower on the western side of the island, landing on a smooth, polished-stone platform covered in intricate carvings of feathers and wings etched into the surface.

The outpost served as a lookout, with a three-hundred and sixty degree view. One could see as far as the distant green plains of The Timeless Fields to the north, the desert toward the south and the west, and the gleaming ocean off in the very far distance to the east. Athena had a small moment of vertigo as she peered off the edge, and wondered how they planned to get down if not by flying. But then she saw the staircase that was hidden in the centre of the platform, leading into the tower below.

Considering the room she was in now was meant to be her prison, it was rather comfortable. She had a lounge and a bed, private bathing chambers, and a small fireplace. If she had to guess, it probably wasn't supposed to be used to keep someone locked up. There were worse places to be held, of that she was certain, so she tried not to feel resentful.

Tallon had insisted that she did not need to be contained and would stay of her own free will. Of course, Athena did just as Tallon said she would and did not fight back or argue when the Queen asked for the door to be locked and guarded. In truth, she agreed with how the Queen handled the situation; it was the same way anyone would have done if a stranger entered their home – remove the potential threat first, then consider the options. Still, she had been left alone the previous day and night. It was surely noon by now and the only time she had any company was when she was brought food – even Tallon was yet to visit.

Athena sank back into the soft bed, her head nestling into the plush pillows. She gazed at the ornate ceiling, her mind racing. The comfort of the bed was stark in contrast to the turmoil churning in her stomach. Who would have thought that saving a siren would lead to her imprisonment in the Sky Kingdom? She traced the delicate patterns on the quilt, trying to find solace in the luxury surrounding her, even as she awaited her uncertain fate.

A sharp knock at the door jolted her upright. The door creaked open, and a head of white-blonde hair peeked through, eyes scanning the room with a quick, assessing glance. Satisfied, the figure slipped inside, the door closing softly behind them.

Relief washed over her, mingled with a flicker of hope.

'I was beginning to think I would be left here while you all made your escape.' Her voice was tinged with lingering fear. She shifted on the bed, creating space for Tallon to sit beside her, her eyes never leaving Tallon's face.

'Yes,' Tallon replied as she sniffed at some food that was left on the table before making her way over to Athena. She sat down with a sigh, her expression a mix of exhaustion and regret. 'I'm sorry about all of this.'

'Will your people make it to the bay before they change?'

Tallon raised her eyebrows, seeming surprised that Athena still cared despite being imprisoned. 'Yes, my Queen is prepared for us all to depart in the morning,' she said, picking at her nails.

'What shall I be doing tomorrow?' Athena asked, somewhat hesitantly. Her fingers twisting the hem of her dress nervously. The uncertainty gnawed at her – surely, they wouldn't leave her here.

'I am to be told tonight,' Tallon said as she tugged at the feathers still woven into her blonde hair, the last reminder of the beautiful wings she'd once had.

'I see,' Athena said, her face just as grim. Her thoughts churned. She didn't think she was prepared for what answer she may receive. The weight of it all pressed down on her until she felt like she would be crushed under the pressure.

'I am trying everything I can to make my cousin understand,' Tallon said, as she turned to face her, the siren's eyes filled with determination. 'I promise you, I will see you home as you did for me.'

'Thank you,' Athena replied as she offered Tallon a small, grateful smile. She took a deep breath, allowing a glimmer of hope to bloom inside her.

'I asked for you to be let out of this room, to be confined to the castle still, but be allowed to roam,' Tallon continued, her voice softening with regret. 'But the council would not allow it … I'm sorry.'

'It is not your fault.' Athena's heart sank as she placed her hand on top of Tallon's. 'Thank you for trying.'

'Is there anything I can get you? We don't have herbs for tea as you do, but perhaps I can have them bring you some broth or something hot?'

If anything, Athena was simply craving company. The silence of the room felt oppressive. She was so used to being with Alanah that she never realised she had become so accustomed to it. She glanced at Tallon, the weight of her unspoken request heavy on her tongue. There was no way she could ask Tallon to merely sit with her in this room, unable to go anywhere. Especially considering that it was Athena's own queen that had brutalised Tallon and cursed her people mere days ago. She marvelled at Tallon's kindness, struggling to understand how she could even look at her, let alone offer such support at a time like this.

'No, I have everything I need, thank you,' she said, removing her hand. 'I might just have a bath while I await your Queen's answer.'

'Sure.' Tallon nodded slowly. 'I will leave you to it.'

She stood and made her way to the door before turning back one last time. 'I will let you know as soon as she tells me the council's decision.'

With that, Athena's only friend in this place was gone.

She was left alone in the room, this time by her own doing. Tallon had offered her an olive branch, and she had politely shoved it back in her face. She had never had a friend before; she couldn't quite say Alanah was one. Alanah was her mentor, more like a mother than anything. She sighed and stood from the bed. A bath would help her relax while she waited to know the Siren Queen's answer.

CHAPTER FOURTEEN

Thornwell, Southern Mortal Realm

+ REID +

JUST AS MARLO had warned, anyone who had not been able to secure themselves a place inside the wall were locked out and, just as Madame Jessamine had suggested, the slums were chaotic. Reid had tried to confine the few younger boys to Gillian's house – or what he supposed was now their house, since Gillian had yet to return. He'd left almost a week ago.

Reid could only assume that, since he never came back, Gillian had somehow secured a position in the Inner Ring. Oscar and Marlo had left around the same time, though they should reach The Blue Sands in the next day or so, all going to plan. Reid silently prayed to Kasin to protect them on their journey, not that he would have any way of knowing if anything had happened to them.

Reid clutched at the wooden carving of Kasin, its smooth surface worn from countless anxious rubs. Praying to Kasin was something he found himself doing a lot of late, the boys' antics pushing him to his limits. They were wild, like untamed colts, always getting into trouble – climbing trees, sneaking into the market, and playing pranks on villagers. He had failed in finding someone to take them, and failed in convincing them to leave Thornwell and head south with him. His only choice was to stay and make sure they were cared for to the best of his ability. Not that they made it easy for him – often he found himself questioning why he bothered. Yet at night when he watched them sleep, their faces peaceful and innocent, he knew he couldn't abandon them. They needed him, even if they didn't realise it.

The rest of the occupants of the slums had either drifted away, some heading south toward The Blue Sands, and others heading east toward Orabelle Bay. The ones that remained were the worst of the lot. Reid had taken to locking himself and the boys in Gillian's study with how bad the nights had become. Riots, murders, break-ins. He was sure they would be killed – or worse – if he was to let them do as they pleased.

Reid wasn't sure what he would do when they ran out of what little food they had. Without food coming from the Inner Ring anymore, they were left to fend for themselves. Reid wasn't sure what it was like on the inside of the wall, but surely, it was better than this. He had considered maybe hunting on the edge of the forest, but killing wasn't something he thought he could stomach. Not to mention he had no weapons, and it would be a risk heading into witch territory.

No, he had to find a way into the city. Maybe Gillian would be able to pull a few strings with some of his old clients, get them to let the boys inside. If he was able to find Gillian, that was. For all Reid knew, he could have high-tailed it to another city.

He let out a deep breath as he laid his head against the back of the lounge. He casually popped a cigarette between his lips. The bitter taste of nicotine enveloped him, familiar and comforting, like a warm embrace from an old friend. The isolation of a week alone with the boys was gnawing at his sanity, each passing day blurring into the next.

Two of the boys had disappeared, and he had spent too much of his time trying to find them. The five that remained ranged from six years to twelve years. None old enough to help him find food, or to even look after themselves. He spent most nights awake thinking through ideas on places he could potentially take the boys, or people that might agree to help. Most of his days he spent sneaking food from the few vendors that still operated. Oscar was probably right; he should have left with them. As much as Marlo visibly didn't want him around, the awkward trip south with them seemed like a holiday compared to trying to care for the boys.

'Reid!' A panting, red-headed boy skidded to a stop in front of him, causing Reid to drop his cigarette tin. The boy doubled over trying to suck air into his lungs.

'What's wrong, Ivor?' Reid scooped the tin up off the ground, wiping the face of it with the sleeve of his shirt. The engraving still looked as clear as the day he was handed it. It was the first thing he had owned since his aunt died that he didn't steal. He never could work out what the symbol on the front meant, the strange pattern of dots and lines. It reminded him of stars. As hard as he tried, he could never remember the face of the person who gave it to him.

'I was in the market, lookin' for food, when I heard some travellers talkin'. Talkin' 'bout Win'elm.' Ivor breathed heavily for a few more seconds before continuing. 'Win'elm is gone.'

'What do you mean "gone"?' Reid demanded as he rose to his feet.

'They was saying that a few nights ago the kingdom was overrun by witches. That they killed everyone.' Ivor was finally breathing normally. 'I ran the whole way 'ere to tell you. They was saying that the king wouldn't bow to the witches, so they slaughtered everyone and burned it to the ground.'

'Make sure all the boys are inside before sunset and lock yourselves in the study,' Reid ran his hand through his messy hair. He pocketed the cigarette tin and patted Ivor on the shoulder. 'You know you shouldn't be running like that with your lungs.'

'You know smokin' will kill ya.' Ivor retorted. 'Where're you goin', anyway?'

'I need to get into the city, I need to find someone,' Reid replied as he headed out the front door. 'And I don't smoke.'

If the witches had taken Winhelm, then the rumours he had heard circulating the coven that night must be real. They were declaring war on the Kingdoms of Emodorea. It wasn't that Reid overly cared about politics, but if they had so easily wiped out Winhelm, then it wouldn't be long before they made their way south to Thornwell, and that meant that he and the boys were at risk.

As he ran through the streets of Thornwell toward the Inner Ring's wall, a million thoughts ran through his head. The main being what would happen to those not inside the wall if the witches did turn their attention towards the Southern Mortal Realm. The King would never kneel to the Witch Queen, which would undeniably mean that the witches and their demons would invade the South, just as they had done in the North. From what Reid knew, Winhelm had a larger army and was far more protected than Thornwell was, and if the witches destroyed Winhelm then Thornwell didn't stand a chance.

Four guards stood sentinel at the imposing iron gate, their armour glinting dully under the relentless sun. As Reid approached, they stiffened, their spears clinking against their breastplates in a sloppy, synchronised motion. Their expressions, however, betrayed their disdain for the sweltering gate duty. Beads of sweat trickled down their brows, and the oppressive heat shimmered in the air.

The Southern Realm was a harsh mistress, its desert landscape unforgiving. The nights offered little respite, cooling only slightly, and true relief only came briefly during the winter months. The heat today clung to the land like a curse, making the guards' task all the more gruelling.

'You there, boy.' One of the guards stepped forward, his hand resting on his sword hilt. 'You have no business being at the wall, move along.'

'Please, I need to speak with Gillian Arcosé,' Reid called out, stopping a safe distance from the guard. Reid fumbled over Gillian's last name, the syllables feeling foreign and the sound of it leaving a bad taste in his mouth. He wasn't even sure that Gillian was aware that Reid knew his last name, let alone had the guts to speak it out loud to a palace guard.

'No one is allowed to enter or leave without the King's approval,' the guard replied, eyes narrowing slightly. 'Something I doubt you would be able to get.'

'Please, it's a matter of life and death that I speak with him. Can he not be brought to the gate?' Reid pleaded, his voice tinged with desperation. The guard's expression hardened, a silent refusal to the frantic request. Behind him, the three other guards exchanged bemused glances, their chuckles echoing in the still air.

Before Reid could react, a swift blow landed on his head, sending him reeling. He stumbled sideways, the world spinning as he crashed onto the unforgiving stone ground. Pain radiated through his skull and he tasted blood, the metallic tang mingling with the dust of the courtyard.

'Be gone, before I lose my patience.' The guard's voice was cold and final as he turned away and continued talking to the others. Their laughter a cruel reminder of Reid's humiliation.

Reid slowly pushed himself to his feet, his head throbbing from the blow. He resisted the urge to rub his aching skull, knowing it would only invite more mockery. The stone ground beneath him was rough and unyielding, much like the guards' indifference. He cast a wary glance at them, their backs now turned, and swallowed his pride. He knew better than to try to speak to them again; he'd only end up with more bruises.

Instead, he wandered along the edge of the wall, putting enough distance between himself and the guards until they vanished from sight. He paused, craning his neck to trace the towering stone structure that loomed above him, its height daunting and unscalable at over four stories. There was only one gate entrance on this side and he didn't fancy heading around to the eastern entrance and facing another set of guards. He doubted their response would be any different, and the prospect of further humiliation was not worth the effort.

'I see Kasin has been doing his job for you, then?' A voice came from the shadows. 'Apart from you being on this side of the wall, of course, and that nasty bump on your head.'

Reid spun around to face the person chuckling behind him. To his surprise, it was the old man from the shop. The one who gave him the miniature carving.

'Why aren't you in there?' Reid gave a vague gesture over his shoulder.

'It seems my shop was on the Outer Ring, after all.' The old man laughed. 'When they finally finished the wall, that is.'

Reid peered behind him, only now realising that he had wandered onto the clean, stone path instead of the dirty cobblestone he was used to.

'I'm sorry.' Reid didn't know what else to say. Other than the brief encounter he had in the old man's shop last week, he didn't know him. He idly fiddled with the wooden carving in his pocket, right next to the metal cigarette tin, as he tried to clear his thoughts.

'You look troubled. Would you like to come in for some tea?' The old man offered.

'I don't want to hassle you any more than I probably already have,' Reid said, remembering how the old man had let him slip out the back of the shop to avoid the guards.

'Nonsense, indulge an old man, would you?' He didn't wait for Reid to reply as he turned to head back into his shop. Reid took one last look at the wall and decided a cup of tea couldn't hurt.

'It's a shame what happened in Winhelm,' the old man said as he sat two cups and a pot of tea down on the table.

'How do you know about that?' Reid asked as he carefully inspected the tea cup he'd been given. The delicate porcelain was cool to the touch, and its surface was adorned with intricate designs. Tiny scrolls, each one meticulously painted, wrapped around the cup in a continuous pattern. The scrolls seemed to tell a story, their edges curling gracefully as if caught in a gentle breeze. The craftsmanship was exquisite, with each scroll detailed down to the faintest ink strokes, giving the impression of ancient wisdom captured in miniature form. Something tingled in the back of his mind as he ran a finger over the artwork.

'An old man hears many things,' he replied. 'Especially when people think he's too senile to understand what they're talking about.' He gave a slight grin as he poured himself a cup of tea and sat down. Reid hesitantly poured his own, mimicking the way he had just seen the old man do it, careful not to clink the seemingly ancient china.

'I'm sorry, I haven't even asked your name,' Reid said as he let the tea sit in his cup.

'Oh, my name isn't important at the moment.' The old man pulled a silver flask from his pocket and poured a dash into his tea. He offered some to Reid, who declined politely, unsure of what exactly he was drinking.

'My name's Reid,' he offered after a moment of silence. 'What is it that you know about Winhelm?'

'Both a great deal and also nothing at all.' The nameless old man rubbed his beard as he thought about what he had heard. 'I heard the witches attended an audience with King Artor and that he refused the Queen's demand to kneel before her.'

Reid sat quietly, sipping the bitter tea as he waited for more. He had no idea why people enjoyed drinking this stuff, it tasted like mud and smelt like damp leaves.

'I also heard that the witches burned the entire kingdom to the ground, leaving no one alive after King Artor refused,' he went on with a chuckle. 'But if that's the case, where did the stories come from?'

From the way the old man was chuckling, it seemed as though it was all amusing to him. Everyone in Winhelm had been slaughtered, which meant that roughly half of the human population was gone. Winhelm was possibly the only ally that Thornwell had, and yet they hadn't sent word for help because it had happened so suddenly.

'Why is this funny to you?' Reid slammed his cup down harder than he had intended, shattering the pretty scroll patterned porcelain across the table. The old man looked slightly taken aback by the sudden outburst. 'People are dead, our allies are dead. What are we going to do if the witches decide to turn on us next?'

The old man's face turned stern as he crossed his arms, an eyebrow raised.

Reid sighed in defeat. 'How am I meant to protect the boys if I can't get them into the city?'

'My question is, how am I going to replace a cup that's thousands of years old?' The old man gestured to the broken pieces in front of him. He stood picking a few of them up, ignoring Reid's offer of an apology, as he moved them to the workshop in the back. He muttered about lost loves and something about humans not caring for heirlooms and keepsakes.

Reid took the chance to look around the dimly lit and overly cluttered shop, its shelves lined with ancient artefacts and forgotten treasures. Each item seemed to hold a story, a piece of history that had survived the passage of time.

'Is that what you were doing, talking to the guards earlier?' The old man asked when he returned a few moments later. His face had returned to the same calm as earlier and he offered the flask to Reid once again, who took it this time. He topped up the old man's cup before taking a long swig.

'Yes, my old …' Reid searched for the word. 'My old landlord left us and ran to the city before they closed it off. I can't keep caring for the boys. I need them to get inside the city, to someone who's more fit to look after them.'

'Would your landlord have been any help, with caring for the boys, I mean? If he left you all by yourselves in the first place, why would he offer you help inside the wall?' A fair question to ask, one that Reid had been asking himself since Oscar left.

'I'm not sure,' Reid admitted, more to himself than the man in front of him. 'He's the only person in there I could ask for help, though.'

'Why not just leave, head south, away from Thornwell?' The man probed. Another question that Reid had often asked himself these past days.

'I can't leave the boys.' Reid's only answer. The same explanation he'd given O when he had asked.

'Well,' the old man grinned mischievously, his eyes twinkling with a hint of madness. 'I can't help you get into the city, but I can offer a small piece of advice. The witches will come, but they will send their demons and followers first, before they make their move.'

'How do you know that?' Reid asked as he fiddled with his carving in his pocket.

'I am much older than you think. I have seen what they can do.' The man stood from the table. 'It's getting late now – you should get back to the boys.'

'Thank you for the tea,' Reid said as he stood, 'and the advice.'

Even though telling Reid that tiny bit of information wasn't exactly going to help him, at least if anything came they would be expecting it.

'Reid,' the old man said as Reid reached the door. 'Caring so much for others doesn't have to be your weakness. One day soon, it might just be what makes you strong.'

CHAPTER FIFTEEN

Nonnelle, Sky Kingdom of Nonnelle

+ ATHENA +

ATHENA WATCHED AS the light faded from the sky window above her, shadows and darkness consuming her room. The moon's luminescent glow cast a silver sheen, allowing her to see just enough to light the few candles that lay about the place. It was a full moon tonight; she could feel the power inside her, it called to her blood. She longed to be out celebrating under the open sky.

Throughout Brielle Forest, the witches would have gathered to celebrate, their chants rising with the moon. The healers and others who summoned their powers from the moon and water would be reciting their rituals, ensuring their powers remained strong. She was sitting on the lounge, gazing at the stars overhead, when two figures appeared in her doorway.

'Queen Nerophine has summoned you to the hall.'

Much to Athena's surprise, it was Peita that entered.

'She's asked for you to be quick, as everyone is waiting.'

'Of course,' Athena said, making her way to the door; with one last look at the open sky above her, she left the room that had been her prison for the past day and a half.

The walk seemed endless; the palace was much larger than she had imagined. The corridors felt claustrophobic, with only a few sky windows high above casting narrow beams of light. She had always pictured the sirens' home to be open and airy, with plenty of spaces for flight. Yet, since their arrival, she hadn't seen a single siren take to the air. Instead, they moved through the halls with their wings folded neatly behind them, more earthbound than she had expected.

'When we get in there, try to only speak if you're asked a question,' Peita warned as she fell into step beside her. 'Not many of the council members like your kind.'

'You couldn't possibly tell me if it's good or bad news I'm getting?' It was worth a shot to ask, she thought.

Cilla silenced Peita with a sharp look that could have intimidated even Alanah. Peita gave her an apologetic shrug as they stopped before the closed doors of the throne room.

As the doors swung inward, Athena was greeted with a burst of bright light and a cacophony of voices. It was clear from the numerous tables and sirens that they were having a feast of some sort. As Athena and her escort began to make their way toward the dais, an ominous silence fell over the crowd. Sirens turned to stare, some with eyes burning with hatred, others quickly averting their gazes in fear.

At the end of the grand hall, Nerophine sat regally atop a magnificent crystal throne, its facets catching the light and casting rainbows across the room. Tallon stood by her side, a silent sentinel. Nerophine looked much more queen-like than earlier, when she had ordered Athena to be locked away. Athena's gaze flickered to Tallon, wondering if she had once looked as majestic when she still bore the form of a siren. Other than the short black hair that the Queen had, the pair could have been considered twins, their resemblance uncanny.

It seemed the sirens were not accustomed to having clothes to fit a humanoid body, so Tallon sat beside the Queen draped in what appeared to be a makeshift robe of some sort. It was very different from the set of leather pants and loose shirt that Athena had donated for her to wear. Clearly, the Queen wanted no part of her beloved cousin looking like her – like a witch.

The trio walked forward through the masses of bird-like women until they reached the base of the dais. Peita and Cilla bowed low to their Queen before stepping back behind Athena. She looked at her friend as the Queen stood and tried to gauge the situation, the outcome, but Tallon's face was unreadable. Perhaps even she did not know what her cousin would decide.

'Athena of the witches,' Nerophine began, 'What your Queen has done to our people, to my cousin, is unpardonable.' She spoke not only to Athena but to everyone in the room. Athena couldn't help but wince at the mumbled curses that came from the crowd. She merely bowed her head, unable to meet even Tallon's eyes.

'My cousin has asked me to spare you,' the Queen continued, her voice cold and measured. 'She has told me that it was you and two others who helped heal her wounds.' She paused, her gaze piercing. 'It was also you who assisted her in returning to us safely. For that, I am grateful.' She glanced at her cousin, who gave a slight nod in acknowledgement that what she had said was true.

'But my people demand justice against your kind,' Nerophine continued, her tone hardening. 'And I, too, would like nothing more than to rip your false Queen's head from her shoulders.' Her declaration was met with a roar of approval from the gathered sirens. 'Many of my fellow council members have urged that you be made an example of to your Queen, and all of witch kind.'

Athena cringed against the onslaught of cheering that followed the Queen's words. They did not know her, yet they hated her. Hated her kind enough to warrant slaughtering her as a way to avenge the curse Queen Isadora had set upon them. She hung her head in shame. Athena could not help what her Queen had done, nor could she excuse her actions. If it were Alanah, or her mother or father, she would want to exact revenge on anyone she could blame.

'I accept the consequences of Isadora's actions.' Athena's voice shook with nerves. 'Though you ought to know that I no longer consider her my Queen. I had no part in what she has done and I do not intend to return to her service.'

Nerophine considered here, the Siren Queen's head cocking to one side in a distinctly bird-like manner. 'If you do not consider her your Queen, then why is it that you accept the consequences of what she has done?' Nerophine asked as she rose and moved down the steps toward Athena.

'I accept my fate, whatever it is,' Athena answered, 'because what has been done to Tallon, what will happen to all of you, is inexcusable. If it would give Tallon some sort of closure to see a witch, even if that witch is myself, be punished for the crimes of another, then so be it.'

The Queen stopped in front of her, her feathered wings folded gently behind her, a soft rustling sound accompanying the movement. Nerophine tilted her head slightly to one side, her sharp, avian eyes narrowing in contemplation. Her posture remained poised, yet there was a certain stillness to her, as if she were weighing each thought with the precision of a hunter.

'Lies!' Someone from the crowd called out.

'We can't trust their kind,' another voice added.

'I will not be welcomed back if the Queen knows I saved the siren she brutally disfigured,' Athena countered. 'If I am to be killed, or to be imprisoned here when you leave, it would be a better fate than what Isadora would offer.'

Nerophine reached out a slender hand and gripped Athena under the chin, her talon-tipped fingers scraping the skin ever so slightly. She stared into her eyes, and Athena felt a shiver run down her spine. The Queen's gaze was piercing, as if she could see into the depths of her soul. Her heart pounded in her chest, fear and defiance swirling within her. She fought the urge to look away, determined to meet Nerophine's scrutiny head-on. Thoughts raced through her mind – would the Queen see her sincerity, her desperation? Or would she see only an enemy, a witch to be punished?

'I've decided,' Nerophine said at length, glancing over her shoulder at Tallon, Athena's chin still grasped in her hand. 'That this witch, Athena, shall accompany us to the east.' She dropped her hand and made her way back to her seat beside Tallon.

Athena stood frozen, disbelief etched across her face. Murmurs of dissent rippled through the room, the sirens' discontent palpable. She couldn't fault them; a witch had shattered their lives, stripping them of their freedom to soar the open skies and condemning them to the dark, watery heart of the ocean. But what would she do once they got to the ocean? She couldn't follow them after that.

+ TALLON +

Tallon descended gracefully, her movements fluid and silent. She placed a reassuring hand on Athena's shoulder, her touch firm yet gentle, offering a silent promise of support amidst the tension.

'Isn't this great? You'll be able to stay with us 'til we get to the ocean.'

Athena blinked and nodded her head, seeming to come back to reality.

'Yes, thank you for your persistence with your cousin.'

Tallon scrutinised her new friend's face, her sharp eyes catching every flicker of emotion. Something was off; Athena should be relieved that she wasn't being left behind. Without the sirens, there would be no escape from this lofty kingdom. Tallon's brow furrowed as she sensed the unease radiating from Athena, a silent storm of confusion brewing behind her swirling red eyes.

'I'm fine,' Athena's voice broke the silence, drawing Tallon's attention back to the conversation. 'Honestly. I'm just thinking over the fact that I will be considered a traitor to the witches.'

'I am sorry about that.' Guilt gnawed at Tallon, her voice soft but sincere. 'I am forever grateful for what you, Alanah, and Elsbeth have done for me.'

Tallon's thoughts swirled with regret and gratitude. She was thankful for the bond they had forged, but the weight of their situation pressed heavily on her heart. She squeezed Athena's shoulder gently, feeling the burden of the choices they had made.

'It is something that should never have been necessary from the start.' Athena's words struck something deep inside Tallon, her voice filled with unwavering defiance. Tallon couldn't shake the feeling that she owed Athena far more than she could possibly repay. Athena had shown her kindness, had seen her as more than just a siren or an enemy. Tallon admired Athena's ability to look beyond the surface, to see the person within, and she would do everything she could to make sure the other sirens did the same in return.

'You should get a decent sleep, we leave at dawn.' Tallon dropped her hand and added, 'I believe you will be flying with Peita again, if you're okay with that.'

Tallon noticed Athena cringe at the thought of flying again. They would soon be flying from Nonnelle, soaring over the Forest of Brielle and following The Wandering River, hoping to reach the bay before the curse claimed more sirens. Tallon shared Athena's clear doubts about their chances. The forest was treacherous, and if any sirens lost their wings, their mission would be doomed. Travelling as a large unit meant they had to move slower to accommodate the young and the old, adding to the peril of their journey.

Tallon's heart ached with worry, but she steeled herself, determined to help lead them safely through the skies as best she could.

'Yes,' Athena said, a show of bravery. 'I like Peita, I think we will be fine.'

Tallon smiled, her eyes softening in a way that lately seemed to be reserved solely for Athena, as she gestured for the witch to follow her out of the throne room.

'I'm glad to hear that,' she replied, her voice warm as she led the way back to the visitor quarters. 'We have a long journey ahead of us, I'll come get you at dawn.'

Athena nodded as they finally reached her chamber, her eyes sparkling with flecks of red as the full-moon's light washed over them from the sky windows.

'Goodnight, Athena,' Tallon's voice was as soft as a whisper as she watched Athena close the door behind her, the siren's thoughts a whirlwind of worry and hope. With a final look, Tallon turned and headed down the hallway back to her own quarters, her mind already planning for the challenges that lay ahead.

CHAPTER SIXTEEN

Alanah's Hut, Forest of Brielle

+ ELSBETH +

ELSBETH LINGERED AT THE threshold of Alanah's hut, her heart a tumultuous sea of indecision. The sun had set over an hour ago, leaving her in the pale light of the rising moon. Shadows danced around her, whispering secrets of the night. She tilted her head back, allowing her unbraided, blonde hair to cascade down her back like a waterfall of silk, shimmering faintly in the moonlight. The cool night air kissed her skin, sending a shiver down her spine as she stood there, caught between the comfort of familiarity and the unknown that awaited within.

The full moon was a time the witches relished in, especially those driven by the moon's power, as Elsbeth was. She stood still, allowing the moonlight to wash over her, feeling its power seep into her very being. She inhaled deeply, the air filling her lungs with a sense of calm and certainty. Alanah was inside, waiting to confirm what Elsbeth already felt in her bones. The signs were unmistakable now. The subtle changes in her body, the whisper of new life growing within her, mirrored the experiences of other women she had known. She was sure of it – she was with child. The realisation brought with it a mix of emotions, but under the full moon's watchful eye, she felt a strange sense of peace and anticipation.

Elsbeth felt a bittersweet relief knowing the child was Raynor's, even if she hadn't seen him in over two months. There had to be a reason he had not come to find her. The Fae Queen had most likely forbidden any of them from coming into the forest, out of fear of Isadora. She resolved to find him herself, even if she had to travel to Osteria alone. If he did not want to go with her, she would still leave Emodorea. She had to escape to another world, a safer world for her and her unborn child. Isadora would never let Elsbeth or her child live if she discovered the truth.

The door swung open, seemingly of its own accord.

'Will you stop hovering out here and come inside already?' Alanah called from somewhere inside, her voice carrying a hint of exasperation.

'Sorry.' Elsbeth murmured, tearing her gaze away from the moon as she stepped into the hut, the warmth and familiar scents wrapping around her like a comforting embrace.

She settled herself at the table near the kitchen, her fingers tracing the smooth, clean surface. She had insisted on staying to help Alanah tidy up the hut after Tallon and Athena had left a few days prior, before the sun had risen. Hopefully, the pair had found their way safely to Nonnelle in time to warn the sirens.

Alanah bustled over, her eyes twinkling with a mix of mischief and wisdom.

'They will be fine, stop fretting over them,' she chided, her voice carrying the no-nonsense tone of someone who had seen it all. She set a cup down in front of Elsbeth with a flourish, the aroma of freshly brewed tea wafting up. Elsbeth smiled to herself, *Alanah and her tea,* she thought.

'So,' Alanah began. 'It seems we have another little witch on the way.'

A girl. She was going to have a girl. She guessed that it was a positive thing; if it was a boy, the chances of him having powers were few. A girl witch – and part fae, at that – would be a powerful being. It had been a long time since a witch was born with a fae father. Sure, some witches came to them from male-born witches that bred with human or fae females. Sometimes even sirens or mermaids. They were usually weaker, thanks to their fathers' diluted witch blood, and were often considered more like the humans who served the covens than an actual witch. This child was the daughter of a witch and a fae prince. Elsbeth had to leave.

'I take it from the look on your face that you're not upset by this news?' Alanah quipped, leaning back in her chair with a knowing smile. Her eyes sparkled with curiosity and a hint of amusement, as if she already knew the answer but wanted to hear it from Elsbeth herself.

'No,' Elsbeth replied, her voice soft and steady. 'I am excited, but there are other emotions, obviously. I do have to find Raynor – he deserves to know he has a child on the way.'

'I'm sure he will be just as happy as you are,' Alanah offered, her voice softening with a rare touch of tenderness. She had been one of the few who met Raynor and witnessed the bond between him and Elsbeth. Those memories of their time together, before his visits became infrequent, usually around celebrations, lingered in her mind. Isadora had destroyed too much in this world since she had taken the crown. If she were to take the other realms as her own, Emodorea would not survive.

'I will not stop you when you leave,' Alanah said, her voice firm yet tinged with regret. 'I wish I could come with you, but I am needed here.'

Elsbeth nodded, understanding the sacrifice Alanah was making.

'I know,' she replied softly. 'Your place is here, protecting our covens and our home.'

She had considered asking Alanah to come with her. Not just to find Raynor, but to go with her to a new world, too. She had spent countless hours in the library, pouring over every book she could find about the other creations the gods and goddesses had made, especially books that Brielle herself had written. The nights were long and filled with fervent prayers to Brielle, pleading for guidance, for a way to escape to a safer world. There had been no response, not that she had expected one. Brielle had been silent to the witches for years now. It was as if she had abandoned them.

'Norella took our coven north a few days ago,' Elsbeth mused as she changed the topic, her brow furrowing in thought. 'I think she suspects something, as she told me I was not allowed to go with them.'

She had found Norella waiting outside her door after returning from Alanah's the morning Tallon and Athena left. Her sister had been leaning against the door frame, her posture tense, her fingers gently drumming the wood as if hesitant to knock. She had been startled when Elsbeth came walking toward her from the hall. Obviously, she hadn't expected her to be awake that early, or to be outside before the sun had risen.

'Yes, I heard they were sent to speak to King Artor,' Alanah's eyes narrowed slightly, a flicker of concern crossing her face. 'It seems that Winhelm has fallen.'

'Yes, from the talk I have heard in the coven, they burnt the city to the ground.' Elsbeth's words hung in the air, heavy and acrid, like the smoke that must have risen from the charred ruins. She was saddened by what her coven had done, which confused her. She was a witch; she was meant to be bloodthirsty, ruthless, and unyielding. Instead, she felt a profound sense of shame at the news. Perhaps it was because she was pregnant that she felt this way. No, she realised, this feeling had taken root long before the life inside her had. The day her mother died, something inside her shifted, something she now realised didn't live within her twin sister.

Norella had told her that she wouldn't go with the rest of their coven to the north – and Elsbeth knew it wasn't because Norella suspected her to be pregnant. No, it was because Norella considered her to be *weak*, a burden to the coven should she have gone with them. The unspoken judgement stung.

Something of Elsbeth's train of thought must have shown on her face because Alanah gave her a curious look. 'Your mother would never have wanted you to be a part of that,' Alanah said sternly. 'She would have wanted peace to remain throughout the lands, as was Queen Brielle's wish long ago.'

Elsbeth felt a lump form in her throat as she looked gratefully at the healer. She had taken so many risks for her these past few days. Alanah had even sent her apprentice to help an enemy because Elsbeth had asked. A ball of guilt formed in the pit of her stomach. If anything happened to Alanah, it would be solely her fault. She prayed to Brielle that they were doing the right thing, defying their Queen's wishes, and she prayed that Isadora would not find out what they were planning – what *she* was planning.

'Alanah, have you heard of any way to get to the other worlds?' It was a long shot, but she had exhausted every other option she could think of. When Alanah raised her eyebrows in question, she continued, 'I have read about how the gods created more than just Emodorea, they made other worlds. Different worlds. If they had a way to travel between them, then surely there would be a way for us to do so, too.'

Alanah thought for a long moment before she answered. 'There were stories of a time when the mermaids could travel between our world and others. The mermaid Orabelle was said to have abandoned this world to stay with a human lover she had found in another world. That was until her mother, Merlian, decided that she was to be brought back so that she could rule in her stead.'

'How did they do it? Travel between worlds, I mean,' she asked, sipping her now cold tea.

'The rumours said there was an underwater cave that held what they called the Pass. The mermaids could freely travel between worlds before Orabelle decided not to return. Once her mother had her found and brought back to Emodorea, Merlian gave her life to seal the Pass shut.' Alanah paused. 'I did hear a story, once, that said the Pass opened once a year, but the other side was so iced over from the power of it that it was difficult to get through.'

'Oh.' The Pass was hidden somewhere underwater in the eastern ocean. Even if she had a spell that would allow her to breathe underwater and she somehow managed to get the Pass open, Elsbeth was sure Isadora would catch her before she got that far.

'Those are just stories, mind you. Merlian was a powerful mermaid; if it did take her life to seal the Pass closed, you can be certain that she would have left a way for her ancestors to access it. She never cared for humans, but the love she had for Orabelle was unrivalled. She would have left a way for her to get back to her lover had she needed to.'

Elsbeth had never travelled very far from the forest. When her mother was the Queen, there had been no real need to leave the Forest of Brielle for any reason. Once, she travelled to The Tretara Range to give a newborn to the Soulless – the tribes of wild mixed-breeds who lived there. That was the extent of her knowledge of Emodorea beyond the covens. She could hardly fathom how long it might take to reach the shore of the eastern ocean, considering that it took them four days just to reach the base of the mountains.

'Perhaps,' Alanah said as she stirred her tea, 'one of the seers would have known if us witches had a way to travel between worlds.'

Frustration slipped into Elsbeth's voice, 'Perhaps, but, thanks to our *Queen*, they're dead.' If they were the only ones who had known, then she was at a loss.

'Yes, they are dead.' Alanah smiled mischievously. 'But their bones remain.'

CHAPTER SEVENTEEN

Thornwell, Southern Mortal Realm

+ REID +

THE NIGHT HAD FULLY settled in by the time Reid returned, the inky darkness wrapping around him like a shroud. He had spent hours pacing alongside the towering wall, eyes straining to find any entrance other than the western and eastern gates. As he approached the run-down house, the faint flicker of candlelight still danced through the front windows, casting eerie shadows on the ground. When he reached the base of the stairs, he paused, his jaw tightening in frustration. The boys had ignored his warnings and clearly hadn't gone to the study below as directed. With a growl of irritation, he stormed up the steps, each footfall echoing his rising anger.

'What in Emodorea do you think you're doing?' He demanded as he ripped the front door open, his anger exploding much more than he intended it to.

Three of the five boys were sitting in the living room playing with some rocks on the floor, the other two he could hear in the kitchen. Most likely scavenging the last of their food supplies for themselves.

'Get downstairs right now!' Reid yelled at the three on the floor, all of whom promptly stood and made their way to the stairs, muttering about how annoying Reid was for interrupting their game.

The other two in the kitchen barely acknowledged his presence when he entered, their focus entirely on the last of the food they were devouring. Crumbs littered the table and floor, evidence of their hastily eaten bounty. The pair had gotten into the bread and jam that Reid had thought he had hidden from them. There was hardly enough left for one of the other boys, let alone three of them. The once full loaf was reduced to a few scattered slices, and the jam jar, though it had already been less than a quarter full, was now empty. The sight made Reid's stomach churn with frustration. The kitchen, usually somewhat in order, now looked like it had been ransacked by a family of rats. Reid's patience was wearing thin.

He walked toward them and ripped the jar from the older one's hands.

'Ivor, I told you I wanted everyone downstairs and locked inside by sunset.' Reid's voice was a low growl, barely masking his frustration. He slammed the now empty jar onto the bench beside them, the sound echoing sharply in the quiet kitchen. His eyes bore into Ivor, who looked up with a mixture of guilt and defiance as he continued to lick the sticky jam off his fingers. He'd trusted Ivor to follow his instructions, to keep everyone safe in his absence, and now that trust felt shattered.

'If I were Gillian, he'd have broken your fingers and forced you to go without food for a week!'

'We were hungry!' Jinn spat.

Reid's hands clenched into fists at his sides, his tanned knuckles turning white with the effort to keep his temper in check as he turned away from the boys. It would do none of them any good if he started acting like Gillian. The weight of responsibility pressed heavily on his shoulders, and the sight of the empty jar near him on the bench was a sharp reminder of just how fragile their situation was. He breathed out once, twice, before turning back around to face them.

'I'll get some food and bring it down for us.' He pulled Jinn off the other bench where he sat. 'Just get downstairs with the others, please.'

The two boys exchanged looks as they slid out the doorway, as if they expected Reid to punish them for what they had done. He leaned against the counter and waited until he heard the door click shut at the base of the stairs.

What am I going to do? He thought to himself as he searched through the cupboards for any remaining food to feed all the boys for the night. He would worry about himself in the morning.

There wasn't much to find; a few bags of dried dates, some dried meat that he guessed someone had been saving for a moment such as this. His scraggly hair hung in his face while he worked, annoying him to the point where he contemplated cutting it all off. None of the knives they had would be close to sharp enough for him to do a decent job of it, but surely, it would be better than how it looked now. He'd worry about it later.

After tonight, they would have two choices: starve, or somehow find some more food. That meant stealing it from other people who probably needed it just as much. The thought chewed at Reid, twisting his stomach into knots. He knew there were plenty of other kids in the Outer Ring who were most likely worse off than he and the boys were.

A pang of guilt shot through him, but he quickly pushed it aside. No, he couldn't think about that, they weren't his problem right now; the five he had with him were all he could be concerned for. He didn't have the strength to care for so many people. Not right now.

Reid's mind was a storm of conflicting emotions. He hated the idea of taking from others, he always had. He only did it because Gillian forced him to. Yet, the desperate faces of the boys flashed before his eyes, their trust in him a heavy burden, even if they sometimes made him want to pull all his hair out. He took a deep breath, trying to steady himself. The kitchen, with its lingering scent of bread and jam, felt suffocating. Reid knew he would soon have to make a decision, one that would likely test his resolve, and his humanity.

He was almost to the stairs when a blood-curdling scream from outside stopped him in his tracks. He stood frozen in place until it stopped, as if his body reacted on its own. Before he could think about what he was doing, he had placed the food near the step and was at the front door. After hesitating a few moments at the handle, he flicked the lock and stepped outside into the dark. There was more screaming from close by, maybe a few houses down. The ground was shaking as he peered into the darkness, trying to work out what was happening.

'Run!' A man came sprinting past, his voice a desperate shout that barely reached Reid's ears before he vanished into the darkness again. The urgency in his tone sent a chill down Reid's spine. Moments later, more figures emerged from the shadows, their faces twisted in terror. He hadn't realised there were still this many people around town. They flooded past him, shoving and pushing each other, eyes wide with fear and their breaths coming in ragged gasps, all trying to get to the front, to get away from whatever was behind them. The night was suddenly alive with the sound of their flight – cries of alarm, the thud of feet on the ground, and the occasional sob of someone who had fallen behind.

More screams came as Reid stood on the steps of Gillian's townhouse, his heart and mind racing in unison as he watched, waiting, to try and see what was there. Whatever was coming, it was enough to drive the entire Outer Ring into a blind, desperate frenzy.

A prickle ran over his tanned skin as the wind changed direction, carrying with it a new, unsettling scent. He stilled, his senses heightened, and then he smelt it. A crimson mist floated toward him, swirling and undulating like a living entity. The metallic taste settled on his tongue as he opened his mouth in awe.

They never had creatures come out of the forest. They were usually controlled by the witches and often kept to the darker, thicker parts of the forest. But now, as Reid stood frozen, he realised this was what the old man must have been talking about when he said their demons would come. This thing that was killing everyone was nothing like what Reid had imagined. It was a nightmare made flesh, a monstrous silhouette against the dim street lanterns. Its eyes, glowing with an eerie, unnatural light, locked onto Reid's.

A shiver ran down his spine as their gazes met. The creature's eyes were filled with a hunger that sent a wave of dread over him. He could feel its power, its intent to destroy, and it was far more terrifying than any story he had ever heard.

It tore through the last few people that were too slow to get away, their screams cutting through the night air. The creature stood four houses away from him, its monstrous form looming in the moonlight. Reid hadn't moved since he locked eyes with it, his body frozen in place by sheer terror. He fought against the overwhelming urge to run back inside. If he did, it would just lead this thing straight to the boys. His mind raced, assessing his options the best he could, while his body trembled from fear.

It was easily eight feet tall, almost two feet taller than he was. He had nothing to fight it with, not that he should have even considered that as an option. He didn't know how to fight, apart from the occasional street brawl that Oscar dragged him into. The creature's red eyes glowed ominously as it began to move toward him, its movements slow but deliberate, each step echoing with menace.

His hand automatically went for the cigarette tin in his pocket, a habitual gesture in moments of stress, but instead his hand closed around the little wooden God. He could feel the creature's gaze burning into him, its intent clear and deadly.

Run. That was his only option. He was fast, he knew he'd be able to get a few blocks at least before it might begin catching up to him. A few blocks were all he needed, he just hoped the boys were safe and smart enough to stay locked inside until morning. The wooden god became warm in his hand, almost as if it were alive, offering him a sliver of comfort. Reid made his choice.

He leapt from the steps of the house, landing in a crouch on the pavement, and dared one last look at the beast. The creature was almost human – almost – if he squinted, maybe. It moved on two legs, but that was where the similarities stopped. Its body was black and covered in thick, tar-like muck that oozed and dripped with every step. As it walked, its footprints left the ground scorched, the earth sizzling and smoking in its wake. Smoke swirled around its hands where it held a mace and chain in one, a sword in the other. Reid's heart pounded in his chest as he watched it advance. The air seemed to shimmer with heat, distorting the creature's outline. The acrid smell of burning earth and flesh filled his nostrils.

The night air whipped past him as he took off in a sprint, his feet pounding the pavement. Reid pushed himself harder, faster. He launched himself around the corner at the end of the street as he heard the beast roar. A shiver ran up his spine and he knew that he needed to move faster. Reid had made a mistake assuming it was slow just because of how it was standing there, staring at him. It had obviously been sizing up its prey a lot better than he had.

The forest, a voice seemed to whisper in his head.

If he needed to go where the voice whispered, he was going the wrong way. He was heading to the southern end of the city – he needed to turn around. He pivoted to his right and headed down past the tavern that Oscar had insisted on staking out. If he could just loop around the creature wide enough that it stayed behind him ... and hope it didn't pop up in front of him somewhere.

He could hear it now, closing in on him. Its footsteps were heavy, each one a thunderous boom that reverberated through the night, but it was fast. Too fast. It felt like its breath was on his neck, hot and rancid, as he prayed for his legs to move faster. He rounded the corner into the marketplace and straight into several people who were using the stalls to hide. He realised with a sinking feeling that half the town had to be hiding here. It had been stupid to lead it this way, he should have known people would be here. He stopped for a moment, gathering himself, his breathing coming in ragged gasps. Hidden eyes watched him from under tables and inside hay-loaded carts.

He couldn't tell them to run, they wouldn't make it. Though he had no idea what he was meant to do once he got to the forest, he had to make sure the beast followed him straight through and didn't have the time to stop. There was no way he could kill that thing without a weapon. It had weapons of its own – though it hardly needed them. It was death on two legs, sent by Krah to take him to Wynlara.

His moment of reprieve was short-lived as an eerie silence fell over the square. He knew it was behind him before he turned around, the skin on the back of his neck prickling with dread and sweat. The air felt thick, almost suffocating, as he braced himself.

The voice in his head told him to move.

He ducked and rolled forward, hot air ruffling his hair as the mace swung, just missing his head. His body moved as if it knew exactly what to do, and he took off across the marketplace, leaping over stalls and carts in his way.

The roof ... the voice was there again.

Reid listened as he leapt up onto a cart that was parked next to one of the buildings. He gripped the drainpipe with his hands, the cold metal biting into his skin as he began scurrying his way up. The rusted gutter creaked under his weight, and sharp edges tore into his palms as he pulled himself up onto the rooftop, blood beginning to trickle down his wrists.

He gritted his teeth against the pain as he looked out over the town. From here, he could see the dark expanse of the forest – the rooftops of the houses stretched out before him, a precarious path that would get him almost the whole way to the edge of the Outer Ring. The night air was cool against his sweat-drenched skin as he left the marketplace behind him.

Back on the ground, the beast was relentless, its glowing eyes never leaving Reid as he made his way over the roofs. Reid could hear the creature's heavy footsteps, a constant reminder of the danger that pursued him. Its long legs easily kept pace with him, each stride powerful and unyielding. Even as it had to round corners and navigate obstacles, it maintained the same line, its focus unwavering. The night air rushed past him as he leapt from one building to the next.

'What am I meant to do when I get to the forest?' He asked whoever it was that was watching over him. He was breathless, he hadn't had to run like this in a long time. Not since he was younger and terrible at stealing. His legs burned, and his ankles hurt from keeping him upright on the sloping rooftops.

Trust, the voice whispered into his mind.

Reid allowed himself to trust the voice. It comforted him, even though he had no idea what or who it was. Following the voice's instructions, he managed to reach the edge of the forest a few moments ahead of the beast. Unwilling to lose his lead, he slid from the final rooftop, landing with a thud on the ground, and dove through the tree line. The light from the moon disappeared as he was swallowed by the forest, but it was from shock that he stumbled when he was met, not by utter darkness, but by a faint, blue glow.

This way ...

The light lured him further into the forest, keeping him ahead of the beast – which he could now hear crushing the ground beneath its feet as it stumbled in the underbrush. Deeper they went, past the abandoned camp of the witches he used to trade with. All that was left was the empty fire pits, their charred remains a stark reminder of the life that once thrived there. Makeshift huts, constructed from branches and tattered cloth, stood in disarray, their walls sagging and roofs caved in. So quickly the forest had taken over since he was last here. The ground was littered with the remnants of the witches' lives – broken pottery, discarded tools, and the piles of bones, picked clean by scavengers, lay scattered around the campsite. He hoped the pungent smell of rotting wood and something more sinister surrounding the campsite would deter the creature from his trail, even just a little.

The light was moving faster now, he was almost sprinting through the forest in the dark as he pushed to keep up with it. His feet seemed to instinctively know where to step, deftly avoiding roots and rocks that could send him sprawling. As he reached a small clearing, the blue glow suddenly erupted, illuminating the dense foliage. Time stood still as he moved to the centre, where a large rock sat, bathed in the ethereal light. His breath caught as he saw it – a black handle protruding from the stone, ominous against the glowing backdrop. The air around him felt charged with energy, the faint hum of the forest amplifying as he got closer. The handle beckoned him forward with an almost magnetic pull.

Take it. The voice urged, and Reid's fingers itched to touch the handle. He stood beside the stone, his hand reaching toward it, but he hesitated. Behind him, the creature snarled as a loud crack of electricity split the air, pushing it back from the clearing. The force of it made Reid's hair stand on end, the smell of smoke sharp in his nostrils.

Now! Take it now!

Without another thought, Reid's hand shot forward, gripping the handle. The moment his fingers closed around it, a surge of power coursed through him. He pulled with all his might, the stone resisting for a heartbeat before giving way. The handle came free, and with it a blade of shimmering blue light erupted from the rock.

The clearing thrummed with power as Reid pulled the sword from the stone. Power radiated through his body as he stared at the weapon in his hand. It was beautiful. The black metal handle was cool to the touch, adorned with intricate carvings that spiralled up the length of the blade. The blade itself was a striking deep blue, almost otherworldly, and it seemed to glow in the moonlight streaming into the clearing. The light danced along its edge, casting shimmering reflections that painted the surrounding trees in hues of blue. Reid could feel the sword's power resonating with his own, a perfect harmony that made him feel invincible.

The invisible barrier around the clearing fell, and the beast stepped out of the tree line. Its sword gleamed, held aloft with a deadly grace, while the heavy mace dangled at its side. Reid turned to face the demon that had followed him this far from the city. Tendrils of black smoke coiled and wreathed around its muscular frame, and it snarled at him, baring razor-sharp fangs – a challenge.

The fear was still there, but it was as if the power that was now inside him pushed it aside. Whatever, *whoever*, it was that led him to the clearing was still around him, he could feel it. The beast walked toward him, hissing a god-awful sound. Reid ground his teeth against the noise that pierced his ears. This thing was far from any animal or human he had ever seen.

Kill it.

A tingle ran down Reid's arm in response to the voice. His muscles tensed; he could do this. He stepped toward the beast, the sword twirling a few times in his hand, the sword catching the light in a dazzling display. He swung the sword upward, meeting the beast's descending strike with a resounding clash. The force from the other blade knocked him down as he struggled against the strength of the beast. Gritting his teeth, he gripped the sword with both hands and pushed back, muscles straining. With a swift roll to the side, he narrowly avoided the beast's blade as it plunged into the ground where he had just been. Scrambling to his feet, he staggered back a few steps.

He had no training, no clue what he was doing. The only thing that kept him going was the voice in his head guiding his every move. It was oddly comforting to have it there, even if he had no idea what or who it was. Again, the demon lunged at him and again he evaded it. He wasn't tiring, but neither was the thing before him. The relentless creature drove him back, inch by inch, toward the ancient stone where he had first drawn the sword.

He slashed and jabbed as best he could, each movement driven by sheer determination. His strikes landed only a few glancing blows, the rest were effortlessly deflected by the demon's swift and precise blocks. His back smashed against the stone in the centre of the clearing when the beast landed a particularly savage kick. As the beast closed in on its prey, Reid raised the sword to protect himself. He closed his eyes and prayed to Kasin to save him.

A burst of blue light shone from the blade as the creature lunged for the kill. It was blinding as it wrapped around the beast in front of him. The sword slipped from Reid's fingers and clattered to the ground as the light encased the creature's body. It consumed it, transforming it into a glowing, blue silhouette. Reid raised his hands to shield his eyes from the searing light, watching as it burned its way through the creature until it suddenly faded away, leaving him standing alone in the dark clearing. The only things remaining now were the serene glow of the moon, and the blue sword lying at his feet.

CHAPTER EIGHTEEN

Southern Reaches, Forest of Brielle

+ REID +

THE ONCE VIBRANT, emerald-green grass in the clearing was left scorched where the creature had been incinerated by the strange, blue light. Reid pushed himself off the stone that he was leaning against and picked up the sword, studying it properly for the first time. He twirled it around, taking in every inch of its glittering length.

With the bright glow of the moon as his light, he ran his fingers over the intricate pattern etched into the blade and hilt. A mess of vine-like swirls snaked their way down the length of midnight-blue metal to the hilt, where smaller symbols joined to form a strange design – one Reid had been familiar with for years. He thumbed the cigarette tin inside his pocket.

Though the sword had come from the stone, it was unscathed, as though it had just been forged. The metal was cold to touch, but he could have sworn it was glowing when he destroyed the beast.

The sword will not always glow.

Reid spun, searching for the voice, his heart rate picking back up as he clutched the sword in his hands.

'Who are you?' Reid called, scanning the clearing for movement.

I am more of a what *than a* who.

The voice wasn't speaking out loud – it was in his mind. The thought of someone being in his head made Reid's stomach churn.

Do not be afraid.

The sword hummed with power as a softer blue light protruded from it and a ghostly figure formed in front of Reid, seeming to come from the blade itself.

'Kasin,' Reid breathed as he saw his little wooden statue now life-size before him.

It is a pleasure to finally meet you, Reid. The figure floated across the ground toward him. *I have been watching you for a long time. I knew you were the one I was looking for when you accepted the statue I offered you.*

The figure altered its form into the old man from the shop. With a sly smile, it was suddenly Kasin again. Broad-shouldered, with long hair that hung below his shoulders, the top half pulled up out of his face. A broadsword was strapped to his side, along with a quiver and bow on his back. His clothes looked to be lightweight, but Reid was sure it was a type of armour. It hugged the being's body, a perfect fit. Before him stood what Reid guessed was a well-trained warrior, yet he had a softness to his face that didn't seem entirely trustworthy to Reid.

I will not harm you – I merely want to talk. The god leaned against the stone near Reid, casually crossing his arms over his chest.

'Why can I hear you in my head?' Reid asked, lowering the sword, but he didn't dare to put it down. He wasn't sure exactly what he could do to defend himself against a god, but it was a comfort to have it there.

Unfortunately, I cannot speak on your plane, at least not in this form. Kasin gestured to himself and the moonlight shone straight through him, reminding Reid that the god was made of pure light. *At the moment we have a small connection, one that allows me to speak to you directly.* Kasin nodded at the small carving. *However, as we spend more time together, we'll soon be able to connect with one another on a different level. But that's something we can discuss later.*

Reid remembered over the past week hearing minor warnings here and there and nodded as he realised it was Kasin from the beginning.

'The old man spoke to me, though,' Reid said, tilting his head in question at Kasin.

Some mortals are weaker than others, it was not hard for me to control the old man as if it were my own body. Kasin smiled at him. *If I was in my pure godlike form ... I fear I do not know what would happen if you gazed upon it.*

Reid had heard stories about mortals that saw a god's pure form. To see such a powerful entity with human eyes was said to end in death. He did not wish to find out if the stories were true.

'What is it that you want from me?' Reid asked as he twisted the sword in his hands, focusing on anything except the figure before him.

Millennia ago, when we decided it was time to leave the mortal world to their own devices, I was asked to name a protector in my place – to choose someone who would watch over the different races. It would be their duty to protect the world from the dark beings that may try to take it over with our departure.

'If you were worried about these dark beings taking over, why not just stay here yourself?' Reid asked, sinking to sit on the grass. He was more exhausted than he had realised, with all the running and almost dying.

Kasin tilted his chin in thought for a moment before he replied. *It wasn't a matter of choice, really. Beings such as ourselves had no place living amongst the different races of Emodorea. We would slowly but surely lose our strength, our powers. There are other worlds which we reside over, and we can also move between the different worlds – or create entirely new ones, should we please.*

But some of us did not want to leave this world. We relished in what we had started here, such a peaceful harmony amongst all the creatures. I was not the only one to leave a subordinate in my wake. Thora created her sirens and their enchanted kingdom in the sky, and Typhonis created the sirens' sisters, the mermaids, and left them his realm in the ocean.

Kasin went on, *Zadea, with the bit of magic she possessed, created an enhanced race of beings you know as fae. They perhaps were one of the better creatures we created. She left them with her powers of knowledge and longevity. They also seemed to get her beauty, too.* Kasin's eyes smiled as he spoke about Zadea. *She was the one who had the idea for me to leave a protector, someone I could enter and give my powers to. Just in case the world needed saving.*

The wind rustled through the trees as Kasin stared up at the moon. Reid sat on the ground before him, like a student listening to his teacher, trying to absorb everything that Kasin told him, to believe that this was happening and it wasn't a dream. He kept looking at the scorched earth at his feet where the monster had been turned to dust.

The time came, and I chose a fae, one that Zadea had been rather fond of, to be the first. Kasin's Protector is what the others in Emodorea came to know him as. He was used in the start to be a buffer zone for the different races. It was due to him everyone came to believe that the world would survive in peace. When it was time for him to pass on – many thousands of years later – I chose another. This time it was a siren, Nyxillia, the granddaughter of Sirennea, the first of the sirens. She never left the Sky Kingdom, though there didn't seem to be a need. The races each kept to their areas. The only issues that ever arose appeared to be with the mortals that were left. Kasin sighed as he looked down at Reid.

I chose a different race each time, every thousand years or so when the previous one passed or became useless – although never a human. The gods have always feared the humans would harbour a dark hatred for the other races, due to their lack of power in comparison. It seemed too likely, given access to my power and longevity, a human may use it for revenge against the rest of Emodorea. As time passed, I got lazy, there was less and less reason for Emodorea to have a protector. After I sensed that the last protector had died, a fae named Shilo, I left the world to its own devices.

'I don't understand,' Reid sat with his hands in his lap, fiddling with the hilt of the sword. 'If everything was okay, why come back now?'

Brielle, a Witch Queen we took with us before we left this world and made her one of us, came to me with conflict in her heart. She spoke to me of how she feared evil had at last penetrated our beloved Emodorea, that it was her kind that the darkness had finally sunk its teeth into. She begged me to return, to choose a new protector that would be able to stop the impending doom she feared would overrun this world.

I did as she asked. I have been searching the world over for a new protector for the past hundred years or so, looking for the perfect being that I could inhabit and gift my powers to. The world I returned to was different from the one I left. There was unease throughout the lands. The sirens seemed unheard of, the mermaids were considered a myth. Fae and witches consorted with each other during festivals, though neither had much to do with mortals.

There were also new breeds – half-breeds that were considered weak by their parent races for not being pure. I had all but given up hope of finding someone with a pure heart that I knew would not be corrupted by the power I would give them. That was when Zadea suggested looking at humans. That perhaps there would be one that was born with a kind heart.

Kasin stepped forward from the stone and smiled down at Reid. She was right. As I passed through Thornwell seventeen years ago, marvelling at the size the once small town had grown to, I heard you. Your soul sang to me as your mother gave her life bringing you into the world. You were such a strong babe. I chose you then, though I did not know it at the time. I was so sure my protector could not be a human. That you would not be strong enough, mentally or physically.

I continued my search throughout the other realms, but I kept coming back to you. That day in the shop when you accepted a carving of a god that you barely knew anything about was the day that I made my choice. This seventeen-year-old mortal that began to pray to me, when all other races barely acknowledged the gods anymore, would be named Kasin's Protector.

Reid straightened at Kasin's words. *Kasin's Protector.* It was all too much for him to take in. Last week he had simply been Reid, a street rat that a rich thief had taken under his wing. The fact that this god wanted him to be a saviour of Emodorea was beyond his belief. There was no way someone like him would ever be able to save the world.

Do not doubt yourself, Reid, Kasin said. *You will become more powerful than you could ever imagine.*

'What exactly is it that you want me to do?' Reid asked, rubbing his temples. It was late, the boys were probably wondering where he was, where their food was. That is, if they had locked themselves inside as Reid begged them to do. No doubt the villagers would think he was dead by now, too. 'That thing ... what was that?' he looked toward the stained ground.

That was a demon sent by the witches. A beast that was probably once fae. A few have given themselves to the witches in hopes they will be spared if Isadora takes over. What I want you to do is stop that from happening.

'You want me to stop the Queen of the witches.' The words sounded dumb, even before they had left his mouth. He was a weak mortal. There was no way he would be able to defeat a witch, and the Queen of the witches at that. Even Erikah scared him half to death, and she was just a normal witch; if normal was even the right word.

We will stop her together. You will have my powers to aid you. Kasin looked pointedly at the sword in Reid's hand. *You also have a god's blade in your possession.*

Reid turned the blade over in his hand. 'A what?'

A god's blade. It is a blade that was forged in our home world from a precious metal called milanite. Witches are the closest thing to Immortals in this world. We did not create them, as we made the others. They were forged from a darkness that was in this world when we began creating life.

Brielle was the first that spoke and took on a physical form. She chose the light, and many followers after her did so, too. Each of the original covens decided to be what they are, pushing the darkness that gave them their powers back into the earth. They can be wounded, but killing them is a lot harder.

Standard weapons might seem to end their lives, but they would only be re-awakened by the darkness. The witches possess their specific weapons, imbued with poisons or curses that, if used the right way, can end a witch's life permanently. The only defence we have against them is milanite. An ancient metal that destroys the darkness that is their life source.

'This is one of your blades, then,' Reid stated more than asked, as he already knew the answer. 'How is it here, in this world, if you cannot be here in your form?'

It was left by Shilo long ago. This part of the forest was enchanted by the Witch Queen, Graciella Wraithe, when she came into power around the same time I chose Shilo to be protector. They were close – I believe one of her daughters is his child. When a protector was no longer needed, the pair chose to embed the sword into the stone should it ever be required against the darkness once more. Graciella enchanted this clearing so that none would stumble upon a weapon to use against her kind. Shilo agreed with her, to protect his child.

'But I found it.' Reid ran his fingers over the cold metal.

Yes. You found it because time has come when it is needed. Do you accept? Kasin asked.

'You mean, I have a choice?' Reid had assumed that he wouldn't have a say in this. That the god would do as he pleased, regardless of what Reid wanted.

The god gave a small chuckle. *Of course, you have a choice. I cannot force this upon you.*

Reid choked on his laugh. A choice, after he had practically just forced him into battle with a demon fae. Perhaps if he was named Kasin's Protector, the king would have to let him and the boys, no, *everyone*, on the outside of the wall … inside. How could the King deny someone who was truly blessed by the gods refuge inside the city?

'If I say no, what will you do?' Reid asked as he stood up.

Kasin's face dropped slightly. *I would have to continue my search and pray that I find another before Isadora destroys Emodorea. I'd also have to take that blade back.* He eyed the sword that Reid had become rather fond of holding.

'I always assumed I'd be living in the Outer Ring, struggling to survive.' He had to accept, if not for Emodorea, then to simply protect himself and the boys. 'I can't promise I'll be able to defeat her. But, I mean, it's not every day a god offers you a mighty sword and the ability to wield his power.'

Kasin laughed loudly at that, his voice rumbling in Reid's head. *No, I suppose not.*

CHAPTER NINETEEN

Witch's Keep, Forest of Brielle

+ ELSBETH +

THE WHOLE PLAN was ridiculous from start to finish. Elsbeth had no idea how Alanah, of all people, had come up with it. Witches could come and go from the throne room as they pleased, but respect for the Queen had to be upheld at all times. Even the slaves did not dare to touch the throne for cleaning without seeking Isadora's permission first. Yet, here she was, standing before the throne in the middle of the night as she waited for Alanah to join her before they did much more than just touch the throne.

She was sure they were going to get caught, and she was yet to come up with an excuse for what they were doing. Alanah had decided that the only way they would find out about passages to the other worlds was to talk to the seers. In other words, Elsbeth had to take one of the skulls from atop Isadora's throne so that she and Alanah could perform a ritual to awaken the spirit that most likely remained inside the bone. Most likely – meaning Alanah could be wrong about the whole thing.

It was a gamble, but Elsbeth was short on options. She had to know there was a way to escape from Emodorea, a way to raise her unborn child in a safe place. Even if that meant a world with no magic. Alanah had readily agreed that it was the only choice, knowing that Isadora would likely kill Elsbeth and the child out of fear.

She hovered in the shadows before the throne as she decided which skull she would choose. One of the side ones was the obvious choice, they would be less noticeable than the centre one. Hopefully, Queen Isadora wouldn't have to use the room for anything for a few days; they'd be able to put the head back before anyone realised it was missing.

'Have you picked one yet?' Alanah's voice whispered as she stepped out of the shadows beside her.

'I was going to take the left one,' Elsbeth whispered back. 'Though, for some reason, the middle one seems to want me to take it.'

Alanah nodded silently as she moved toward the throne. In her hand, she held a hessian sack that she had filled earlier with a few herbs from her garden. She had told Elsbeth it was to keep any dark spirits at bay that may be within the skull, at least until they were able to summon the seer back.

Elsbeth held her breath as the older witch stood on the seat, barely able to reach the skulls at the top. She perched one foot onto the armrest and pushed herself up before grabbing the bones that surrounded the skulls for balance. With one foot on either armrest for support, she began moving the centre head back and forth in a twisting motion.

The room was silent apart from the grinding noise from where Alanah was slowly but surely removing the skull. She was taking her time to ensure that the head didn't crack from the motions. Elsbeth was nervous – several people could walk in at any given moment. She wished Alanah would be less careful and just pull the skull free so they could leave. It felt like she was being watched from the shadows.

A sharp pop echoed around them as Alanah finally wrenched the skull free from atop the ancient chair. They let out simultaneous sighs of relief as the witch climbed down, the bag now bulging from the head she placed inside. She deftly tied the top with a woven fennel string, its earthy scent mingling with the room's stale air, a protective charm to ward off any evil spirits that may try to escape – or worse – enter the skull.

The door behind them clicked open, shattering the silence with the sudden burst of laughter of two witches. Their hushed whispers filled the room as they slipped through the doorway, closing it softly behind them. Elsbeth and Alanah quickly ducked behind the throne, pressing themselves against the cold stone to stay out of sight. Elsbeth's hands shook as she waited for them to be caught.

The whispering and giggles grew louder, echoing around the empty room as the two witches drew nearer to their hiding spot. Alanah held a finger to her lips, her eyes wide with urgency, as if the need for Elsbeth to be quiet wasn't already painfully clear. Elsbeth's breath caught in her throat.

She clutched the edge of the throne, her knuckles white, every muscle in her body tense with the fear of being discovered.

The pair of witches had reached the bottom of the dais, their footsteps halting abruptly. The room fell silent again, except for their heavy breathing, the whispers and giggles now replaced by an eerie stillness. Elsbeth battled with curiosity and caution as she brushed off Alanah's restraining hand. She had to know who was in the room with them and whether they posed a threat. Slowly, she inched forward, peering around the bottom of the chair. She caught sight of the witches, their faces partially obscured by the shadows of the room.

Witches were free to come and go from the throne room as they pleased, sure, though not many bothered being here without reason. If these two were here, they were either hiding from the festivities that were happening downstairs or on patrol for Isadora. Given their laughs and whispered words, Elsbeth was sure it was the former. She watched them closely hoping to get a glimpse of who they were.

As she edged around the seat, the giggles of the two witches grew louder, echoing off the stone walls as they ascended the stairs. She pulled herself back around next to Alanah, shaking her head in frustration; she hadn't had time to see who they were. A heavy thud followed as the witches collapsed onto the throne together. Alanah raised an eyebrow at Elsbeth – a knowing look in her eyes. It was clear what was happening.

A soft moan escaped one of the witch's lips as the clouds parted, allowing the moonlight to spill into the room. The pale light cast the pair's intertwined shadows across the floor, making the reason for their presence unmistakable. Elsbeth fought the urge to run from the room. She didn't need to bear witness to this intimate moment; it was clear the witches were seeking privacy. Though why they didn't just go to their chambers was beyond her.

'Erikah,' one of the voices whispered in earnest, the name hanging in the air like a forbidden secret. Elsbeth's breath caught in her throat as she listened. 'I can't believe you stayed away for so long.' The words were followed by a long, heavy silence, the kind that seemed to stretch on forever.

Elsbeth could almost feel the tension between the pair before they finally broke apart, their breathing laboured and uneven.

'You know I hate being here,' Erikah replied, her voice full of frustration. 'I only come to see you. I would have come sooner, had you not gone north.'

Her words sounded like they were filled with longing and reproach. The silence that followed was thick with unspoken emotions that even Elsbeth noticed, their separation evident in every breath they took.

'I had to go north,' the other murmured between kisses, her voice breathless. 'Our Queen demanded it.'

'You know I don't consider her my Queen,' Erikah replied boldly.

'You know I would have to kill you if anyone else heard you say that,' the whispered voice was cut off with a slight suckling noise, the weight of the threat mingled with the intimacy of their moment.

'Why do you follow her?' Erikah asked again, her voice cutting through the intimate noises. It was clear that this conversation was not something the former wanted to be talking about just then, as they huffed in annoyance.

'Please, we have limited time together,' they pleaded. 'Do we have to spend it discussing politics?'

'I don't want to discuss it with you,' Erikah replied, her words muffled as she kissed her partner deeply. A small whimper escaped her lips when she broke away and continued, 'I just need to know why you aren't against her, with what she is doing to our covens, to our world. Brielle would not be on board with this.'

'Can we discuss it tomorrow? My body has missed you too much right now.'

A moan escaped one of them as the throne shifted slightly, nudging into Elsbeth and Alanah's hiding spot. It was clear where this encounter was headed.

Alanah absently placed a hand on Elsbeth's knee as the pair huddled behind the throne. A silent question as to what she wanted to do. Elsbeth weighed the options in her mind. Did they continue hiding until the couple left, or did they allow them to know they were there and risk confrontation?

She had known the risk when they had decided to do this, but she had never thought the person that would catch them out would be ... she shook her head. She looked at Alanah, who was still waiting for Elsbeth's decision. Elsbeth was sure that Erikah would not speak of them being here should they expose themselves, but the other ... she had no idea about. She nodded to Alanah – they would take the risk – before she stood and coughed, stepping out of the shadows into the moonlight that still filtered through the stained-glass windows.

Neither witch on the throne moved as the two made themselves known, Alanah absently holding the bag behind her out of sight. A petite witch with long, sandy blonde hair in two tight braids was sitting with her knees on either side of the other one. She looked over her shoulder to where Elsbeth and Alanah now stood facing them, her freckled covered face wrinkled into a small smile.

'Can I help you?' she said as she continued to stare at them over her shoulder, blocking the other witch's view of them.

'It's been a long time, Erikah,' Elsbeth said, crossing her arms. The other witch all but pushed Erikah off her as she stood up. Erikah stepped aside, a slight grin still playing on her lips, as a mirror image of Elsbeth stepped forward. The two sisters didn't say anything for a moment as they stared at one another. Norella looked sheepishly at Erikah before looking back at Elsbeth, unable to find words to explain.

'You're here for the full moon ceremony, I take it?' Elsbeth spoke to Erikah, though her eyes never left Norella.

The freckled witch leaned casually against the arm of the throne, her posture relaxed but her eyes alert, and nodded. 'It seems my coven dispersed themselves amongst the others when the trading from Thornwell stopped, thanks to our majesty.' Elsbeth could taste the hatred in her tone. She smiled; she had always liked Erikah, even if she was one of the more bloodthirsty amongst them.

'What are you doing here?' Norella suddenly found her voice as she stared her sister down.

'I could ask the same of you,' Elsbeth replied, glancing between Norella and Erikah. She had always had her suspicions about who Norella wished to spend intimate time with, but never would have guessed Erikah, of all people. It was common for their kind to enjoy partners of any gender, so that wasn't what shocked her about her sister. It was the tenderness that Norella seemed to have toward Erikah as they had sat in the chair, unaware they weren't alone.

'That's none of your business,' Norella crossed her arms, matching her sister's look. It was just like Norella to be straight on the defensive. 'I never questioned you about sharing your bed with that Fae Prince.'

'I'm happy for you, Norella, if this is what you want.' Elsbeth smiled, each second felt like an eternity as she stood there, acutely aware of the need to leave. Norella hadn't noticed that Alanah was carrying a bag, or even seemed to see her standing there. She knew Erikah would not say anything, but Norella ... Norella was a different story. Her loyalty to the Queen was unwavering, and Elsbeth couldn't be certain where her sister's allegiance would lie if it came down to a choice between her and their Queen.

'Nothing is happening.'

Erikah winced at Norella's words, and she edged away from her slightly. Norella seemed to notice the movement, and her stern face faltered for but a moment before she turned back to Elsbeth.

'What are you two doing in here? You hate this room.' Norella's tone was full of suspicion.

Elsbeth's heart tightened with anger and sorrow. Norella should hate the room, too, if she ever truly cared for their mother. This was where Isadora had claimed her bloody victory, where Hesta had taken her final breaths. They could do nothing but sit and watch, bound by the rules of the challenge. The memory of their mother's death was seared into Elsbeth's mind, a wound that had never fully healed.

Her gaze wandered over to where the bloodstain had remained for weeks, a grim reminder of that fateful day. Isadora had finally ordered it to be cleaned, but Elsbeth knew it was a deliberate act of cruelty. The Queen had left it there to taunt the twins, to see which one would break first under the weight of their hatred for her. Elsbeth's eyes met Norella's, and she saw a flicker of something – regret, perhaps, or guilt? But it was gone as quickly as it had appeared, replaced by the familiar mask of indifference.

'I was replenishing the Queen's medicinal herb stock, for when she returns from the festivities.' Alanah held up the bag she carried with her. The bag, which held the skull from atop the throne the two had just been sharing, swung slightly with her movement. 'Elsbeth was just keeping me company.'

'Elsbeth, it has been so long. I would love to have a drink with you,' Erikah said as she moved forward, away from the throne. Norella reached her hand absently toward her as she passed by; Erikah in turn twisted her shoulder ever so slightly to avoid the touch. Elsbeth watched the exchange with conflicting emotions. She forced a small smile, trying to mask her unease.

'Erikah …' Elsbeth watched as Norella's eyes glazed over, the pain evident in her expression. Her voice trembled as she turned away, trying to hide her tears. Elsbeth could see the struggle in her sister, the way she fought to maintain her composure.

'Leave before I notify the Queen of your presence and find out the true reason you are here,' Norella said, her voice hardening.

Erikah hesitated, her eyes lingering on Norella for a moment longer before she turned and walked away, stopping at the door to wait for Elsbeth and Alanah. Norella stood beside the throne, alone, shoulders unnaturally stiff. Elsbeth was torn between comforting her sister and leaving while the option was there. She wished she could reach out, offer her something, but she knew now was not the time for this battle. Without another look at Norella, Elsbeth turned on her heels and led the way from the castle.

CHAPTER TWENTY

Thornwell, Southern Mortal Realm

+ REID +

THE MARKETPLACE WAS DARK when Reid returned. He couldn't stop his hands from shaking as he made his way back through the carts he had accidentally tipped over, still scattered around. Shadows were beginning to emerge as it became clear that the threat was gone for now. He kept replaying the conversation he'd had with Kasin, going through every detail, trying to believe what had happened. How in the world had a god chosen him – a common street rat, an orphan, and a lying thief?

Reid sighed.

Then, there was the milanite sword that now weighed heavy in his hand. He had no idea what Kasin expected him to do with the blade; he wasn't a trained swordsman, and he doubted King Oswald would let him in to train with the guards.

People muttered as Reid walked by them. A few offered silent thanks to him by the nod of their head or a brief smile. Most scowled at him as they tried to piece back together their stalls in the dark, many refusing to waste what little oil they had left by lighting their stall lamps. Reid considered staying for a moment to help clean up, but decided he'd done enough for them for one night. Plus, he needed to check on the boys.

'You there!' A guard appeared at the market entrance. His lantern held up to the face of a stall owner. 'Why is everyone out at this hour?'

'Can't ya see that someone's destroyed our stuff?' the man replied as he pushed the guard's lantern from his face. 'Let us clean up before the rats spoil our wares.'

'Who would have been able to cause this much damage?' The guard pressed another villager, a woman this time. Her eyes grew wide as three more guards appeared behind her.

'I'm ...' she stammered, 'I'm not sure.'

'Someone has to know something,' the guard walked to the centre of the marketplace.

Reid ducked into the shadow of a doorway.

Two doors up, Madame Jessamine's door creaked open. Her full-bodied figure emerged into the moonlight. She didn't notice Reid as she sauntered past him toward the guards. She tugged her shawl around her shoulders as she entered the light of their lanterns.

'Excuse me,' her voice was like honey. 'I might have an answer for you.'

The guard looked her over head to toe before scowling.

'You better not be wasting my time, whore.'

'I have information.' Madame Jessamine didn't falter at the insult. 'For a small donation to my institution, that is.'

'You'll offer the information for free,' the guard demanded. 'As it is your king that asks.'

'Well,' Madame Jessamine spoke softly. 'I shall tell you, but I cannot confirm how accurate my information will be.'

The guard mulled it over for a moment, his gaze sweeping across the bustling market, taking in the curious onlookers. Reid watched as, after a tense pause, he gestured to the guard behind him. A small bag of what were presumably coins was tossed through the air, landing at Madame Jessamine's feet with a soft thud. Her eyes briefly caught Reid's as she bent and scooped the bag up, hastily wedging it into her corset.

'Well, I can't be certain what I saw because it looked like a demon from Wynlara.' Madame Jessamine looked the guard in the eye. 'But the boy that it was chasing is surely the source of this destruction.'

'And where can this boy be found?'

'Head down Gibbon Street. It's a rundown yellow brick building on the left, his name is Reid. Brown hair, about seventeen.' Madame Jessamine curtsied to the guard. 'If any of your men would like some entertainment before they head back, I'd be happy to offer them a substantial discount.'

The guard held his arm out, blocking the path of the two men who moved to follow Madame Jessamine, eager for any chance to have their urges satisfied. His stern expression and firm stance made it clear they were not to proceed. The men halted abruptly, exchanging annoyed glances before stepping back.

'We won't be taking part in your frivolity tonight.' The guard turned and ushered the others down the path toward Gibbon Street.

Reid stepped from the shadows as Madame Jessamine walked back to her door. She stopped beside him for a moment, placing her hand on his shoulder gently.

'You understand,' she spoke quietly, 'that it was in my best interest to tell them.'

'I understand,' Reid replied through gritted teeth. 'Thank you for telling them the wrong house colour, at least.'

A small smile played on Madame Jessamine's lips as she patted his shoulder one last time and disappeared through her doorway.

Reid turned, racing back through the streets, attempting to get ahead of the guards. It wouldn't take them long to realise they had the wrong house and, with his description, be turned toward Gillian's run down, terracotta coloured house with broken roof tiles and boarded up windows. Madame Jessamine might have given Reid a head start, but he knew it wasn't enough time to get the boys out before the guards got there.

As he rounded the corner of Gibbon street, Reid's face fell. The guards were making their way down the steps of the red brick house and across the road to Gillian's.

'Hey, there!' Reid panicked and called out to the guards.

'What do you want, boy?' the guard barely looked his way.

'Who are you looking for?' Reid took a step toward them, making himself more visible to their lights.

'None of your concern.' The head guard replied as they walked up Gillian's steps.

'Well,' Reid choked out. 'That's my house you're at.'

The guards stopped and turned toward him. The head guard descended a few steps, making his way back towards Reid.

'Reid, is it?'

'Yep.' Reid gave them what he hoped was one of Oscar's cocky grins. 'What can I do for you?'

'You can explain what you were doing, causing a mess in the marketplace earlier tonight.' The other guards joined him in the street, hands ready at their waists. Their eyes widened as they noticed the sword in Reid's hand, glinting ominously under the streetlights.

'I'm not sure I recall,' Reid replied, tapping his chin. 'Could you be more specific?'

'Don't play dumb with me,' the guard spat. 'We were told on good authority that you were the cause of the damage.'

'You were also told that there was a demon chasing me.' Reid stood with his arms crossed, the sword lazily draped over one shoulder. 'Are you also planning on finding and questioning it, too?'

'You smart-arse. I bet that whore was working with you to get some free coin.' The guard drew his sword. 'You can either drop your weapon and come with us, or we'll take you by force. You and anyone who is an accomplice.'

Careful. Kasin's voice filled his head.

'I'm always careful,' Reid replied smugly.

'What's it going to be, boy?' The guard took a step toward him, sword raised.

The door at the top of the stairs cracked open, a sliver of light spilling out. Ivor's red-head poked through the gap. Before the guards could turn to see, Reid swiftly placed the sword at his feet, his movements quick and deliberate

'Okay,' he said. 'I surrender.'

Ivor cocked his head to the side in confusion.

'I'll come with you, there's no one else with me. I live alone.' Reid hoped Ivor would understand and go hide with the other boys. He looked up in time to see the door close without a sound.

'We should do a search of your house just in case.' The head guard nodded to two of the other guards who proceeded up the stairs and kicked in the front door. The head guard and the one remaining moved to take Reid's sword and tie his hands. A few moments later, the other guards re-appeared, shaking their heads.

'What do I do now?' Reid was asking Kasin, his voice barely a whisper. However, it was the guard who answered.

'You'll be taken to the King.' The guard barked as another stepped forward, his rough hands rummaged through Reid's pockets.

The priest prays to me. He will help you. Kasin replied.

Reid and the guards walked back to the Inner Ring in silence, the first light of dawn beginning to creep over the horizon. Reid's pockets were empty for the first time since he could remember; the guards had taken the little statue and his cigarette tin. The early morning air was cool, but a cold sweat clung to his skin. Though he was fully clothed, Reid suddenly felt completely naked to the world, exposed and vulnerable. Each step echoed in the quiet streets, the guards' presence a constant reminder of his predicament, their stern faces and unflinching grip making escape seem impossible. As they neared the Inner Ring, the sky began to lighten, casting long shadows that seemed to stretch endlessly before them.

CHAPTER TWENTY-ONE

Witch's Keep, Forest of Brielle

✦ NORELLA ✦

'The mortals of the Northern Realm have been dealt with,' Norella told Isadora as the pair stood on the balcony. Below them the covens gathered, their murmurs and movements a distant hum. Norella's gaze swept over the assembled witches, seeking one face in particular, but to no avail.

Norella had returned from the raid of the Northern Mortal Realm the day before the full-moon. Her own coven suffered only two losses and a dozen or so injuries that needed attending to by the healers, but otherwise they were unscathed. The raid had been brutal, but Norella's warriors had proven their mettle once again, emerging victorious despite the challenges. The coven's strength remained largely intact, ready to follow any orders that were given next. Norella had watched as first her cousin, Lorelai, was pierced through the heart by a wayward arrow; Kirra was foolishly running to her aid when she was decapitated by a long sword. They had both disintegrated into shimmering, silver dust before Norella's eyes. The fallen witches would be mourned, their sacrifices honoured as they returned to the darkness from which all witches once came – never fully gone. Their essence would wait to be reawakened.

'I cannot believe that fool Artor did not kneel,' Isadora fumed as she ungracefully leaned against the stone railing. Norella kept her posture formal, waiting for the Queen to continue. 'All he had to do was agree to live under my rule, but the stubborn old bastard had to defy me and have his entire kingdom slaughtered.' There was no hint of remorse for what she had ordered Norella and her coven to do.

Norella knew the Queen's annoyance was purely practical, a frustration over lost resources rather than any moral consideration. Norella understood this mindset, it was one she had adopted herself. Emotions were a luxury she could not afford. Her duty was to the Crown, and she would carry out Isadora's orders without question.

The slaughter of Artor's kingdom was a necessary act of obedience, a demonstration of their power and the consequences of defiance. Norella knew that, yet a small part of her couldn't help but feel a pang of regret. Not for the mortal lives lost – she had long since steeled herself against such emotions – but for the strategic loss. Artor's kingdom could have been a valuable asset, a stronghold in the Northern Realm. Now, it was nothing but ash and bone.

'What about King Oswald?' Isadora asked, referring to the mortal that sat on the throne of Thornwell. 'What have our scouts reported of that situation?'

Norella's eyes darkened at the thought of Oswald. She sighed, her frustration evident in the tightness of her jaw. She didn't have a lot of information to share with the Queen, thanks to the scouts not being able to get into the city.

'Well, they built a wall. They've enclosed all the wealthier residents inside the wall and left the poorer ones to fend for themselves.' The image of the mortal king, smug and secure behind his fortress, ignited a fire within her. A coward, hiding behind his walls while the rest of the realms fight his battles. The witches would eventually tear down those walls and burn him at the stake. The thought of battle, the clash of steel and the smell of blood in the air sent a thrill through her veins.

'There is one thing,' Norella cautiously went on, 'one of the first berserker fae we sent into Thornwell wound up missing.'

'Missing?' Isadora's eyebrows arched as she crossed her arms and waited for Norella to continue.

Norella took a deep breath, her fingers drumming lightly on the hilt of her sword. Her eyes flickered with concern, the mystery of what she was about to say gnawing at her. She clenched her jaw, the muscles in her neck tightening as she fought to maintain her composure.

'The other berserkers that were linked with him say he's dead, but we haven't been able to find his body. They tracked the scent through the city and back into the forest. When the trail ended, there was no trace of the beast, instead they found a human scent mixed in with the berserker's.'

'It was probably just chasing its next meal,' Isadora said dismissively, waving a hand as if to brush away the concern. She turned away from Norella, her gaze sweeping over the mass of witches that had formed below them. The full-moon festivities had brought the majority of the covens into the keep. Isadora had asked them to stay for an extra day or so while Imogen and Zala took stock of their numbers. Norella watched as the Queen's eyes glinted with dark satisfaction. 'Never mind the demons we lose. Behold the empire I have forged.'

'Imogen last told me they had counted around two thousand in the vicinity of the castle right now,' Norella said proudly as she moved to stand beside her aunt. 'Twice that are said to be travelling as we speak.'

'Four thousand is not nearly enough,' Isadora's hands paled as they tightened on the rail.

'We have sent word to all our covens across Emodorea,' Norella said. 'We should expect them to respond with their numbers any day now.'

'I should hope so. How am I supposed to conquer the world if I have no army?'

'You will have an army, my Queen,' Norella reassured with a bow as the Queen pushed past her to head back inside.

Going to war against the mortals was one thing. They may have managed to kill two of Norella's coven members, but in general, fighting against mortals usually only left the witches with a few minor wounds. King Artor had gotten lucky this time around, and Norella was sure it was more lack of awareness from her fellow witches that got them killed, than any actual skill on the humans' behalf. The real challenge would be going up against the fae.

Similar to witches, the fae lived long lives and were well-honed warriors. They possessed the ability to shift into different creatures, and a select few were bred from witches and had magic. The only ones allowed within Osteria were those that were of the royal blood, the purest of all by far, and those that had the appearance of being pure fae. Taking the fae's land would not be easy; they would likely lose many witches. The fae could be formidable enemies to the witches if they chose. Though, like what happened during the witch raid in the North, it was likely that a fae killing a witch would just mean she would lose her physical form. Her dark essence would return to the earth, waiting to be reawakened.

The only thing strong enough to kill the darkness within a witch for good was gods' metal and a selection of methods known only to witches high enough in the ranks to need to know. However, if the situation wasn't handled correctly, there was the possibility they would lose the war. Not that it was truly possible for the witches to lose. Under Isadora's reign, they had already succeeded in diminishing the Northern Mortal Realm and squashed any chance of the sirens joining the rebellion. Soon they would take the Southern Mortal Realm, and then the only thing really standing in their way was Osteria and the Fae Queen. Norella's resolve hardened. She would lead her coven to victory, not just for the Crown, but to ensure the witches took their rightful place as rulers over Emodorea.

'Have someone draw a bath for me,' Isadora called over her shoulder. 'A hot one.'

Norella waited a moment after the door to the throne room closed before heading inside off the balcony. She stopped before the throne and stared up at the still-missing skull. Elsbeth had been lucky that the Queen hadn't needed to use the throne today. She surely would have noticed the centre skull missing from above her head.

She'd kept quiet about what she had seen the night before, mostly in hopes that Erikah would forgive her if she kept it from the Queen. A small part of her didn't want to see her sister in trouble, even if she brought that trouble upon herself by not submitting to Isadora. Her attitude toward the Queen was the main reason she had decided not to take her north with them on their mission. Elsbeth seemed to forget that it so easily could have been hers and Norella's skulls adorning the throne alongside their mother's, instead of the three seers'. The Queen had won the challenge for the throne as per witch law and could have claimed Hesta's entire bloodline – some would argue that her claim on the throne would be even more secure had she done so. Yet, she had allowed her nieces to live.

Norella shook her head, her blonde hair swishing from side to side against her cheek. It was useless, her mind was a muddle of where her loyalty should lie. She had a duty as Second to her Queen, her aunt. On the other hand, her twin, the one who shared the same blood and bone as she did, seemed to have pit herself against Isadora.

Elsbeth didn't trust Isadora and, in turn, didn't trust Norella. She was hiding so many secrets of late, things she would never have kept from Norella when their mother was alive. Turning away from the throne, Norella moved towards the door, stopping only to order one of the servants to prepare a hot bath for their Queen in her chambers. She needed to speak with Erikah.

She hadn't seen her lover since she left with Elsbeth and Alanah. Sighing as she paced up the stairs toward her chambers, she reminded herself Erikah would be around for another few days as they prepared the covens for whatever battle may come. There was time for her to mend the rift she had caused by dismissing their relationship so harshly.

CHAPTER TWENTY-TWO

Witch's Keep, Forest of Brielle

✦ ISADORA ✦

As soon as the servants had left, Isadora sank deep into the steaming hot bathtub, ordering her maid to allow no one to enter her chambers until dinner. The hot water covered her opaque skin, turning it slightly pink with heat. She breathed out a heavy sigh as she tried to relax.

The marble tub was big enough to fit herself plus two others comfortably, should she feel like it. Its smooth, cool surface gleamed under the soft glow of candlelight, inviting yet imposing. Trust was a rare commodity for her, and sharing her bed was an even rarer occurrence. Her private chambers were a sanctuary, a place where vulnerability was not an option. Only her maid and Norella were granted access and even then, it was a privilege bestowed sparingly and with great caution. The heavy, ornate door to her chambers remained closed to all but the most trusted.

It likely stemmed from the relentless scrutiny and the lack of privacy she endured whenever her mother was present. Always watching, always sending handmaids to ensure she was doing the right thing, adhered to proper conduct, and practised her magic. She shuddered with relief as she dipped her head below the water, letting herself sink to lay on the bottom of the tub, looking up to the water's surface.

The sounds from the castle disappeared as the water covered her ears and her red hair spread around her like wild flames. It was stupid of Artor to allow his kingdom to perish because of his defiance. He should have kneeled. Humans were such a pathetic bunch, always saying they were so hard done by, thanks to the gods not granting them any gifts. They never seemed to notice that they were the most abundant of the races in Emodorea, breeding like the wild hares that roamed her forest. If they could have looked past their disagreements and banded together, Norella's witches might not have been able to trounce the North.

Her mind drifted to the lives lost in the Northern raid. Norella had mentioned it was a distant cousin of hers and a fledgling witch. It was a shame their bodies had returned to the darkness so quickly, all that wasted power. Isadora's thoughts lingered on the potential that had been lost, the raw energy that had dissipated into the earth.

What if there was a way to harness that essence, to siphon the power of the fallen instead of letting it return, waiting to be reawakened? The notion was both thrilling and dangerous, a forbidden path that could grant her unparalleled strength. She recalled a ritual, ancient and complex, that could draw the very life force from the deceased witches, channelling it into herself. Such power could tip the entire war decisively in her favour. It was something she would need to mull on, but the idea left her body tingling with anticipation.

The next part of her plan, however, was already in motion. The beasts were taking the Southern Mortal Realm slowly, starting with the outskirts of Thornwell. King Oswald would kneel, she knew he would. He was cowardly compared to Artor. Once her beasts and witches broke through the wall, Oswald would hand over his crown to save his hide. She would enjoy feasting on his fear as he watched her burn his wife and children just to prove her point.

The surface of the water reflected her glowing red eyes as if it was a mirror, her reflection slightly distorted around the edges like a fractured glass. She stared at herself for a long time before her head broke the surface once more. The bathwater had cooled noticeably in the short time she had been underwater, a chilling reminder that winter was drawing near. She stepped out of the tub, her feet meeting the cold, unforgiving stone floor. Standing naked in front of her actual mirror, she observed her reflection. Her wet hair cascaded over her shoulders and down her chest, the fiery strands clinging to her pale skin and partially veiling her exposed breasts.

Over the years, she had often wondered when her body would begin to show the signs of her age. She was over two thousand years old now and still ... she admired herself. Her skin was all but flawless, a smooth canvas unmarred by time. Her curvier areas still sat where they did when she was twenty, defying the centuries that had passed. The only part of her that felt old and worn out was her mind, burdened with the weight of countless memories and experiences. She traced a finger along her arm, marvelling at the resilience of her physical form, even as her thoughts drifted to the weariness within her.

She had seen and done much in her many years in Emodorea. Some that she wished she could forget – not out of regret, though. No, she would not change anything she had done. She simply wanted peace of mind and to not be reminded of her actions constantly. It was enough that she had endured her sister's rule for five hundred years or so. Not to mention, she always saw Hesta's face in her nieces' – mainly in Elsbeth. Although the two sisters were identical, Isadora found it easier to have Norella remain around her once she cut her hair short. Elsbeth chose to keep her hair long, like Hesta's. She sighed as she called for Anika to attend her.

Anika had chosen well, Isadora mused as she wandered through the masses of witches gathered in the throne room. It was mid-afternoon when she finally emerged from her chambers and told Norella to summon the coven leaders. She was going to speak to them of her plans, even though she was sure most of them had gleaned enough information from her talkative coven members.

The assembled witches parted before her, forming a path through the room like a river splitting around a stone. As Isadora glided forward, the soft rustle of her skirts was the only sound, drawing all eyes of those she passed. A few marvelled at her dress as she passed them by. Had she been entertaining another realm, such as the fae she often sought to take to bed, her attire would have been more whimsical, more seductive. But this meeting amongst coven leaders called for a different kind of presence. She could feel hungry gazes following her, a mix of admiration and envy. Isadora relished the attention, but she wanted more than their desire; she wanted their unwavering obedience. Her sharp eyes met those of the coven leaders, silently conveying that she was in charge and would not be defied.

Her dress was a striking compromise of the two. It began with two small shoulder pads of leather, just like the armour most witches wore, held in place by a thin silver chain. The chain crisscrossed over her shoulders and the top of her breasts, leading to a bodice that hugged her tightly in a simple, corset-like style. This bodice, crafted from the same leather, left her stomach bare, showcasing her toned midriff.

Two silver chains were clipped to the base of her bodice, looping loosely around her ribs and supporting a sheer, draped skirt that hung low on her hips. The skirt had high slits on either side, allowing the fabric to float gracefully around her as she moved. Her long legs were clad in short, tight leather pants that left little to the imagination but provided the flexibility required for combat. Thigh-high, leather-armoured boots completed the ensemble, adding an extra layer of protection and style.

As always, she left her hair unbound and hanging to her waist in a red flowing wave. Anika had smudged coal around her eyes, making the red in her irises burn like fire, enhancing her fierce and commanding presence. The witches around her couldn't help but be captivated, their eyes following her every move as she made her way through the room.

As she ascended the stairs, each step echoed through the throne room, amplifying the anticipation that hung in the air. The crowd of witches knelt before her, their heads bowed in a unified sign of respect to their queen. The sight of them, a sea of reverence and loyalty, sent a surge of satisfaction through her.

Taking her seat upon the throne, she felt the cool, carved wood beneath her fingers, a tangible reminder of her power. The room was silent save for the faint murmur of whispered adoration. After a moment, Norella stood and walked forward, taking her place on Isadora's left-hand side, and she couldn't help the thrill that travelled her spine, electrifying her senses. This is what she had always craved, always deserved. The weight of the crown, the admiration of her followers, the absolute authority – it was all hers, and it was *glorious*.

'My sisters,' Isadora's voice echoed throughout the quiet room, 'the time has come for us to bring our covens home.'

The witches around her slowly stood, a few muttered amongst themselves. It had been centuries since the witches were called home to the castle. All this time they had been allowed to roam freely throughout the forest and the rest of Emodorea.

'King Artor and the Northern Mortal Realm has fallen,' Isadora continued, she was sure most of them already knew, but it didn't dim her satisfaction in confirming it herself. 'It is time that we band together and prepare to conquer the rest of Emodorea!'

A ripple of excitement surged through the room. The coven leaders, all fifty of them, erupted into cheers and whistles, their faces alight with agreement and bloodlust. Isadora's power swelled within her, her eyes gleaming as she took in the onslaught of support from her followers. This was the moment she had been waiting for, the culmination of her plans and ambitions. The sight of their fervour, their unwavering loyalty, filled her with a heady mix of pride and power. With a graceful motion, she raised her hand, and the witches fell silent once more, their attention fully on her.

'Now that the North is ours, we will turn our attention south. We have proven that no mere mortal stands a chance in the face of our might, and they will have no choice but to bow down before us or face the same fate as their foolish Northern brethren. You can rest assured, there will be plenty of blood, humans, and war for those of you who will be sent south.'

She raised her hand to summon a servant over to her. A young man, maybe in his early twenties, made his way toward her from his place by the wall. She held her hand out and took his supple wrist between her fingers.

'Let us start with a celebration feast to prepare us for what we will share in the Southern Realm!' Isadora sliced her long nails up the man's arm, who – to his credit – barely whimpered, before greedily drinking from his open vein. A roar went up from the witches around her as they smelled the iron in the air. She shoved him down the steps toward them when she had taken her fill, and the few closest to him pounced, wanting their share in the Queen's blood bag. Isadora grinned down at them, his warm blood running over her chin. The mess below her was a sea of gleaming red, as the coven leaders' own eyes glowed to match hers.

+ NORELLA +

The throne room, once a cavernous expanse, was now filled with the coven leaders from all fifty of the great witch clans that were spread throughout Emodorea. The air crackled with the hum of the ancient magic that flowed through each and every one of them. Gathered around the base of the throne were the witches from the ten highest-ranking clans. Each one of them draped in different colours from midnight blue to sunset orange, all varying in age and beauty. Their faces now smeared with fresh blood.

From where she stood beside her Queen, Norella's eyes glided over every one of the coven leaders who had made the trek back to the keep in the centre of Brielle Forest at their Queen's behest. All but one. Elsbeth had not shown herself at the meeting. It was true most of their coven likely viewed Norella as their true coven leader, rather than Elsbeth, but Norella never thought Elsbeth would disobey a direct order from their Queen – no matter her true feelings about Isadora. Elsbeth had been pushing the boundaries of late, sure, but to not show up at all …

If Isadora noticed, it would not end well for Elsbeth; she was lucky enough that the Queen had not seen one of her prized skulls was gone. Norella avoided the temptation to look at the top of the throne, focusing her eyes on the rest of the room as the coven leaders began to gather around the tables brought in for the meeting.

They formed semicircles, each taking their seat on the ancient wooden benches, naturally finding those that they were familiar with. Sister finding sister, friend finding friend, and those that were new coven leaders all mingled with one another, silent power plays at work as each tried to assert themselves as the leader of their group.

Food and wine was served, filling the throne room with smells of herbs and roast meat. As the witches all dug in, most not used to this kind of food, Norella held out a hand for the Queen as she descended the stairs to join the head of the first table where her closest allies sat.

'I will have Norella begin to organise the covens into battle regiments,' Isadora said as she sipped at the wine a servant placed before her. 'Once we have reached our full strength in numbers, we will be ready to assert our dominance over all Emodorea.'

'Where do we head first?'

Norella's head jerked up at the voice. The chair at the opposite end of the table was pulled out abruptly as Erikah plopped herself down, her goblet sloshing as she did so. A few of the other witches gave her reproving looks, but none dared utter a word.

Norella leaned forward ever so slightly to see past the five witches separating her and Erikah. She thought she had seen her head of strawberry-blonde hair amongst the crowd earlier, but had figured she imagined it. Norella thought that Erikah, like Elsbeth, would not bother to show for the meeting. She hadn't been able to find Erikah after she left last night with Elsbeth and Alanah. Come to think of it, Norella hadn't seen either of them since then, either. Not that it was completely out of the norm – she made a point to avoid Alanah whenever she could. The old witch had always favoured Elsbeth over her, even when they were children.

'I will send a coven or two to Winhelm to claim the land as ours and make sure that there is no uprising amongst any of the outlying villages,' Isadora replied. 'Then, we will organise to head south in a month, to Thornwell. I hear they have built a wall to keep us out.' The Queen grinned wolfishly.

Norella noted that Isadora didn't tell the witches that the wall was enough to put a slight halt on her plans. Originally, Isadora had wanted to leave early the next week to take out Oswald. Norella had explained that they would have to be cautious about what army he may hold inside the wall; he had enough time to call for recruitments from The Blue Sands and other areas while they were in the North.

'Why not the fae lands?' Erikah leaned forward, her long hair falling onto the table in front of her. Norella raised an eyebrow at her, which Erikah deftly ignored as she continued. 'Why not take Osteria by surprise?'

That was the other option that Norella had laid before the Queen; to head north in search of the fae capital known as Osteria, the City of Vines; a place of legend and mystery. The downside was that they could wander for weeks throughout The Timeless Fields and probably never find it. Even some fae had been forbidden from the knowledge of where it was.

Osteria was said to be a living city, with structures made of intertwining vines and flora that could shift and change its position to deter unwanted visitors. The city was rumoured to be an ethereal beauty, with luminescent flowers that glowed in the moonlight and ancient trees that whispered secrets of old. Even when fae left to travel through Emodorea, there was a chance they wouldn't find it again for a long time. Only the royal bloodline possessed the knowledge of where the city was at any given time, even then, it was more of an instinct than an actual map. It was a sanctuary and a fortress all at once.

Isadora had shut the idea down within seconds of the suggestion leaving Norella's lips. The fae with their ancient magic and deep-rooted connections posed a significant threat to Isadora's plans. Norella knew that engaging them directly could lead to a costly and prolonged conflict. Humans, on the other hand, were less formidable opponents, making them easier targets.

'The human lands,' Isadora continued, 'are the largest in all of Emodorea. Once we control these areas, none will likely stand against us. Then, we can search for Osteria.'

Erikah was silent at the other end of the table, Norella could almost see the argument forming in her mind. She all but melted with relief when Erikah raised her wine toward the Queen, the others at the table following suit. Erikah stared at Isadora, her lip lifting ever so slightly into a grin before she downed the rest of her cup.

As the light faded outside the castle, the talk around the tables went from war and strategy to drunken laughter and gossip. Isadora had dismissed Norella after the food had finished, too taken by the attention from the other witches to care for whether she stayed or left. She searched the floor for Erikah – she needed to make amends with her. She'd been foolish with her words.

Her eyes locked onto the other witch as she slipped from the throne room. Norella followed her, weaving her way through the throng of revellers.

She caught up with Erikah in a dimly lit corridor, the flickering torches casting long shadows on the stone walls.

'Erikah, wait,' Norella called out.

Erikah stopped but didn't turn around. 'What do you want, Norella?' she asked, her tone cold and distant.

Norella took a deep breath, trying to steady her nerves. 'I wanted to apologise for what I said last night. I was out of line, and I didn't mean to hurt you.'

Erikah finally turned to face her, eyes blazing with anger. 'Out of line? You were more than out of line, Norella. You all but dismissed our relationship, in front of the two people who'd least judge us. Do you have any idea how humiliating that was?'

Norella winced at the memory. 'I know, and I'm sorry. I was frustrated with Elsbeth, and I ... it wasn't fair of me.' She reached out to clasp Erikah's hand in her own.

'Fair?' Erikah's voice rose as she swatted the affection away. 'You think an apology is going to make everything better?'

'Can't we just go back to how things were?' Norella pleaded.

'Back to the way things were ...' Erika's face hardened. 'I don't want things to go back to the way they were. Hiding in the shadows, stealing kisses after dark. Pretending I'm not in love with you every single day.'

Norella's shoulders slumped. 'I don't mean ... I just want to make things right between us.'

Erikah shook her head. 'And what of your beloved Queen? Would you ever choose me over her?'

'Erikah, that's not ...' Norella sighed.

'Not what? Not fair?' Erikah clenched her fists, tears welling in her eyes. 'Your loyalty to her blinds you. You can't see the difference between right and wrong when all you care about is following orders. Sometimes, loyalty isn't about obedience; it's about knowing when to stand up for what's right. And it hurts because I love you, but I can't stand by in the background and watch you lose yourself to blind allegiance.'

With that, Erikah turned and walked away, leaving Norella standing alone in the corridor, the last ounces of kindness sucked out of her as the witch's form disappeared into the darkness.

CHAPTER TWENTY-THREE

Southern Reaches, Forest of Brielle

✦ ELSBETH ✦

THEY HAD ASKED ERIKAH for her help, as she too was a daughter of Typhonis, her lineage marked by the same ancient power that coursed through their veins. Alanah had seemed wary of the outsider, but had trusted Elsbeth's judgement on the matter. The ritual they were about to undertake was a delicate dance of incantations and invocations to summon a spirit from beyond. This was no ordinary spirit, but one who had met a harrowing end, its soul scarred by the violence of its demise. Erikah's presence, with her deep connection to the arcane, would be the key to easing the arduous process, ensuring the spirit's safe passage into their realm.

The three of them ventured deep into the forest, their path winding through the dense foliage until they reached a secluded clearing that Graciella herself had blessed. The moment Elsbeth stepped into the space, she felt her grandmother's magic resonate within her. Her blood sang in harmony with the lingering power that seeped into the freshly scorched grass, the towering trees, and the ancient stone at the clearing's centre. The air was thick with the scent of something otherworldly mixed with the familiar metallic tang of blood. They quickly surrounded themselves with the protection herbs and spells that Alanah had meticulously prepared, their aromas mingling with the residual magic in the air. Alanah, her movements deliberate, placed the sacred skull in the centre of their little triangle, its hollow eyes seeming to watch over them as they prepared for the ritual.

Together, the three witches chanted the ancient words that Alanah had taught them.

'Libele da pneritus apoex dis kosmeta, enkalebit makretur da alyncula dat denogis. Det Krah odiux da adelors lo Wynlara.'

For Erikah and Elsbeth, this was their first time performing such a ritual. Alanah however, had undertaken this sacred rite once before, long ago, before Graciella's mother had been Queen. The incantations for this occasion were more precise, tailored to the unique and delicate circumstances they now faced.

The bordering forest had started to warp, as if time inside their little triangle was bending. Their hands held tight to one another; Alanah had warned them of the consequences if they broke their triangle. The wind swirled around them, quicker and quicker, until they were all leaning into each other to hold their places. Still, they chanted the ancient words over and over.

They'd found themselves in the eye of the storm that surrounded the clearing, a calm amidst the swirling chaos. At the centre of their triangle stood a young woman, both ethereal and commanding. The air about her seemed to hum with latent energy, the remnants of the storm's fury held at bay by their combined magic.

'You dare to summon an oracle such as I from trying to get to Krah's domain!' She hissed, her voice had echoed eerily from the centre of the triangle. Her eyes, like burning coals, bored into them with an intensity that had made the air around them crackle.

'Are you Ravina, the oracle?' Alanah had asked the shimmering figure before them.

'I am the spirit that inhabited the body of the witch you once called Ravina,' the woman responded, her voice a chilling whisper that seemed to come from everyone and nowhere. 'Why have you dragged me back to the living plane?'

'We are seeking a way to another world.'

Erikah stifled her shocked cough at Alanah's answer. They hadn't told her about their reasons for calling the dead spirit back.

'You seek what is known as the Pass,' Ravina's spirit intoned, her spectral form flickering in and out of sight. 'Why would one of our kind wish to leave Emodorea?'

Alanah had warned Elsbeth of giving too much information to a spirit. They were not the same as their living forms. A witch's spirit was dark and full of cunning and malice.

'I want a way to escape.'

Alanah all but slapped Elsbeth with the look she had given her, but Elsbeth continued nonetheless. 'The Queen who killed you and your sisters is destroying this world. I want a safe place for myself and my baby.'

The spirit looked toward Elsbeth, her face seeming to soften at the word baby. 'You bear a powerful fate for your future bloodline. The life of this child will change the future of Emodorea, should it survive.'

'It will not survive if we stay here,' Elsbeth begged. 'Please, tell me where to find the Pass.'

Alanah had warned her to choose her words carefully, that spirits were known to try to strike a bargain. She had told Elsbeth to not promise the entity anything in return for the knowledge they sought.

'In return for the way to the Pass, I ask payment from you.'

Elsbeth did not look at Alanah, she knew that the witch was shaking her head. 'What do you ask of me?'

The spirit moved forward until she was in front of Elsbeth. 'Burn my skull and those of my sisters who remain upon that throne. We cannot be completely free to enjoy our life in Krah's kingdom with part of our spirit still trapped in this world.'

Both Erikah and Alanah looked at Elsbeth in alarm then, but the witch ignored them and agreed to the terms.

The following evening, Elsbeth and Alanah sat in the cosy confines of the cottage, the flickering candlelight casting dancing shadows on the walls. They sipped their tea, the warm liquid doing little to soothe their frayed nerves as they considered the full weight of what exactly Elsbeth had agreed to do. What she had committed to do would be deemed treason, a crime punishable by death. If caught, she would face execution, and those who aided her would share the same grim fate.

'I'm sorry I agreed to the terms,' Elsbeth said at length. 'It was my only choice – I need to get myself and my unborn child away from this world, from Isadora.'

'I understand why you did it,' Alanah replied, placing a hand on top of Elsbeth's. 'I just wish there was some other way.'

'I don't want you to help me with this,' Elsbeth said defiantly. 'I will take the skulls and burn them myself, then I will leave and head to Osteria.'

'The Queen will have you hunted and killed,' Alanah said. 'You know she will send Norella after you, just to prove she has the power.'

'If my sister is the one to hunt me, perhaps I stand a better chance than if she were to send Imogen or Zala,' Elsbeth replied as the door to the house opened and closed quietly. Neither witch needed to look to know who had entered.

'You missed the meeting,' Erikah said, pulling up a chair. 'Norella noticed, but I'm not sure if Isadora did.'

Elsbeth held back any question she had about why Erikah had chosen to grace them with her presence. After the assistance Erikah had provided the previous night, it was clear she had no intention of running to Norella or Isadora to betray them. The trust forged in the crucible of their shared ritual was fragile but genuine, a silent pact sealed by the gravity of their actions. Elsbeth was beginning to understand why her sister had feelings for this witch.

'Norella will get over it. She leads my coven better than I do, anyway,' Elsbeth said as she pushed a cup of hot tea toward Erikah.

'So,' Erikah said after a long gulp, 'when are we going to get these skulls?'

'*I'm* going to get them tonight, while the Queen is asleep,' Elsbeth replied. '*You* will be pretending that you haven't become friends with me.'

'Don't be silly,' Erikah scoffed, her freckled nose crinkling as she grinned. 'I'll help you escape from Emodorea because I want to come with you.'

'You can't be serious,' Elsbeth said as she put her cup of tea down with a soft clink. 'What about your coven? What about Norella?'

'My coven has been living without my rule for a long time, they handle themselves just fine.' Erikah took a long pause before speaking about the latter.

'As for Norella'—she sighed, picking at a chip in her cup—'I love her ... but she has chosen Isadora too many times for me to continue this charade of a relationship.'

'I'm sure Norella is just confused about the situation,' Elsbeth offered. 'I mean, I always had my suspicions. I don't understand why she felt the need to hide it from me.'

'She has had two hundred years to work out her confusion over being involved with me,' Erikah replied, her face hard.

Two-hundred years Norella had kept the secret of her lover from Elsbeth. They had been together before Hesta died, and she had not spoken a word of it to her sister, her twin. She wondered with a twinge if perhaps it was because Elsbeth had confided in her about the Fae Prince too many times and had asked Norella continuously why she didn't have a male in her bed.

'If you wish to come, I will be leaving to find Osteria as soon as the skulls are burned. I want to be as far from here as we can by dawn.' Elsbeth offered Erikah the chance to back down. 'We won't ever be able to return to the Forest of Brielle while Isadora is Queen.'

'I do not need to return,' Erikah said. 'Besides, I heard what you and Ravina spoke about – your child's survival could very well be the saviour that Emodorea will need once Isadora's plans come to fruition.'

CHAPTER TWENTY-FOUR

The Wandering River, Forest of Brielle

As the last light of day began to wane, Elsbeth and Erikah had almost made it to the forest's outer edge. They had reached the bank of the Wandering River just as the sun dipped below the horizon, casting a golden glow over the rapidly moving water. They had just dropped their satchels to the ground when the sky overhead turned a deep, ominous shade, blanketing them in darkness. Both witches instinctively lifted their gazes, their expressions mirroring the darkening sky. Elsbeth's stomach twisted into a knot, a visceral panic gripping her as she feared Isadora's sky legion were upon them. With a sudden whoosh, her terror was swallowed by awe and confusion as colossal shadows of wings danced across the ground before them. Through the break in the tree line that bordered the wild river, Elsbeth could just make out the sirens as they flew overhead. Erikah hissed as she realised what they were.

Elsbeth's hand drifted to the other witch's shoulder, signalling her to relax. Relief washed over her; Tallon and Athena had completed the journey to Nonnelle in time, then. She wondered where Athena was now as they kept watching the skies, whether she was with the sirens or making her way back to Alanah. She hoped it was the former – the thought of Isadora's wrath if anyone witnessed Athena with the sirens made her stomach churn with dread.

The legions of bird-women passed over them before turning and soaring down toward the clearing. Erikah froze, her eyes widening before she ducked back into the tree line behind an aged oak, urgently tugging Elsbeth with her. Elsbeth's heart raced, she didn't know if they had been seen or if the sirens had simply chosen to land at this clearing by the river due to the setting sun; she knew it was one of the few open spaces for miles. The uncertainty of what was to come clawed at her.

'Elsbeth!' The call echoed through the twilight as the first wave of sirens landed on the green-grassed edge of the river. A blonde figure stepped out from the arms of one of them, followed closely by a familiar face, cheeks flushed crimson from the biting wind. Ignoring Erikah's urgent grip, Elsbeth shrugged off her friend's hand and stepped boldly from the shadowy treeline into the open clearing.

'Athena.'

'What in Emodorea are you doing this far north of the Keep?' Athena's eyes widened with worry and confusion. She glanced nervously over Elsbeth's shoulder, as if expecting danger to emerge from the shadows. 'Is Alanah with you?'

'No,' Elsbeth shook her head, her expression a blend of weariness and regret. She gestured behind her, motioning for Erikah to join them. 'It's a long story. This is Erikah.'

Athena introduced herself in turn, and Erikah gave a tight smile in response as she watched the rest of the sirens land – more of them than the small clearing could handle. Many, it seemed, had already started to succumb to the curse. Around two-hundred sirens stood before them, a haunting assembly that tugged at the seams of reality. Elsbeth had never seen so many sirens in one place before. Some had lost their wings, reduced to ghostly whispers of their former selves, while others had begun to take on a disturbingly human appearance. The transformation was unsettling, a mix of elegance and eeriness that made her skin prickle.

Isadora's estimations of the siren population in Nonnelle had been woefully inaccurate. The Witch Queen had spoken of a potential legion, fearing that the sirens had hordes of warriors ready to rebel against the witches. Standing before Elsbeth now was a mere fraction of what Isadora had suggested. These two-hundred souls were just a glimpse of the once fabled race.

'I see you made it in time to help your people,' Elsbeth said, her voice a mix of relief and lingering tension as she turned to Tallon. 'I'm glad.'

'I wouldn't have made it at all without your help,' Tallon replied, a glint of gratitude sparkled in her eyes as she bowed slightly in thanks. 'Though we are past the time-frame that bitch, Isadora, gave us.'

A rare moment of vulnerability and unspoken understanding passed between them. Their connection forged through the heat of survival and a mutual disdain toward the Witch Queen.

'So'—a new voice interjected—'I have you to thank for saving my cousin.'

Elsbeth's gaze shifted past her two companions, drawn to the source of the voice. Emerging from the centre of the sirens, a figure stepped forward with an air of unyielding authority. Among the few who still retained their complete form, this siren was striking. Short, raven-black hair framed her tanned, angular face, bearing the uncanny resemblance to Tallon.

The sirens shifted uneasily, their movements a ripple of anxious energy, as she made her way through their ranks to where the witches stood. This was without doubt Queen Nerophine.

Elsbeth didn't wait for an introduction before bowing deeply to the Queen. Her mother had taught her many things, the most important was to show respect to other monarchs, regardless of their race. The weight of that lesson now sat heavy on her shoulders as she faced the Siren Queen. The almost faded light from the sun that had since disappeared below the horizon, casting long shadows as Elsbeth's form remained unwavering. This act, she hoped, would speak volumes about her intentions and the respect she held for such a ruler. It would not end well for them if they insulted a queen with this many of her warriors with her.

'You'—Queen Nerophine stopped beside Tallon, within arm's reach of Elsbeth—'are the daughter of Hesta.'

'One of,' Elsbeth replied, 'Your Majesty.'

'It was your sister, then, that did this to my cousin?' Nerophine's powerful voice was laced with accusation as she gestured to the recently healed scars that covered Tallon's arms. The angry red lines were stark against her skin, a permanent reminder of the cruelty that befell her.

Elsbeth could feel Erikah's gaze boring into her each time it flicked between the queen, Tallon and herself.

'I'm ashamed to admit it,' Elsbeth confessed, her voice tinged with regret as she glanced briefly at Erikah. 'She did so under the directions of her Queen.'

Queen Nerophine's eyes narrowed, a dangerous glint flashing within them.

'Another, it seems,' she observed coldly, 'that does not consider Isadora to be her Queen.'

Elsbeth's eyebrows raised in surprise as she turned her gaze to Athena. Now surrounded by soft twilight, the trees rustling, and the river's roar dulled as if Dagmar, the Goddess of Earth and Life herself, held her breath. Elsbeth could feel the damp earth beneath her boots, the secrets that seemed to whirl through the air between them.

'You as well then, Athena?' Elsbeth's voice was tinged with disbelief, yet there was an undercurrent of respect for the healer witch's bravery. Not just for renouncing fealty to the Witch Queen, but to defy Alanah, to break the healer oath of loyalty to the crown.

'In the short time I have spent with Tallon, I have come to realise what a true Queen is,' Athena said, her voice unwavering as she bowed to Queen Nerophine.

Athena straightened, her gaze met Elsbeth's with a steady resolve. A mix of admiration and trepidation swelled within Elsbeth as she glanced at the ancient forest behind them.

'Any ruler would be more suitable than the one on our throne.' Erikah finally spoke, her voice breaking the tense silence as she stepped up beside Elsbeth. The weight of her words hung heavy in the air, resonating with a truth that couldn't be ignored. The shadows of the ebbing night seemed to darken in response. This moment, this act of defiance, seemed almost monumental. Erikah and Athena's words were not just mere statements. They were declarations, a challenge to their very reality. As the cool evening breeze whirled around the three witches, it seemed to carry away the last remnants of doubt, leaving only the stark, raw truth of their rebellion. This was a turning point, one that could shape the destiny of them all.

Elsbeth and Erikah found themselves seated amongst a small circle of sirens. A fire burning at the centre crackled and snapped, sending occasional sparks up into the dark night, as the flickering flames cast dancing shadows around the clearing. Around them, the rest of the sirens, all in various states of transition, had begun setting up for the night, their movements quiet and deliberate. The soft murmur of their voices mingled with the quiet roar of the river and the night sounds of the forest to their backs, creating a symphony of whispers.

'Dare I ask what the pair of you are doing so far from your covens?' Queen Nerophine asked as Elsbeth was handed the plate of food that was being passed around the circle, taking it from the hands of the one Athena had called 'Peita'. The wooden plate was laden with roasted forest roots, their earthy sweetness enhanced by the fragrant glowroot spice, a rare seasoning known for its warm, nutty aroma, that grew only on the western edge of the forest. Freshly caught fish from the Wandering River, scaled and meticulously cut into thin strips, some sizzling over the open flame, while the rest was left raw, ready to be eaten with a marinade of silverleaf and moonberry extract, giving the flesh a slightly tangy taste.

'We have someone we need to find,' Elsbeth replied simply, tasting a wild berry that had been dusted with a white powder that gave it a spicy kick as it burst in her mouth. She wasn't sure how much she wanted to, or should, share with the Queen of the sirens. No matter how much Athena seemed to trust them. Elsbeth sighed as she savoured the taste, taking a few pieces of marinated fish before passing the plate along to Erikah.

'So tell me,' Elsbeth continued, brushing off the rest of the Queen's unanswered question, 'What happened after you left Alanah's hut? I feel like that might be a story worth hearing more than ours.'

Athena recapped what had happened over the days she had been gone, her voice steady but laden with exhaustion.

'We had planned on being out of the forest by tonight,' Tallon added to Athena's story, her tone marked by frustration and a hint of sorrow. 'But as you can see, almost half have suffered at the hand of the curse.'

'Have any'—Elsbeth was almost too embarrassed to ask—'grown tails?'

'A few have started to develop scales on their bodies,' Tallon replied, a deep frown etching lines of worry on her forehead. She lifted her tunic slightly, revealing her stomach where white, diamond-like scales snaked their way up her torso, glinting ominously in the firelight. 'Nothing more than that yet.'

The sight of the scales made Elsbeth's breath catch. To witness such beauty bringing forth so much anguish was a cruel reminder of life's unforgiving irony.

'It is why we are following the Wandering River,' the Queen said solemnly. 'I fear that we will not make it to the sea in time. It has already taken us almost four days to make it this far.'

'The first started losing their wings within a day of flying,' Tallon added, a pained expression crossing her face, 'it has forced us to slow to a snail's pace compared to our normal flight time.'

Elsbeth nodded, understanding that they would likely end up swimming the last leg of their journey. The thought of having to wade through the murky waters herself to reach the Tretara Range on the other side was enough to send a shiver down her spine.

'What of you, Athena?' Erikah asked as she picked at a burnt fish that the siren with the stern face had handed her. 'Where will you go from here?'

'I cannot return to Brielle,' Athena answered, her voice tinged with regret. 'I am travelling as far as Orabelle Bay with Tallon and the others. My father owns a fishing boat there – it has been a few years since I saw him last.'

Elsbeth could see the pain of past separations and the hope of a long-awaited reunion flickering in Athena's eyes. It made sense that Athena's father was from the Eastern villages. Not many witches had dark skin as vibrant as hers. The fact that Athena knew her father was a bit of a surprise, even more so that he was still alive – it confirmed Elsbeth's earlier suspicions of how young the witch was.

'Now,' Tallon declared, 'you must tell us your story. What happened after we left you?'

Ten long days had passed since Athena and Tallon had left Alanah's hut, headed for Nonnelle. Elsbeth didn't quite know where to start. She glanced around the circle that had grown as more sirens sat to join the meal. Each of their faces seemed to be etched with their own stories of struggle and resilience. Where should – or could – she begin to recount her own somewhat harrowing journey over the past ten days?

'Well, I'm not sure if you have heard, but Isadora has claimed the Northern Mortal Realm. King Artor and the people of Winhelm are no more.' Elsbeth's voice wavered as she shared the grim news. Silence encased the campfires that were close to their own, the gravity of her words settling heavily in the night air.

'She has made plans to send witches south to Thornwell in the coming month,' Erikah added, her tone sombre as the quiet deepened.

'You do not plan to stand with her?' The stern siren's eyes narrowed, her gaze sharp as she scrutinised Elsbeth and Erikah, clear disdain written all over her face.

'I love blood and war just as much as the next witch.' Erikah grinned, either completely oblivious to the fragile alliance they were potentially building, or uncaring, Elsbeth wasn't sure. 'However, I disagree with what Isadora is doing. The gods and goddesses left our world in a somewhat peaceful balance. Isadora is tipping that balance, and not for the better.'

Other nearby sirens nodded their agreement, while the stern faced siren grunted neither in approval nor disagreement.

'Cilla,' Queen Nerophine spoke to the siren that had taken to glaring toward Erikah with burning hate in her eyes. 'Can you check on the sentinels near the forest edge?'

With a huff, the siren stood and stalked away from the rest of the group.

'Where are you both headed?' Athena asked as she added some herbs to the hot water passed to her by a young child, one of the many now making their way around the campsites helping to clear away plates and hand out cups.

'We are going to The Timeless Fields,' Elsbeth said, her hand absently going to her stomach, feeling the faint swell of new life beneath her fingertips.

'You are in search of your child's father,' Queen Nerophine mused, indicating Elsbeth's slightly rounded stomach. 'You must not be far along.'

'It is early, yes.' Elsbeth admitted, a gentle smile tugging at her lips. The thought of Raynor brought a warmth to her heart, mingling with the anxiety of their journey. 'Prince Raynor is who we seek, I am hoping the fae find us soon after we enter their land. I do not wish to wander about looking for Osteria for long in my condition.'

Elsbeth recounted the oracle Ravina's declaration about her unborn child, her voice tinged with pride and fear. She explained how she, Erikah, and Alanah had ventured into the heart of the forest under the cloak of darkness. They needed to gather the remaining two seers' bones and burn them with the third, a trickier task than they had initially hoped. They had all been on edge, praying to Brielle and whatever other Eternal that would listen, in hopes that they would not let the trees pass their secrets on to Isadora.

'It turns out'—Erikah laughed—'a one-hundred-year-old skull stinks an awful lot when it *eventually* burns.'

'I'm almost certain Isadora knows by now what has happened.' Elsbeth said, turning solemn as her voice dropped to a grave whisper. A shiver ran down her spine as she contemplated the wrath Isadora was capable of unleashing. 'It's just a matter of what she will do when she finds out it was me.'

'Us.' Erikah interjected. 'It wasn't just you.'

'You are her niece,' Tallon said, her voice filled with curiosity. 'She favours your sister, why not you?'

Elsbeth shrugged, a bitter smile now tugging at her lips. She had wondered the same thing for the past hundred years, the mystery gnawing at the edge of her thoughts. The answer always eluded her, buried beneath layers of family dynamics and Isadora's twisted ambitions.

'It's your hair,' Erikah told her, as she shoved the last of her fish into her mouth.

'What?' Elsbeth fingered the thick braid that hung heavy over her shoulder, tracing it to the soft ends that reached past her waist.

'Norella told me that the reason she keeps her hair short is that it reminds Isadora less of your mother.' Erikah continued, barely concealing her grin. 'Though I always thought she kept it short so that I wouldn't have anything to pull on.'

Tallon let out a snort.

'Of course,' Queen Nerophine smiled, a knowing glint in her eye as she ignored her cousin and Erikah. 'With your long hair, you are the spitting image of Hesta – it's how I recognised you.'

'Isadora's vanity knows no bounds,' Erikah sighed dramatically, 'must she ruin all the fun things in my life?'

'She never mentioned that to me,' Elsbeth whispered, her fingers absently twirling the end of her braid around her finger. The gesture was almost hypnotic, a small anchor amidst the swirling revelations stampeding through her head.

'It's odd that she would think that way,' Athena said, shaking her head in disbelief. 'She is the one who killed your mother for the throne. You would assume she would not care if you look like her.'

'If I'm not mistaken,' Queen Nerophine quietly added, 'Isadora hated Hesta, even though they were half-sisters.'

'It did seem that way for most of our childhood,' Elsbeth sighed, 'she was never exactly *Aunty Issy*.'

'Can you imagine!' Erikah laughed loudly, her mirth breaking through the sombre mood. Elsbeth and Athena joined in, their laughter a shared defiance against the shadows of their past. The thought of Isadora playing aunty was something else entirely.

'I remember when we were really little, before either of us had gotten our powers, Norella and I tried to convince Isadora to wear one of our flower crowns.' The memory surfaced and was leaving her mouth before Elsbeth could think better of it. 'She got so frustrated at us for calling her the "queen of the flowers" that she nearly set the entire field of wildflowers on fire. Alanah was furious that half her medicinal stock was gone.'

Erikah snorted, tea flying out her mouth and nose, 'Norella never told me that!'

Elsbeth smiled, a spark of mischief growing within her that she hadn't felt since she was younger.

As the night deepened, the sirens slowly moved away, each to their own beds while the small group of unlikely companions continued to share their stories, the queen even sharing some of Hesta before Elsbeth was born. Tales that Elsbeth listened to fervently, clutching at the precious memories. Even the surrounding trees seemed to lean in, eager to listen to the tales being shared.

CHAPTER TWENTY-FIVE

The Wandering River, Forest of Brielle

+ ATHENA +

ATHENA HAD WATCHED as Elsbeth and Erikah settled in with the sirens for the night. There was little doubt that Isadora had discovered the missing skulls and pieced the facts together by now. The concerns Elsbeth had voiced earlier were ones that Athena now harboured herself. Despite the older witch's reassurance that Alanah would be fine and that Isadora wouldn't harm the head healer, not with war unfolding before them, Athena couldn't shake the gnawing unease.

She rolled over in her makeshift bed, a mess of itchy blankets one of the sirens had supplied for her the first night of their journey. Erikah, the freckle-faced witch, snored peacefully between her and Elsbeth, her cheeks rosy from a little too much of the siren wine.

The other two had found it easier to get to sleep than Athena had. She supposed it was because the witches were used to living in camps around the edge of the forest, never having a proper bed. Since becoming Alanah's apprentice, Athena had lived in the small hut with the older witch and all the comforts that afforded. But now, Athena envied them their seeming ease with pebbles sticking into their backs, and tiny feet of unknown origin crawling over their skin. Dawn wouldn't be far off, and she had yet to get a wink of sleep.

She watched the guards change shifts for the night before she rolled to her other side to where Tallon was asleep. The pair had become good friends, despite what had happened. She was glad to have someone to talk to on her journey to the East, and that she wasn't their prisoner because of Isadora's actions.

As she rolled onto her back and closed her eyes in a futile attempt to at least rest if she couldn't sleep, an ear-piercing scream ripped its way through the camp. The sound was so sharp, so jarring, that Athena's heart seemed to stop mid-beat. For a moment, she lay there, utterly frozen, the scream still echoing in her ears. Her mind raced, a thousand possibilities flooding in, each one more terrifying than the last.

The scream was followed by another less violent cry for help. Tallon jolted awake and was on her feet within seconds, her eyes scanning the camp for the source of the scream. She took off running, Queen Nerophine and her two guards, Peita and Cilla, close behind her as they all ran toward the far side of the camp.

'Come on,' Athena said, rousing Elsbeth. 'They might need our help.'

Elsbeth glanced down at Erikah as she rose to her feet to join Athena. The witch was still asleep, seemingly undisturbed by the noise. They left her there and ran to join the others.

The night was dark and heavy, the only light to guide them from the dying embers of the long forgotten fires scattered around the clearing. They stumbled and clutched each other for balance before coming to a stop at the back of the circle of sirens.

'What's happened?' Athena asked, grabbing Tallon's arm after they pushed their way to the front of the circle. On the ground, where Queen Nerophine knelt, was a young siren, her body shaking and eyes fluttering.

'She was fine before we went to bed,' one of the other human-looking sirens told them, her voice trembling. 'I mean, she'd lost her wings and talons like most of us and had a few scales on her body, but nothing like this.' She looked away from her friend, almost in disgust.

The siren on the ground writhed, her every movement a struggle against the advice from Tallon to stay still. Athena knelt on the other side of her, looking to the Queen for approval before reaching out to touch her.

The siren's legs had webbed themselves together in a long, muscular tail covered in hard, emerald-coloured scales that glinted in the dim light from the fires. The tail, powerful and sinuous, seemed to ripple with an unsettling energy. Athena gently removed the tatters of the siren's dress, revealing more iridescent scales that crept up her torso, disappearing under her bodice. The transformation was both mesmerising and horrifying, a testament to the curse's relentless grip.

Athena carefully brushed the siren's hair out of her face, her fingers trembling slightly as she tilted her head to expose her neck. In the fading moonlight, three thin slits became visible on either side of her neck. Faint, but unmistakable.

'Gills.' Elsbeth fell to her knees beside Athena in disbelief. Isadora had done it; she was so powerful that she could cast a shifting curse of this scale. The sight was enough to send chills down anyone's spine, a stark reminder of the dark magic at play.

'It won't be long now,' Tallon whispered, her hand going to her own throat as if to check.

'You have to get into the water,' Athena whispered to the siren. 'You won't be able to breathe for much longer on land.'

The siren's eyes widened in sheer terror, but as she opened her mouth to reply, all they heard were sharp screeches and hisses. Athena watched as Tallon exchanged a bewildered look with her cousin, confusion etched across her face.

'The language of the Mer.' A bleary-eyed Erikah stumbled into view, her voice filled with disdain. 'Such a gods-awful sound.'

They all looked toward Erikah, waiting for a further explanation. Mermaids were reclusive, and kept to themselves most of the time. Athena had grown up in Thames, on the edge of Orabelle Bay, and had never seen one; and by the look on all the sirens' faces, none of them had either. The people of the small towns peppered along the shoreline of Orabelle Bay were probably the only ones who could claim to sight mermaids with any regularity.

'I don't know much,' Erikah went on, 'and for the life of me, I never learnt to understand them, but I know that is what their voices sound like above water. Possibly below water too, except, of course, they'd be able to understand each other.'

'You mean we are all going to sound like that eventually?' Tallon asked.

'Yes,' Erikah replied.

Athena placed a comforting hand on the siren's featherless shoulder.

Upon Queen Nerophine's demand, Peita and Cilla moved swiftly to carefully lift the tailed siren in their strong, still-feathered arms. They carried her with a gentleness that belied their stern exteriors as they made their way down the riverbank to the water's edge, the river whispering its welcome.

'Also, the fact that one of you has turned means you have run out of time,' Erikah added.

'What do you mean?' demanded Cilla, her voice strained under the weight of her tailed sister.

Erikah crossed her arms. 'You will have to move slower to accommodate the mermaid, now, and less of you have wings than yesterday, too. Although I'm sure you don't want to admit it. You'll have to walk from here on. Since she has changed, it won't be long before the rest of you do, too.'

Queen Nerophine stood, watching as the tailed siren, the first to become one of their sisters of the sea, was lowered into the cool, flowing water. An audible sigh escaped the siren's lips as the river embraced her, the current seeming to ease the pain of the transformation. The surrounding sirens watched in solemn silence.

'Those of you that can fly, I'm ordering you to go.' Her voice thundered through the quiet clearing. 'Take the young ones that haven't turned yet and fly as fast as you can towards the bay.'

'My Queen—' Peita began, but Queen Nerophine cut her off with a sharp glance.

'I will stay with those of you that cannot fly,' she declared, her voice leaving little room for argument. 'We will walk the length of the river and stay with those that complete the curse's transformation.'

'No,' Tallon interjected as she also stood for all to hear. 'As Second to our Queen, I will lead those that cannot fly to the ocean. Our Queen must be protected, she must fly with the others to the safety of the bay.'

A murmur of agreement rippled through the sirens that stood around them in a circle.

Athena watched as the Queen's eyes narrowed. The tension thick between the cousins as they seemed to silently argue about what to do.

'You know what is at stake Tallon,' Queen Nerophine's voice was almost too quiet for anyone but those closest to her to hear. 'I cannot abandon those who need me.'

'And I cannot allow you, our *Queen,* to risk your life.' Tallon shot back, her tone firm but laced with concern. 'You are the beacon of our people. Without you, there is no hope.'

'I will not be a coward,' the Queen replied through gritted teeth. 'My place is here, walking alongside those who are suffering.'

'And my duty is to you, cousin. Let me bear this burden. You are more than just a leader, you are our symbol of hope and if you fall, I fear all may well be lost.'

'I will stay with them as well,' Athena stepped up beside Tallon. 'I'm no warrior, but I know Thames well, and I can help with any that need healing along the way.'

The Queen glanced between the two of them, before finally nodding in defeat, reluctant acceptance in her eyes.

'Gather what you can carry without weighing yourself down. We leave in ten minutes.'

A flurry of wings filled the quiet morning as the sirens took to the sky, leaving the grounded sirens and the newly transformed mermaid behind. Athena and the others stood solemnly, the weight of the curse's effects hanging heavy in the crisp morning air. The small flock soared toward the horizon, where the sun was beginning to crest. Athena watched as the silhouettes of the sirens faded into the golden light, a bright reminder of the sacrifice and bravery etched into this dawn.

CHAPTER TWENTY-SIX

Thornwell, Southern Mortal Realm

+ REID +

REID HAD SAT in the dimly lit cell at the base of the castle for the past five days, his only visitor the King's high priest, the sole observer to his ever-growing despair. If you were to ask him how many days had passed, he would have told you that he lost count, but it felt like an eternity. The air was thick with the musty scent of damp stone and decay, mingling with sweat and the faint, acrid smell of mildew. The days and nights blended together, the only light a dim flicker from a torch down the hall. The walls, cold and unyielding, seemed to press in on him. The priest would sit across the room from him on a wooden stool and take notes on his behaviour, while Reid sat on the hard bed, which, though unforgiving, was still better than the floor at Gillian's.

When the priest had appeared on Reid's first day in the prison, he was certain this was the priest Kasin had told him – no, had promised him – would believe him, or at least have faith in Kasin. And so Reid had spent the better part of the day explaining to this priest who he was, everything that he'd already told to the guards, and answering all his questions as politely as he could. But so far, Reid wasn't getting any signs that the priest believed a word he was saying.

He was still yet to meet the King, even though he asked every day when the priest arrived.

'Soon,' the priest would say before handing him a small loaf of dense rye bread, its dark crust a tapestry of toasted grains, and a small pot of honey. The honey carried a scent close to what Reid imagined the wildflowers in The Timeless Fields smelt like. Apparently, it was the only food they seemed to want to waste on him.

Reid expected today to be no different, although he thought the priest was later than usual, he couldn't be sure – maybe he just woke up earlier than he usually did. But his stomach said otherwise with how hungrily it growled when the door eventually clicked open, echoing through the silence like a promise. The scent of the anticipated meal – the mix of warm nutty bread and the floral, sweet allure of the honey – failed to greet his senses. The priest's hands were empty, devoid of the comforting offerings Reid had become dependent on. The air seemed colder, the room darker, and his hunger more acute in the priest's absence of sustenance.

'Today is your last chance to convince me that you harbour the god Kasin inside you,' the priest said as he paced the room.

'I've told you, he isn't harboured inside me.' Reid leaned back on the bed. 'Kasin comes and goes as he pleases, he is a *god*.' Perhaps if he emphasised the word, they would understand. Kasin had been quiet since they had arrived. He did say that projecting himself as he had in the forest took a great deal of energy, though Reid had hoped after this long he would have returned.

'So, we are expected to believe that out of everyone in Emodorea Kasin may have chosen to be his Protector, he chose you'—the priest eyed Reid suspiciously—'a common street rat.'

'Apparently, not so common.' Reid smirked, more so to himself – or Kasin, if he was listening. He was sure the god was always eavesdropping.

'If you could do something to prove that you are what you say you are,' the priest asked cautiously, his eyes seeming to gleam with some hidden malice. 'Perhaps call the god forth to speak to us himself.'

'As a priest, you should know that mortals cannot set eyes upon a god's true form,' Reid countered. The priest huffed at that; his round belly jiggled as he moved about the room in frustration. As he strut past Reid, the oppressive scent of incense and old parchment, mingling with the underlying odour of sweat from the priest's anxious movements, wafted over him. He scrunched his nose.

'What more could I offer you?' Reid asked, desperation seeping into his voice. 'They have already taken the milanite blade from me. Where else would I have gotten a god's blade, besides from an actual god?'

The priest's eyes twitched, he stopped pacing and rushed toward Reid, pinning him to the bed as he leaned over him, his face close enough that Reid could feel his hot, sour breath on his skin. His eyes, once merely suspicious, now glinted with intense mania.

'Kasin!' He screamed in Reid's face, his spittle flying as he called for the god he claimed not to believe was there. 'You must show yourself if you wish to save the boy.'

'Save me?' Reid demanded as he shoved the man away from him. 'What in Zadea are you talking about?'

'The King has said that if you cannot prove you are Kasin's vessel, then you shall be trialled before the council for impersonating a god.' The priest's eyes gleamed with unholy delight, as his lips curled into a sneer. 'Which, if I have my way, and you're prosecuted, I'll take great pleasure in making an offering of your body to Krah.'

'You can't be serious,' Reid exclaimed. 'You're a priest! You're meant to be helping me.'

They were going to kill him, all because Kasin would not show himself to them. The priest, of all people, should be the one on his side – but he wanted him dead more than anyone, from what Reid could see. Despite the priest having spent the previous days bringing him bread, talking to him, offering counsel on the matters of the gods and goddesses – the Eternals, as he had learnt they were called – the priest was now threatening his life. Was this all a scheme?

'You will be brought before the King and council at dusk – they will decide your fate.' The priest smirked as he moved to the door. 'Until then, no food will be served to you.'

The lock clicked into place as Reid rushed toward the door, banging and shouting after the priest through the small, barred peep-hole as he waddled away up the stairs and out of sight.

Kasin! He called into the darkness of his mind, praying that he would finally respond to him after hearing what the priest had said. *Come on, I know you can hear me.*

Nothing. His head was as quiet again, a void of emptiness, just as it was before he had been given that little statue from the shop. The figurine and his cigarette tin were the other objects they had taken from him when he arrived. Anxiety gnawed at his insides without the carving of Kasin to hold, to feel connected to the god, without the familiar cool metal of the cigarette tin in his palm. It surged through his veins, an uncontrollable, relentless tide that left him gasping for breath.

Please, Kasin, a softer approach, one filled with more dread and doubt than he had let himself feel the past few days. He had been sure that once the priest arrived, he would be released and the King would meet with him. But now he had just about reached breaking point, especially with Kasin being oddly quiet in his mind. Though, he was confident he could still feel the god's presence lingering amongst his thoughts.

Reid's hands shook violently as he raked them through his sweat drenched hair, the sheer thought of his potential fate making his chest tighten. While the thought of being found guilty and put to death caused him a great deal of fear, the thought of what would happen to the boys, *his boys*, played on his mind. They were still out there, alone, for the past week. He had prayed to Kasin every night since he had been brought here, prayed for the god to protect them for him. To watch over them and make sure they didn't do anything stupid. Yet, his pleas seemed to echo into the abyss that was now his mind, met only by the god's unusual silence.

CHAPTER TWENTY-SEVEN

Thornwell, Southern Mortal Realm

+ REID +

Dusk arrived a lot quicker than Reid anticipated. He had just closed his eyes to sleep in an attempt to drown out the pains of hunger when his escort arrived.

Instead of the priest, a fair-skinned woman appeared as the door to his cell swung open. She lingered in the doorway, her lips curling in disdain at the squalor within, as though the mere air inside repelled her.

'Wash your face, then follow me,' she commanded, her voice slicing through the grim silence.

The guards outside his door watched with indifferent eyes as he emerged, wary and uncertain. The woman led him with brisk steps up the narrow staircase. As they stepped into the dim afternoon sun, he squinted, feeling the weight of the orange sunset sky, and the impending doom it might bring.

The woman offered no explanation as to who she was or why she had been the one to collect him and not the priest. Her shoulder-length, obsidian hair hung in tight curls that framed her face with an elegance that was unknown to Reid. She wore a long, flowing lavender dress that swished around her ankles, the delicate fabric at odds with the bleak surroundings. It was clear the lady was not a maid, given what she wore and how she held herself. There was an undeniable air of authority about her – her posture straight, her steps measured and precise. If she was nobility, then why was she sent to retrieve him – and alone, at that?

Trailing behind her, he navigated the brightly lit castle with a sense of awe. Every sandstone pillar was adorned with a blazing torch, casting a warm, golden light that bridled the space between it and the next. The ceiling soared above, far higher than any of the buildings he had been to in the Outer Ring, its surface painted in a brilliant blue that seemed to mock the sky itself.

'It was painted so that even when it is dark or stormy, we may glimpse our beautiful blue skies outside,' the woman said when she noticed he had stopped walking to stare up at the masterpiece. 'My great-grandfather commissioned the piece. I believe he had a strong love for Thora, and that is why he chose the most beautiful sky in Emodorea as his ceiling.'

'Why not just leave the roof open?' Reid asked, still looking up. 'It isn't like we ever get rain.'

The woman tilted her head, her eyes twinkling with a hint of amusement as she studied him.

'Perhaps he was afraid of what lurks in the dark outside.' She stepped closer, letting her words linger with a mischievous smile.

Reid's eyes never left the ceiling as he replied, 'Could be.'

She giggled softly, turning on her heels and continuing down the corridor, her laughter echoing in the halls.

She led him further through the labyrinthine castle, past sprawling gardens now cloaked in twilight. The sun had now completely set, leaving the sky a deep indigo. Young women chased children around, their laughter mingling with the evening air as they coaxed them indoors for supper and baths. A few older folks wandered through the passageways, arms laden with books, occasionally darting around Reid and the woman. She glanced at him from time to time, her expression unreadable, as though she was contemplating something. Reid shifted uneasily. He wasn't used to being around women; the only ones he had ever had much interaction with were either the witches or the ladies at Madame Jessamine's.

They must be scholars of some kind, Reid thought to Kasin, another attempt to get the god to respond to him. He wasn't shocked when Kasin still didn't reply, he just continued to pray that he would show up before the council decided to have him sacrificed.

'Quite the lovely place, isn't it?' she remarked, pulling Reid from his thoughts. Her voice was laced with an undertone he couldn't quite place.

He simply nodded in response, taking in as much of the bustling scene around him as he could.

'Do you always walk so quietly?' she added, her tone playful. 'Or is it just with me?'

'I guess I'm just used to avoiding attention.' The words slipped out before Reid realised he was speaking. A light blush rose up his cheeks as her sea-green eyes lingered on him.

They climbed a continuous flight of stairs until Reid was sure that he would run out of air. He had never even considered that a building could be so high. Every so often, there was a window he could peek out of. He could see the whole way to the forest out of some, and others, the desert between Thornwell and The Blue Sands.

'The council and King Oswald are in here waiting for you,' she said as they stopped before a dark, cherry wood door. Reid's body went rigid at her words.

'Don't look so pale,' she joked as she pushed the door open for them to enter.

'Ah, Elisavet, finally, you have joined us.' A stocky man rose to greet the woman, as did the other council members who were seated around the table.

'Uncle,' Elisavet replied as she greeted the man with a quick peck on the cheek. She moved into the room and took up a position on the far wall, next to the priest. Reid thought it interesting he wasn't considered high enough rank to be seated at the table.

Elisavet's uncle stood before Reid and looked him over from head to toe. Reid could see that he wasn't impressed with what he saw – from the other council members' looks, neither were they. He didn't know what they expected him to be, perhaps a burly man instead of the somewhat gangly boy on the verge of manhood.

'Don't you know to bow before your king, boy?' one of the older councilmen to his right said.

Reid looked over the man standing before him – the King, he supposed. The King's face was crinkled with lines that spoke of years spent in silent contemplation and weighty decisions. His eyes, a piercing blue, held a depth that made Reid uneasy, as though the King could see through his very soul. Reid had never set foot inside the castle, and the King never seemed to leave. How was he meant to have known the man before him, with no crown on his head, was the King?

Reid's eyes wandered to the back of the room. Elisavet. Reid let the name of the woman swirl around in his mind. No, Princess Elisavet, he corrected himself. The King had sent his only niece to retrieve him from the cell – was that normal for royalty to do? She met his gaze, her eyes flicking meaningfully between Reid and her uncle. She was leaning ever so slightly forward, her body silently gesturing at him.

Reid snapped back to attention, she was trying to silently tell him to bow. So he did, or at least he did what he assumed was a bow, to the man before him. 'Apologies, Your Majesty.'

The council members mumbled to one another as the King accepted Reid's apology with a slight nod of his head.

'You are not what we expected Kasin's Protector to look like,' the King went on as he moved back to his seat at the head of the table. Reid stood just inside the doorway, unsure whether he was meant to stay there or take the empty chair at the other end of the table, set away from the council members and the King.

'Well,' the King said, 'take a seat.'

Reid noticed Elisavet try to hide her smile as his face turned crimson.

'The priest tells us that you cannot produce evidence that Kasin has chosen you to have his powers,' the same older councilman said.

'Come now, Lord Tokil,' the man to the King's right said, 'give the boy a chance to explain himself, instead of believing wholeheartedly what a simple priest had to say.'

There was a quiet sound of protest from the direction of the wall as Reid's head snapped up from where he had been looking at his hands in his lap, searching the table for the source of the voice. The man who had spoken leaned backward in his chair, hiding his face behind the man next to him, the one he referred to as Lord Tokil.

'I've been trying to contact Kasin since you locked me up,' Reid said as he tried to see past Lord Tokil. 'You took my milanite sword – was that not enough evidence?'

'I'm afraid, merely possessing a sword that is made of a mythical metal isn't enough for us to accept this outrageous claim,' Lord Tokil said as a matter of fact.

'Perhaps,' the hidden-faced man spoke again, 'if you were able to show us the creature you *killed*, we would be more inclined to believe you.'

'As I told the priest and the guards,' Reid answered as he folded his hands on the table in front of him, 'after I pulled the sword from the stone in the forest, the beast attacked. But when Kasin told me to kill it, a light burst from the sword and incinerated the creature. I'm sure the clearing is still blackened from what happened.'

'And then a *god* decided to show himself to you,' the voice finished, the evident smugness rubbing Reid the wrong way.

'No, a god's true form would kill anyone who looked upon it,' Reid said evenly. 'He appeared as an apparition of sorts, not a solid form.'

The lords looked around the room, seeming to size up whether any of the others believed the story. Reid glanced toward Elisavet, who was concentrating so intently on Reid that it shocked him into looking away, heat creeping up his neck.

'If you cannot produce any evidence,'—the priest interjected—'then I am bound by duty to Kasin and the other deities to punish you accordingly for impersonating one of them.'

Around the table, a mumble of agreement ran through council members. The one that remained hidden from Reid's view was the only one that kept quiet on the matter. The King nodded his agreement, at which point Elisavet opened her mouth as if she were going to argue in Reid's defence – but self-preservation appeared to win out.

Please Kasin, Reid begged the god, *how do I prove what I say is true?*

There was still no reply. Reid was sure that Kasin had not abandoned him, not at a time like this. Perhaps he was busy checking on the boys, like he had begged him to while he sat in the cell. At least that's what he hoped as he listened to the men before him decide his fate.

'So, it's agreed,' King Oswald said to the priest, 'you will perform your ritual at sunrise.'

'Uncle, please,' Elisavet stepped forward. The King held his hand up to silence her, which, to Reid's surprise, she ignored. 'Are you willing to risk angering the gods if you are wrong, and end up killing Kasin's chosen one?'

The King looked as if he would consider his niece's words, but a tan hand placed itself on his shoulder, a head leaning in to whisper something into the King's ear. 'I'm sorry, Elisavet, the council has voted.'

Reid stood like the rest of the council members as they moved to leave the room, the brown-haired man who had spoken to the King at the head of the pack. Reid was still unable to see his face, but he couldn't shake the feeling that there was something familiar about him as he watched him leave.

CHAPTER TWENTY-EIGHT

The Wandering River, Forest of Brielle

✦ ELSBETH ✦

Elsbeth and Erikah hadn't stayed with Athena and the sirens very long after dawn spread across the land, painting the river in soft hues of pink, orange, and red. It had been a brief departure, the two witches bidding farewell and good luck to Athena and the sirens before they set their sights on the Wandering River. They made their way down to where the river narrowed, its once expansive width now confined to a murkier, more manageable passage.

The water was treacherous, swirling with unseen currents and veiling the riverbed in an impenetrable shadow. Carefully, they waded into the rushing water, using jagged stones that jutted out to brace themselves as they made their way through the shallowed section. Each step was taken with measured precision, their clothes becoming heavy as the water threatened to drag them away. The only benefit either seemed to gleam from the entire ordeal was the renewed strength being in the water seemed to bring them. Elsbeth sent a silent prayer to Typhonis as thanks for sharing his affinity to water with her. She was certain Erikah had done the same, though likely littered with the string of curse words flowing from the witch's lips as she stumbled along in front of her.

Osteria was said to be a city of secrets. Elsbeth didn't know where to begin searching for the hidden city and, in turn, Raynor. Each step as they trudged their way along the base of the Tretara Range seemed to echo with whispers of old magic, the kind that made the hair on the back of her neck stand up. There were rumours of the fae knowing when outsiders entered their lands; it was said they often found travellers who sought them out first. She could only hope they were found by Raynor's allies, or by the Prince himself.

'So,' Erikah said as they made their way around the base of the mountain range, 'do you think he will be happy when we find him?'

Elsbeth's mind raced. Of course, she wanted to believe that he would be happy; she wanted to believe that they had shared more than just their bodies during the years they had been together. But, if she was honest, the question that Erikah asked so effortlessly had been one that she had been asking herself for days now. What if he wasn't happy to see her? What if he shunned her, and their child? Worse again, what if he wanted to keep the child with the fae, as sometimes happened when half-borns resembled their fae parent, and tried to force her to leave the baby? The thought of all the horrible outcomes made her nauseous.

'I think he'll be happy about it,' she finally answered, her voice a lot more confident than the thoughts that swirled through her mind.

'Well,' Erikah offered, as if she sensed Elsbeth's ill-ease, 'I'd be happy if it were mine.' Elsbeth smiled at the thought of sharing parenting duties with her sister's former lover.

'I'd be a good mother,' Erikah went on, 'share all my spoils of war with her.'

'What if it's not a girl?' Elsbeth asked. 'What if Alanah got it wrong and it's a boy? What if they don't have an affinity for any of the elements?'

Erikah thought for a moment as she clambered over a small rock mound that was in their way.

'I think I'd treat them the same. And if my coven didn't like it, I'd leave them, even if I were their leader.'

Bold words, but Elsbeth wasn't surprised that Erikah felt that way. In the few days they'd been travelling together, Elsbeth had become accustomed to her raw honesty and way of thinking. It was a pleasant change from all the devout followers of Isadora.

They continued walking in silence, something they both seemed happy to do most days. The surrounding terrain turned from the dense green of the forest to a barren, snow-covered mountain. In the far distance, they could see the brilliant greens that would be The Timeless Fields. For now, they had a two-day journey across the base of the Tretara Ranges, the place where the Soulless – those half-breeds not kept by either of their parents – reigned supreme.

CHAPTER TWENTY-NINE

Southern Foothills, The Tretara Range

+ ELSBETH +

THE TRETARA RANGE wasn't somewhere that people in Emodorea chose to travel to willingly. The surrounding land at the base of the peaks barren and uninhabitable, it marked the border between the Northern Mortal Realm and the Land of The Fae. It ran from the rocky ocean shoreline in the North, right down to the edge of Brielle Forest, separated only by the Wandering River.

The mountains themselves were perilous, the ground covered in spine-riddled, dense shrubs and vines that sprouted poisonous flowers crawling their way across the known path, snaring unsuspecting victims. The weather was teeth-chattering cold and the air thin. Ice concealed the path as it rose higher, making every step treacherous to those that were unfamiliar with the terrain. Blizzards hit almost every night over the winter months, and summer storms made the ground swamp-like.

But all of that was the least of Elsbeth and Erikah's worries as they set up camp when the sun began to set. The stories the surrounding villages told of the Soulless were enough to rattle even the most bloodthirsty witch in Brielle Forest. There were reasons people in Emodorea chose to take a longer path when travelling to avoid the mountain range.

'Do you think any of them come down this far?' Erikah asked as they gathered small bits of wood. Their pile was dismal, most of the sticks and leaves around were wet from the water that ran down from the peaks.

'If winter wasn't about to set in, I'd be inclined to not have a fire,' Elsbeth replied, dropping her pile on the patch of dry dirt they had cleared.

'In all my years, this is the closest I have ever been to the Tretara Range.' Erikah looked to the highest point of the mountains, her eyes taking their time to search the few caves she could see.

'I've been once,' Elsbeth said as she squatted with her flint rocks in either hand, 'when I was younger. Mother sent me to leave one of our impure.' The word 'impure' felt heavy on her tongue.

'What do you suppose the Soulless do with them?' Erikah asked, sitting in front of the small fire as it was starting to smoke.

'I assume they either leave them to die or take them into their clans – haven't you had to bring any babes from your coven up here?'

'Only one of my sisters has borne a child,' Erikah shrugged. 'It was a male – half-human, so he was given to his father. A mortal that lived in a village near Thornwell.'

None from Elsbeth and Norella's coven had borne a child since Anise Wraithe, a distant cousin of theirs, over a century ago. They were rare among witches, mainly because many didn't want to forgo the bloodlust for the months they were pregnant. Elsbeth herself hadn't planned to be pregnant, but hadn't taken any actions to prevent it from happening. She was glad the father was fae and not a human, though. These days, too many humans were descendants of sirens or mermaids that didn't get their mothers' traits, and the mongrel blood didn't blend well with the witches.

'I want to be moving before sunrise,' Elsbeth changed the subject. 'I'll take the first watch, if you want to get some rest.'

'I'm not sure I'll be able to sleep knowing what's in those mountains.' Erikah leaned back against the boulder so she was facing the range.

'As long as we don't draw attention to ourselves, I'm sure we'll be fine.' Elsbeth tried her best to reassure her. 'I feel as though the stories we hear aren't all that true anyway – you know how humans can overindulge in bending the truth.'

It didn't take long before Erikah was snoring across the fire – Elsbeth was sure the whole of Emodorea could hear the witch. She smiled to herself and leaned back against her rock, a cup of mint tea in her hand. The warmth of the fire, mixed with the cool night air, created what was becoming a rare moment of tranquillity. As she gazed up at the star-strewn sky, the chaos of the day melted away. Elsbeth took a deep breath, savouring the rare peacefulness.

'Elsbeth,' Erikah whispered. 'Elsbeth, wake up.'

Elsbeth's eyes flickered open as something rough grabbed at her, the icy chill of the night air clawing at her senses. Her vision was bleary, the cold making her sluggish. Erikah was close by, she could smell the familiar herbs she always had entwined in her hair. Her gaze locked with a pair of golden eyes flecked with red mere inches from her face. A rush of adrenaline surged through her veins as she startled and tried to scoot back against the rock that she had leaned against earlier.

Her heart pounded wildly as the shadows seemed to press in around her, each breath drew in more of the frigid air that bit at her skin. Her mind raced – what creature had those eyes? The oppressive darkness around them amplified her terror, shadows of figures crowded around them both.

'You fell asleep,' Erikah hissed at her. 'Why didn't you wake me if you were tired?'

'I don't think this is the right time,' Elsbeth said as the figure in front of her tilted its head, watching her. She tried to summon her magic, to summon the water from the ice and snow around them, but her hands were bound behind her back and her feet together in front of her. Without being able to make the signs, she was utterly useless. To her left, Erikah was in a similar position.

A deep, rough voice spoke from the other side of the fire in a language Elsbeth didn't understand. The accent was thick and deep, similar to the Northern humans', but it wasn't their language that these beings spoke. She glanced at Erikah, but the other witch shrugged, indicating she didn't know what they were saying either.

'You will come with us,' the deep voice was so heavy with the strange accent that Elsbeth could barely comprehend the whole sentence. Then, the two creatures hauled the witches to their feet and cut the ropes between their ankles.

The golden-eyed one pushed them from behind, forcing them to shuffle up the little goat track that had been hidden by the shrubs. In the dark, Erikah and Elsbeth exchanged a glance of confusion.

CHAPTER THIRTY

Thornwell, Southern Mortal Realm

+ REID +

THE PRIEST HAD the guards move Reid from the council room to the courtyard, where he would spend his last night tied to the post in its centre. He kicked and fought against the guards all he could, but it was useless. With their sheer brute strength, they easily diffused any of his attempts to escape. Whatever the man had whispered in the King's ear had swayed him from listening to the sense that his niece spoke.

The guards tied his hands and feet to the post, as the priest had instructed. They forced him to stand with his back against the stiff, unrelenting wood, unable to sleep or sit down as the hours of waiting threatened to swallow him. Not that his rigid body would likely have let him do either, even if they hadn't tied him up. His mind was frantic with the thoughts of what would come in the next few hours.

Dawn wasn't far off, now – but there was still time for Kasin to show himself. At least, Reid hoped Kasin would show himself. Surely, the god wouldn't make such a spectacle of choosing him just to let him die at the hands of a wayward priest.

'Reid,' a voice whispered through the fading darkness, a warm hand gripping his from behind the post. Prickles made their way down his neck where her breath touched his cool skin.

'Elisavet?'

'My uncle is wrong for doing this to you,' the black-haired princess appeared in front of him, her hand reaching up to cup his chin, nails running along his cheek before she dropped her hand. His skin burned where she had touched, an unfamiliar ache formed in the pit of his stomach, longing for her to put her hand back. Her green eyes stared up at him, though she wasn't much shorter than him. 'I think the priest is doing something to stop Kasin from being able to rise within you.'

'What do you mean?' Reid whispered, his voice hoarse from yelling at the priest, at the guards, at anyone who had dared to walk by. Was it even possible for a simple priest to prevent a god from doing whatever he wanted?

'There are enchantments that a priest or priestess can perform to dull a being such as Kasin.' Elisavet stepped in close to Reid. Her scent was intoxicating, like the desert roses that grew outside the city.

'It doesn't take much if one has the right talisman.' Her hands reached around him, fingers brushing his skin with a feather-light touch, as she pressed herself against his chest. Reid swallowed hard, his heart pounding in his ears, hoping it was still too dark for her to see how red his face had become. She leaned in closer, her breath warm against his neck, sending another shiver down his spine. Each word she spoke hung thick in the air. 'A relic of the god can be used for *or* against him.'

'Hey—' Reid grunted as her fingers began reaching down the side of his pants. He wasn't sure what was happening – it seemed she would defile him right there, in the open for anyone awake at this hour to see. 'Hey, stop!'

She stopped, looking up at him through thick black lashes as he squirmed.

'I'm not sure this is … proper.' He didn't know how to word it – he felt like an idiot for stopping her. Oscar would have told him so, too. Gods, why would he think of Oscar right now? Elisavet was beautiful, probably one of the most beautiful girls he had seen in Thornwell. The way her fair skin seemed to glow under the fading moonlight, combined with her black hair and brilliant green eyes, she did something to him that he hadn't felt before. He'd never felt such an intense pull before now, an inexplicable blend of awe and yearning. He couldn't deny the lingering glance she had stolen on their walk to the council room. His eyes had trailed her every movement, captivated by her presence as much as he was by the artwork and sheer size of the castle. He had thought it hard to not stare at her more throughout the meeting – but he'd never imagined she'd noticed him in the same way. He'd only ever heard O talk about girls like this before. Shit, there he was thinking about damned Oscar again.

She laughed at his obvious discomfort. 'This'—she pulled her hand from his back pocket, one he never checked and almost forgot was there—'is probably what the portly priest is using to keep Kasin quiet.' She held out her hand before him. It was a piece of wood wrapped in a strange herb that he had never seen before.

'Is that my carving of Kasin?' Reid asked, barely making out the shape of the little head that she held in her hand.

'Just the head – I'm sure he probably kept the rest aside in case you found this,' Elisavet said as she began unwrapping the vine-like herb. 'He's used falrose. It's a herb that is meant to work against the gods and goddesses. It's not lethal, of course, I'm not sure anything could kill a god, but it is powerful enough to inhibit their magic ... for a little while, anyway.'

Reid watched as she pulled the rest of the falrose from the carving head and tossed it into a torch nearby. She held the little statue up for him to examine.

'How did you know?' Reid asked, brow furrowing. 'Better yet, why didn't you say something earlier?'

'I wasn't sure. I had to do some quick reading to see if it was possible before I took the chance to come here,' Elisavet grinned at him. 'I couldn't be caught if I wasn't sure you were telling the truth.'

She stepped toward him, eyes sparkling as she whispered in his ear, 'Though, I'm delighted you are.'

He closed his eyes, torn between the tantalising caress of Elisavet's voice and the urge to reach out and call to Kasin. He prayed that Elisavet had opened up the channel between them once more.

Kasin, please. He begged once more, his eyes still held tightly shut.

'Reid,' Elisavet's voice murmured from where she remained in front of him, he could faintly feel her breath on his skin still.

A familiar presence crept into his mind once more, almost groggy but undeniably there, and Reid smiled. Elisavet gasped and stepped back as Reid's eyes shot open, a bright blue light shining from within them before they faded to his usual deep brown.

'I wasn't sure you were still with me,' Reid spoke aloud to Kasin.

Be grateful, short words from Kasin, it was clear the herb had affected the connection.

'Thank you,' he said now to Elisavet. 'Kasin says he is grateful too.'

Elisavet gathered herself enough to nod in acknowledgement.

'What do we do now?' Reid asked, either Kasin or Elisavet, he didn't know. He just wanted an answer.

Wait, Kasin replied. *Wait for the priest.* Kasin's words were still short, but Reid understood what he wanted.

'I could untie you, you can prove your innocence now,' Elisavet offered.

'No,' Reid said softly, his voice barely above a whisper as he leaned down toward her. 'Thank you. Go now until the ritual.' He dared to brush his lips lightly against her cheek. A delicate blush bloomed across her neck, almost as red as the desert roses she smelled like. She gave him a small, grateful smile before slipping away into the night, her footsteps silent and ghostly, leaving behind only the faint trace of her floral scent and the warmth of her skin lingering on his lips.

CHAPTER THIRTY-ONE

Thornwell, Southern Mortal Realm

+ REID +

THE HIGH PRIEST entered the courtyard moments before the sun began to rise, the King not far behind. Word had seemingly spread of the hastily arranged ritual, as other lords and a few Inner Ring townspeople filtered into the viewing area.

Reid had spent the last hour silent, allowing Kasin to replenish his diminished strength from the falrose herb. He could feel the god's power bubbling below the surface of his skin, as if begging for Reid to grant him the right to release it and control his body. Something Reid knew he would agree to if Kasin asked.

Reid lifted his head as the priest made his way into the centre of the small crowd that had gathered. Elisavet appeared next to the King and whispered something in his ear that caused the King to shake his head in response. Her gaze flicked to Reid, where it remained as the priest began speaking.

'My King, Lady Elisavet, my lords.' The priest nodded to each in turn. 'As the sun rises in our skies this morning, we will offer this boy to Krah, God of Death, ruler of Wynlara and husband to Dagmar, Bringer of Life and Goddess of Earth, on behalf of Kasin. As a favour for sacrificing this swindler, this boy who dares to impersonate Kasin's Protector, we will ask the gods to bless us in this coming pandemic of witches and demons.'

A small cheer rose from the lords that joined them – all except one. Reid could tell that the lord standing hidden in the shadows to the side, away from the others, was the one that had done the same the day before.

'We shall spill his blood for our soldiers to bathe their weapons in,' the priest continued as he drew a knife from his belt. 'The blood will ensure Kasin has blessed us with his protection while we are at war, a symbol of his gratitude for our apprehending this charlatan. Our soldiers will fight harder and longer, knowing the gods are with them.'

Inside his head, Reid felt a small tremor as Kasin laughed. The god's voice smooth as he asked Reid for control. He could feel the god's presence ripple as the priest moved closer with the blade. In the short time Kasin had been with Reid, he had never mentioned controlling him, but Reid knew it was possible after Kasin admitted to possessing the old man's body from the shop. There was a part of Reid that had even wanted Kasin to ask him.

They didn't believe me like you thought they would, Reid said silently to Kasin as he watched the priest stop in front of him, his arms out to the sides, showing the long, curved blade that was in his hand.

'Kasin,' the priest called out, 'our God of Protection, our saviour! Today, I gift on your behalf a sacrifice to Krah, of one insolent enough to think themself higher than you!'

Another roar went up from the crowd of onlookers. The high priest smiled as he turned a full circle, brandishing the gleaming blade for all to see. 'We pray that you accept this offering!'

Reid felt Kasin's response as the priest lifted the blade to his throat. It was like an invisible force shoved Reid backward, but his body didn't physically move. He gave in to the feeling as his mind slipped away and Kasin took over his body, fully trusting whatever the god was about to do.

Reid's eyes flew open, glaring down upon the priest. The knife stopped mid-motion, drawing just the slightest bit of blood. It was strange, as if Reid was watching himself, from afar, but also watching the scene unfold through his own eyes. Was this how Kasin felt when he wasn't controlling Reid?

'I do not accept your sacrifice,' Reid's voice, broadening as it harmonised with Kasin's, boomed across the courtyard and the knife clattered to the ground as the priest stumbled backward. A few of the lords fell to their knees as they realised who was speaking to them.

'I sent Reid here to you as my subordinate, I named him my Protector,' Kasin continued to speak through Reid. 'You dare to defy my will? Do you think so little of me? Do you think that I would allow someone to pretend to fulfil my holiest duty?'

Blue light seared through the ropes that bound Reid's feet and hands to the post. His body stepped forward, toward the priest, Kasin's powers seemingly replenished. The priest cowered before the god. Part of Reid didn't want Kasin to do anything to the man, or those that voted for this outcome, but he also didn't want them to get away with it.

'H–how are you here?' the priest managed to stammer.

'It would seem,' Kasin spoke over the priest, directly to the King, 'that your high priest has not been truthful with you.'

'I have only ever been honest with you, my King!' The priest whirled to where the King had stepped forward, ever so cautiously. 'This has to be some trick – perhaps a spirit has taken over the boy's body.'

The King seemed to consider the thought for a moment, ever reliant on the conniving priest.

'No, Uncle.' Elisavet moved from the shadows and placed the head of the carving into the King's hand.

'What is this?' the King asked as he held the little head up to examine it.

'That,' Elisavet said, 'is what Jerola used to contain Kasin's powers inside Reid.' She stared pointedly at the man, seemingly no longer afraid of the consequences she had mentioned to Reid earlier. A few of the surrounding lords gaped at the blatant use of the priest's real name. Not even the King dared use it in fear of being unholy.

'How dare you accuse me of such a thing!' The priest blustered, his face and neck blotching.

Elisavet ignored him and continued, 'Jerola used the carving of our great Kasin that Reid carried with him and wrapped it in falrose!'

'Lady Elisavet speaks the truth,' Kasin confirmed. 'She proved her devotion by sneaking out here before dawn and burning the remnants of the herb in order to free me.'

'I never did such a thing! This is a plot against me, against your crown, Your Majesty!'

'Whom, may I ask, could stand to benefit from such a plot?' the King questioned as he signalled the guards.

'Your niece and this street rat!' The priest grabbed the knife from the ground and held it before Reid. 'She must be after your crown, if she defied orders and came here to rescue this ... this thing!' He waved his arms at Reid.

'The only person I can see here that has committed any form of treason is you, Jerola,' the King said. 'If my niece hadn't been so zealous about Reid telling the truth, we might have just slain Kasin's Protector and exposed ourselves to his wrath.'

'My lords,' the priest turned to the other men in the yard, 'you voted with me. You don't truly believe this boy is harbouring a god inside him, do you?'

'Why would you try to hide the fact Kasin had returned to us to begin with?' The brown-haired man who had sat beside the King in the council room finally stepped out from the shadows. From far inside his mind, Reid snapped to attention at the man's voice once more. But adrift in the fog of his consciousness as he was, it was like looking through the stained-glass windows that obscured the view into Madame Jessamine's. He simply couldn't place the man – though he was sure he knew him.

'I did not keep Kasin from you! The boy could not provide evidence that Kasin had chosen him.' The priest looked disgusted at the thought. 'Why would a god choose a street rat over someone more divine?'

'Ah,' the man countered, 'so it was simply because Kasin did not choose you.'

The high priest spat in response, and the guards moved to arrest him after a simple gesture from the King.

'I waited a long time to choose my protector.' Kasin turned Reid's body to speak to everyone. 'I have followed Reid since his birth, and he has not once strayed toward the path of darkness, always putting the care and protection of others above his own agenda. Unlike your head priest here, it seems.'

The priest writhed against the guards' grip as they made to drag him away.

'It would seem,' Kasin spoke to the priest now, 'that you aren't as divine as you thought. I hereby strip you of your prestige as high priest – any affinity you have, or thought you had, with the divine plane will be removed from you. The gods and goddesses will no longer answer you.'

The priest slackened in the guards' arms, his face drained of colour. Whatever Kasin had done to him evidently took effect immediately. Jerola was a priest no more.

CHAPTER THIRTY-TWO

Ma Dessa's Tribe, The Tretara Range

+ ELSBETH +

'Did you see those eyes?' Erikah asked before the creature behind them shoved her forward, a silent order to shut her mouth.

Elsbeth trudged along the uneven, rocky path, each step taking them further from her intended destination. They were being marched high up into the mountains where the air grew thin, and the terrain became increasingly treacherous. Her mind buzzed with anticipation, the darkness within her screaming at her to fight, to kill. Elsbeth knew exactly what Erikah was talking about – how could she have missed them? Golden eyes with flecks of red.

Such eyes were unmistakably those of witches, and yet, their shape and colour bore an uncanny resemblance to Tallon's. But how could that be, when the creature possessing those eyes was undoubtedly male?

The group ascended higher, the clouds wrapping around them like a shroud concealing their destination. Elsbeth's heart pounded in her chest, both from exertion and the unsettling revelation that she might not make it to Raynor. The path ahead seemed endless, winding through jagged rocks that threatened to trip them at every turn. The chill of the mountain air bit at her skin, but it was the unknown that truly ate at her.

As they climbed, Elsbeth tried to focus on the back of Erikah's head. Her gaze narrowed in on the symbol for Typhonis on the back of her neck, the three-pronged trident tattooed there just after her sixteenth year. She could see it glowing faintly in the dark, so similar to how her own must look. Both witches were trying to draw power to them, instincts preparing them for battle.

Her thoughts swirled with questions. Witches' eyes were a rare, telling sign, and the implications of a male possessing them were profound. Of course, there were males born to witches, but there had been no recorded cases of them ever possessing a hint of the darkness. Nor were many ever left alive. Usually, they were handed off to the fathers or, much to Elsbeth's displeasure, left at the Tretara Range to suffer whatever fate the gods willed upon them.

As daylight began to filter over the ridge, they were marched onto a ledge overlooking a field of thick, dense clouds. The mist swirled around their feet, damp and cool, masking the expanse of whatever lay below them. The rocky path they had been navigating vanished into the whiteness behind them, a path known only to those that inhabited the lifeless mountains.

As the sun rose higher, the clouds began to thin, slowly revealing their surroundings. The field of clouds below faded away to reveal a large stretch of lush green meadow. From where they stood at the top of the ridge, they were able to see the entire plateau. Stretching far below from where they stood, all the way to a sheer drop that loomed to the east, where the sun was rapidly growing.

Elsbeth didn't hide her curiosity as she took in the scene before her. Along the mountainside to the north, she could just make out caves, some natural, some man-made. Curtains made from what seemed to be animal hide and vines hung over makeshift doors and windows, some pulled back, presumably to let the morning light in.

The two witches were pushed along toward another steep incline, the stone staircase uneven and jagged beneath their feet as they descended toward the green expanse below. The path wound its way precariously through the mountain's craggy terrain, the view of the plateau dipping in and out of view. Steam rose from bubbling hot pools that were dotted throughout the mountainside. Strange, otherworldly beings lounged in the pools, their curious eyes following the witches' every move.

They soon reached the bottom, where they were ushered through a cluster of huts made from stone and wood. The smell of exotic spices and unfamiliar herbs filled the air as they followed a paved path, dotted with market stalls holding various woven garments, raw meats and tropical plants. Alongside them, the earth abruptly fell away into a dizzying void.

'Arhias,' an older woman's voice rasped, 'Vos iter dexo serga parum.'

She'd spoken not in the language the others had earlier, not even in the common Emodorean language, but in the witches' native tongue. It was something that Elsbeth hadn't heard since her grandmother was alive. The rich, lyrical words resonated deep within her, awakening old memories. With the number of mixed blood witches in their covens, the ancient language was all but forgotten, save their spells and chants. Hearing it now, so unexpectedly, was like a haunting melody from a long-lost song. The woman's voice wove through the air, each syllable a reminder of a heritage that had almost slipped into oblivion.

'Ma Dessa.' Arhias intoned, his voice resonating with the formal cadence of the ancient tongue. He stepped forward toward the woman, his posture respectful. 'We caught these two at the base of our mountain path.'

'So, you thought it wise to bring them to our home?' The old woman didn't move from where she sat facing the clouds. Her words were a string of sounds that Elsbeth strained to translate, the forgotten language familiar yet distant in her mind.

'They are witches,' Arhias replied. His speech, though fluent, held a slight hesitation, as if acknowledging the weight of tradition each word carried. 'I didn't think it was proper to let them freely wander our mountains.'

'We weren't wandering your mountains,' Erikah retorted, the native language rolling smoothly off her tongue. The fluidity with which she spoke stunned Elsbeth as her head whipped to the strawberry-haired witch. 'We were passing from Brielle Forest to The Timeless Fields. We have no interest in being in *your* mountains.'

Elsbeth could taste the sharp tang of disdain in Erikah's voice, each word dripping with impatience and frustration. They were losing time, the minutes slipping away like grains of sand through an hourglass. The urgency of their journey seeped back into Elsbeth's mind – find Raynor before Isadora found them.

The Pass, the place that Ravina had told them about, was located within the folds of Zadea's mountain. It lay somewhere south of The Timeless Fields, marking the delicate tri-border between the Fae Lands, Brielle's Forest, and the vast expanse below the Sky Kingdom.

'Why would a child of Hesta be heading to the land of the fae?' The old woman's voice cut through Elsbeth's thoughts like a knife, crisp and clear from her spot on the ledge, catching her off guard. She seemed content to sit there and not move as she switched easily to the common tongue.

'You knew my mother?' Elsbeth's voice was barely a whisper, her eyes fixed on the back of the woman's head.

'Aye, I knew her, and your grandmother.' The woman finally stood and moved away from the edge of the cliff with a reluctance that hinted at her attachment to the spot. As she turned, the sun washed over her face, causing her blue eyes to sparkle with soft red swirls. 'Though my power may have faded these past few centuries, I am still witch enough to sense my sister's blood.'

'You're Odessa,' Elsbeth murmured, her gaze tracing the contours of the woman's face, mentally comparing them to the old paintings she had seen in her grandmother's chambers when she was younger. 'You're Graciella's sister.'

The woman's features were a blend of familial traits – more of Isadora's high cheekbones and delicate chin, but with the unmistakable eyes of her lineage. Those eyes, a striking mix of blue with soft red swirls, were a trademark of their family, something Isadora hadn't inherited from the Wraithe side. Those icy blue eyes met her own, and a shiver of recognition tingled down her back, secrets and unspoken truths pressing down upon her.

'I am Odessa Dran,' the old lady replied as she approached Elsbeth and lifted her chin in her calloused fingers. 'You look so much like my *adelor*, my sister. Come, we will eat breakfast at my home.'

'Ma Dessa—' Arhias started, his voice faltering as the old woman motioned for Erikah and Elsbeth to be cut loose.

'I won't hear it, Arhias.' Odessa cut him off sharply, turning her stern, weathered face toward him. Her eyes, glinting with authority, left no room for argument. 'My word is the law, you have brought two witches into our camp without my permission. I will handle them how I see fit.'

Elsbeth and Erikah, freed from their bindings, fell into step behind Odessa. Arhias remained near the edge of the cliff, his face scowling in frustration.

Without sparing him another glance, Odessa's voice carried back to him, 'I'll deal with you later for acting without permission.'

CHAPTER THIRTY-THREE

Ma Dessa's Tribe, The Tretara Range

+ ELSBETH +

'We were told you were dead,' Elsbeth said as they sat around the hearth inside Odessa's hut. They had expected to be led to one of the larger cabins in the camp, but Odessa's home was of average size. It was the last one in the row of five, the only wood-built homes on the plateau, and its garden was the clouds. The room was dimly lit by a few flickering candles, their soft glow casting shadows on the rough, oak walls. Shelves lined the walls, crammed with jars filled with curious substances, dried herbs, mysterious powders, and preserved specimens. Elsbeth had spent enough time with Alanah to know that the contents of these jars were likely used for healing spells and tonics.

The floor was covered in woven mats, worn and frayed with age, but still vibrant with intricate patterns. The scent of incense hung in the air, a heady mix of sandalwood and something more elusive, almost like the essence of the earth itself.

'It is what most would have believed,' Odessa's blue eyes, with their soft red swirls, sparkled with an enigmatic blend of wisdom and weariness as she regarded them while she stirred the contents of her onyx-coloured pot; the smell that came from it made Elsbeth's stomach rumble. 'Death is but a whisper in the life of a witch.'

'Queen Graciella barely spoke of you after you left.' Erikah said, leaning forward to examine the contents of the pot.

'The laws dictate that one shouldn't speak of a deserter,' the older witch replied as she shooed the freckle-faced witch away from the fire. 'Your mother hadn't yet become queen when I left.'

'Grandmother never said you deserted our coven, we were told you died in an attack by the Soulless,' Elsbeth said as she took a bowl of food from Odessa.

'I was pregnant when our coven tried to expand to the mountains.' Odessa sighed as she sat down. 'Your grandmother ordered us to push north, as our covens were becoming too large for the forest.'

The two witches ate in silence as they waited for Odessa to continue with her story.

'I came across a small band of tribes people not far from this plateau when I went into labour. My baby was going to come earlier than expected.' Odessa looked out her window toward the clouds. 'The people were peaceful and didn't want to fight, but they weren't willing to give up their land to the witches either. Graciella left me with my two closest coven sisters to deliver the baby, while she and the others left to claim new territory. Only a few escaped, they didn't expect so many of the Soulless to be there when they found the plateau.'

'Why is none of this in the history books?' Erikah asked. 'I've read almost everything in the castle library, and no book speaks of any war in the mountains – only warnings to stay away from the mutant half-breeds that live here.'

'They prefer to be called the Soulless – and you'd do well to remember you are enjoying their hospitality,' Odessa said. 'Perhaps it's because Graciella had a loss that day, and she did not want her people to know.' Odessa shrugged. 'Either way, when Graciella returned to where she had left me and my sisters, she found I had given birth to a baby boy – a true "half-breed", as you so eloquently put it. She ordered me to leave him behind for the Soulless, as is witch custom. When I refused, she tried to take him from me. But even in my weakened state after the long birth, she couldn't pry my child from my arms.'

'What did you do?' Elsbeth was on the edge of her seat, her hand on her belly. She imagined she could feel the heartbeat of her own child in her palm.

'Some of the Soulless were watching the encounter. I guess some sympathised with me – or my boy, at least – because the group converged on the little grove we were supposedly hidden in, causing Graciella to flee with her remaining witches, including my own coven.' Odessa's voice softened. 'They brought my baby and me back here to live with them. I guess it was only supposed to be temporary, but I've been here over nine hundred years now.'

'Your baby?' Elsbeth all but whispered the question.

'You met him,' Odessa grunted as she pointed over her shoulder to where Arhias hovered outside the hut.

'But he's …' Erikah's jaw dropped open.

'Yes, he's part siren. Turns out his father was the son of a siren and a human, but lacked the siren traits … at least from what I recall, anyway. The only thing that Arhias inherited from his father is his eyes – except the red swirls of our ancestors.' Odessa smiled and Elsbeth's heart warmed, despite Arhias' rough treatment of them earlier.

'Does he have magic?' Erikah asked as she peered at the man outside.

'Not as strong as a true witch – he has an affiliation with plants. Can make anything grow, anywhere. It's why our plateau is so abundant with life.' Odessa smiled again.

'I can't believe that my mother didn't tell me you were alive,' Elsbeth said quietly.

'I was under the impression that Graciella thought the Soulless had killed me.' Odessa replied as she patted Elsbeth's knee. 'I chose to desert them, to go against my Queen's orders. They had every right to forget me.'

'If you had come back, even after my mother was made Queen, things might have been different.' Elsbeth stood and walked to the window facing the garden of clouds.

'Different how?' Odessa asked.

'Do you know what is happening down there?' Elsbeth turned to her great-aunt.

'I'm assuming Hesta has lost the plot, especially if you're running from her.' Odessa nodded toward Elsbeth's belly, the unmistakable bulge beginning to show.

'Queen Hesta was killed just over a hundred years ago by Isadora,' Erikah said softly, filling the heavy silence when Elsbeth couldn't find her voice. 'Isadora challenged her to combat for the crown.'

Odessa's face remained impassive, but her eyes darkened with a mix of grief and resolve as she absorbed the information. Suddenly, the door burst open with a forceful gust of wind.

'It's you!' A whirlwind of feathers and hair blew into the hut, radiating pain and fury. A bronze-haired demon girl, her eyes burning with rage, turned upon Elsbeth. 'I could smell you from across the camp!'

She snarled, a torrent of what one could only assume were curse words erupted from her lips, spoken in the strange language the others had used earlier when they were first captured.

Elsbeth stared wide-eyed at the girl who stood before her, stunned by the sudden and violent intrusion. The serenity of Odessa's hut now teetering on the brink of chaos as Erikah growled, moving to put herself between the pair.

'Avella,' Odessa stood, 'what is the meaning of this?'

'That bitch is the one that came through our camp the other week.' She pointed her sharp nailed finger toward Elsbeth, feathers ruffling down her arms as she moved. 'The one that led that army of witches and shifters into Winhelm!'

'That was not me,' Elsbeth said softly, her voice barely audible over the storm of accusations.

'I would remember your scent anywhere. You killed my entire tribe!'

'Elsbeth has only arrived today,' Odessa said as she placed a hand on Avella's shoulder in an attempt to calm her. 'Arhias, come in here, please.'

Arhias entered the room, and as Elsbeth's gaze fell upon him, the familiar Wraithe family traits became prominent. His blonde hair and pale skin, while common among the northern people, now held a deeper significance. What truly captured her attention were the particular swirls of red in his golden eyes – so much like her own. For the first time, she saw beyond the superficial resemblance to the northern folk; as she recognised the distinct markers of her lineage, the undeniable proof of their shared blood.

'I couldn't stop her.' Arhias apologised, his voice tinged with frustration as his mother scowled at him. It was then Elsbeth realised he hadn't just been lurking trying to eavesdrop, he was standing guard. The whirlwind of a girl had simply overpowered him, her sheer rage enough to storm through before he could react. The embarrassment on his face was clear.

'It is her, I swear,' Avella insisted. 'The smell, the looks, the only difference is your hair is longer – but I'm sure that's some witch magic at work.' She spat the word *witch* like it was a bad taste in her mouth.

'Norella,' Erikah said to the small crowd now assembled in the tiny hut. 'Elsbeth's twin.'

'I don't believe them!' Avella had tears welling in her eyes. 'I deserve vengeance for my people!'

Odessa moved to be beside Avella, a gentle hand placed on her shoulder.

'Retribution is deserved, yes, but actions taken in haste often echo with regret for a lifetime.'

'I am not proud of what my sister witches have done,' Elsbeth said, her voice steady as she stepped to the side of Erikah to be seen by Avella. Her gaze met Avella's and she hoped the sincerity of her words would cut through the hostility, revealing the truth of her intentions. 'I have chosen to leave them, to leave the forest of Brielle. We both have.'

'This is why you are heading for The Timeless Fields?' Odessa asked.

'Prince Raynor is the father of my child. I intend to find him and, whether he chooses to accompany us or not, I am leaving this world. I want a better life for my child, and peace cannot be found in Emodorea while my aunt reigns.'

'We are heading to The Pass. It is inside Zadea's Mountain,' Erikah added. With a nod from Elsbeth, she continued, 'A seer told us how to open it. We plan to leave Emodorea for a world without magic, where Isadora can't follow.'

'It seems there are many things our people do not know about the world below our mountains,' Odessa mused, taking her seat when she seemed sure that Avella had calmed down. 'Perhaps you can spare the time to stay a day or two to enlighten us.'

Elsbeth hesitated, her mind racing. Every minute they spent here gave Isadora more time to potentially find them. 'We can't afford to delay,' she started, her voice uncertain.

'Would a day or two really make a difference if it means we're well rested and fed?' Erikah interjected, her tone gentle but firm. 'We're running on fumes, Elsbeth. We need our strength, and gods knows I would die to have a bath and a decent meal.'

Arhias, sensing her reluctance, stepped forward. 'If they stay here, it could be dangerous for us,' he argued. 'We are exposed and vulnerable if this Witch Queen does send spies.'

'If they're staying, I'm leaving.' Avella growled. 'I came here for protection, to find a way to seek retribution for my people.'

'We do not turn away those in need, nor do we act out of fear. You chose to bring them here, Arhias, now you have a duty to uphold. If you leave, Avella, that is your choice, but know that unity is our strength.' Odessa's voice sliced through the tension.

Elsbeth considered for a moment; it was another day's hike from the mountain range into The Timeless Fields, and Brielle knew how long until they'd stumble upon Osteria. The pragmatic part of her knew Erikah was right, though she didn't like the idea of intruding on their peaceful village.

'It would be nice to have a decent rest and food for a day or so.' She admitted finally, a reluctant smile crossing her lips as she looked at her great-aunt.

CHAPTER THIRTY-FOUR

Ma Dessa's Tribe, The Tretara Range

+ ELSBETH +

ELSBETH AND ERIKAH spent three days resting on the plateau with Odessa and the rest of the Soulless tribe. They had mostly been welcomed, though a few wary glances and whispered conversations reminded them that not everyone was happy with the new guests. While Avella had accepted that Norella, and not Elsbeth, attacked her village near the foot of the mountain, she seemingly refused to accept the idea that the two newcomers were welcome among her people.

During the day, Elsbeth had wandered through the village, marvelling at the seamless way the tribe lived with one another. Erikah had been glued to her side the entire time, despite Elsbeth insisting that she was okay and didn't need to be, for a lack of better term, babysat. She'd had a brief respite from the witch when Erikah had disappeared to check out the hot pools. But Erikah returned a few hours later to resume her post, carrying the scent of minerals and earth on her now purified skin.

The nights were cool and filled with the sounds of distant wildlife, and the occasional soft chant of a tribe member or two. The sky, free from any obscurities, was an endless canvas of twinkling stars. Elsbeth found herself enjoying the calm nights and the rhythm of daily life on the plateau perhaps a little too much, yearning for relief from the chaos they had left far below.

'It's time we leave,' Elsbeth told Odessa and the others during dinner on the third night. 'First thing tomorrow, I would like to be taken back down the mountain.'

'Are you sure this is what you want to do?' Odessa had expressed concerns at the idea of the two trying to leave Emodorea. No one knew the consequences of travelling between worlds – and to one without magic, of all things. But Elsbeth knew in her heart it was the only way to truly keep her child safe from the wrath of Isadora's revenge.

'We have spent enough time here.' Elsbeth placed a hand on her aunt's. Odessa's hut had become a sanctuary of sorts, where she'd learned more about the tribe's ways and the Soulless than she had ever thought possible. She would miss these few evenings they got to spend together, sharing tales of old battles, lost loves, and family secrets. 'It's time we continue what we set out to do.'

'I too, will be leaving in the morning,' Avella announced.

'Why am I not surprised?' Odessa turned to the young woman at the other side of the table, eyes soft with understanding. 'I saw it the day you got wind of Elsbeth's scent.'

'What does my scent have to do with anything?' Elsbeth raised an eyebrow at Avella, curiosity overriding the guilt that she just couldn't seem to shake.

'You smell of your sister'—Avella snapped, her nose crinkling in disgust—'I can follow your scent to her, to her demons.'

'It would not be wise to hunt down a coven of witches,' Erikah chimed in, her amusement clear in her tone. The light from the candles flickered across her freckled face, the shadow of a smile hidden on her lips.

'I don't want the coven – I just want the one witch.' Avella spat, her glare directed at Erikah. Tension crackled in the air as she pushed her chair away from the table.

'My sister is … dangerous.' Elsbeth chewed her lip. 'There is a reason she is the Queen's Second.'

'I have nothing left to lose.' Avella's expression was cold, her golden eyes darkening as she spoke. 'If I do not seek revenge, what honour remains for my people? I must fight for them. For their memory, and for justice.'

'I would beg you to reconsider.' Odessa sighed, a note of resignation in her voice. 'But I know you will just do as you please, anyway.'

Avella nodded, her expression softening slightly as the old woman smiled at her. 'Thank you for the meal, and the hospitality you have given me and the few who remain from my tribe.'

'What are we, if not family?' Odessa's smile was warm, her voice reminding Elsbeth of her mother's. They all watched in silence for a moment as Avella slipped from the cabin.

'Arhias will show you the way back down the mountain to where he found you.' Odessa spoke again to Elsbeth and Erikah. 'From there, it won't be long before you enter the land of the fae.'

'Hopefully, it doesn't take us long to find Raynor.' Elsbeth rubbed her stomach where the small bump was growing beneath her shirt.

'You are always welcome back here if you change your mind.' Odessa squeezed her hand with a warm smile.

'We should go to bed.' Erikah stood from the table. 'It'll be a long journey tomorrow.'

'Yes.' Elsbeth stood and cleared away the remaining plates before kissing her aunt on the cheek and heading to bed.

The sun rising over the edge of the plateau was something Elsbeth thought she would never get tired of seeing. She wasn't sure if it was the hormones from being pregnant, or if she was actually sad to say goodbye to Odessa and the others, but a small tear escaped her eye as she gave the old woman a quick hug goodbye. With one last look at the green grass, she turned and followed Erikah and Arhias through the boulders and toward the back of the mountain.

With the sun hidden on the eastern side, they walked the perilous path in silence and darkness. Arhias had warned that there would be other mountain folks out at this time for morning hunts, but he doubted they would come across any.

Odessa had explained that the mountains were home to many tribes, each with their own customs and traditions. From what Elsbeth gathered, the tribes seldom saw eye-to-eye. Most chose to exclude those with parents from one race or another, holding fast to outdated prejudices. Odessa's tribe was the only one that accepted anyone who wanted to be a part of it, which is how the remaining few from Avella's tribe had ended up there.

Avella had vanished before the first light of dawn kissed the sky, her departure as quiet as it was resolute. While she hoped that Avella travelled well, the thought of her crossing paths with Norella sent a chill through her veins. She didn't want to imagine what Norella would do to Avella if their paths crossed.

Back at their original camp, they bid farewell to Arhias, who didn't bother to mutter a response before he turned and headed back up the mountain, disappearing amongst the rocks after a few steps.

'Well,' Erikah said, stretching, 'any idea where to head once we hit those green fields?'

'No idea,' Elsbeth admitted. 'I'm hoping that the fae have people watching their borders and send word that we have arrived.'

'Then what? We pray to Brielle that Raynor is the one they inform?' Erikah replied as the two headed away from the mountain range.

'I think we'd be better praying to Zadea,' Elsbeth said to lighten the mood. The truth was, she could only hope that it was one of Raynor's fae that found them; otherwise, it could be a long time before she would get to see her lover.

The world before them burst into a wave of colour as the sun peeked over the mountains, painting the sky in hues of gold, pink, and orange. The warmth of the sun was a welcome contrast to the biting cold they had endured in the peaks. The marshland surrounding the Tretara Range spread out before them, a patchwork of green and blue, shimmering under the sun.

As they approached the edge of the marsh, it was clear to see where the border to The Timeless Fields lay. It was as if they were stepping into another world as the bogs dried out and turned to beautiful, emerald-green grasses. Wildflowers of vibrant purple and pink dotted the landscape, their petals opening to greet the sunlight and filling the air with their sweet, intoxicating perfume. For miles, all the pair could see were open fields and dazzling flowers.

'This place is beautiful.' Erikah closed her eyes for a moment and took a deep breath of the wind that blew toward them.

Elsbeth nodded her head in agreement. In other circumstances, she would have considered it a perfect place for her baby to grow up – if Raynor accepted the child, that was. However, the doubt still lurked in her mind that he would not want a half-breed child.

'Well, let's try and find a city or something to get word to Raynor.' Erikah hefted the small food pack Odessa had given them up onto her shoulder.

Far to the south, the lone mountain could be seen. It was the only place in Emodorea that was shared amongst more than one race. It was said to be the home of the Goddess of Knowledge herself, Zadea. That was their next destination, with or without Raynor.

CHAPTER THIRTY-FIVE

The Wandering River, Orabelle Bay

+ ATHENA +

ATHENA AND THE SIRENS' journey east had slowed considerably over the past few days. Nevertheless, Athena was hopeful that Queen Nerophine and those who could still fly had made it to the bay safely and were awaiting their arrival. Having finally emerged from the dense forest, the group found themselves moving through open plains, but the fishing villages bordering the vast eastern ocean still lay about a day's walk away.

All but Tallon and a small group, including Cilla, had completed the transformation from wings to tails. Athena watched as those who had grown their gills and tails swam warily along in the river beside them. The younger ones, filled with curiosity and energy, occasionally surged ahead, testing their new tails against the current, adapting quicker to the changes than their elders. Tallon smiled at the sight – a gesture that gave Athena a glimmer of hope that perhaps things wouldn't be so bad for the sirens after all.

'We should camp outside the village for the night,' Athena suggested, drawing Tallon's attention. 'Those in the water should head into the bay while it's dark, to avoid commotion with the townspeople.'

Tallon was silent for a long moment before she replied. It was clear to Athena that the siren had never ventured this far east before. It had been just shy of two decades since she herself had left, but everything seemed different now. She noticed the change in the air, more humid and heavy with every step closer to the ocean. The ground beneath her feet had begun to soften, becoming sandier, filling her sandals with the rough, annoyingly familiar grittiness. The dense oaks of the forest had given way to tall, thin trees crowned with plumes. Despite the turmoil Tallon and the sirens were enduring, Athena could see a spark of excitement flickering in Tallon's eyes.

'You don't think the townspeople would be accustomed to seeing mermaids?' Tallon finally replied.

'No.' Athena shook her head, remembering the stories her father had told her when she was little – tales woven with adventures and mysterious encounters. 'The mermaids haven't been seen willingly for years now. If people were to see a tide of mermaids swimming out of the river mouth, it would be more than enough to raise some questions.'

Tallon's brow furrowed. 'We'll need to be cautious, then. We don't want to alert the wrong person.'

'Yes,' Athena agreed, her gaze sweeping over the group. 'We'll need to find a way to blend in when we arrive. But that will be easier with a smaller group.'

Tallon nodded her agreement. 'We shall stop and make camp for the night as soon as we can see the ocean.'

Athena watched Tallon closely as they strode side by side along the sandy bank, the sunlight filtering through the trees, casting dappled shadows on her friend's face. Since Tallon began to develop mermaid traits, Athena's concern had only grown. Her progress had slowed immensely after the diamond-hard scales appeared, which now shimmered faintly in the daylight. Even the others, who had yet to complete the curse's transformation, were changing more rapidly than Tallon. Athena could sense the unspoken worry in Tallon's eyes, mirroring the concerns she herself felt. Queen Nerophine had shared these worries and had asked Athena to keep a close watch on her cousin.

Tallon confided in Athena that she thought she would be the first to transform as her wings had been removed, though now Athena could see that she was worried whether she would even be affected the same way as the others. Perhaps it was a cruel twist of the curse for failing to negotiate with the witches, maybe Tallon would be condemned to live on land, separated from her family. Athena grimaced at the scars that marred her friend's shoulders, peeking out above the tunic – a stark reminder of the haunting brutality caused by her people.

As the river began to widen, a soft breeze blew past them, tugging at Athena's long brown hair and dousing them all in the sickly sweet smell of the briny Sea of Typhonis. Athena breathed in deeply, sighing contentedly as the salt in the wind settled on her skin. The last time she had breathed this salt-heavy air, she had been but a child in the eyes of the witches, waving goodbye to her father as she left to become a healer's apprentice. The memory, tinged with the bittersweet scent of the sea, flickered in her mind as she reversed her steps from that day. Soon, she knew, they would see the ocean and the peaceful fishing village that rested by its calm waters.

'It's gorgeous,' Tallon breathed when the Sea of Typhonis swept into view as they crested the final hill that overlooked the Bay of Orabelle. The waters shimmered with a silver glow, catching the last rays of the setting sun, far to the west. Small waves broke gently on the rocky edge of the bay's mouth, their rhythmic sound as soothing as the sirens' song against the quiet of the evening. The scent of saltwater and seaweed mingled with the earthy aroma of the sand and rock. Thalatroses called out as they circled above, their cries echoing across the tranquil landscape, the sky a mirage of pinks and orange reflected in the calm waters. Home.

'It is a thing of wonders,' Athena agreed, finding the sight of the ocean was even more breathtaking than she remembered. The river, now turned to salt, sparkled under the fading light, and it was a good sign that the sirens – no, mermaids – hadn't yet complained about the taste. Athena still wasn't sure what to call them now that they had transformed.

'I feel as though we will remain known as sirens, even among the mermaids,' Tallon said, either sensing Athena's question or wondering the same thing herself as they watched them from afar.

Before Athena could respond, Tallon continued, a lightness in her tone that hadn't been there earlier. 'If we set up down there, we'll be out of sight of the village but still next to the river.'

Athena agreed. The clearing Tallon pointed to looked like a perfect haven, a place where they could find some semblance of peace for the final night. They called for the rest of the group to meet them near the bank, and Athena took a deep breath. Standing on the cusp of the sea, the promise of both a new beginning and the ghosts of her past taunted her like the waves that tickled the edge of the shore.

CHAPTER THIRTY-SIX

Thames, Orabelle Bay

+ ATHENA +

'This town is incredible,' Tallon's eyes were alight with wonder and astonishment as they stepped into the heart of Thames. The village was already buzzing with activity, the air alive with the clatter of carts rolling over cobblestone streets and merchants calling out their wares. Even before the sun had fully risen, the market was a riot of colour, with stalls piled high with fresh fish, vibrant textiles, and handmade crafts. 'I've never seen so many humans in one place before.'

Athena shared Tallon's amazement. She had almost forgotten how lively Thames could be. The village was one of the larger fishing and trade settlements along the eastern coast and was considered a neutral ground, untouched by the claim of any one Emodorean realm. It was here, amidst the hum of daily life, that her parents had met and where she had often wandered as a child, drawn by her mother's love for her human father. The familiar scent of the sea and the exotic fruits of the marketplace brought all those memories flooding back, grounding her in the present as she tried to navigate the swirling tide of her past.

As they ventured further into the town, Athena couldn't help but notice the lack of fae and witches; who could usually be seen around this time of year stocking up on fish and other supplies the humans dragged from the ocean. However, the streets, bustling with human and half-breed activity, felt strangely devoid of the sisters she had grown accustomed to.

Athena eyed the boats far out on the bay, already hauling in their catches with a practised rhythm. The ocean, so near and yet strangely distant, called to her with an almost magnetic pull. It had been a few years since she last felt the sea breeze on her face, the salt air filling her lungs. The bay was much calmer than she remembered.

'I hope the others got into the bay last night without any issues.' Athena's eyes flicked to where Tallon now stood beside her, the wonder slowly ebbing from her face to be replaced by sharp lines of worry.

Late last night, under the cover of darkness, Cilla and the others finally completed their transformations. Tallon had stood at the water's edge and insisted that they go while they could. No one knew how long it might take for Tallon to also succumb fully to Isadora's curse, and Athena could tell it was eating her friend up inside. The others, after much arguing from Cilla, finally swam off into the depths of the bay, leaving Tallon and Athena alone at the campsite. Queen Nerophine and those who had flown with her had not met them as they had expected, causing Tallon to sit awake for the rest of the night, waiting and watching, as if praying for some kind of sign from her cousin.

All they could hope was that the others found sanctuary in the bay, away from the prying eyes aboard the fishing boats. Athena had no idea, however, what she was meant to do to help Tallon. Other than the silver scales covering her upper body and legs, she was yet to possess any other traits that would suggest she was becoming a mermaid.

'Are you going to meet your father this morning?' Tallon asked as she stopped to eye a cart full of fresh fruit. She picked one up to inspect the brown, fur-like skin as she waited for Athena to answer.

'I wasn't going to right away, no,' Athena answered, absently taking the fruit, its hard rough shell familiar as she handed it and a few of the copper pieces she had to spare over to the vendor. 'I was hoping to go once you had left, save the hassle of explaining myself.'

As the vendor expertly sliced a small square off the end, revealing a pure white flesh beneath the touch exterior, Athena watched with amusement as Tallon's eyes glazed over with excitement. The man grabbed a short sharp rode and pierced a hole into the thick skin, and handed it over to Tallon who grabbed at it eagerly.

'You drink it,' Athena said as the pair thanked the vendor and continued their walk through the market stalls.

Tallon looked hesitantly between Athena and the furry fruit, before she tentatively took a sip of what Athena knew was a cool, sweet liquid.

'What is it?'

'It's a palm fruit.' Athena gestured to the trees that lined the bay and surrounding hills. 'It has many different names and uses. Alanah trained me to use its water for purification.'

Tallon stopped mid-drink and moved the fruit away from her lips. 'Should I be drinking it?'

Athena laughed as she took the fruit and had a drink herself, savouring the sweet taste she had missed so much. 'It's not just for remedies and such, it's also a refreshing drink, and you can eat the white layer on the inside too.'

Tallon gave her a playful push and took the nutty-tasting fruit back from her to finish the rest of the water. In Nonnelle, the sirens weren't privy to the delicacies of Emodorea, Athena had noticed that during her short stay and the conversations she had with the sirens during their journey. Instead, they had a bland diet of meat, roots and whatever fruit they could grow or find nearby without travelling too far into the other realms. She knew from the contented look on Tallon's face that she was enjoying this new experience immensely.

'So, if we aren't going to find your father'—Tallon asked as she looked for somewhere to open the fruit, clearly curious about what was inside—'what are we going to do?'

Athena held out her hand for the fruit. 'Well, I was going to say we could get a few supplies and head out along the rocks. At least that way, if you change before nightfall, we won't be around anyone.' She took her herb knife and cracked the fruit in half as if she had done it a million times before, then sliced off a piece of the hard-white flesh and handed it to Tallon to try.

'I'd have thought after all this time you would have forgotten how to do that,' a deep male voice laughed from behind them. Athena froze, the marketplace noise seeming to fade into the background, leaving only the sound of her own breath and the thud, thud-thud, of her heart. She glanced sideways, her eyes fixed on Tallon's reaction as the siren turned to face the speaker.

'Come now, Athena, don't pretend like you don't remember me.' The voice was deep, smooth, and carried a hint of playful arrogance. She shivered as the voice rumbled through her like the thunder does over the open sea. 'After all, some memories are too delicious to forget.'

'Jirimka.' Athena turned, her knife still in her hand. 'I didn't think you'd still be around here.'

The man had dark skin that seemed to absorb the morning light, and short curly black hair that framed his face with an effortless charm. His stubble, a few days' growth, added to his rugged allure. Athena's heart raced as she took in his familiar features, a flush creeping up her neck, threatening to expose her thoughts as old memories flashed by.

'Turns out the travelling life wasn't something I wanted in the end.' His eyes, deep and knowing, locked onto Athena's as she finally looked up at his face. Her breath caught in her throat as the corners of his lips rose into a smirk. The intensity of his gaze sent a shiver down her spine, old feelings she had buried long ago threatening to surface.

'Jirimka.' He held his hand out to Tallon. And just like that, the storm under her skin was gone, her thoughts scattered to the wind as she honed her features into a scowl.

'I'm Tallon.'

Athena eyed Jirimka as Tallon awkwardly shook his hand, careful not to let her shirt sleeve slide up her arm. Athena had found the tunic when they first arrived at the markets; it barely covered all the diamond-scales that had appeared on Tallon's skin.

'I never expected to see *you* return here,' he spoke to Athena again, his voice carrying a playful lilt, his arms folding at his chest. Athena couldn't help but notice how much he had changed, and yet remained the same.

'Well, I'm only here to … see a friend off,' Athena sighed, sheathing her blade with a practised motion. 'So it would seem we are both surprised today.'

'I assume you will be going to see Tyrus while you're here.' Jirimka's eyes never left her as he spoke, a mischievous glint in his eyes.

'Why would you assume that?' Athena raised an eyebrow.

'Because'—Jirimka stepped closer, his voice dropping—'no matter how much of a witch you are, you always had a soft spot for your pa.'

Athena's skin felt hot as she realised just how close he had gotten to her. She held her ground, attempting to keep her tone even. 'Maybe I did, but that was a long time ago. I'm not a child anymore.'

'Some things never change,' Jirimka said, his smile widening as he reached out a hand toward her face.

Athena stilled, her breathing shallow. His fingers wrapped around a strand of her hair that had come loose from the braid, and he tugged it … hard.

She growled and swatted him away, turning her back toward him and grabbing Tallon's arm.

'You're right,' she called over her shoulder. 'Some things don't change. You're still an immature arse.'

Tallon beamed at her friend, a bemused look on her face.

'I've never heard you swear before.' Tallon smirked.

'Yes, well.' Athena stomped her way through the crowds of people.

'Is he'—Tallon's brow furrowed—'an ex lover?'

Athena felt her face turn crimson as she scoffed. 'It was a stupid … never mind. No, it was nothing.'

'I've missed our talks,' Jirimka laughed as he jogged to catch up to them. 'A shame your friend isn't spending more time in the village – it's been void of anything but humans lately.'

'How do you know I'm not human?' Tallon demanded, planting her feet in the sand and crossing her arms, a slight shine from the scales under her sleeves glinting in the sun.

'Call it a sixth sense.' Jirimka smirked.

'Jirimka is part fae.' Athena glared at him. 'Which is why I didn't expect to see him back here with everything that's been happening.'

'I haven't seen a siren before. I always figured you'd have these brilliant wings on show.' Jirimka moved his hands as if to show what he meant by wings.

Tallon's eyes glowed yellow. If she had feathers, Athena could have sworn they would have bristled at his words.

'Sorry,' he said, placing his hand on his heart. 'I can see I've said the wrong thing. Perhaps the rumours milling around are true after all.'

'What rumours would they be?' Athena asked.

'The ones about your Queen,' Jirimka replied as he followed them.

'She is not my Queen,' Athena hissed at him. 'Not anymore.'

'I see,' he replied smoothly. 'So, you're one of the ones that caused all the ruckus amongst the covens.'

'Can we go somewhere quieter for the day?' Tallon cut in before Athena replied. 'I'd like to be away from all these people.'

'You're more than welcome to have breakfast with me,' Jirimka offered. 'I'd love to catch up some more with Athy before she decides to run away from me again.'

'Athy?' Tallon raised her eyebrow at her friend.

'No one calls me that anymore,' Athena chided. 'Not that anyone but you ever did.'

'Oh, don't be like that, Athy,' Jirimka joked, adding to Tallon, 'She never complained about it before.'

'I never said I liked it, either,' Athena muttered as they followed Jirimka back through the market.

'You're still as captivating as the day you left,' he replied, his voice softening. Athena wasn't sure, but she was sure the playful edge was gone. 'It hasn't been the same since.'

CHAPTER THIRTY-SEVEN

Thames, Orabelle Bay

+ ATHENA +

'So, you two were a thing, huh.' Tallon glanced between Athena and Jirimka, a sly grin on her face as she sipped her juice. They sat in Jirimka's cosy hut, just out of the village, the space filled with the scent of herbs and sea air.

'No,' Athena answered just as quickly as Jirimka answered, 'Yes.'

'A-huh.' Tallon looked at her friend over the rim of her cup and waggled her eyebrows.

Athena's cheeks flushed as Jirimka smirked at her from the kitchen. 'It seems we remember things a little differently,' he said, shooting her a teasing look.

'We never declared that we were together,' Athena said.

'Only because you didn't want to,' Jirimka interjected, his tone teasing, but Athena saw a hint of hurt flicker in his eyes.

'So, what did you do?' Tallon asked him, pointedly.

'What?' he stumbled, shocked that she assumed it was his fault they didn't work. 'Why do you think it was me?'

Tallon shrugged, her eyes twinkling, 'Just a hunch.'

'He's right,' Athena sighed. 'I didn't want anything to tie me to here since I knew I was going to the keep.'

'As I told you,' Jirimka said from the kitchen, his voice carrying a mix of frustration and longing as he sliced the fresh fruit, 'I would have gone with you.'

The hut went silent as he stopped cutting. 'I would have waited for you to return.'

'It's not that simple, Jiri,' the name rolled off Athena's tongue before she could stop herself. The familiarity of it hung in the air, heavy with unspoken emotions. She could almost feel his heart break a second time as he released her stare.

'It never is with your kind,' Jirimka said, breaking the silence as he put the plate of food on the table before them. 'I'm sorry we don't exactly have the meat you'd be used to in Nonnelle, but the fish is fresh.'

'It looks good,' Tallon said, clearly trying to change the topic as Athena stared at the table, suddenly overly interested by the delicately carved patterns. 'I've never had fish before.'

'No, I can't imagine you would have much reason to fly this far east,' he offered, pushing the conversation along.

'Most of us never even make it as far as the forest,' Tallon said as she picked up a piece of fish so tender that it almost crumbled away in her hands. 'However, a few years back, a group set out to the west, over the barren plains, to see what they could find.'

'What did they find?' Jirimka asked.

'We don't know'—Tallon moaned slightly at the taste of the fish—'they never came back.'

'So are the rumours true, then?' he asked after a moment.

Athena looked to Tallon before answering. The siren nodded as she shoved more of the fish into her mouth, savouring the sour taste the lemon gave it.

'Depending on what rumours you heard, yes,' Athena answered hesitantly.

'The crazy bitch actually did it.' He sat back in his chair and put his hands behind his head. 'She cursed your entire race to become fish-people?'

'So it would seem,' Tallon replied, pushing the plate of exotic fruits away from her.

'So'—Jirimka leaned forward—'why is it that you haven't changed?'

'Jirimka!' Athena shot him a glare that screamed, *Shut your mouth!* He locked eyes with Tallon, who steeling her face, silently shrugged her jacket off, exposing the diamond-hard scales along her arms and exposed chest. She turned, showing him her back and the pale red marks where her feathers and wings once were. Tallon looked away in shame as she pulled the jacket back over her shoulders, and Athena's heart ached for her friend.

Jirimka's eyes softened for a moment, the storm within them calming ever so slightly.

'You're not the only one who's been shamed,' he said quietly. Athena looked away as Jirimka brushed his hair over his ear, revealing what was once clearly sharp and defined like the fae, now cruelly cropped. 'We all bear scars that we would wish to hide.'

'The difference,' Tallon said, her voice trembling with a sudden rage that shocked even Athena, 'is that I had my wings, my *world*, ripped from me by some barbaric bitch!' Tallon shoved the table away, the sound of it scraping against the floor caused Athena to wince.

Jirimka nodded slowly, the pain of his own memories evident in his expression as he replied, 'And I had a mother who decided that if I didn't look like my ancestors, I wouldn't be accepted by them.'

The room was heavy with shared pain, their wounds laid bare. Athena felt for them both, the depth of their suffering unfathomable. The two beings, strangers to one another, brought together by her. Her past and her present; bound by trauma and a fierce determination to not be held back by the shadows that haunted them.

Tallon breathed out slowly, as if unsure of what to say. Her anger, though still visible in her eyes, seemed to dissipate into the heavy silence. Jirimka stood, gathering the plates, his movements slow. Athena remained quiet, the weight of their shared secrets pressing down on her. She felt the unspoken words linger in the air, a fragile thread connecting them all, each bearing their scars proudly.

'She was right,' Jirimka said as he dumped the plates into the sink with a heavy clatter.

'Who was?' Tallon asked softly, still facing the table, not prepared to look at him.

'My mother.' He breathed heavily for a moment. 'My father's people, my kin, denied my existence when I travelled to find them, and my mother refused to acknowledge me once I returned.'

The sound of dishes scrapping in the sink ended the discussion, leaving an eerie silence in its wake. Tallon stood mutely from the table, her thoughts clearly elsewhere. She nodded to Athena in acknowledgement before making her way outside, likely seeking solace and space to think.

'That was years ago, Jiri,' Athena said quietly as she finally stood from the table, her steps deliberate as she crossed the small room to stand beside him. 'Tallon's wings ... what happened to her was as recent as the last fortnight.'

Jirimka turned to face her, the space between them charged with unspoken emotions. 'You would think that fifteen years of not seeing you would have changed my mind,' he said, his voice laced with longing and frustration.

Fifteen years had seemed like nothing to her since she left. At eighteen, her powers had finally come in – much later than most witches – and her mother had been so pleased to have a daughter with an affinity for the moon and water. She eagerly sent word to the keep, knowing how few and far between healers were among the witches. Alanah had readily accepted the request for Athena to study under her, and that had set her on a path away from everything she knew.

'Jiri,' Athena whispered, her voice barely audible. Her body ached to move closer to him, the pull of the old emotions so strong and insistent. But now was not the time to reminisce or rekindle old flames, so she held her ground and stayed where she was. Her heart heavy with the weight of what was left unsaid. The years may have passed quickly, but the memories and feelings had remained, lingering like the familiar salt that clung to their skin.

'I missed you.' He took a step toward her, and more than the physical distance between them seemed to shrink. 'I sent letters.'

She needed to step away from him, but her feet remained rooted. This wasn't something she needed right now, despite the longing in her heart.

'You never replied.' The words were tinged with hurt. 'To any of them.'

She swallowed hard, guilt ebbing its way into her mind. She never replied because she didn't want him to come chasing after her. Her duty to her coven was clear; train with Alanah, perhaps one day replace the head healer and have her coven, her *family*, move into a higher position within the witch community. It was not written in her future to be with a human, even if he was half-fae.

'I had my reasons,' she murmured. 'It wasn't about you, Jiri. It was about my duty, my obligations.'

'Some things are worth breaking the rules for, Athena.'

Her heart ached at his words, torn between the life she was meant to lead and the one she had left behind. For a moment, she let herself imagine what might have been, before reality pulled her back. 'I couldn't let you risk your life for me, to make you wait. It wouldn't have been fair. We both had to move on.'

'Don't tell me that you met someone else,' his eyes darted briefly toward the door that Tallon had left through. 'Don't tell me that you've decided to chase after a *bird*.'

'It's not like that.' Athena blushed, her cheeks turning a soft rose under her dark complexion. 'I owe Tallon a debt for what Isadora has done to her and her people.'

The last couple of days had made Athena wonder if there was anything between her and Tallon. They had become close, but Athena wasn't sure if it was a romantic feeling she had when she looked at the siren or if it was merely a strong friendship. Regardless, it was a bond that tugged at her heart, reminding her of an old connection she'd long since lost.

'So, will you leave when she joins her family in the sea?' Another step toward her, the gap between them now so small, it was almost non-existent. It had been so long since she had felt this nervous around anyone – almost fifteen years, to be exact. Yet, she still felt her stomach swirl and her head spin when he got close.

'I don't know,' she whispered, her eyes dipping toward the ground in shame. 'I cannot return to the forest. I cannot return to the witches. Isadora will have my head.'

She honestly didn't know what she was going to do after Tallon left to join the others. She would see her father; he would be an old man now, easing into potentially his last years. What was there to do apart from travel away from the forest, perhaps aid a small village somewhere? Maybe she could even charter a boat from The Blue Sands and discover a new world. The possibilities were endless, but each idea seemed to be weighed down by memories and unresolved feelings. The pull of the sea and the whisper of unknown lands called to her, promising both adventure and freedom from living in fear of Isadora.

'So, don't leave.' A warm, rough hand cupped her chin, lifting her gaze to meet the ocean blue eyes flecked with silver that she had long missed. 'Fifteen years is long enough. It's time to come home.'

'I don't have a home,' she whispered, a single tear rolling down her cheek. It had been fifteen years since she had felt the calluses on his hands against her skin. Fifteen years and she had not once forgotten the sensation, the way it made her blood hot.

'You will always have a home with me.' His voice was a soft promise as he gently lifted her chin a little higher. His eyes seemed to hold the entire ocean within them, swirling with emotions; Athena felt a pull, as if being drawn into the very depths of his gaze. The loose curls framing her face swayed gently with the movement, and as he leaned in closer the world around them faded away. The stands of her hair brushed against her cheeks, falling away as he brought his lips down to meet hers. The kiss was a fusion of years of desperation and longing, the undeniable spark of rekindled emotions, leaving her breathless and dizzy.

Suddenly, she forgot to hold her ground.

'She's been out there for hours.' Athena murmured, leaning her head back against Jirimka's chest as they sat on the sand at the far end of the bay. Tallon had disappeared from the hut while they had their brief reunion, and it had taken them over an hour of searching around the town to finally find her.

She was perched on the edge of the rock wall, her feet dangling in the water, singing a hauntingly beautiful melody that seemed to echo through the evening air. The gentle waves lapped at the rocks, harmonising with her song, creating a serene yet melancholic atmosphere.

'Do you think they'll come back for her?' Jirimka asked as he wrapped his arms around Athena. The wind had picked up, carrying a chill that hinted at the coming season's change. Soon, the bay would be shrouded in icy mist, and the once bustling fishing ships would become scarce as the villagers grew weary of what lurked in the deep. Trade on the land would slow, with travellers preferring the safety of their homes over the risks of the road. Not to mention what would happen with the impending war that Isadora promised.

'Queen Nerophine is her cousin.' Athena sighed, leaning into the warmth of Jirimka's embrace. 'She wouldn't leave Tallon behind, but we don't know what's happening out there.'

Tallon's voice floated on a phantom breeze back to them. It was sweet and melodic, yet filled with a profound sadness that Athena had never experienced. She sang of a sister lost to a tormented sea god, and the ruins of a castle on the ocean floor. Then, as her voice dipped toward the end of the song, she sang about a saviour from another world, descended from the lost sister and the ocean god, who would come to free them from their ocean chains. It was a tale of loss and redemption, echoing in Athena's heart and stirring a yearning for the unknown future that awaited them.

'We can't stay out here all night,' Jirimka said, his voice barely audible now over the distant crash of the waves as Tallon's haunting song drifted away from them again.

Suddenly, a piercing scream shattered the calm and Athena's heart leapt into her throat as she watched Tallon slip from the rock and plunge into the dark water.

'We don't have to,' Athena said as she jumped to her feet. She kicked off her boots, the cold, wet sand numbing her toes as she sprinted to the rock wall. Jirimka followed behind her, his footsteps pounding on the rocks as they ran. The pair raced along the rocks as fast as they could, the sound of waves crashing around them, frigid water spraying against them. When they reached the end, Athena began climbing down – the jagged rock edges cutting into her fingers – to where Tallon's body was banging against the rock edge, the water churning around her.

'Tallon,' Athena reached down to grab the siren. Her heart pounded as she extended her arm, straining to reach her friend. Jirimka was suddenly beside her, his strong hands moving swiftly and surely. Together, they pulled the limp siren onto the flat rock, the sea spray whipping into their faces.

'Did you see them?' Tallon croaked, eyes rolling before she convulsed. Jirimka held her firm as she clawed at her legs, the skin peeling away under her sharp nails.

'She's changing. This is what happened to the others.' Athena dragged herself away, avoiding Tallon's thrashing body.

'They're coming!' Tallon's eyes shot open. Athena and Jirimka looked away as her legs finished fusing together, the sight too gruesome to behold.

Screeching came from the water as bubbles began to appear around the rocks.

Athena grabbed Jirimka and moved them away from the edge as two heads appeared in the water.

'Peita!' Athena gasped excitedly. The siren responded with a smile full of teeth, and a low growl from her throat.

'It's true,' Jirimka said as he eyed the sirens in the water. 'Mermaids can't speak human.'

The other head came into view and hissed at him.

'They might have tails, but they're still sirens.' Athena warned. To the hissing siren, she added, 'Look after her for me, Cilla.'

In response, the two sirens reached out of the water to help the newly changed Tallon down from the rocks and into the icy darkness. Athena leaned down, her heart heavy with sorrow and relief, and carefully kissed Tallon's brow. The siren placed her hand on the witch's cheek, a silent farewell filled with understanding and thanks, before allowing her sisters to pull her down into the depths of the sea, vanishing into the cold, unforgiving abyss.

CHAPTER THIRTY-EIGHT

Thornwell, Southern Mortal Realm

+ REID +

ELISAVET BECAME ALL but glued to Reid's side while he roamed freely around the Inner Ring. He spent most of his time trying to find the man who had spoken out against the priest, both in the council chamber and in the courtyard the week before, when Kasin had finally returned to him. He was almost sure he knew who the voice belonged to, but Reid had yet to see the man again.

When Reid pressed Elisavet for information, she danced around the question, mentioning that the man had slipped into the city just before the gates shut, a visiting friend of her uncle's. Her eyes fluttered and a subtle blush coloured her cheeks as her words painted a picture of a man esteemed by the lords and beloved by the court ladies. Reid could see the puzzle pieces falling into place, but he needed more – if only he could corner the man for a private conversation, he was sure they knew each other.

'Why are you in such a hurry?' Elisavet's arm intertwined with his, her voice a silky purr. 'Don't you want to see more of the city before you head to training?'

Reid's morning routine over the past week had become a blend of exploration and duty; the city's sights in the early dawn light, followed by relentless training with the new guards. Despite the prestigious title of Kasin's Protector, the King's orders still bound him to a rigorous regimen. The weight of the responsibility hadn't lessened, only shifted in form. He felt as though he was more the King's underling now than he was Emodorea's saviour.

'I don't mean to be in a hurry,' Reid said, shifting slightly to create a sliver of space between them, though he kept her arm hooked in his. 'I just want to – no, I *need* to get in as much training as I can.'

'Oh come on, Reid,' Elisavet looked up at him, her green eyes sparkling with a blend of mischief and sincerity, her lips forming a delicate pout, her voice a soft, teasing melody. 'Surely you can spare a few moments for me?'

Her ease with him was disconcerting; the image of a princess on the arm of a street rat was something he never imagined. Oscar would never believe it if he told him.

In just a week, Elisavet had shown more interest in him than anyone else ever had. Reid wasn't used to girls talking to him, let alone a princess who seemed so comfortable with him. Her casual demeanour made him nervous – though there was a part of him that wondered if her fascination stemmed from his status as Kasin's Protector, rather than genuine interest.

'What is it?' Elisavet asked as Reid stopped abruptly.

'There is one thing I would like to do this morning before training,' Reid replied as he turned to face her with a determined look.

'Yes,' Elisavet breathed, her eyes wide with anticipation. She tilted her head up toward him, twining her fingers insistently into his.

'Can you show me where Lord Avere lives?'

'Of course,' Elisavet's smile faltered only for a moment before she bounced back to her usual self. 'We can stop by their bakery for a tart on the way back to the castle.'

'If you're sure there isn't anything else you are meant to be doing this morning, of course.' Reid said, though his steps followed her lead as she guided him down a narrow side street that meandered toward the castle.

'Don't be silly. I have all the time in the world,' she replied breezily, her voice light with amusement. Her fingers tightened slightly around his arm, grounding him in her presence. 'How do you know Lord Avere? I thought you'd never been into the Inner Ring before.'

'I haven't. Well, I mean, there was once or twice when Gillian brought me with him for work,' Reid said, navigating the polished cobblestone road beside her. 'I don't know Lord Avere personally – I know his daughter, Marlo.'

'How did you come to know Marlo?' Elisavet's voice lost some of its playful lilt, her eyes darkening ever so slightly at the name. A flicker of something else, almost imperceptible, flashed across her features, but Reid wasn't sure what it was.

'It's hard to explain,' Reid said and glanced sideways at her, catching her sour look.

'She always was very popular with the boys in town.' Elisavet spoke almost enviously of the younger woman. Her lips tightened for a brief moment before she forced a smile. 'She was always the first onto the dance floor with the high lords' sons at castle events. So I'm sure whatever you two—'

'No, gods no, not like that!' He exclaimed, his cheeks flushing with embarrassment. The thought that she believed he knew Marlo the way Oscar did was mortifying. The girl was nothing but snarky toward Reid.

'I only met her once when she left town with my best friend, Oscar,' Reid went on. 'Though she looked oddly familiar. No clue why.'

'Oh, that's why you want to see her father, to explain what happened to her?' Elisavet nuzzled in closer to his side.

It was bewildering to him how quickly her mood had shifted. He wasn't used to the overwhelming amount of social interactions he had been dealing with since coming to the Inner Ring, especially not the interactions with Elisavet. The sudden shifts from lightheartedness to whatever this other emotion was were a new and perplexing dynamic for him to navigate. He couldn't shake the feeling that her interest in him was far more complex than it seemed.

'Yes, I should have done it sooner. Everything's been so chaotic since I arrived,' Reid said. 'I feel terrible for not having gone to him yet. I'm sure he's worried sick about where his daughter has been for the past few weeks.'

'I'm sure he will be grateful to you for telling him.' She grinned and pulled him even closer as they walked the last block to Lord Avere's home.

The bakery was fancier than any of the bread stalls he had seen outside the wall. Here, the aroma of fresh-baked goods mingled with the sweet scent of pastries, and the storefront gleamed with polished wood and intricately carved signage. It was an actual shop, its windows showcasing an array of beautifully crafted loaves and confections, not just a cart with goods piled on the back of it.

Elisavet waited with a smile Reid found puzzling, her eyes sparkling with anticipation as he pushed the door open for her – something she seemed to like, and was easy enough for him to do. The inside of the building was warm and inviting, filled with the soft hum of morning chatter.

'Welcome, Lady Elisavet,' a cheery-eyed, older man stepped out from the kitchen to stand behind the counter. 'What can I do for you this morning?'

'I've brought a friend that would like to talk to you,' Elisavet replied as she turned to introduce Reid.

'Ah, Kasin's Protector!' The old man's voice boomed with hearty laughter. 'Tymon Avere.'

He gave a mock exaggerated bow to Reid, a warm smile crinkled the corners of his eyes.

'Lord Avere,' Reid started, unsure how to word what he needed to say, 'I have news – well, sort of – about your daughter.'

He watched as the old man's grin disappeared. From somewhere in the back of the shop came the clatter of metal hitting the ground, and a young woman, barely older than Reid, appeared at the baker's side.

'What's this about, Marlo?' she demanded, her voice tinged with worry. 'We haven't heard from her since the gates closed.'

'She left town a few weeks ago,' Reid spoke carefully as he ran his hand through his hair. 'She went with Oscar.'

'Went where?' the woman pressed, her eyes narrowing. 'And who is Oscar?'

'Last I heard they were heading for The Blue Sands. Marlo had been asking Oscar for a while to run away with her,' Reid explained, his voice tinged with unease. Beside him, Elisavet inhaled sharply.

'How long is a while?' demanded the woman. Curious eyes around the room darted toward them.

'Merla, please calm down.' Tymon attempted to soothe the young woman, his tone was gentle but firm. 'We both know Marlo was the wilder of you two, she obviously took after your mother a lot more than I realised.'

'You want me to calm down? Calm down, when we've just been told that Marlo, *Lady* Marlo, has run off with some common street rat!' Merla hissed at her father, her fists clenched in her apron, her voice rising with anger and frustration.

'Might I remind you, Lady Merla,' Elisavet interjected politely, 'that the "street rat" as you call him, Oscar, was a close friend of Kasin's Protector?'

Reid cringed at the way she emphasised *Kasin's Protector*, as if he were the god himself, rather than just Reid.

Merla faltered for a moment, her anger giving way to a flicker of fear. 'I apologise, Lady Elisavet, Lord Reid,' she said, her voice softer. 'But you must understand my concern. My fifteen-year-old sister has run away from a safe place – and with some strange man, at that.'

Being called *Lord Reid* still hadn't grown on him. The title felt foreign, heavy, and he much preferred the simplicity of just being Reid. He understood why Merla was angry about the situation. Yet, Tymon's reaction – calm and resigned – spoke volumes. It was clear this wasn't the first time Marlo had sparked concern with her impulsive nature.

'From my understanding,' Reid offered, 'the Blue Sands is probably going to be the safest place around. Perhaps they will sail south and find new land somewhere, without the witches and the war.'

'Perhaps you are right, my boy,' Tymon agreed as he patted Merla on the shoulder, a small attempt at comfort.

'I can't believe this!' Merla tossed her apron onto the counter in frustration and stormed from the room.

'Forgive my daughter for her abruptness.' Tymon sighed as he rubbed his temple. 'It has been hard on her since their mother left us.'

'Well,' Reid said after a long moment of awkward silence between them, 'I'm sorry I can't offer anything more. I just wanted to let you know where she had gone, in case you wanted to follow her that way before anything happens to the city.'

'Thank you, I appreciate it,' Tymon said, before he grabbed Merla's apron and headed back to the kitchen.

'Come on.' Elisavet pulled Reid from the shop. 'It doesn't look like we're going to get one of their tarts today.'

CHAPTER THIRTY-NINE

Thornwell, Southern Mortal Realm

✦ REID ✦

ELISAVET LEFT HIM at the gate to the barracks, promising to meet him for lunch and leaving before he could tell her he had made other plans. He had seen the tower inside the castle that the man with no face disappeared into often. Today at lunch, he wanted to visit it and hopefully find him. For one, Reid needed to thank him for what little help the man offered toward proving he was the Protector Kasin had chosen, but mostly he just wanted to know why he seemed so familiar to him.

A sword clashed against his shield, knocking him off balance as a relentless attack from Orrin – his sparring partner – brought his attention back to the training grounds. He was regularly caught off-guard during training, either from Kasin whispering in his head or his thoughts drifting beyond the sword's edge. Today was no exception. The distraction left him vulnerable, a chink in his otherwise steadfast defence. Orrin's strikes came fast and heavy, a physical reminder of how much weaker Reid was than the rest of the new recruits.

'Pay attention,' Orrin whispered as their instructor walked to the other side of the arena. The young guard was only slightly taller than Reid, but he had been raised to be a fighter. His muscles were sculpted and defined from countless hours of rigorous training, even before he'd been old enough to sign up as a palace guard. Broad shoulders and a powerful chest framed his lean physique, giving him both strength and agility, and his skin bore the faint scars of a life outside the Inner Ring. With every movement, his toned body seemed to flow with a lethal grace.

'Sorry,' Reid murmured, launching into a series of strikes that clanged against Orrin's shield. Each blow was met with a firm, calculated resistance, Orrin countering with practised ease. Despite the demanding routine, Reid was glad he had been paired with Orrin for sparring practice. Orrin's technique pushed Reid to refine his skills, making the gruelling hours spent in the training grounds feel worthwhile.

Although he had been training for such a short time, his skills had developed impeccably fast. Every swing of his sword felt more fluid, every block more precise. He couldn't shake the feeling that it was Kasin's gifts at work, rather than his own natural talent. He was a pick pocket, after all – a thief, a street rat – not a warrior. The whispers and side long glances from the other trainees hinted they thought the same. He wasn't sure if he would ever truly feel he deserved the title Kasin had bestowed upon him.

Orrin's shield bashed into him with brutal force, sending Reid sprawling onto the ground, his sword skidding out of reach. Chuckles came from the other fighters surrounding them as he lay there, winded, staring up at the sky.

Well, that was graceful, Kasin's voice echoed in Reid's mind, *Perhaps, next time, you could try staying on your feet?*

Thanks for the tip. I'll be sure to add "not falling" to my list of skills to master. Reid rolled his eyes, hoping the god could feel the irritation rolling off him.

A single bird circled lazily overhead, its song a lilting serenade. Reid's thoughts drifted to the feather his aunt had given him and the stories she had told him when he was younger. A shiver ran down his spine, a strange tingling at the edge of his consciousness.

Shaking his head, he pulled himself back to reality just as Orrin's shadow loomed over him, offering a hand to pull him back to his feet. The moment was fleeting, but the eerie melodic tune of the bird lingered in his mind.

Time passed quicker than expected, and Reid found himself back in his chambers before he knew it. The room was a far cry from the cramped cell where he had been imprisoned for a week. The spacious quarters offered a private bathing room with a bath built into the floor, a luxurious feature he had never seen before. At Gillian's, bathing meant they had to fill a bucket with cold, often murky, water and do the best they could with that. Bathing had been a rare chore, with the frigid water discouraging any regular attempts at cleanliness.

Here, though, the bath remained warm throughout the day, kept at a pleasant temperature by servants who diligently topped it up with buckets of hot water drawn from the springs beneath the castle. He marvelled at the consistent warmth, a small mystery he had no desire to solve. As he slid into the soothing water, his aching muscles finally beginning to relax, Reid couldn't help but appreciate the unexpectedness of his current life.

His peace was interrupted by a series of insistent knocks at the door. Reid sighed, closing his eyes and hoping to ignore whoever was on the other side. It was probably just Elisavet, early as usual and ready to go to lunch. But the knocking continued. So, reluctantly, he stood, water dripping from his body as he grabbed a towel and wrapped it around his waist. The knocking persisted, becoming increasingly more rapid. He took a deep breath and opened the door, bracing himself for the interruption.

'I'm sorry, I wasn't expecting you until lunch. I'm not exactly dressed for company,' Reid finished tying the towel around his waist, then looked up – and straight into the face of Gillian. His face paled as he stood there, rooted to the spot.

'Just put some clothes on,' Gillian said, unimpressed as he strolled into the room, completely at ease. 'We have some things to talk about.'

Reid scrambled to dress himself, his mind spinning. How had he not recognised the man earlier? He'd heard Gillian's voice every day for years, yet had not connected it with the nameless man influencing the King. Once dressed, he joined Gillian in his small lounge area. It seemed that he had been right in thinking the man with no face was familiar to him.

'How did you get here, how did you become a lord in such a short time?' Reid wasted no time in asking the questions that were darting through his mind. The pieces were starting to fit together, but there were still so many unanswered questions.

'A lot of people owe me a lot of favours.' Gillian smirked, arms crossed casually. 'I'm more interested to know how *you* became the chosen one of Kasin.'

A lot of people owe him favours, huh? Kasin's voice dripped with mock praise. *Must be quite the charmer to wrangle all that influence.*

Reid didn't bother hiding his grin as the god's laugh rumbled inside him.

'According to Kasin, he chose me the day I was born,' Reid replied shortly. The bitterness in his voice was unmistakable as he added, 'You left us outside to die.'

Gillian had been at the King's side this entire time and had not spoken one word to him. Had not asked where the others were, had not offered to aid Reid in convincing the council he was telling the truth.

Hurt flickered in Gillian's eyes for a moment before he replied, 'I'm neither your nor their father. Besides, I left you and Oscar in charge when I departed, did I not?'

The sting of betrayal cut deeper than Reid had anticipated. 'We were under the impression you would return. We didn't realise that you were saving your own hide and never coming back.'

'Well, look at you.' Gillian raised an eyebrow. 'All brash and bold since you have a title now. Quite the transformation from the helpless orphan I found on the street.'

Reid's lip twitched. 'I guess having a god at my back does that to a person. I'm not the boy you once knew, Gillian. Unlike you, I don't run away from my problems.'

'I didn't run away.' Gillian's glare found Reid. 'I have always had a place here. I simply chose to spend most of my time in the Outer Ring because that is where my money was made. Do you think I could have pickpockets in here and get away with it?'

'So that's all any of us were good for? Stealing so that you could make money.' Reid almost spat at him, he was so infuriated.

'What happened to Oscar and the others? I didn't see the guards bring them in when they brought you to the priest.'

'You were at the meeting when I asked the King to bring the boys in,' Reid said coldly. 'He refused. And Oscar left the day before they brought me in with a girl he's been seeing – Lord Avere's daughter. Last I saw them, they were headed to The Blue Sands.'

'Why didn't you go with them?' Gillian asked.

'Because I had people that would most likely die without my help.' Reid looked away. His voice was barely above a whisper when he eventually spoke again. 'Though I'd say by now they probably already have, thanks to those things roaming around out there and your lack of help.'

The room fell into an uneasy silence, both men lost in their own thoughts. Reid's mind raced with so many questions about the week he was locked up, but he doubted Gillian would give him a straight answer; it had never happened before.

'So,' Gillian broke the silence, 'the great Kasin has decided that a simple orphan such as you will be the one to save the world.'

'It would seem so.' Reid half smiled at the thought of being more significant than Gillian ever allowed him to think he would be. 'Why didn't you show your face to me that day in the council room?'

'To be honest, I didn't want you announcing to the King that you knew me.' Gillian sighed. 'I thought if you did that, he would think this whole thing was a plan I enacted to move up the ranks within the council.'

'Ah, I see. So, to save yourself and keep your secret, you let them torture and almost kill me.' Reid wanted to be angry but found he was growing bored with Gillian's predictability.

He seems like a real gem. Kasin said drily. *Are we going to keep him?*

Undecided.

Reid wasn't impressed by the situation, but he wasn't surprised by Gillian's actions either. If his years in the slums of the Outer Ring had taught him anything, it was that people would scheme, steal, lie and even kill to survive; a habit that Reid never developed, even though it might have made his life easier in some ways.

'If I could have done something more, I would have,' Gillian said. 'I helped you with the priest, did I not?'

Reid scoffed at him. 'The only thing you did was to side with me once you were certain that Kasin was real. Before that, you stood in the shadows and waited to see the outcome.'

Gillian didn't say anything more; he simply sat back in the chair, a smirk appearing on his face.

'So, I'm assuming I don't call you Gillian here?' Reid stood from the chair. It was almost noon. Elisavet would no doubt be arriving soon to go to lunch.

'I'm known as Lord Brione Ascot,' Gillian said as he watched Reid pour himself a glass of water. Kasin snorted.

A knock sounded at the door, lighter than Gillian's and less demanding.

'Expecting someone?'

'If you must know,' Reid said, 'it's Lady Elisavet.'

'Ah.' Gillian gave him a look. 'Am I interrupting private plans? It's not often that a Lady would meet in a Lord's private chambers. What would the King think of his niece visiting your rooms unaccompanied?'

'Not that it's any of your concern,' Reid said impatiently, 'but we are going to lunch.'

Reid walked over to the door and waited for Gillian to join him. 'And the King does know, he is the one who insisted Elisavet show me around the city.'

'I doubt that's all the King insisted upon.' Gillian laughed as he opened the door.

'Oh, sorry,' Elisavet said as she faced Gillian and not Reid at his door, 'I was expecting Lord Reid.'

'Indeed, you were.' Gillian stepped past her.

'I will see you again, Lord Brione,' Reid said with a nod of his head, indicating the conversation was not over.

'I'm sure you will, Lord Reid.' Gillian smiled. 'Have a good lunch, Lady Elisavet.'

'Lord Brione.' Elisavet nodded as the man left them both by the door.

CHAPTER FORTY

Thornwell, Southern Mortal Realm

+ REID +

THE TAVERN THEY ARRIVED at was bustling with activity; it was one of the more popular spots just shy of the palace grounds. It had taken the pair a good fifteen minutes to walk there, Elisavet clinging to Reid's arm, as usual. The wooden sign above the door creaked gently in the breeze as they entered. Inside, the warm glow of lanterns cast a cosy ambience, inviting them in from the hot sun. The scent of roasted meat and freshly baked bread mingled with the sound of laughter and clinking mugs, a welcome escape from the tension of earlier.

'It's a shame what's happening in the Outer Ring,' Elisavet said as they sat down at a tavern table for lunch.

'What's happening in the Outer Ring?' Reid asked as he sipped his cold tea – a new favourite since being inside the wall.

'I'm surprised you haven't heard – it's all the councilmen's wives and daughters are talking about,' Elisavet said as she shuffled closer to him on the bench.

Reid felt the familiar warmth of her presence, the subtle scent of her perfume – a delicate blend reminiscent of the roses that grew to the west of Thornwell. It was comforting yet unsettling, his stomach twisting with a mix of nerves and something else he couldn't quite place. Every brush of her arm against his sent shivers down his spine, his skin tingling with an unfamiliar sensation.

'In case you haven't noticed,' Reid attempted to stay calm as he fiddled with his cigarette tin on the table. Her closeness, the warmth, the perfume, was sending his mind into a spiral of confusion and excitement. 'I haven't been included in a single council meeting since I asked your uncle to bring in the people from outside the wall.'

It was true. The King had since stopped informing him of when the meetings were going to be held. Instead, his days were filled with guard training and accompanying Elisavet throughout the city. Not that he minded much of the latter, the princess was good company.

'Well, they are saying that bodies are showing up on the edge of the forest.' Reid dropped his fork, his heart plummeting as her words registered with him. The boys were still alive, as far as Reid was aware.

They're okay, for now.

'What do you mean "bodies"?' He raised his eyebrows at her, trying to keep his voice down. Even in their secluded booth, they drew attention – whether because of who he was, or the fact that she was the princess.

'Bodies,' Elisavet shrugged her short black bob bouncing as she did so, 'you know, dead ones.'

She said it so casually that it was clear this wasn't news to her. Reid's mind raced, his heart heavy with the fear that his friends might be among those found eventually. The ease with how she spoke about the situation was a painful reminder of how their worlds, though currently intertwined, would likely always remain vastly different.

'I knew more of those things would be coming,' Reid sat back in the chair with a defeated sigh. The King should have listened to me and brought everyone in from outside.'

'I don't blame him for not wanting to bring in the Outer Ring residents,' Elisavet replied, her fingers trailing along his arm, leaving uncontrolled prickles in their wake. 'They would have robbed us all poor by now.'

'They're not all like that.' Reid moved her hand off his arm. 'You're quick to forget that I am one of them.'

Embarrassment flickered through her green eyes as she stilled at his words. 'I didn't mean it like that,' she whispered as she placed her hand back on his, 'I'm sure there are more that are like you.'

Don't fight with her, Kasin spoke briefly. *You need to know more information.*

I thought you'd disappeared from me again, Reid replied. Kasin had been oddly quiet apart from a few words here and there.

You're on a date with a princess, Kasin said smoothly. *I didn't want to …
interrupt.*

How considerate of you.

Kasin was right. Reid shouldn't argue with Elisavet. She was the King's
niece; she had access to the information he needed. It was clear she thought
they were friends. In truth, she was probably one of his only friends apart
from Orrin. Reid couldn't afford to alienate her, not when her assistance was
so crucial. Despite the strange mix of feelings her presence stirred within
him, he knew he had to keep his focus and make the most of her being
around. For now, he needed to play it smart, keep his eyes on the bigger
picture.

'What if,' Elisavet interrupted his thoughts, 'I asked my uncle if we could
go check out your old home? I'll tell him there are some things you need to
collect. Maybe you can check on the boys while you're there?'

'You'd do that?' Reid asked, absently putting his hand on top of where
Elisavet's sat.

'Let's go somewhere quieter,' Elisavet suggested, her eyes lingering on
where their fingers touched. She squeezed his hand, lingering just a bit too
long, and her eyes sparkled with a softness that almost sent him reeling.
The subtle brush of her fingers against his sent a tingle up his arm, heat
flaring up his neck.

Oscar would be screaming at him to go wherever she wanted. After all,
she was a princess, and she was quite pretty, with her dark hair and bright
eyes. The thought of Oscar's voice in his head made Reid's lips twitch with
a faint, amused smile.

Reid stood hesitantly as Elisavet tugged him to his feet. He was suddenly
acutely aware of the precarious balance he needed to maintain. It would be
awful to reject Elisavet's feelings outright, especially considering what she
had just offered him. Perhaps if he gently conveyed that he wasn't looking for
anything serious – especially with the weight of Kasin's responsibilities and
the impending doom of the witches that were hanging over him – it would
ease the tension. He wanted to ensure that her feelings were respected, but
the chaos and uncertainty of his current situation left little room for deeper

commitments. The last thing he wanted was to hurt her. Yet, despite his resolve, it was difficult to resist the urge propelling him to follow her, the magnetic pull of her presence drawing him in.

Hopefully, you're better at this than you are at sword fighting, Kasin's deep chuckle lingered as Reid felt the god's presence disappear from his mind once again, their connection closed from Kasin's side. Reid internally snarled at the god's lack of empathy.

He thought back to what Gillian had said earlier about the King probably encouraging Reid to court Elisavet. Reid, however, was conflicted. He had no idea what he wanted from Elisavet. While he didn't want to lead her on, he couldn't ignore the way his skin flushed whenever she looked up at him through those thick, black lashes.

'Elisavet,' he said as she made to leave their table. 'We should probably talk about us.'

Her eyes glimmered as she smiled at him. 'I'd love to talk about us.'

Though the god had left, he was sure he heard his familiar deep chuckle, perhaps he had chosen the wrong words. Reid considered how to explain it better to Elisavet as she dragged him from the tavern and away from the busy streets.

She had miraculously found a quiet spot in one of the western streets, not too far from the servants gates into the castle. It was just the two of them, nestled in a small recess in a wall beside the Tea House, the bustle of the city feeling like a distant hum. Elisavet positioned herself facing the street, so her back was against the wall, settling into the space with an ease that seemed almost natural. The dim light of the afternoon sun cast a warm glow around them, creating a moment of intimacy that was unexpected. She'd pulled Reid in close, the proximity making his heart race.

'So'—Elisavet played with a curl of his brown hair—'what about *us* did you want to discuss?'

'Umm, well ...' Reid ran his hand through his hair, brushing her fingers out of the way as he did. The gesture was both nervous and intimate.'I just wanted to make sure you knew where we stand.'

'Reid,' she whispered, her voice low and breathy, 'doesn't this just feel ... right to you?'

His skin prickled as her warm breath lingered against his ear. This was not going as he planned, and it wasn't as easy as he'd hoped. He knew he should stop it, but his damn body wanted to do its own thing. Her fingers traced a slow, deliberate path along his arm, igniting a fire that was hard to ignore. The intensity of her gaze, the way her lips had brushed against his ear as she whispered, made it nearly impossible to resist. But there was something ... something he couldn't place that was holding him back. He was torn between the logical voice in his head and the primal urge to give in to what was happening.

'You know I have to find the Witch Queen as soon as Kasin is satisfied with my training.' His hands moved on their own as they found her hips. Her dress clung to her figure, the fabric slick and snug against her skin in the oppressive afternoon heat. He wasn't sure why his body wanted her so badly when his brain told him it was a bad idea. 'We can't do this.'

'What is this, exactly?' Her nails ran along his jawline. His eyes closed as a low, unfamiliar sound found its way up his throat.

'We can't be together, not properly.' He sighed, raising a hand to tuck a loose strand of hair behind her ear, his touch lingering just enough for her to blush. 'Not yet.'

There it was, two little words that just slipped out. Reid could already see Elisavet clinging to those two little words in hopes that they would be something more. He had no idea how to explain to her that while he enjoyed her company, and it was clear that his body wanted hers, he just didn't feel like there was anything more to offer emotionally.

He stilled as her lips suddenly connected with his, her body pulling him against her so hard that he was sure she would be crushed against the brick wall. It was harsh and filled with heat, not at all what he expected kissing to feel like. It was intoxicating, the bitter taste of lemon lingering on her lips from earlier dulled his senses as she pressed her tongue into his mouth. He pulled back slightly before both Kasin and Gillian's words resurfaced in his mind. He internally swore as he tried to relax and let the kiss deepen into a wave of pleasure wrapped in regret. Perhaps he wouldn't survive the fight with the Witch Queen. Maybe he wouldn't have to break the Princess's heart.

CHAPTER FORTY-ONE

Witch's Keep, Forest of Brielle

+ NORELLA +

ISADORA WAS FURIOUS, and the entire forest knew about it. Her anger radiated through the trees, startling birds from their nests and sending creatures scurrying into their burrows. She had been so caught up in preparations for heading to Thornwell that she had been oblivious to the fact that someone had stolen from her. The fact that it was her own niece – her own flesh and blood – who had the shameless audacity to steal from her, only fuelled her rage further. Leaves trembled in the trees as her wrathful energy pulsated through the air, and even the ancient oaks surrounding the keep seemed to bend away from her fury.

The curtains in the throne room were still burning when Norella finally appeared before her. The acrid smell of smoke mingled with the opulent scent of incense, creating a disorientating blend. Norella's heart pounded, each step echoing ominously in the vast, dimly lit room as she made her way toward her Queen. She could feel the heat from the flames on her skin, adding to her growing unease. Uncertain about what the Queen would want from her exactly, she kept her eyes lowered, avoiding her gaze.

'You know, when my mother named Hesta as her heir, despite my obvious power, I didn't act out like this.' Isadora gestured to the missing skulls above her as she sat with her legs draped over the arm of the throne. A glass of what Norella only assumed was wine laced with herbs was dangling in her fingers near the floor.

'I understand, you must be furious with my sister.' Norella knelt before her Queen. 'I am disgraced by what she has done.'

'Yet'—Isadora swirled her glass around—'you still call her *sister*.'

'A bad habit,' Norella said slowly. 'Elsbeth is nothing but a traitor to our covens. She and whoever helped her.'

'Oh, I know who it was that helped her.' Isadora almost seemed delighted as she continued. 'The only other coven leader who hasn't appeared at any meetings. Even her coven cannot tell me where she is.'

Norella knew who she meant without her having to say. Erikah had been absent since the declaration of war against the Southern Mortal Realm. It had taken Norella a few days to realise it was more than a coincidence that both her sister and Erikah had disappeared simultaneously. Considering how angry Isadora was, Norella was glad she had kept quiet about seeing Alanah with them. Brielle knew they would need the old witch's healing abilities soon.

'Erikah,' the Queen turned her head to look at Norella at last. 'Your lover has also betrayed us.'

Norella did her best to keep her face neutral. Over the past days, she had tried to wipe Erikah from her mind, with little success. Their last moments together replayed in her mind over and over until she wanted to claw her own brain out to end the torment. She had no idea where the pair were going, nor why they did what they did, apart from Elsbeth harbouring an intense hatred for their aunt after their mother's death. She attempted to mask the turmoil that raged within her as her stomach twisted into knots.

Isadora took a sip from her glass. 'You will not be going south with the rest of the covens.'

'What would you have me do instead? Elsbeth's coven are still adjusting—'

'Imogen's coven,' Isadora casually corrected her, 'will be heading south ahead of us to scope the area. I want *you* to hunt down the pair who betrayed me – betrayed *us*.'

'I have a few select witches from my coven I can trust to—'

'No.' Isadora cut her off and sat upright, wine sloshing over the edge of the cup. 'You will go alone. You will bring only their heads back to me. I require new throne adornments and have no use for chit-chat with either of them.'

'You want me to kill Erikah,' Norella whispered. 'And Elsbeth.'

'Unless I have reason to doubt your loyalty, also?' Isadora leaned forward, her eyes glowing.

'Of course not.' Norella stood. 'My Queen.'

'Good, I'm sure you can have yourself packed and ready to leave by sunset.' Isadora waved her hand in dismissal.

'Yes, my Queen.' Norella bowed before making her way to the door.

'Oh, and Norella,' Isadora called as the servants pulled the doors open, 'don't bother returning if you don't have their heads. I'll assume they aren't dead if you do.'

Norella gave her a slight nod before she slipped through the barely open doors and disappeared toward her chambers. The hallway was dimly lit, with shadows stretching along the walls, whispering secrets of the past. Only once in her chamber did she pause, lingering on what to do next. She would pack light, only the essentials for spells and food. Her hands moved quickly, gathering vials of potions, herbs, and a small, worn book of incantations. She'd decide on her weapons later, not that she was sure she'd even be able to use them. The thought of using them on Erikah ... on her *sister*.

She sat on her bed for a long moment after having packed, contemplating what her sister and Erikah had allegedly done. There had been a time, before Isadora was Queen, that she and her sister would share everything with one another. Now, it was like they were from different worlds. She sighed as her eyes drifted to her mirror. Different worlds, but the same blood ran through their veins. Now she had been asked – no, she had been ordered – by her Queen to destroy that bond for good.

A piece of parchment caught her eye; it poked out from behind the corner of her mirror, its edges slightly crumpled. She leaned toward the dresser and picked it up, the paper rustling softly in her hand. Her name was scrawled across the front in Elsbeth's neat handwriting. A cold realisation washed over her. She planned this. Elsbeth had planned to leave without a word to Norella, without a word to anyone.

Rage suddenly boiled inside her as she tossed the letter back down, unopened. The parchment fluttered to the floor, curling as if recoiling from her fury. To hell with her note, and to hell with whatever bond Norella thought they might have still shared. Isadora was right. Elsbeth and Erikah were both traitors to the covens. They had humiliated Norella and disgraced their families by going against the Queen. The thought burned in her mind, the betrayal cutting deeper with each passing moment. Her hands clenched into fists, her nails digging into her palms as she fought to contain the tempest of emotions swirling within her.

She would do as Isadora demanded. She would hunt them down and return with their heads as a way to show the Queen and the covens that she was loyal to the crown, that she was not to be underestimated or associated with the traitors.

CHAPTER FORTY-TWO

Wandering within, The Timeless Fields

+ ELSBETH +

THE TIMELESS FIELDS were a living tapestry of colour and motion, forever changing, yet constant in their beauty. As the two lone witches wandered their way through the vast fields, vibrant hues of wildflowers painted the landscape. Herds of large deer moved gracefully in the distance, their russet coats glinting in the sunlight. A chorus of sounds swirled around them – the rustle of leaves, the distant call of birds, and the whispering wind weaving through the tall grasses. It was a place so teeming with life and magic that it was clear why the fae kept the lands so fiercely guarded from the rest of Emodorea.

Since they had left the Tretara Range, Elsbeth and Erikah had travelled the realm for almost three full days, with no sign of any fae. They came upon plenty of villages and farms, yet these places, with their cracked walls and empty streets, bore the eerie silence of abandonment. The air was thick with the scent of desolation; dry wells and barren fields offered no respite. Not a single hint of fae magic flickered in these desolate lands. The promise of the magnificent city of Osteria still eluded them, like a mirage on the horizon. Their journey felt increasingly like a quest through a forgotten land, untouched by time yet marked by the echoes of its former inhabitants.

'I would have thought,' Erikah said as the pair stopped for lunch under an old pine tree, 'that someone would have found us by now. Aren't the fae meant to find travellers before they get too far into the land?'

'As far as I can tell,' Elsbeth replied, unrolling the map that Odessa had given her, 'we have almost covered half of the realm.'

'Exactly.' Erikah stuffed some berries into her mouth, savouring the sweet taste. 'So why haven't we been stopped yet?'

Elsbeth thought for a moment as she etched their newest spot onto the parchment. 'Perhaps, with the war Isadora is starting, they have moved on?'

'To where?' Erikah asked, gesturing over the map.

'Well, no one really knows much about the fae,' Elsbeth replied as she accepted the water skin Erikah handed her. 'I mean, they border the Northern Sea. They could have a whole fleet of ships, for all we know.'

'They have been in The Timeless Fields since the gods were here.' Erikah leaned back against the tree and closed her eyes. 'I really can't see them packing up and leaving because of a little war.'

Elsbeth's scoff cut through the quiet. The word 'little' seemed laughable, a far cry from the enormity they both knew Isadora was capable of. Her mind raced with the possibilities of Isadora's grand machinations – plans that would likely ripple through every realm. As she swallowed the fear rising in her throat with another mouthful of cold water, she clung to the fragile hope that she was wrong. That Raynor and his kin hadn't abandoned Emodorea just to avoid a brewing clash with the witches. The thought of conflict ate at her insides, an unwelcome spectre.

'Well,' she said, 'we know that not all of them have left. Isadora has her shifter-fae that have always been under her command. Surely, they would have mentioned it if their kin had decided to leave?'

The shifter-fae, a unique and often ostracised group, had long pledged their allegiance to Isadora. Elsbeth had seen them around the keep frequently enough over the past century to know what and who they were. They chose to live among the witches, rejecting the opulence of the royal court for a life of service and relative freedom. These fae possessed the rare ability to change their forms, a gift they used to aid Isadora. Their dual existence in the shadows of both Emodorea and Wynlara made them equally feared and pitied by the other fae.

'Perhaps they have been cast out by their kin for joining with the witches, even before any talk of war was present,' Erikah offered. 'It wouldn't surprise anyone that the fae would listen to their Queen and discard their kin if she asked.'

Elsbeth knew Erikah was most likely correct. The fae, one of the oldest races of Emodorea, leaving because of a potential war was absurd. They would never give up their land that easily, not without good reason, anyway.

'Elsbeth.' Erikah opened one eye to stare at her friend.

'Mmm?' Elsbeth answered, not looking up from her map drawing. 'What is it?'

'Do you hear that?' Erikah's voice was barely more than a breath as she slowly sat up, eyes scanning the horizon behind Elsbeth.

'No,' Elsbeth replied, her brow furrowing as she tried to refocus on the map. 'I don't hear anything.'

'Exactly,' Erikah whispered, a chill creeping into her voice.

Elsbeth stilled watching her friend stand, before she slowly folded her map and placed it back in the satchel. She rose to her feet, mirroring Erikah's caution. Moments ago, the world around them had been full of bird songs and animals calling to one another in the distance. Now, an eerie silence had descended, like the world itself was holding its breath. The two witches, despite their training as hunters, had become so lulled by their journey that they hadn't noticed the subtle shift. Now, every instinct screamed that something was wrong.

'Something's watching us,' Elsbeth said under her breath as she sidled closer to Erikah. With practised ease, both witches drew their small blades from their belts, the familiar weight a comfort in their hands. This would be the second time this month that they had been caught off guard, a thought that made Elsbeth's grip tighten around her weapon. She knew Erikah was thinking the same thing. All the leisurely wandering had made them soft, and Elsbeth mentally cursed the complacency that had settled in. She scanned the silent landscape, back pressed to Erikah's as she did the same, ready for whatever stalked them.

'You're trespassing ... *witches*,' a deep voice spoke to them from the trees. 'We've been watching you.'

Erikah and Elsbeth exchanged glances. The realisation hit Elsbeth like a cold wave – how had they not sensed the follower? The voice, as yet unseen, had pierced their guard, a chilling reminder of the dangers lurking in even the most serene of places.

'We're looking for Prince Raynor,' Elsbeth said.

'Why would witches be seeking our Prince?' The voice was sharp, higher pitched than the first, heavy with accusation and suspicion. A shadow detached itself from the gnarled bark of a tree, morphing into the form of a fae woman. Her skin, an eerie grey that blended seamlessly with the bark, seemed to shimmer in the sunlight that filtered through the leaves. 'It sounds like a trap to ensure our forces join your war.'

Elsbeth and Erikah stood their ground, blades at the ready, knowing that their intentions were under severe scrutiny.

'We are not a part of the war,' Erikah spat. 'Isadora is no Queen of ours.'

'I find it hard to believe the daughter of Hesta has abandoned her kin.' A male, the one who had spoken first, seemed to materialise from the very air, his half-shadow form flickering in and out of focus like a waning candle. His presence, neither fully seen nor concealed, made Erikah's lip curl in disdain. She had made it known she had never trusted the fae's sly allusions and theatrics, and Elsbeth knew this encounter only cemented her distaste. The air crackled as the witches and fae faced off, each side wary of the other's next move.

'It's true,' Elsbeth said. 'I am Elsbeth Wraithe. Raynor knows who I am. If you could take us to him, I'm sure he'll—'

'You would do well to not give us orders in our land,' the female said.

'Sorry if I spoke out of turn.' Elsbeth dipped her head apologetically. 'But Raynor must see me.'

'Our Prince,' the male interjected as his form solidified, standing a head taller than both the witches, 'doesn't have to do anything.'

'We should kill you both here,' the female cursed. 'Two fewer witches in the war to come.'

'A war we aren't to fight in,' the male replied. The female bowed her head in silence, though not before allowing a low growl to pass her lips.

Erikah matched the other female's growl with a low one of her own. Elsbeth felt her shift behind her as she moved to stay between Elsbeth and the fae who eye'd them with so much hatred.

'We will take you back with us.' Elsbeth felt a chill as the male's eyes roamed over her, his cold grey gaze making her feel exposed and vulnerable.

'Thank you.' Elsbeth tried to maintain her composure, bending slowly to gather her things. But the male's sharp retort shattered any pretence of civility.

'You misunderstand, witch,' the male said. 'We will take you with us as prisoners. You shall go before the council, and they shall decide what will happen to you.'

Elsbeth sensed Erikah's cautious question as her friend turned her eyes upon the male.

'Is Raynor part of the council?' Erikah asked, eyes darting around as three more fae males appeared from the trees, all the same grey skin tone as the woman. The forest, which had once felt like a sanctuary, now seemed like a trap, closing in around them.

'*Prince* Raynor will only be called if the council deems you to be truthful in what you have told us,' the male replied. 'Cassida, bind them, will you?'

Elsbeth watched as the female stepped toward them, her long white hair flowing like a ghostly veil. The fae's movements were almost graceful as she bent forward to tie their hands together. Elsbeth, feeling the weight of the situation, allowed her hands to be bound without resistance. She knew any struggle would be futile and might only make things worse.

Erikah however, was not as resigned. Elsbeth could feel the tension radiating from her friend. Erikah's eyes blazed with defiance as she cursed at the fae, her voice filled with venom.

'Get your hands off me!' She shoved the taller woman away with surprising force. The fae, Cassida, stumbled back, her expression hot with anger. 'I'll send you to Krah before you put your filthy fae hands on me!'

Erikah's words hung in the air, a bold challenge met with an icy stare from the other female. Elsbeth admired Erikah's courage, but feared the outcome of such defiance.

'Erikah, please,' Elsbeth begged as Erikah drew her other knife from her side. 'I need to find Raynor. We need to go with them.'

'I didn't come with you to escape one captor only to be stuck with another,' Erikah replied as she bared her teeth at the fae, her sharpened incisors making her seem feral in comparison.

'If you do not allow us to bind you, you are free to head back to your forest,' the male spoke again.

'They are in our territory, Bayal,' Cassida hissed at him. 'It is not for them to decide whether they can leave or not.'

'We already have one war bearing down upon us,' Bayal replied. 'I do not wish to have another reason for their Queen to head to our lands.'

The others remained silent as they considered his words and waited for Cassida to respond.

'Erikah,' Elsbeth said quietly as she reached her bound hands toward her sister witch. 'I know Raynor won't let anything happen to us. I need to find him.'

'I can't be kept in chains while I wait for them to tell me I'm going to be killed,' Erikah whispered back to Elsbeth, an odd fear in her eyes.

'It is only while we travel to Osteria,' Bayal said as he took the rope from Cassida. 'It will not be for more than an hour or so of walking. Once we are there, you will be given a room to wait in while the council meets. I do not wish to fight you, witch.'

'See?' Elsbeth offered. 'It won't be that bad. Raynor will come and talk to us – I promise you.'

Erikah looked at the fae around them before looking back at Elsbeth.

'Well, I suppose it is a compliment that five of them have to chain us both for a short walk.'

Elsbeth's worried face softened, knowing it was the best she was going to get from Erikah. She could see why her sister had loved her.

Cassida hissed in annoyance as Bayal gently wrapped Erikah's wrists in the same rope tied to Elsbeth.

'This way,' he said as the others began moving into the trees.

'Aren't you worried that we will know how to find your city again?' Erikah asked.

'You won't remember how to get there,' Bayal replied. 'That's part of its charm.'

The ground beneath Elsbeth's feet was unforgivingly cold and damp, her feet sinking slightly with each step into the soft earth. The pine forest around them was dense, the tall trees casting long, eerie shadows as the group made their way through. The further they walked to the west, following the sun as it began its descent in the sky, the more the scent of sea salt filled her nose. When mingled with the pine needles, it created an intoxicating blend that clung to her clothes and reminded her of Raynor.

Elsbeth's senses were on high alert, the smells sharp and almost overwhelming. She could feel the cool, salty breeze against her skin, hinting at how close they must be to the western ocean. Waves crashing against rocks far off in the distance could be heard intermittently as they wove their way through the trees, the silence among them broken only by the occasional snap of a twig underfoot. Cassida kept a firm grip on their bindings, her touch cold and unyielding.

Darkness enveloped the group, the dense canopy of intertwined branches above blocking out any remaining light from the setting sun. The fae moved effortlessly through the underbrush, their steps soundless, as if they were an extension of the forest itself. Elsbeth found herself struggling to keep up as her mind drifted to another forest, a place that had always been home. The memory of its mighty oak trees, their ancient power resonating through her, tugged at her heart. The mark on the back of her neck tingled, a constant reminder that Brielle would always, always be with her, regardless of where she was in Emodorea – and, she hoped, any other world.

The pine trees soon disappeared, replaced by tall, rock walls to one side and a sheer drop to craggy rocks below on the other. Every sound seemed amplified, the howling wind, the distant caw of a seabird, the faint, rhythmic crashing of the waves.

Erikah and Elsbeth eyed each other warily as they were ushered behind one another, their faces pressed flat against the cliff face. Elsbeth could feel the biting wind whipping through her hair as it threatened to suck her off the edge. She kept her vision fixed on the fae in front of her, attempting to steady her breathing. Erikah, just behind her, muttered curses under her breath, her grip on the rock wall as fierce as it could be with her bound hands. As they rounded the bend, Elsbeth spotted the dark mouth of a cave ahead, an ominous gash against the sheer stone.

'Where are we?' Erikah called over the noise, running her hands over the cold, damp wall as they disappeared into the darkened cave on the cliff side.

'Heading under The Timeless Fields,' Bayal replied.

'Under?' Elsbeth asked in wonder as she took in the small passageway they were in.

'That's part of the gift that Zadea blessed us with when she created our realm,' he replied. 'Osteria will never be found by those not trusted by our kin. This is just the entrance, we have a little ways to go before we reach the city.'

'I never pictured the fae living underground,' Erikah mused to no one in particular as they continued walking.

'It is the first time Osteria has moved under the earth,' Cassida replied, clear irritation in her voice. 'We fae were not made for enclosed spaces.'

'Osteria moves?' Erikah raised an eyebrow. 'Fascinating.'

'When Zadea created our race and gifted us her kingdom of Osteria,' Bayal continued, 'it was enchanted to move around The Timeless Fields. So it will appear in different areas for different seasons. Or, in this case, the safest spot from a threat.'

'That's amazing,' Elsbeth replied.

'That'—Cassida glared at Bayal—'is something only the fae should know.'

'Perhaps,' Bayal said as they came to an opening. 'Though, is it not better for Zadea's knowledge to be shared? This is *her* Osteria, after all.'

Cassida grunted in response as she fell back from Bayal and the two witches to speak with the others.

CHAPTER FORTY-THREE

Osteria, The Timeless Fields

+ ELSBETH +

THEY HAD TRUDGED ALONG in moderate silence as the two witches became lost within the underground passages. It wasn't until they could hear the thundering sound of water and a soft light appeared up ahead that they realised they had finally reached the city. As the fae ushered them from the tunnel, Elsbeth was taken aback by the view. The towers of Osteria rose majestically before them, their pristine white marble was almost other-worldly in the dim light. Each tower was a marvel of architecture, reaching skyward with an elegance that seemed to defy gravity. The smooth, polished surfaces caught what little light there was, creating an ethereal glow that bathed the surroundings in a soft luminescence.

A long, narrow bridge stretched across a crystal-clear river, the water so transparent that every pebble at the bottom sparkled as if encrusted with jewels. The gentle bubbling of the water over the smooth stones created a soothing, melodic sound that filled the air. The river itself was framed by lush, green banks and bell-shaped blue and white flowers that Elsbeth had never seen before. Each step across the bridge felt like a journey into another world, one where beauty and danger were inextricably intertwined.

The streets they walked through were paved with smooth marble, their surfaces worn by countless footsteps yet still gleaming as if freshly washed. Lush, blooming flowers, similar to those on the riverbank, lined the pathways, their strange scents threatening to make Elsbeth's nose itch. The architecture was nothing short of breathtaking – delicate spires, intricately carved facades, and graceful arches.

Making their way through the gates, Elsbeth and Erikah were greeted by hundreds of fae wandering the streets. The fabric of their elegant clothing was unlike anything Elsbeth had ever seen, apart from on Raynor. It flowed like liquid silver and gold, catching the light in a way that was almost mesmerising.

There were no beggars here, none of the destitution so common in the mortal cities she had been to. Every fae they passed was adorned in finery, their attire a show of the wealth and craftsmanship of Osteria. The air was filled with the murmur of soft conversation and the faint, melodious sounds of fae music drifting from the open windows.

The fae were taller than witches, and beautiful to look at. Elsbeth wasn't sure she had seen so many skin colours before, ranging from the same dark-grey shade as Cassida to pale blue, like the sky after a storm. Almost all had shockingly white hair, save a few that seemed to have darker shades mixed in. Elsbeth wondered if they were sons and daughters of two races.

'We're heading to the centre tower,' Bayal told them as they passed by more shops.

'I never imagined Osteria would be this big,' Elsbeth said, openly marvelling. 'I mean, Raynor spoke of how vast his realm was, but I never pictured this.' She gestured around her the best she could with her bound hands.

'It is home to almost all our kin now that it has moved underground.' Bayal smiled and nodded to a few of the fae they passed by with similar hued skin to his – a soft blue that almost seemed transparent.

'Our Prince shouldn't speak of such things with a witch,' Cassida all but spat at Elsbeth, the words, practically seething through her clenched teeth. Her gaze snapped to Bayal, icy and unforgiving. 'Neither should you, Bayal.'

'Mind your tongue, Cassida,' Bayal replied. 'I know you can smell him on her, just as I can.'

Erikah raised her eyebrows. 'You can smell Raynor even though it has been three months since he saw her?'

'Yes, and that filth in her stomach is—' Cassida's eyes burned as Bayal shot her a look that silenced her.

Erikah and Elsbeth exchanged wary glances with one another, the former moving slightly closer, putting herself between Cassida and her friend.

They'd made their way through the winding streets with their white marble roads and busy shops. Everything in the city appeared to be made of marble. The towers, the streets, and the shops they passed. Osteria was elegant, clean, and so bright for being so far underground.

The streets were lined with poles, each holding a blue flame. Bayal explained that these flames, a gift from Zadea, were eternal, never to be extinguished. As they approached the centre tower, the tallest and most imposing structure in the city, Elsbeth's heart pounded in her chest. They were shuffled inside as two guards stepped forward from behind a desk to take the chains from Cassida.

'These two were caught wandering around up top,' Cassida spoke first. 'Take them to a cell while we speak with the council.'

'What do you mean?' Erikah's anger flared, her eyes narrowing into fierce slits. 'Don't we get to speak to the council?'

'No,' Cassida smiled. 'The council is no place for witches. You will wait until a decision is made and be called forth for the sentencing.'

'You told us we would speak to the council!' Erikah's voice rose in fury. Her fists clenched at her sides, trembling with barely contained rage. She took a step forward, challenging anyone to deny her.

Bayal eyed Cassida warily. 'I'll speak on your behalf. I'll see if they will allow you to plead your case.'

'And what of Raynor?' Elsbeth asked, hands shaking as she was pulled along behind the guards. Before Bayal could reply, the pair were dragged around the corner and led down the stairs.

'I knew it was a bad idea to let them bring us here,' Erikah grumbled, rubbing her wrists. She slumped onto the stone bench in their cell – shockingly the only thing they'd come across not made of marble.

'It's the closest we've come to Raynor since leaving Brielle,' Elsbeth replied. 'I wasn't about to say no and keep wandering around in hopes that he would appear.'

'I'm sorry,' Erikah said. 'I just didn't think we'd end up stuck *here*.' She gestured around at the dimly lit area. They were surrounded by stone walls and had been walked further down into the earth than they thought was possible.

'It's freezing,' Elsbeth said as she sat down next to Erikah on the bench. Both witches shivered as they leaned into one another for warmth.

'How long do you think they'll leave us down here?' Erikah asked after a moment.

'If Cassida has her way, I'd say forever.' Elsbeth half laughed.

'She was rather brazen toward us, wasn't she?' Erikah sighed as she undid one of her braids. 'What a bitch.'

'More so toward me, I think.' Elsbeth leaned back against the cold wall.

'Maybe she has a thing for Raynor. I mean, she did seem annoyed when Bayal mentioned they could smell him on you.'

'Maybe it's a territorial thing. Fae often dislike when their kin mingle with others.'

'Perhaps she's his ex.' Erikah untied both her braids, letting her strawberry-blonde hair fall over her shoulders. She rubbed her scalp, relaxing from the tightness of the last few days.

The thought annoyed Elsbeth, even though she knew that there was a good chance Raynor had been with Cassida. He was a few hundred years older than she was, and they had only been seeing each other for a little while in terms of their age.

'Maybe,' she said at last, closing her eyes. 'I guess we will find out when they call us up for the sentencing, as Bayal said.'

'It's a pity Cassida is a bitch,' Erikah leaned back and closed her eyes too. 'She's easy to look at, for a fae.'

'Easier to look at than Norella?' Elsbeth didn't like to pry, but she couldn't help but ask.

'Honestly'—Erikah laughed—'how do I answer that when she's your identical twin?'

'We're twins,' Elsbeth agreed with a sigh, 'yet I had no idea about your relationship – and you have been together for how long?'

'*Were* together.' Erikah crossed her arms. 'And a little while.'

'Still.' Elsbeth tried to smile. 'How come she didn't tell me?'

'At the start, she was interested in the secrecy – though I'm sure most of my coven worked things out when she shared my tent on her visits.'

'Well, I heard no rumours. Your coven did well to keep quiet if they knew.'

'They know gossip isn't worth the punishment they'd receive.' Erikah smirked.

Elsbeth smiled and gave her friend a little nudge with her shoulder. 'Do you think it's okay to sleep?'

'I can't imagine them doing anything until the council has voted. The fae might be all high and mighty, but they seem to behave pretty fairly.' Erikah patted Elsbeth's knee reassuringly. 'Get some rest.'

CHAPTER FORTY-FOUR

Osteria, The Timeless Fields

+ ELSBETH +

'Elsbeth.' A whisper so quiet she was sure she was dreaming.

'Elsbeth.' Again, a little louder this time. She stirred, realising how deeply she had been sleeping. Perhaps it was Erikah trying to rouse her from her sleep. She hadn't noticed how tired she was. It was likely the pregnancy beginning to wear on her, or that they had been wandering with little sleep since the morning before last.

Slowly, her eyes fluttered open. The blue flame outside the cell flickered steadily, eerie shadows spaying out from it. Erikah's head was slumped on her shoulder; the witch was oblivious to the whisper that slipped its way through the iron bars. Her long strawberry-blonde hair was soft against Elsbeth's cheek, comforting in a way.

Through the iron bars, a whisper snaked its way into the cell, faint but unmistakable.

'Elsbeth, what are you doing here?' Elsbeth's heart skipped a beat as she strained to catch the words.

Her blue eyes glowed in the dark, the flecks of red swirling around as her power surged, crackling beneath her skin like the sea amidst a storm as she searched for the voice. Her gaze landed on a figure, his striking white hair standing out against the dark stone of the cell, and her face lit with hope.

'Raynor,' Elsbeth whispered as she gently pushed Erikah's head off her shoulder and all but ran to the door of the cell. His hand reached through the gap, cupping her chin tenderly. His green eyes glistened as he brought her lips to his, their kiss passionate despite the tiny space between the bars.

'I was hoping you would find us,' she murmured against his lips.

He glanced over her shoulder at the still sleeping witch and raised his eyebrow in question.

'It's a long story.' Elsbeth smiled softly. 'We have much to discuss.'

'Bayal told me that you were here – looking for me,' he replied as his other hand moved to hold hers, his warm fingers lacing through her cold ones. 'The council's meeting did not go well.'

'What do you mean?'

'They feel that with the impending war, having witches in our city is too risky,' Raynor replied.

'So, they're casting us out?' Elsbeth asked, her hands shaking a little at the thought of leaving without him. 'They didn't even let us speak.'

'No,' Raynor said softly, 'they intend to keep you here until they can decide whether ... '

'Decide what?' Elsbeth pressed.

Raynor gave her a grim look. 'They're debating whether to kill you as a message to Isadora or to simply keep you imprisoned.'

Elsbeth groaned, the sound echoing softly in the confined space. She pressed her forehead against the cold bars of the cell, feeling the chill seep into her skin.

'Why did you come here, Elle?'

'We're leaving Emodorea,' she replied, smiling softly at his nickname for her. 'There are some things I need to tell you – I want you to come with me, with us.'

'Elle,' Raynor whispered, his voice thick with sorrow and longing. 'I'm the heir to the throne. I can't abandon my people with this war coming.'

His words were like a dagger to her heart. She saw the turmoil in his eyes, the weight of his duty smothering him as her own had once done. His hand trembled as it reached to cup her face again, his touch both tender and desperate. She could see the battle in his eyes, the love they shared against the responsibilities he felt he could not forsake.

'Sir.' Bayal appeared at his shoulder. 'We haven't got much time left.'

'Please don't leave us here,' Elsbeth said fiercely. 'You have to get us out, even if you can't come with us.'

'Why do you want to leave?' Raynor asked. 'Your aunt is the Queen. You would be safe with her.'

'No, you don't understand,' Elsbeth replied, grabbing his hand. 'We aren't safe near her.'

Her eyes bore into his, pleading silently for him to understand. She placed his hand against her stomach, the unspoken truth passing between them.

'It's ... ' Raynor's voice trailed off, his gaze shifting from Elsbeth to Bayal, then back to Elsbeth, the realisation dawning in his eyes, the connection forming as he sensed the life growing within her. 'It's mine?'

'Of course, it's yours,' Erikah said roughly from where she had roused on the bench. 'Do you think she'd have gone to this much trouble if it wasn't?'

'But we haven't seen each other in months.' Raynor stared at the witch in the back of the cell.

'Three, to be exact.' Elsbeth smiled, more nervous now than she had been the entire trip.

'I don't understand.' Raynor's brow furrowed. 'Why would being pregnant mean you have to leave your coven?'

'A child born from a bloodline of yours and Elsbeth's would be powerful,' Erikah said carefully as she eyed Bayal. 'Isadora would not want such a child brought into the world – especially one with a claim to the throne. It could mean the end of her reign. It could change the tide of the war.'

'It could make your mother decide to fight against the witches instead of choosing to hide away,' Bayal added.

'I don't want my child to be the cause or cure of anything,' Elsbeth replied firmly. The future she envisioned for their child was one free from such burdens, a life where they could just be themselves, without the weight of destiny on their shoulders. 'I won't be letting Isadora kill her, or your mother use her in a play for power.'

'Her,' Raynor whispered, his hand lingering on Elsbeth's rounding belly. 'Yes, I can feel her power.'

'Please,' Bayal urged, 'we can't wait much longer before the shift changes. If Cassida finds you here, she will alert the others.'

'We have a way out.' Erikah joined Elsbeth near the door. 'A way to keep the three of you safe from Isadora.'

'Yes,' Raynor replied as his eyes found Elsbeth's at last. 'Yes.'

Raynor stepped aside, giving Bayal room to work. With swift, deft movements, Bayal picked the lock, the click of the mechanism echoing through the cell. As soon as the door swung open, Elsbeth didn't hesitate. She launched herself into Raynor's arms, sighing as she clung to him.

'I missed you.' She kissed him deeply, pouring all her relief and longing into that moment, completely ignoring the presence of Bayal and Erikah.

'I wanted to come back and see you.' Raynor brushed her hair from her face. 'My mother has banned anyone leaving the realm. There was no chance of me breaking through it.'

'I understand,' Elsbeth said, and pressed her forehead against his.

'Alright, you two,' Erikah cut in. 'Can we get moving, please?'

'Moving to where?' Cassida was standing at the base of the stone stairs, watching as Raynor slowly let go of Elsbeth.

'Cassida.' Raynor's voice was stern as he stepped between the newcomer and the rest of the group.

'I can't believe you.' She crossed her arms, all but invisible next to the stone except for her eyes and hair. 'Why are you choosing that *thing* over your people?'

Elsbeth felt Raynor tense, his fingers tightening around hers. She knew the stigma the Fae Queen and his people would place on a child born from their union – no matter the power it possessed – viewing it as a taint on the royal bloodline. He had broken tradition in his affair with Elsbeth; yet he had continued to see her whenever he could, regardless of the risks.

'That *thing*'—Raynor spoke softly—'is my child.'

'That impurity,' Cassida spat, 'could end this war if you handed it over to your mother.'

'Careful,' Erikah warned, teeth bared as she, stepped forward beside Raynor, both of them now blocking Elsbeth from view.

'You don't scare me, baby witch,' Cassida snarled at Erikah. 'I can feel your power. It will be of little use to you down here.'

The red specks in Erikah's eyes began to glow as she brought her hand to the wall beside her. Elsbeth knew that Erikah would be able to feel the water bubbling beneath its surface, just as she could. It was cold and powerful, calling to them, begging them to set it free. Elsbeth's skin prickled with the anticipation of blood.

'*Neraqua*,' Erikah whispered as she drew her hand away, the water pouring from the wall and folding itself around the witch's forearm. It flowed over her hand and into the form of a whip, an extension of herself. The water-whip writhed excitedly, as if it sensed the fae flesh within reach.

'That's a neat trick,' Cassida said casually. 'I didn't know you witches could do that.'

'Not a lot of us can.' Elsbeth gently put her hand on Erikah's shoulder from behind. 'We don't need to fight.'

'I don't care much for your friend,' Cassida said to Elsbeth over Erikah. 'You, though, daughter of Hesta, could be useful to us.'

'I've told you once,' Raynor's voice was like ice, 'don't make me tell you again.'

'Is this why you refuse to seal our courtship?' Cassida gestured toward Elsbeth. 'Because you would rather play happy families with a witch?'

'Elsbeth and I have been seeing each other for over a century,' Raynor replied. 'It's not as if you didn't know that before agreeing to my mother's proposal.'

'Oh, I knew.' Cassida took a step toward them, away from the wall. 'I just assumed it was a rebellion against your mother. I figured if I were declared yours, that you would stop the nonsense and join with me.'

'You two are betrothed?' Elsbeth looked between them.

'Why wouldn't either of you have said that when you found us above?' Erikah asked, looking between Cassida and Bayal.

'It wasn't my place,' Bayal replied. 'I answer to Raynor. I was asked not to speak of it.'

'We aren't "betrothed", as you say.' Cassida looked at Raynor, a smirk on her lips. 'We are wed. He just refuses to mate with me to seal our fate.'

'You're married!' Elsbeth stepped away from Raynor. Her hands shook as she braced herself on the cold wall, mouth dry with unease. 'Is that why you have stayed away for so many moons? Because ... you have a wife?'

'No, I told you, my mother banned us from leaving the realm,' Raynor pleaded as he reached for her hand again. 'Believe me, if Cassida didn't follow me everywhere, I would have come back to you in an instant.'

'You are the *Prince*.' Erikah's voice was cold. 'Why do you need your mother's permission?'

'It's not as simple as that. I am the only heir to her throne. I am the last of the pureblood Ashshades. If I abandon my duty as the Prince, a lower family will step into my place. They would most likely dethrone my mother.'

'Which is why you should forget this filth.' Cassida flicked her hand at Elsbeth. 'My bloodline is as old as the Ashshade line. If we were to finally join, our offspring would be a force to be reckoned with.'

'I don't have time for this.' Elsbeth's mind swirled with a torrent of emotions – numbness, hurt, anger – all crashing together like storm-tossed waves. A sharp pain settled into a hollow ache in her chest. She shook her head at him, voice trembling. 'I'm leaving. It is your choice to come or not.'

'The only way you're leaving here is if I let you.' Cassida moved quicker than either witch could see, shoving Raynor aside as if he were nothing, and grabbed hold of Elsbeth's wrist.

'Cassida'—Bayal drew his sword—'think about what you are doing.'

'Think about what *I'm* doing?' Cassida laughed as she drew Elsbeth to her chest, towering over the blonde witch as she brought a dagger to her throat. 'You're the one who's helping a traitor to the Crown.'

'Cassida.' Raynor had drawn his own sword. 'Let Elsbeth go.'

'Or what?' Cassida replied, pulling the witch's head back to expose her throat. 'I've heard that witches are hard to kill. If I spill your blood here, will your spirit be reborn like the ancients, or will you simply be the walking dead?'

'We might be different from the ancient witches,' Elsbeth whispered, her throat flinching against the cold steel. 'We don't harbour a completely dark spirit as they did. You can kill me, but only gods' metal will end my life for good.'

'Now, where would the fun in that be?' Cassida whispered into Elsbeth's ear.

Elsbeth felt the cold water swallow her feet first, spreading over her leather pants and continuing up until she was completely submerged. The icy sensation sent a comforting shiver through her body. She felt Cassida pause as the water enveloped her as well before she shoved Elsbeth away, retreating to the wall and grasping at her throat. Elsbeth quickly moved to stand beside Erikah as the water around her seeped back into the earth. Cassida glared at them with a mix of shock and fury, still clutching at her throat and scratching at her mouth and nostrils where Erikah's water was slowly drowning her.

'I told you to be careful,' Erikah said, her pointed incisors glowing as she grinned. 'Do you have a death wish, or were you just born stupid?'

'You can't kill her.' Elsbeth put her hand on Erikah's as Raynor joined them.

'Why not?' Erikah glanced sideways at her. 'She was happy to kill you.'

'It will only add to the war,' Bayal answered as he watched Cassida struggle for breath, an ominous mime submerged in Erikah's swirling power.

'We'll put her in the cell,' Raynor suggested. 'She'll be there until the shift changes in a few hours – longer if no one thinks to check on you two.'

'It doesn't seem like a fair trade.' Erikah glowered before she flicked her hand. The water released Cassida and the fae dropped to the ground with a splash. She landed on her knees, coughing as she expelled any remaining water from her lungs. Erikah reached forward and grabbed her hair, ripping Cassida's head backwards and exposing the fae's face to hers.

'Under different circumstances, we could have enjoyed each other,' Erikah purred, her voice dripping with dark amusement. She ran a nail along Cassida's chin, the touch both threatening and intimate. 'Pity.'

Still gasping for breath, Cassida tore her head away from Erikah and spat at her. Quick as a flash, Erikah's hand slapped across Cassida's face, her sharpened nails slashing it open from ear to lip, and the fae collapsed onto the cold, damp ground. Erikah grinned as she ran her blood-soaked nails across her lips, her tongue darting out to taste the sweet, sticky crimson life-force.

CHAPTER FORTY-FIVE

Thornwell, Southern Mortal Realm

+ REID +

ELISAVET AND REID STOOD outside Gillian's old, run down house. It had taken a lot of convincing on Elisavet's behalf to convince the King to let them head to the Outer Ring. They had only been allowed to go if they took a patrol of guards with them. No one was sure how much the Outer Ring had changed, nor what might await them.

From what Reid could see, it didn't look like much had changed, though it was clear that no one had tended to the weeds pushing through the bricks on the front steps. Not that anyone ever 'tended' to them before; they were usually kept in check by Oscar when he nervously used to pull them out while the two of them sat outside together. Reid silently hoped that he'd open the door and find the boys running around, fighting one another for the last bit of bread – but he couldn't shake the unnerving feeling he had.

'Maybe you should stay here.' Reid nodded toward the guards that the King had insisted go with them. 'It might be safer if you're with them. We don't know what's in there.'

'No'—Elisavet grabbed his hand—'don't be silly. I'd be safer at the side of Kasin's chosen one than a few measly guards.'

Reid walked up the front stairs, Elisavet trailing behind, her fingers still interlocked with his. It was too quiet. Normally, Reid would have been able to hear the boys fighting, but today he could only hear the house creaking back and forth as he stood on the discoloured brick steps. The paint on the door had begun to peel, revealing layers of forgotten colours beneath.

'Something's not right.' Reid paused as he reached for the door handle, his heart hammering in his chest. The silence was heavy, almost suffocating.

'Are you sure we shouldn't get the guards to go in first?' Elisavet asked as she stepped back slightly, hesitation suddenly scrunching her pretty features. 'What if they're ... I mean, wouldn't you rather someone else find their bodies?'

Reid ignored her and pushed through the unlocked door, detaching her fingers from his as he disappeared into the dim entrance hall. Shadows clung to the corners of the room, only broken by faint shafts of light slipping through the cracks in the moth-eaten curtains. The once-vibrant wallpaper now a faded, peeling memory of its former self. He didn't bother to see if Elisavet and the guards were following him as he made his way into the living room. The smell of iron was heavy in the air, its tangy presence clinging to his nostrils and tongue. The room felt like a time capsule, filled with relics of a past life, now forgotten and left to gather dust. As he crossed to the stairs, the creaking floorboards echoed through the silent house. Bounding up them, his heartbeat grew louder in his ears with each step, the metal tang on his tongue growing more intense with every breath he took.

Smears of blood surrounded the frame of the door to the boys' room, as if something or someone had been dragged unwillingly inside. The crimson streaks stood out against the ageing paint, a chilling sight that made his stomach churn. Reid took a deep breath, trying to steady himself as he felt Kasin's calmness flow through him like a soothing balm. His fingers trembled as he reached for the doorknob.

I'm here, let's go in together.

'Reid, please don't, let's just go!' Elisavet was at the bottom of the stairs, a handkerchief of silver silk – woven from the web of the snakytes that roamed somewhere to the west – muffling her voice as she tried to filter the rich iron air through it.

'I thought you wanted to help me,' Reid called back. 'Why do you keep trying to stop me?'

What does she know? Kasin's voice drifted through his head.

'I'm not trying to stop you,' Elisavet all but whispered back. 'I just ... I don't think it's healthy for you to be the one looking for their bodies.'

'Bodies?' Reid called back, his voice full of scepticism.

'I mean the boys.' Elisavet coughed out.

Reid pushed the door and stepped inside the dark room. The god's blade at his side glowed, spreading its soft blue light over the bunk beds. Reid fell to his knees, relief flooding through him at the sight. The boys were all in their beds, seemingly sound asleep.

'It's okay!' He called down the stairs to Elisavet. 'They're all okay.'

Reid …

'Ivor, wake up. Couldn't you hear us downstairs?'

The boy didn't move. The only sound was Elisavet's heavy thudding as she raced up the rickety staircase.

'What do you mean they're okay?' She barged past Reid, reaching out a shaking hand, and grasped the bedsheet, tugging hard. The grey fabric fell away, coiling on the floor like a serpent, to reveal the boy's swollen blue body.

'Ivor!' Reid fell to the ground beside the boy. 'No, no, no.'

Reid, Kasin's cool voice washed over him. *I'm sorry.*

'I told you.' Elisavet put her hands on her hips. 'They're dead.'

'How?' Reid whispered. 'I don't understand.'

'How should I know?' Elisavet snapped, her voice tinged with frustration. She dropped the sheet back over the corpse, her hand trembling slightly. Disgust was etched across her face, her nose wrinkling as she took a step back, unable to tear her eyes away from the lifeless body.

Why was she so shocked when you said they were alive?

Reid's thoughts were a mess. The other boys were all in their beds, all covered with the same grey sheets that Ivor had been. He knew though, without needing to check, that the others would also be gone. Elisavet seemed annoyed at the idea of staying as she huffed and walked out of the room, mumbling something about not being able to be around the smell anymore. Kasin's words replayed over and over in Reid's mind as he sat on the dirty floor. What good was he as a protector if he couldn't even protect the boys?

But who killed them?

'Probably something like that creature I fought,' Reid replied, too tired to converse silently. 'All the guards are talking about the attacks.'

Do you really think one of those creatures killed them and then tucked them in for the night?

'Well …' Reid looked around. 'No … it's too clean for that, I guess.'

Reid sat next to Ivor for a few more minutes before moving to cover each of the boys with the sheets.

'I should bury them,' he whispered to himself.

Where?

'I don't know.' Reid shrugged. 'The garden isn't big enough.'

Perhaps the King would allow them to be buried in the temple's graveyard?

'I don't think the King will allow anything, considering he's just let them be murdered.' Reid fiddled with his cigarette tin. He popped the top open and pulled a poorly rolled cigarette out, placing it in his mouth before leaning against the wall. The feeling of the paper and tobacco on his tongue settled him slightly. Right now, he wished he had some of the herb that Erikah shared with him once or twice. He should have taken the small pouch when she offered it to him on his last visit.

Outside, he could hear the muffled voices of the Princess arguing with the guards. He wasn't able to make out what she was saying, but she was using her *I'm the King's niece* voice. The door downstairs opened and Reid could hear the clanging of metal and shuffling of feet on the stairs. He answered the knock on the door with an annoyed look.

'My Lord,' the young guard started, 'the Princess has requested we move the bodies for you.'

'No,' Reid replied.

'No, my Lord?'

'Where would she have them moved to?' Reid asked. 'There's seven of them.'

'She's asked us to take them to the forest,' the guard replied. 'We've got enough men to take one boy each.'

Convenient, Kasin remarked.

'Don't touch them.' Reid ordered as he stepped around the guard and bounded down the stairs.

'What do you think you're doing?' He asked Elisavet as he shielded his eyes from the bright sunlight.

'I thought you'd wish to bury them.'

'In the forest?' Reid demanded. 'With those things that possibly killed them?

Do we still honestly think this was a berserker-fae's doing?

Reid brushed off Kasin's words as he faced Elisavet.

'I was just trying to help.' Elisavet crossed her arms, her bottom lip pouting slightly. 'But, clearly, the help is unwanted.'

'No,' Reid faltered. He ran his fingers through his hair, the unlit cigarette a comfortable companion between his lips, a habit without a flame. 'Not unwanted, just … I don't want them buried in the forest.'

'We can burn them if you'd prefer?'

It's almost like she has a script.

'No, I mean, I want them to have proper burials. In Thornwell, not in Brielle's Forest.' Reid reached for Elisavet's hand but hesitated, pulling away just before his fingers brushed hers. She spoke again, her voice carrying an edge that made him pause.

'My uncle doesn't know we are here,' she whispered. 'We can't ask him to bury them at the temple without him finding out that I disobeyed him by bringing you out here.'

'You said he allowed it,' Reid replied. 'You said you spoke with him, and he said it was okay as long as we bought guards.'

Seven guards for seven bodies …

Not now, Reid cut Kasin off.

Elisavet's eyes fluttered as they found Reid's. Her face was red and blotchy as tears welled in her eyes.

Reid … Kasin's warning was squashed down as Reid's guilt for causing Elisavet to lie to her uncle consumed him.

'I'm sorry,' Reid replied, he reached a hand toward her. She took it and let him pull her close to him. He buried his face in her hair, salty tears threatening to overflow. 'We'll burn them. I won't have their bodies buried in the tainted soil when Thora could have their ashes instead.'

CHAPTER FORTY-SIX

Zadea's Pass, Sky Kingdom of Nonnelle

✦ NORELLA ✦

NORELLA HAD SPENT FIVE agonising days scouring the west border of the forest, her anxiety growing with each passing hour since she lost the scent near the Wandering River. The dread in the pit of her stomach gnawed at her, a constant reminder of what she had to do when she found them.

When she finally picked up Erikah's scent again, it was like a heady perfume – the sweet memories that came with it intoxicating her as it coated her senses. She paused, drawing a deep breath and savouring the delicate fragrance of wild roses from the desert – Erikah's favourite haunt. Her eyes fluttered closed for a moment, lost in the ecstasy of the memory.

She whispered a few words in her ancient tongue before slowly opening her eyes. A soft, rose-coloured glow led away from her, trailing off into the distant trees, the luminescent aura a beacon leading her straight toward Zadea's Mountain.

Part of her prayed to Brielle that Elsbeth wasn't with Erikah, that they had gone separate ways. Maybe Erikah was heading toward the uncharted wastes to the west. She'd often spoken of travelling, exploring whatever lay past the scorching desert. The other part of her wanted both of them to pay for the pain and torment they caused her in recent weeks. Elsbeth for betraying the coven and causing their sister witches to question Norella's motives; Erikah for abandoning her and the love they had shared for the past two centuries. Still, she was unsure if she would be able to complete the Queen's orders when she caught up to them.

Norella shrugged off the lingering feelings of love and lust, her hunter's heart hardening as she readied to face what was ahead of her. She had visited Zadea's Mountain base countless times, but had never ventured further than necessary. The area was mostly a hunting ground for her, and in the years before Erikah it had also been a place for her dalliances with certain fae females. Now, though, those memories felt distant and irrelevant.

As she climbed, the forest transformed into a tapestry of devotion. Each tree bore decorations and offerings to the Goddess of Knowledge, their presence a demonstration of the fae's deep reverence. These tokens, lovingly placed by the fae who still openly worshipped their deity, added a transcendent quality to the path ahead. Few races besides the witches showed such unabashed adoration, and the sight filled Norella with a strange sense of respect and nostalgia. The air was fragrant, the scent of the fresh flowers, herbs, and other offerings mingling together created a peaceful yet poignant atmosphere.

Norella was still unsure why Erikah and Elsbeth would be here, of all places. There was always the chance that they were just using it as a place to stop for a day or two before heading west. If it were her, she would have gone south and ventured off the continent to one of the lone islands in search of what lay beyond.

A soft laugh floated down the mountain – a sound usually reserved for her. The hair on her arms stood on end as a deeper chuckle soon followed it.

Norella froze, torn between curiosity and dread. The thought of seeing who Erikah was with sent a cold shiver through her. Erikah had always enjoyed the company of both male and female partners but, for two centuries, she had been only Norella's. The idea of Erikah with someone else, after all that time – all they had shared – made Norella's heart clench painfully. She hesitated, unsure if she was ready to face that possibility yet.

'I can't believe we have to go that far inside the mountain.' Erikah's voice carried clearly through the air, a mix of frustration and resignation. Norella edged closer, her senses sharp. 'It's like being back inside that damn cell.'

'It has been many years since even us fae have travelled to Zadea's heart,' a male's voice responded coolly. Norella's eyes slanted with anger as she continued to listen to them from the cover of the trees. 'My mother forbade it after a group of High Court fae sacrificed themselves in the Goddess's honour.'

'Isn't that considered a sacred act among your kind?' Erikah asked as she peered inside.

'Yes,' the male replied, 'though not when they are the last of their line. They did so as an act of defiance against my mother.'

'Come on, the sooner we get down there, the sooner we can sort this out.' Elsbeth's voice rang from deeper within the cave. Her tone was urgent – perhaps she knew that Isadora would send someone after them.

Norella paused, taking a few moments to ensure the fae's sensitive hearing wouldn't pick up on her following them. The forest behind her was a silent witness as she cautiously stepped out of the tree line and into the cave's shadowy mouth.

The light from the entrance faded soon after they began the descent, the temperature growing hotter by the minute – not what Norella was expecting at all. She made a note to thank Brielle for the fact that she could see well enough in the dark. She was sure she would have fallen to her death more than once.

The path they followed clung precariously to the mountain's side, so narrow that even the nimble fae would only be able to walk single file. The ancient walkway, unused for centuries, crumbled in places, forcing Norella to cling to the wall to avoid falling. Each step was a calculated risk, the wooden beams supporting the walkway groaning under their weight.

Elsbeth and the others moved with determination, oblivious or indifferent to the dangers. Norella's heart pounded with frustration at how slow she was moving. The others' apparent disregard for safety felt reckless, almost like a death wish. She couldn't shake the nagging worry that one misstep could send her plummeting into the abyss below.

It took the better part of an hour to follow the trio down into the mountain. No one spoke much, not that Norella was listening if they were while she tried to keep her footing. The feel of solid ground beneath her feet was a soothing relief. She let out the breath she'd been holding and whispered a small prayer to Zadea for sparing her life in her domain. The treacherous descent had pushed her nerves to the limit.

'So, where do you think we need to go?' Elsbeth turned to the fae male. He was looking around, sniffing the air. Norella stepped behind a pillar as quietly as she could and held her breath once more, cursing her lack of caution. She hoped all the cobwebs, dust, and dirt that covered her was enough to mask her scent. 'Raynor?'

'I thought I smelled something,' Raynor replied as he put a hand on Elsbeth's shoulder. 'It sort of smelled like you, but different.'

Norella watched through a sliver between the pillars as Elsbeth and Erikah exchanged brief glances with one another, neither saying anything.

'Let's keep going,' Erikah said, moving toward the doorway at the end of the tunnel. 'Elsbeth is right – the sooner we get out of here, the better.'

Norella waited, longer this time than she had when they entered the cave on the surface. The fae had scented her, whether he realised it or not. Elsbeth and Erikah were with Prince Raynor, the only heir to the fae kingdom. Maybe if she returned with his head instead of the two witches', the Queen would forget Elsbeth and Erikah's treachery. Returning with the Fae Queen's son in chains would be an even more incredible feat than just his head – it would be the bargaining chip her Queen would need to control the fae. Norella grinned as a plan came together in her head.

CHAPTER FORTY-SEVEN

Zadea's Pass, Sky Kingdom of Nonnelle

✦ NORELLA ✦

AS SHE HALTED IN the shadows of a crumbled pillar, Norella's breath caught in her throat. Before her stood the trio – the two witch traitors and the Fae Prince. From the dimly lit cavern, she could only just make out the carvings along the walls. They had led her to a long-forgotten temple of Zadea.

At the centre of the trio hovered a shimmering orb of light, casting an eerie glow across their faces. The orb's light illuminated the cavern. Norella watched, fascinated, for a moment before realisation dawned. Only one of the oracles, who had lived thousands of years, could have told them about this place, but they were all now dead – skulls atop Isadora's throne. Skulls that had since been stolen.

Norella watched as Erikah grasped Elsbeth and Raynor's hands to form a small circle around the orb. Norella's freckle-faced ex-lover took the lead, her voice steady and powerful as she began chanting in their ancient witch language. The words flowed like a river, filled with old magic and forgotten power, and the light between them pulsed and shimmered in response.

'Elsbeth.' Norella's voice sliced through the tension. Erikah flinched, but didn't waver as Norella stepped from the shadows.

'What do you want, Norella?' Elsbeth asked, her tone anything but calm. Norella knew she wouldn't look at her, concentration was always key during a ritual. All three kept their eyes closed as Erikah continued to chant without missing a beat.

'I've been ordered by our Queen to ...' Norella began, her voice trailing off as the weight of her mission pressed upon her. The cavern hummed with energy, heavy with some age-old power that reacted to the echo of Erikah's incantations.

'You're mistaken in thinking Isadora is anything to me,' Elsbeth hissed.

Norella took another step toward the group, annoyance evident on her face. Typical of Elsbeth to reject her attempts at protection. She had been prepared to offer Elsbeth a way out, a chance to avoid the Queen's wrath, yet here her sister stood, defiant as always. The sound of crackling filled the space as the magic of their ritual took form. Norella took another sombre step forward, torn between duty and familial bonds.

'Elsbeth Wraithe, firstborn of Hesta Wraithe, and Erikah Pillar, firstborn of Isla Pillar, you are declared traitors of the Crown,' Norella said while looking directly at Erikah. 'Queen Isadora Mallum has declared that you are to be killed on sight.'

Elsbeth held firm as Erikah stopped chanting to turn towards Norella. Raynor's deep voice took up the repetitive chant, the old language flowing smoothly off his tongue as if it were a part of him.

'Norella,' Erikah spoke calmly. 'Leave.'

'I can't do that, Erikah,' Norella replied. 'I'm ordered to return with Elsbeth's head and that of anyone who helped her.'

'Then don't return,' Erikah replied as she looked to Elsbeth, who simply shook her head. It was clear there was something Elsbeth didn't want Norella to know. Some secret that was now shared between her twin and the witch she had loved. If they were going to keep secrets from her, then maybe they didn't deserve her mercy.

'You could both be forgiven if you return with *his* head.' Norella locked eyes with Elsbeth as her sister turned to stare at her. 'Returning with the head of the heir to the fae throne would be a start at redemption in the eyes of your Queen.'

'She is no queen to us.' Erikah spat.

'Norella, I'm leaving'—Elsbeth flicked her eyes between her two companions—'we are all leaving. You are welcome to come with us. Stay if you wish, but do not hinder our plans.'

'Leaving? To go where, exactly?' Norella threw her hands out, gesturing around them. 'We have a duty to our coven, Elsbeth. A commitment our mother—'

'Do not speak of our mother!' Elsbeth glared at her twin. 'You lost that right when you sided with her murderer.'

'Queen Isadora followed witch law.' Norella kept her tone even. 'You are betraying your duty to our sisters.'

'No.' Elsbeth sighed. '*You* have a duty to the witches. My duty ended the moment Isadora killed our mother, her *sister*, in cold blood.'

'It is the way of our kind, Elsbeth.' Norella's words were harsh, but they needed to be. To go against her coven like this meant that Elsbeth would never be allowed to step foot into Brielle Forest again. Although, if Norella didn't return home with someone's head, she shouldn't bother returning, either.

'The way of our kind ... for one sister to kill another?' Elsbeth spat the words in disgust. 'Isadora could have taken the crown and left our mother's head on her shoulders.'

'Would you truly have bowed to her if she had done so?' Norella stared directly at Elsbeth then. They both knew the answer. Elsbeth never would have allowed her coven to bow to someone else whilst their mother was still alive. 'I told Isadora it was the only way if she wanted the Crown.'

There was a flash – so quick Norella didn't have time to react. Raynor had been fast enough to grab Elsbeth's hand as Erikah broke the circle and lunged for Norella.

'You traitorous bitch!' Erikah had her pinned to the ground. 'Your own mother!'

Blood streamed down Norella's face as Erikah's nails sliced her apart with each strike.

'It wasn't like that!' Norella tried to grab Erikah's hands. 'I was training to be her adviser, so I advised!'

'You shouldn't have advised her on that.' Tears streamed down Elsbeth's pale face, glistening in the light between her and Raynor as it grew brighter, the Prince somehow managing to continue the chant.

'You can't leave, Elsbeth!' Norella rolled to her feet, shoving Erikah to the side in the process. Erikah cried in pain as her back hit a pillar; the familiar crunch of bone echoed through the chamber, followed by her laboured breath. She grabbed her side and stumbled to her feet with a snarl.

'Go. Now!' Erikah yelled at Elsbeth as she put herself between the sisters once again.

'I can't leave without you!' Elsbeth's pained voice rose above Raynor's, who was staring at her intently while he continued to chant, low and rhythmic, his knuckles white around Elsbeth's arms. Norella knew the male was likely at a loss. If he stopped chanting to help Erikah, their moment would be lost – but anyone who knew Elsbeth understood how leaving Erikah would cut her to the core. And the way the Prince was looking at Elsbeth said he knew well enough.

'You have to,' Erikah replied as she unsheathed her dagger, the blade glittering in the pulsing magic. 'Free the both of you from this world.'

'Erikah, don't do this.' Norella wanted to beg her for forgiveness, for her to come home.

'It's too late, Norella.' Erikah spun the dagger, once, twice in her hand.

'There's no coming back from standing against me – against the crown,' Norella warned.

'I don't plan on coming back from anything!' Erikah lunged. They grappled with one another, using every ounce of strength they had to push the other out of the way. With a fierce yell, Erikah managed to shove Norella back. 'Go!' She screamed, her voice cracking with raw desperation.

Norella recovered from the blow, muttering a string of words under her breath as vines broke through the stone floor and raced toward the figures in the centre, encasing them in a glowing cocoon.

Erikah collided into Norella's side, knocking them both to the ground. Norella rolled to her feet, pulling her dagger just in time to deflect Erikah's own. She struggled against her ex-lover, her focus solely on reaching her twin before it was too late. She just needed to break past Erikah, to shatter the barrier that stood between her and her sister – her redemption.

'Move so I can stop my sister from doing something stupid.' Norella demanded. But the pillars began to tremble, and Elsbeth let out a small cry from inside the cocoon as the light burned bright from the orb, blinding them all before extinguishing with a flash.

'What have you done?!' Norella shoved Erikah aside and stumbled towards the tangle of vines as they crumpled to the ground – there was no sign of the witch and the Fae Prince within.

'It's too late,' Erikah replied. 'They're already gone.'

Norella's mind raced, a storm of emotions threatening to drown her. The betrayal cut deep, Erikah's actions a stab to the heart. She had trusted Erikah, believed in their bond. Now that lay shattered, as broken as the tangle of vines before her. Anger flared, but so did a desperate hope that there was still time to undo the damage.

Taking a deep breath, Norella steadied herself. 'I don't want to kill you, Erikah.' She threw her dagger to the side.

'Then don't.' Erikah held on to her dagger but lowered it slightly. 'But if you don't turn around and leave, I'll do what I have to.'

'Erikah,' Norella reasoned, 'we both know who the better fighter is.'

'You might win.' Erikah grinned. 'But I'm willing to die now that Elsbeth and her family are safe.'

Norella drew her twin blades from their sheaths. She spun them in her hands, adjusting to their weight. It had been a while since she had felt the need to use both at once. Erikah hesitated for a moment before drawing her own sword from her hip. It was heavier, and she was slower than Norella when it came to sword fighting, but Norella knew she would hold her ground as long as she could.

'One last chance,' Norella offered.

'We both know the only way you're going back to Isadora is with my head,' Erikah replied. 'So just get on with it already.'

Erikah didn't wait for Norella to make the first move as she swung her sword, the tip of it just missing Norella's chest as she stepped backward out of its reach. Norella responded by striking her blades one after the other at Erikah, who managed to deflect the blows with the same speed Norella delivered them. Back and forth, the witches parried and twirled, moving in a circle around the still dimly glowing light, Erikah refusing to give an inch.

'You can't keep this up,' Norella taunted.

'I hate you,' Erikah replied through panting breaths.

'And I loved you.' Norella swung again, finally knocking Erikah's sword from her grasp. 'Move aside.'

'No.' Erikah brought her fist up and moved to her fighting stance.

'You have no weapon, Erikah, and you're far from any water source.' Norella let her blades hang at her sides.

'I've done what I needed to do.' Erikah relaxed as the light behind her dimmed finally, leaving nothing but an empty space where the others had been. 'Elsbeth and Raynor are safe. However, you might be in a predicament with your Queen.'

Norella screamed in rage and swung her blades, the midnight-blue metal flashing through the dimming cavern. The scent of blood filled the air as Erikah fell to her knees, crimson splattering from her lips as she choked on the warm liquid. The life in her blue-grey eyes sputtering out. Norella's eyes cleared, and she threw herself forward, catching Erikah's body as it crumpled. The blades had done their job; Erikah's head slid from her neck and rolled toward the centre of the temple.

'All you had to do was stand aside.' Norella clutched the lifeless, headless body to her chest. Her stomach threatened to empty itself as she looked to where Erikah's head lay. Her spirit wouldn't return to the darkness. The gods' metal in her twin blades had severed the darkness from within her. 'I didn't have any other choice.'

There's always another choice. Erikah's words from another time, another place, echoed in her head. She was right. Norella had a choice, and – as always – she chose the Crown. She would always choose the Crown. She set Erikah's body on the floor and readied the hessian bag.

CHAPTER FORTY-EIGHT

Witch's Keep, Forest of Brielle

+ ISADORA +

THE COVEN LEADERS had all assembled for her in the throne room. Isadora stood facing her throne, disgusted in herself and Norella that they hadn't noticed her missing ornaments immediately. They had been a symbol of her reign, a sign that no one should oppose her. Soon, Norella would return with two new decorations for her throne that would serve as a warning to any willing to betray her in the future.

'My sisters,' Isadora turned to face them. She wondered if this was what her mother had felt when she addressed the covens, with all of them looking upon her with such awe. No, it wasn't awe that was on the faces of the leaders before her – it was fear, wonder, and excitement. So different than she remembered from that day, all those years ago.

†

The witches had gathered, just as Graciella had asked them. Her two daughters, the eldest just over six hundred years old, and the younger not far behind, stood at the front of the group. Both leaders of their covens.

It was a blood moon, the perfect time to announce her retirement from the throne. Many would expect her to choose Hesta as she was the eldest, though more would want her to choose Isadora, the stronger of the two.

Hesta, the smart one, the loyal one who was kind to everyone, would make a brilliant leader. Isadora, the stronger one, the more cunning one who was cruel beyond compare, would make the witches more powerful. Though Isadora knew Graciella feared such a dark creature would not be a good leader, nor the right leader for her people.

It was clear that no one in the room, perhaps not even Graciella herself, knew who would be named as her successor. They all waited patiently as she made her way to her throne, nodding at them as she sat. Her Second, Alanah, stood to her side.

'Sisters.' She spoke clearly, her voice even. 'Today is a prestigious day for our covens.'

A murmur rippled through the coven leaders. It was as they had assumed, Graciella was picking her heir and finally stepping aside after reigning for over two thousand years.

'My daughters'—she motioned for them to step forward—'it is time I chose which of you will lead our covens into the future.'

'Isadora.' Graciella looked toward her younger daughter, flame borne of her ice. 'You have grown powerful these recent years. Perhaps more powerful than even I.'

Another murmur of acknowledgement from the gathered witches.

Hesta fidgeted beside her sister, almost itching to take a step away from her mother.

'Thank you, Mother.' Isadora bowed her head to the Queen, the first acknowledgement she had given Graciella in many years. 'I have worked hard to hone my abilities.'

'It is because of that drive, that fire, which you possess that has made this choice particularly hard.' Graciella continued, 'For though you have immense power, and in turn respect from the other coven leaders, I fear that you have demons that haunt your heart and mind.'

The crowd around them fell silent. Hesta's eyes flicked between her mother and her younger sister. She had always assumed that since Isadora's powers had become strong, her mother would choose Isadora as a replacement, regardless of her status as the firstborn and bearing the Wraithe name. She'd told Isadora this herself, many times.

'Hesta.' Graciella turned from Isadora, who glared toward where Hesta stood, rage burning in her eyes. 'You are the eldest. Though you might not be as powerful as your younger sister, your earth magic runs deep and your heart beats true. It is to you that I bequeath my crown.'

Hesta, just as shocked as most of the leaders, held her breath. She waited for her sister's outburst that was to be expected with such a declaration. Graciella glanced between her two daughters. One so full of rage that her hair seemed to grow flames, the other somewhere between dazed and apprehensive.

Alanah, reading the situation from afar, moved from her spot beside the throne. 'Let us thank Brielle, Mother of Witches, for bestowing our new Queen upon us,' she declared. She gently removed the crown from her cousin's head and placed it on Hesta's, before kneeling at the new Queen's feet – as was the custom.

The coven leaders followed suit one by one, falling to their knees before Hesta, until only Hesta, Graciella and Isadora remained standing.

†

The witches before her now, some familiar faces from that day, others daughters of them, stood patiently as they waited for her to continue.

'It is time that we march south to Thornwell. It is time to conquer the Southern Mortal Realm as ours!' Isadora's eyes burned a brilliant red as the power within her surged to break free. Tendrils of hair that hung around her face turned to flames as her sister witches let loose their roar of agreement.

'We will march our forces to King Oswald's walls and tear them down,' Isadora continued. 'We will destroy any who stand in our way.'

Isadora could feel the bloodlust in the air around them as they began chanting her name. To hell with Brielle and what she stood for; this was Isadora's time. This was her chance to make history and bring forth the true rulers of Emodorea. This was a new dawn, one where the witches would rise.

Chapter Forty-Nine

South-Eastern Borderlands, The Forest of Brielle

+ REID +

REID TRUDGED THROUGH THE dense undergrowth, the afternoon sun casting long shadows across the forest floor. His senses were filled with the thick scent of pine and decay as he followed the King's guards to yet another bloody mess. The victim lay sprawled on the ground, eyes wide in terror, a brutal reminder of the relentless beasts plaguing their land. He wasn't sure why they put up the charade of 'investigating' anymore. It was clear what was happening, and even more clear that they had no way to stop it.

Isadora had made her first moves against Thornwell not long after she destroyed Winhelm in the North. The creatures were sent ahead of the witches. They had done their job, picking off the weak mortals that remained outside the walls of Thornwell for the past few weeks. Reid begged the King to take in everyone left outside, only to be denied at every turn.

Gillian, moonlighting as Lord Brione, had done nothing to help Reid plead his case. As a result, Reid had again felt useless and alone, trapped inside the walls, with only Elisavet to keep him company. The Princess, however, was another problem entirely.

The King had decided to send a small group of guards with Reid to check and report back on the bodies dragged into the forest. Kasin had muttered something in Reid's head, a cynical edge to his words as he mused about the King's possible intentions. The notion of being used as bait for a beast didn't sit well with Reid. He scanned their surroundings warily, muscles tense, ready for anything. As Kasin's Protector, Reid had a duty, but he knew he wasn't fully prepared. His training was far from complete, and he still needed to sharpen both his mental and physical skills. The uncertainty gnawed at him as they ventured deeper into the forest each time.

The guard that was beside the body waved to him to come over. Reid stretched, pushing himself off the tree where he slouched, watching the guards move around nervously. None of them seemed genuinely interested in the task at hand. Some were so completely revolted that they refused to be anywhere nearby, choosing instead to stand guard with their backs facing the mess of a body.

'This is pointless,' Reid said as he went over to the guard who summoned him. 'We should head back before it gets dark.'

A few of the guards within earshot nodded their heads in agreement. None of them wanted to be out after sunset. It was hard enough to get inside the walls as it was, let alone after dark. Moreover, the chances of surviving out here in the night were slim to none, with the creatures prowling around and the threat of witches showing up at any moment to wreak havoc.

'We need to get as much information as we can for the King,' the captain responded, stepping forward to where Reid stood now next to the body. 'No one has seen what kills these people.'

'You forget that I fought and killed one,' Reid replied and turned away. 'We should be preparing to blockade the city or evacuate south.'

'Hasn't your *god* seen them before? Can he not shed some light on our situation?' The captain said as he squatted beside the remains of the woman.

'First of all, he is your god, too,' Reid snapped. 'Secondly, don't you think I've tried asking him exactly that. It's not like we have conversations all the time; speaking with him is tricky. Most of the time, he only appears when *he* wants to. He is a god, after all.'

Mystique, drama, and divine timing – ever heard of them? Kasin's voice drifted in.

Speaking of divine timing … Reid hoped his smirk filtered through the connection.

The captain all but rolled his eyes. He was one of the many who seemed not to believe that Kasin had returned. Generally, only those who had been blessed by the gods worshipped them – few humans still believed in them, and fewer still gave offerings.

A distant howl brought every soldier to their feet, some reflexively drew their swords in anticipation and fear. The sun had all but disappeared over the tree line to the west, and they were farther from the wall than they had ever travelled. It was as if the beasts had gotten smart and dragged their kills further away to draw them out. Reid gave the captain an *I told you so* look as the familiar feeling of Kasin reaching out took over him.

Run.

Reid wasn't sure if he heard Kasin's voice in his head or if the words slipped from his own mouth. He didn't wait to see if the others followed before he darted off through the forest toward the city. He risked a glance over his shoulder as he wove his way through the trees, taking a slightly different path to the one they had taken earlier, this time more direct.

He skidded to a halt. The men were falling behind. He often forgot the gifts Kasin had given him made him faster than normal humans. There wasn't much he could do to make them move quicker, but perhaps he could buy them some time if he was at the rear. Everything in his body wanted him to bolt, to leave the stragglers to their fate. The captain was doing just that as he dashed past Reid, well ahead of his men.

I thought he wanted to see a beast? Kasin's witty remark came as quick as the next wave of howls, no longer in the distance.

'Hurry, get to the city,' Reid called to the trailing men as he drew his sword. He had trained every morning and evening since the King decided to allow Reid into the castle. Still, he prayed they would get to safety before he would have to put himself or the others in danger.

As the last of the straggling men passed by him, Reid finally saw the monstrosity that was hunting them. They'd heard tales of Isadora's demons, but nothing could have prepared him for the creature emerging through the trees. It was a grotesque vision of nightmares, its very presence chilling the air around them.

It was bigger than any wolf he had seen before, its black fur matted with mud and debris, as if it had just crawled out of the swampy ground they stood upon. Its feral gaze settled on Reid, and it began to practically foam at the mouth. Balancing most of its weight on its hind legs, standing almost human-like, a droplet of drool trailed from its maw as it stalked towards him.

Don't panic.

Kasin's attempt to calm him didn't help much, as a slight shudder of fear ran down Reid's spine. Another howl came from deeper in the forest.

The pack, Kasin warned.

The rest of the men had all but disappeared into the trees behind him, none stopping to see if he was following. He hoped they got as far away as possible. The city ruins of the Outer Ring would be their best chance. Spinning his sword in his hand, he turned back to face the beast that was now mere feet away from him, teeth bared and snarling.

As it lunged for him, he moved just in time to avoid being gutted by its claws. Its head jerked back toward him, jaws snapping shut where his arm had been moments ago. Again and again, he moved, avoiding the creature by only seconds. Déjà vu washed over him as he remembered his first battle with one of these beasts.

The creature wasn't tiring, not like he was. He wished Kasin had blessed him with endless stamina, not just speed and agility. There was no way he could keep this up, he hadn't even swung his sword yet, and it was already beginning to feel like a dead weight in his arms.

Warmth spread down his side as his body moved by itself to the left. He hadn't been paying attention. Its claws had managed to slice him open just under his ribs. It would have been worse if Kasin hadn't taken some control and moved him. Something he had never done without asking first. The sword fell loose in his grip as he clutched his side. Blue light slowly began to glow from inside the wound, stitching the skin back together, another of Kasin's gifts. He didn't wait for another attack before sprinting off through the forest.

Make it to the wall … to the wall. Kasin's voice was now a familiar friend in his head, only ever coming in simple phrases but forever a growing presence in his mind. It urged him on through the night, protecting him by leading him away from the beast in hot pursuit.

Reid's sight was set on the city wall, on safety. He ran hard, his feet lifting higher with each stride, though the snarling was closing in on him; it felt like the beast's hot breath was on his neck. He knew he was slowing down, as if the muddy ground beneath his feet was trying to swallow him up. His heart pounded in his ears, or was that the beast's heavy footsteps looming? He shook his head and willed himself to push harder, even though he could tell that he was slackening, could tell he wasn't going to make it. He had to do something, had to give himself more time.

About seventy yards from the wall, he turned to the left and pulled up short behind a wide oak tree, covering his mouth with his hand to quiet his breath. He knew it wasn't far away when it let out an ear-splitting howl. Pushing back into the tree, he prayed for the moon to stay hidden a little bit longer, and for the shadows to cover his tracks. The abandoned houses on the outskirts of Thornwell were all that stood between him and the wall now. If he made a break for it, he would only have seconds before the beast would be upon him. Maybe, if he was quick enough, he could make it back to Gillian's old place and hide in the basement there to wait it out instead. He hoped the soldiers had gotten inside the wall with the bit of extra time he had spared them.

Hot breath filled the air around him. He'd missed his chance. It was too late for him to make a break for it now, the creature would get him before he got anywhere near the old town. Where was Kasin when he needed real help? He hadn't asked for much after Kasin named him *Kasin's Protector*, but he was still yet to see another manifestation of the god since their first meeting. The ground crunched under the weight of the creature that stalked him on the other side of the tree. His hands stilled as they closed around the hilt of his sword, Kasin's gift, and he closed his eyes, praying to Kasin to save him.

A whistle and a thud were all he heard with his eyes shut. He dared to open them, peering into the darkness. Nothing. Not a sound. Still clutching the sword firmly, he stepped out from the shadow of the tree. The body lay at its base, not three feet from his hiding spot – if you could call it such. It had slowly transformed back into its pure form. From the looks of the facial features, it was a shifter-fae. One of undoubtedly many that decided to work for the Witch Queen.

Is it dead? He asked Kasin silently.

His heart pounded as he crouched down beside the fallen creature, a silver arrowhead sticking out its back; a clean kill, by the looks of it, straight through the heart.

Filthy creature, Kasin mirrored his thought as Reid bent to pull the arrow out. He looked around, not sure if he should be standing there or moving back into the shadows. The forest was eerily silent, the usual chorus of nocturnal creatures absent. Another distant howl echoed through the trees – there would be more of them coming. He had to get to the city.

CHAPTER FIFTY

South-Eastern Borderlands, The Forest of Brielle

+ AVELLA +

THE SCENT OF SOMETHING familiar enveloped Avella, taking control of her senses. Her hair lifted, floating around her in the cold air, the tight braid now loose and tangled. Unslinging her bow from her back, she scanned the forest below with keen eyes. The tension palpable as she slowly raised her bow.

The howl came again – her string was tight. She released the arrow, watching as it disappeared into the dense tree line. Silence followed as Avella leapt down from the branch she was perched on, landing gracefully on the ground below, and vanished into the trees.

The rustle of movement ahead marked the spot where her arrow had hit its target. The pack would be close behind; shifter-fae never hunted alone. Avella knew she had to retrieve the arrow before the pack found their dead comrade.

This was the fourth she had come across in the days since she had left the Tretara Range. She had skirted a few covens of witches, making sure she stuck to the outskirts of the forest as she made her way south. She had heard the witches' keep was just south of the centre of Brielle Forest, but hadn't wanted to risk any unnecessary conflicts before getting there. The witch covens she had come across had been smaller than she expected, though they each had one or two shifter-fae with them, as well as something else ... some other beast that was barely recognisable.

With a quiet sigh, Avella moved forward, each step careful and measured. She kept an arrow knocked in her bow, eyes darting through the shadows of the forest. The silver arrow was valuable, but more importantly, it carried her scent. Leaving it behind would be an open invitation for the pack to hunt her down. The thought of them tracking her scent caused an uncomfortable chill to creep over her.

The forest had gone quiet, the usually boisterous nocturnal creatures seemed to sense the death in the air and had disappeared for the night. The sound of the far-off growls from the rest of the shifter-fae pierced the now silent forest. She needed to act quickly, reclaim the arrow, and disappear before the pack closed in. Spending the night evading them wasn't a challenge she looked forward to.

She stopped just before the small clearing, dropping to her haunches in the undergrowth when she saw a man standing over the beast, her silver-tipped arrow in his hand. From where she crouched watching him, she could see that he was breathing heavily, almost as if in a state of panic or shock. She needed that arrow, and she needed to find somewhere safe for the night. Taking out one of those things from a distance she could handle, she wasn't sure how she would go taking on a pack of them up close. She tensed, unsure what to do. What if he was one of them?

The man turned, his eyes seeming to bore directly into her hiding spot. Her heart raced as she scooted back slightly, drawing her short dagger from her boot. She could take him; she just needed to get it over with before more turned up. Just as she stepped out from the undergrowth, he turned away, oblivious to her presence. There was no way one of them would have missed her hiding there.

He was taller than she was, but not by much, and had the muscle tone to show he had at least trained in some form of combat. His skin, deeply tanned, stood out in contrast to the paler complexions she was used to seeing in the north. Most likely because here, in the south, it was almost always sunny and hot. The winter rarely brought any snow or ice, which had clearly left its mark on him.

He reached into his pocket and pulled out a cigarette tin. He thumbed one out and raised it to his lips without lighting it, just holding the butt of it in his mouth. His exhale was shaky, revealing a momentary vulnerability.

'I'll take my arrow back, if you're done examining it.'

The smoke fell from his mouth as he stumbled over the beast's prone body, landing on the ground with a thud. She stepped forward with her hands visible, an attempt to look less threatening.

Her bronze hair framed her face, the few loose curls blowing gently in the breeze. She slipped her blade back into her leather boot and put her hands on her hips. Her chest noticeably deflating as she let out a long sigh. 'I'm honestly not going to hurt you. I just want my arrow back and to get out of here before more of those things arrive.'

'Who are you?' he asked, scrambling to his feet, his hand hesitating on the deep blue sword at his side. 'What are you?' His voice was deep and smooth, given how shaky he seemed when she first appeared. His brown hair was tied back out of his face, his eyes such a deep brown one would think they were black.

'A thank you would be nice.' Avella stepped forward and snatched the arrow from his other hand, her feathers ruffling on her arms as she moved. She knew she was probably freaking him out. Most mortals from this part of Emodorea hadn't seen her kind before; some hadn't seen any other races, save the witches, of course.

'You have wings,' he said, completely forgetting the dead shifter at his feet.

'No,' she responded as she cleaned the arrow on her pant leg. 'I have feathers. I cannot fly.'

She watched as his eyes seemed to glaze over, like he was internally battling what to say next.

'You're a siren,' he whispered.

Her eyes burned in pure hatred of the word. She whirled on him, pinning him against the tree.

'I am not one of those *things*!' She spat the words at him in disgust.

Another howl came from the west, closer this time. She released his throat, fingers trembling slightly as she stepped away, her instincts screaming at her to flee. The forest was still, every shadow a potential threat, every rustling leaf a harbinger of danger. Avella's muscles coiled, ready to spring into action at the slightest provocation.

'We need to get inside the wall of the city,' he said, whether to himself or her, she wasn't entirely sure.

'Do what you wish. I'll be heading that way.' She pointed in a roughly north-westerly direction, away from the city he spoke of. 'I passed a coven of witches on my way down – I don't intend to get stuck fighting them.'

She knew those howls were different to the shifter-faes'. She had no desire to be caught in the witches' crossfire – no desire to have to battle whatever those other demons were that travelled with them in the cages.

'You'll never outrun the shifters if they catch your scent.' His tone was matter-of-fact. It was an open invitation, giving Avella the choice to go with him or continue on her own. Avella hesitated, weighing her options. She had just met this man, but she felt his words held a ring of truth – as much as she wanted to deny it. She knew he was right. If she tried to go it alone, she'd probably be running all night, trying to stay ahead of them. And if she didn't encounter more of the shifter-fae, or these new demons, there was always the risk of running into the witches. These days, it was hard to tell what was worse.

'They aren't shifters ...' She began to explain the witches had other beasts with them, ones that were likely once shifter-fae but had been changed into something akin to demons, but he had already turned to leave, heading toward the tree line. She turned northward, her heart hammering in her chest. The dangers of the forest tonight were all too real. She steeled herself, knowing that survival demanded every ounce of strength and cunning. The forest in front of her loomed dark and foreboding. With a shudder of annoyance, she made her choice.

CHAPTER FIFTY-ONE

Thornwell, Southern Mortal Realm

+ REID +

You need to get to the wall, Kasin urged.

No, she will change her mind. She will come, Reid replied. He could almost feel the god roll his eyes in response. He had never seen a siren before, or anyone with mixed blood like her.

Reid had navigated his way through half of the abandoned houses, weaving his way toward the wall. His mind wandered as he took in the dilapidated surroundings. Suddenly, she was beside him, the girl from the forest. He couldn't help but study her with a mix of curiosity and fascination. The exoticism of her features, the colourful feathers, the iridescence of her skin, even the way she moved – it all drew him in, making him want to learn more about the mysterious girl who had seemingly appeared out of nowhere.

'Avella,' she said, falling into step beside him.

He raised his eyebrows, glancing sideways at her, his pace not slowing.

'My name,' she said again. 'Is Avella.'

'Reid.' He stopped short of the wall, his mind buzzing with questions.

'I will come with you to your city,' Avella said, her voice firm. 'If only to be safe for the night. Tomorrow, I will take my leave.'

They were standing at the western gate, the shadows of the old man's shop where Reid had first met Kasin looming nearby. Reid raised his fist and pounded against the wood, the sound echoing in the quiet night.

'What is it?' Avella asked, studying his face.

'The guards are unlikely to let us in,' he replied, pounding on the gate again with more urgency. 'If they even answer. It's me, Reid!'

The silence stretched for a few moments longer, tension building as they awaited a response. Avella glanced around, as if looking for another way in.

'We're under orders to not let anyone in or out!' A familiar voice yelled back through the gate.

'Orrin?' Reid replied. 'Come on, you know it's me. Let us in, it's not safe out here.'

'I'm sorry, Reid, truly.' Orrin's guilt seeped through the strong oak. 'They'll hang me if I disobey.'

'It's okay.' Reid sighed. How could he blame Orrin for doing his job? 'Just make sure they let us in at sunrise.'

'Yes, sir.'

'Where do you suggest we go in all ... this?' Avella gestured around them at the run-down buildings, most barely recognisable as such. The surrounding structures were little more than shadows of what they once were, the desolation of the Outer Ring evident.

'I have one place that we should be able to lock ourselves inside well enough,' Reid replied before heading off down a backstreet away from the wall.

Are you sure you want to head there? Kasin asked gently.

Don't have anywhere else I can think to go, Reid replied, his steps heavy with the weight of necessity and memories. Reid's thoughts were a storm of past and present as he took in the streets that were once his home. Each step drew him closer to a place he knew all too well, and yet wished he didn't have to revisit.

They didn't speak as they walked. Avella stayed a respectable distance to the right of him, fiddling with an arrow. He'd never seen anything like her. Other than the witches, no races travelled to their part of Emodorea. The fae had little need to interact with humans, and the sirens were all but secluded in their Sky Kingdom. He imagined this is what the sirens would look like if he were to see one, except he expected they would have great wings to carry them through the skies. Much like the stories his aunt told him. His mind wandered to the feather he kept beside his bed in the palace.

She noticed him looking at her and fixed him with a hard stare. 'What?'

'Nothing, I just ...' He had to choose his words wisely if he didn't want to offend her. 'I've never seen anyone like you before.'

She huffed at him. 'Well, I've seen plenty of your kind.'

He chuckled to himself as he stopped before the rubble that was once Gillian's. It hadn't been much to look at before the wall went up, now barely the frame was standing. Even when he and Elisavet visited, it had been more together than this. He shivered as he remembered the boys seemingly asleep in their beds. Upstairs wasn't accessible, the guards had made sure of that when he and Elisavet left after putting the boys to rest. Gillian's study would have to do for the night.

The stairs were still there, barely. Reid grabbed the railing and gave it a fair shake, watching as a few of the steps came loose further down. The entire structure seemed fragile, teetering on the edge of collapse. It was clear that they'd taken a significant beating when the house had been destroyed.

He could almost hear the groaning protests of the wood as it strained under the stress of time and neglect. Taking a deep breath, Reid weighed his options, knowing that any misstep could send him crashing down. It was a gamble, but he didn't have much choice.

Avella didn't wait to see what his plan was. Instead, she bounded past him over the stairs and landed quite gracefully on the basement floor. She turned to where he was still waiting at the top of the stairs.

'Are you coming or what?' She gave a half-smirk before disappearing into the office room.

Locked in the basement of what used to be his home, Reid waited patiently for sunrise. They barricaded the door with anything they could find, and Avella sat intently staring at it. Her small blade, drawn from her boot, twisted in her hands, her movements rhythmic and tense.

The dim light from the lantern they lit cast a warm glow, illuminating the room's rough, unfinished walls. Avella's pale skin seemed to almost sparkle under its soft light. The silence between them was heavy, filled with unspoken fears.

Every creak and groan of the old house above them had them tensing and staring at the ceiling until it stopped. Time seemed to stretch endlessly, each minute feeling like an eternity as they waited for the first light of day, which was still hours away.

'So,' Reid asked, quiet enough that only the two of them could hear, 'if you're not a siren, then what are you?'

Avella turned her blue eyes upon him; her face showed little emotion as she answered him.

'My mother was a siren.' She quietly cursed the woman to Krah. 'My father was fae, or so I'm told.'

'You don't sound happy about either of those things,' Reid replied as he stretched out his legs where he sat against Gillian's old desk.

'Would you be happy if both your parents cast you out because you weren't considered *pure*?' she asked darkly.

'Would you be happy if your mother died giving you life?' Reid shot back at her.

It wasn't something he often thought about; he had never known his mother, only her sister, who had raised him for the earlier part of his childhood. Even the memory of his aunt was vague and distant, more of a concept than a person. He didn't know who his father was, and if his aunt had known, she'd never told him.

A few of the memories he clung to of his aunt drifted back to him. Her caring yet stern guidance and her strength were what shaped him into who he was, but the unanswered questions about his parents still lingered like ghosts in the recesses of his mind.

'It's different,' Avella said as she looked away from him. 'Your mother cherished her baby's life over her own. My parents valued their lives more than their child.'

Reid watched her silently, allowing what she had said to sink in. She wasn't wrong, though it wasn't like his mother had a choice in the matter. She died giving him life, but he was sure she wouldn't have chosen that if she'd had the chance. He let his eyes roam over her while she looked down at the floor, playing with a piece of discarded paper. Her hair fell around her face, now almost completely loosened from her braid, casting shadows over her features, highlighting the delicate curve of her jaw and the slight furrow of her brow.

'My father,' she continued without looking up, 'or his kin, left me at the base of the mountains in the middle of the night. When my tribe found me, they said I was blue. They had no idea how I survived the blizzard that tore through the mountains that night.'

'If you're from the mountains,' Reid asked, 'why are you on this side of the forest?'

'I was tracking that thing I killed in the forest,' she replied as she stood and moved toward the desk he was leaning against. 'They attacked my tribe a moon ago with the witches, before they ransacked Winhelm.'

'You said they aren't shifters?' Reid asked.

'Some are the shifter-fae, yes, the ones that turned to the witches in hopes they'd be spared if they helped in the war to come.' Avella shuffled through a few bits of paper on the desk, revealing maps marked with circled locations. Her fingers absently traced the circles, eyes focused but distant. Reid could see the defiance in her stance.

'Only three of us are left – from my tribe.' Avella turned her attention away from the paper and tugged open one of the desk drawers. He listened as the drawer's contents rattled about while she continued. 'Thankfully, Ma Dessa took us in. We were much safer on her plateau than we were in the lower mountain area. I picked up the scent of those things not long after we had two witches arrive at camp. I've been hunting them for over a fortnight now and tracked their pack down this way.'

Finally, she seemed to find what she was searching for. Reid watched as she pulled a dust-coloured bottle from the drawer, her expression one of relief. She moved back around to where Reid sat, sliding down to join him on the floor. She sighed, the tension in the room easing momentarily.

Her shoulder was warm against his, an oddly comforting presence in the dark room. As Avella popped the cork on the bottle and offered him the first drink, Reid felt a pang of nostalgia. He'd only drank once before, coaxed by Oscar on a night of youthful rebellion. The memories of the hangover the next day had been enough to deter him for a few years, but the thought of his friend made him reach for the bottle she offered.

'Thanks.' He took a deep breath and brought the bottle to his lips, the warmth of the liquor spreading through him, mingling with the memories of simpler times. The night seemed a little less daunting with Avella beside him, and for a moment he allowed himself to relax, to find solace in the unexpected company. 'I'm eighteen today.'

'Well, then'—Avella grabbed the bottle back—'happy birthday.'

CHAPTER FIFTY-TWO

Thornwell, Southern Mortal Realm

+ REID +

CELEBRATING HIS BIRTHDAY was something that Reid had never done. To be honest, until Kasin had mentioned the day of his birth in the woods, he hadn't known the exact day to celebrate; plus, it was the day his mother died. He reached for the bottle again and took another long drink of it.

'What was a human doing that deep in the forest anyway?' Avella asked as he handed her back the bottle. 'Especially alone and that close to sunset.'

'First of all, I wasn't alone. There were palace guards with me,' Reid replied. 'Secondly, I am not just a *human*. I'm *the* human.'

Kasin rumbled softly in his head, as if he were laughing at the cockiness that came with the drinking.

'*The* human?' Avella eyed him from head to toe.

'Kasin's Protector, at your service.' He bowed to her from where he sat.

'Am I supposed to be impressed?' She raised her eyebrow at him as she had another drink. 'Surely the God of Protection could have chosen one more deserving than a human?'

'Oh, give me that.' Reid huffed, snatching the bottle from her hand. Avella's lip circled slightly in amusement as he puffed up, trying to prove he was more of a big deal than she gave him credit for. The slight smirk on her face said it all – she was unconvinced, but entertained by his efforts.

All this power is going to your head. Kasin laughed.

Please, if I let it go to my head, your ego would have competition. Can't have that, can we? Reid replied.

Ah, a mortal keeping me on my toes.

Reid swore out loud at Kasin, his words slurring slightly.

'Oh, I wasn't cussing at you,' Reid said when he noticed Avella glowering at him. 'It's the god – he's in my head.'

'Right,' Avella replied and shifted slightly away, clearly unconvinced. 'Never drank before?'

'No, Gillian never let us.'

At the tilt of her head and the confused look on her face, Reid explained. 'Gillian was the owner of this house. He took me in when my aunt died. He ran a sort of ... boys' home.'

'So from the slums of the city to a place in the palace, and a god that ...' Avella paused for a long moment, the scepticism lingering in her gaze, 'lives inside you?'

'A part of being chosen by Kasin is that he can communicate with me through my mind. So it's like his subconscious and mine are connected somehow – or something like that anyway.'

Something like that, Kasin agreed.

'We don't hear much while in the mountains.' She wiped her chin as a dribble of whisky trickled down it, her lightly feathered arms ruffling as she moved. 'Who am I to not believe a god?'

'Well, I wouldn't say that *I* am a god,' Reid smirked as he turned his head to face her. He could almost feel Kasin sigh in annoyance.

Maybe I should add flirting lessons to your divine duties.

I think it's time for you to go check on your loyal followers or something, Reid growled internally. He could hear Kasin chuckling to himself as Reid closed the connection between them, something he had been practising over the past few days.

'Oh no, you never implied that at all.' Avella rolled her eyes. For a moment, her blue irises glowed with what Reid could have sworn was a faint red ring, but it vanished just as quickly as it appeared. She blinked, suddenly looking away, as if startled by her own reflection in his eyes.

'What's wrong?' Reid asked as he leaned forward, trying to catch another glimpse of her eyes. There was something about them that was familiar, yet like nothing he'd seen before.

'It's nothing,' she said as she combed her fingers nervously through her hair, letting it fall over her face, blocking her eyes from his view.

Maybe it was the whisky, or perhaps it was because of the closeness they shared in the dimly lit basement, but Reid suddenly felt a warmth run through him as he stared at her. It was different to when he was around Elisavet. The Princess made him nervous, but not in the same way. There was an unspoken connection between Avella and him, a shared vulnerability that drew him in.

'Can you stop staring at me, please?' Avella asked quietly, her voice breaking the silence.

'Why?' Reid asked, his eyes still begging for her to face him again. The attraction he felt for Elisavet had always been a quiet, controlled presence, surfacing only when he allowed it to. But this ... this was different. It was raw and unfamiliar, a heat that surged through him uncontrollably. He felt his cheeks redden, betraying his inner thoughts.

The room seemed to shrink around them, the tension heavy. Reid's heart pounded so fiercely he was sure Avella would be able to hear it, each beat echoing the confusion and intensity of his feelings. Her closeness stirred a string of emotions he hadn't anticipated. He wasn't sure why, but something about this girl – this half-siren, half-fae, beautiful creature – drew him in.

'Why would you want to look at me?' She fiddled with a curl of her bronze hair, not meeting his gaze.

Reid swallowed another mouthful of whisky, the burn coursing down his throat, giving him a moment to gather his thoughts. 'Why wouldn't I want to look at you?'

She stilled, the question hanging in the air as her golden feathers prickled down her arms – Reid longed to touch them. His cheeks still flushed, he could feel the intensity of the moment – the warmth between them undeniable. Avella's eyes met his briefly, a flicker of uncertainty crossing her face before she looked away again.

'Because I am a miscreation. Because people outside the mountains think my kind are monsters. Because I am different.'

His heart rate spiked, his nerves frazzled. His fingers brushed her hair as he gently turned her chin toward him.

'I think those people are idiots,' he whispered, his voice barely above a murmur.

Her blue eyes flicked up at him, the red glow faintly circling the outside of her pupils again. The subtle glow mesmerised him, a simple, beautiful sign of her otherworldly nature that both intrigued and unsettled him.

'I think you're too drunk to know what's good for you,' she whispered back.

'I might be drunk, but I'm not blind,' Reid replied, a hint of a smile playing on his lips.

The corner of Avella's mouth lifted slightly at his reply, a small, almost reluctant smile breaking through. She tilted her head so that his hand moved from her chin to her cheek. Her skin was soft and warm, but he could feel the dampness of his palm, betraying his nerves. He watched her close her eyes for a moment, both of them acutely aware of their closeness, before a brief moment of courage overtook his senses.

He felt the heat of a blush creep over her skin as his lips found hers, the warmth of the kiss igniting a spark that sizzled throughout his body. The kiss was brief and sweet, leaving a lingering warmth between them. Reid pulled back just enough to see her eyes again, searching for a reaction. The taste of stale whisky mingled with something else, something he couldn't quite place. Perhaps it was the essence of her magic, a reminder of the fragile yet intense connection they shared in that moment.

'What?' A nervousness had replaced her harsh attitude from earlier. It was probably the alcohol inhibiting her senses. She gulped. 'What is it?'

'I think you're beautiful,' Reid whispered as he ran his thumb over her cheekbone. His eyes stared into hers, a brilliant blue, causing her skin to flush a delicate rose colour again. Reid's thoughts raced, a storm of emotions swirling within him. He had no idea how that had just happened. Unlike with Elisavet, he didn't feel betrayed by his body. His mind was screaming at him to do it again – the warmth of her lips lingered on his, a tantalising reminder of the unexpectedness when she'd returned the kiss. He felt a strange exhilaration, unsure what had driven him to make such a move.

The whisky had certainly loosened his inhibitions, but there was something more – a genuine attraction to Avella that he couldn't ignore.

She leaned past him, her arm brushing across his chest, shaking him from his inner thoughts. She grabbed the bottle and drained the last of it.

'You could have shared,' he said, glancing down at the empty bottle she'd dropped.

'I think you've had enough, don't you?' she replied, eyes drifting to his lips.

Reid's hand found hers, his thumb making small circles on her palm. It was softer than he had imagined it to be, and much warmer than Elisavet's. With how tough she was, he'd expected that she'd have a fighter's hands, like Orrin's.

Not the time to be thinking of Orrin, he chided himself. Guilt ebbed its way into his thoughts, *or Elisavet.*

'Do you want to kiss me again?' Avella asked. She didn't look up from where she watched his hand play with hers.

'Do *you* want me to kiss you again?' Reid asked, his gaze locked onto her, his voice soft but steady. The warmth of her touch, the way she didn't pull away from him, made his pulse quicken.

Her eyes softened as they met his, flicking ever so slightly down to his lips and back up again. A soft, rose hue tinted her cheeks as she leaned in closer, her breath mingling with his, a silent invitation. She whispered a breathless 'yes' and that was all he needed.

He pulled her toward him. Warmth filled him as he kissed her again, this time longer but just as soft as the first kiss. Her arms wrapped around his neck as he deepened the kiss; his tongue gently found its way to hers, and she moaned.

They were both breathing heavily as Reid broke away, though only long enough to shift his weight and pull her on top of him.

Her body was warm against his as he moved from her lips and began kissing between her neck and shoulder. His hands slid under the hem of her tunic, thumbs making gentle circles on her hips, feeling the soft texture of her skin and the slight ruffle of her feathers as goosebumps prickled her skin. It was so utterly different from anything he had allowed himself to do or feel with Elisavet. Everything about this woman made him want to forget about what was happening in the world above them. Here in the basement, in his old home, there was only the two of them.

'Wait,' she pushed her hands against him. His lips lingered on her collarbone as he looked up at her, his hands still holding her in place. He could feel the tension in her muscles, the slight tremble in her breath, and it only made him want to hold her closer, to hold on to this fleeting sense of belonging.

'Did I do something wrong?' His eyes searched hers for any sign of regret or discomfort, hoping he hadn't just overstepped and damaged the fragile connection they had just begun to explore. Maybe he had pushed her too far, too soon. They had only just met, after all. He pulled back slightly, the warmth replaced by a wave of uncertainty.

'No,' she whispered, 'I don't think so, I just ...'

Reid's eyes roamed her face, his hands not letting go but stilling against her. He could almost see the torment in her eyes, could sense her hesitation, feel the heat of her pressed against him, and reality slowly seeped back into his thoughts.

'It's just that we're both pretty drunk.' Her voice was soft, laced with nerves.

Reid gently brushed her hair from her face, tucking it behind her ear, his fingers lingering against her warm skin. Her eyes met his, and for a moment, the world around them seemed to fade away. A silent understanding passed between them.

'It's not that I don't want to,' she said, running her hand along his jawline. 'I just, I've never ...'

'It's okay,' Reid whispered softly, his voice gentle as he shifted out from under her, giving her space. 'We should probably get some sleep anyway.'

The moment hung in the air, the intimacy of their exchange leaving Reid feeling hot and flushed. Avella turned to lean her back against the desk again, visibly sighing with relief.

'You don't think anything can get through that door?' She glanced back at the door nervously, her fierceness now dissipated with the effects of the whisky.

'I'll stay awake and keep watch if you like.' Reid made to stand up.

'No.' Avella reached out and grasped his hand in hers. 'Sleep would be good for both of us.'

Reid hesitated for a moment before he eased back into his spot. He pulled her to him as he leaned back against the desk. They'd be able to get a little sleep before dawn came, so long as the door stayed locked. She wrapped an arm around his waist and leaned her head on his shoulder.

'By the way,' he whispered into her hair when her breathing had slowed to an even rhythm, the rise and fall of her chest soothing at his side. 'I haven't either.'

CHAPTER FIFTY-THREE

Thornwell, Southern Mortal Realm

+ REID +

ELISAVET WAS WAITING by the gates as they swung wide for Reid to enter. She was fidgeting with her hair, tugging at the ends of her short curls when he stepped through the wide wooden doors. She rushed forward to meet him, throwing her arms around him, her face full of concern as she buried it into his neck.

Reid felt Avella stiffen beside him. They hadn't had a chance to speak about what had happened last night. When he'd woken this morning, head pounding from the whisky, Avella was already awake and waiting in the living room of Gillian's house. Reid had tried to ask if they should talk about it, but she had brushed it off as harmless drunken antics and told him it didn't mean anything.

Reid coolly stepped out of Elisavet's embrace, manoeuvring her so that she was at arm's length. She frowned up at him as she reached forward to brush his shaggy hair from his eyes.

'I was so worried,' she gushed, stepping toward him to place her palms on his chest. 'When you didn't come back with the guards, I asked my uncle to send a search party to find you, but he refused. And then Orrin said he spoke with you and—'

Her voice broke into a sob, her hands balling his tunic into a tight clutch.

'I'm fine—' Reid said, his hands wrapping gently around her wrists. 'We're fine.'

Her head snapped up at his words. She wiped at her face, her eyes suddenly dry of tears as she stepped around him.

'Who are you?' Elisavet demanded as she eyed Avella.

'This is Avella,' Reid said. 'She is ... ah, she ...'

Lost for words? Kasin's voice crackled through Reid's mind, causing him to wince in pain.

Not helping.

'I killed one of the shifter-fae that was hunting Reid,' Avella finished for him.

'You.' Elisavet eyed Avella before returning her gaze to Reid. 'She killed one of those things, not you?'

'Yeah, actually,' Reid replied, running his hand through his hair, a lopsided grin tugging at his lips. 'If she hadn't turned up, I'd probably be another body in the forest.'

'So, she saved your life,' Elisavet said slowly, 'and then you ... what, decided to bring her here with you this morning?'

'Well, no, I was going to leave after we woke up this morning,' Avella said.

'*We* woke up?' Elisavet glowered.

'Yes, Reid took me to his old home to—'

'You took her to your house?' Elisavet's hands clenched at her sides as she turned to face Reid.

'It was the only place I could think of where we could barricade ourselves in, and then we started drinking and—' Reid stopped himself, his skin heating up as he remembered the feeling of Avella's lips on his, her soft skin, her warmth.

'Drinking and what, Reid?' Elisavet demanded.

'And now I'm hungover and in need of breakfast,' Avella cut in. 'You did say we could have food when we got here.' She turned to Reid.

Elisavet's eyes narrowed as she also turned to Reid, clearly displeased with Avella's interruption. Reid shifted uncomfortably, caught between the two women.

'I suppose, the least we could do is offer you some breakfast,' Elisavet's smile was too sweet, like honey with a hidden sting. 'And a bath.'

Avella caught Reid staring at her, and he saw a hint of defiance in her eyes as she sauntered past Elisavet with her own sinister smile.

'A bath would be nice,' Avella replied finally, her eyes lingering on Reid as she stopped beside him. 'Wouldn't it, Reid?'

With an annoyed Elisavet at his side, Reid led Avella through the Inner Ring, her eyes wide with bewilderment as she took in the vastness of

Thornwell. The city was just waking up around them, its narrow streets lined with vibrant shops that were beginning to open for the day. Elisavet was in her usual spot, her attempts to link arms thwarted by Reid's constant gestures. He pointed out various shops and where the training yards were, his hands always in motion, an effort to distract and to keep Elisavet at bay. Despite his best efforts, she still managed to try linking her arm through his several times, her persistence unwavering.

Avella remained silent, her gaze seeming to drift from the colourful banners fluttering in the breeze, to the intricate patterns on the cobblestone streets.

'Reid, ah, sir,' Orrin said as he approached them when they reached the doors to the palace. 'King Oswald would like a word with you, and ah ...'

'Avella,' Reid supplied.

'Yes, sir. He would like a word with the both of you.'

'Sir?' Avella quipped as they fell into step behind Orrin.

'Yes,' Elisavet beamed, finally managing to grasp Reid's arm. 'Reid is Kasin's Protector, after all.'

'I've told Orrin he can call me Reid.' He smiled sheepishly at Avella as she rolled her eyes at him.

'Don't be silly.' Elisavet patted Reid's arm. 'You are a lord now, the servants and guards must defer to you appropriately.'

Reid didn't need to look back at Avella to know that she was likely scoffing at the Princess's words.

Orrin marched them up the tall flight of stairs that led to the council room, bowing slightly as he closed the door behind them.

'He lives,' King Oswald declared, standing from his seat amongst the council members. 'How did you manage to kill it?'

No time for pleasantries then, Kasin muttered.

'I didn't kill it,' Reid said, crossing his arms. 'But thanks for noticing I'm not dead.'

'Oh, come now,' the King chuckled as he walked over to clasp Reid on the shoulder. 'My darling niece would have never let me live it down if you had died.'

Reid felt Avella shift uncomfortably beside him.

'This is Avella,' Reid began.

'She comes from outside the wall,' Elisavet interjected. 'Reid brought her here this morning.'

The King's gaze sharpened, his eyes scanning Avella from head to toe, lingering on her feathers.

'Avella is the one who killed the beast,' Reid said, an edge of pride in his voice.

'How did a half-breed manage to kill such a creature?' One of the other lords at the table interjected.

Avella's feathers bristled at the words, but she held her ground, her eyes narrowing as she met the man's gaze. 'I shot it through the heart with a silver-tipped arrow.'

The room erupted with quiet murmuring amongst the council, some clearly in awe, while others did not bother to disguise their disbelief.

'I believe Kasin's Protector,' Gillian spoke up from the far end of the table. 'If he says the girl killed the creature, then so be it. We should be thanking her for such a feat.'

Elisavet huffed in annoyance beside Reid. It was clear she was not happy about Avella being here. Reid gave her a confused look before the King spoke again, drawing his attention away from the Princess.

'Yes,' he said, 'I agree. Let us thank this young lady who has rid our forest of another of those ghastly things.'

Reid had offered for Avella to use his room to freshen up, but thanks to Elisavet's thinly veiled jealousy, the Princess now had the pleasure of sharing her spare room with Avella.

The trio sat in Elisavet's chambers at a small table that had been brought, now adorned with an array of delicacies – freshly baked bread, fruits glistening with juice, assorted cheese, and steaming meats. Three chairs were also placed around the table, two of which Elisavet had dragged next to each other as Reid arrived for their late breakfast. Elisavet's displeasure with the entire situation was noticeable as she gripped her fork tightly, her knuckles turning white as she attempted to stab a piece of fruit from her plate.

'As I told you last night'—Avella spoke to Reid, almost ignoring the fact that Elisavet was there—'I am only staying until I know it is safe to continue my hunt.'

'I truly wish you would reconsider my offer,' Reid said, trying not to stare at Avella. The golden light from the midday sun streamed in through the tall, arched windows that lined Elisavet's room, glinting off Avella's bronze hair, making it shimmer like spun gold – distracting Reid.

'What offer is that?' Elisavet asked as she placed her hand on Reid's arm tentatively, her eyes flickered between the pair.

Avella glanced away from Reid, her fingers idly picking at her food. Reid seemed to notice Avella's change in mood and shifted away from Elisavet as he reached for the pitcher to refill his glass. He avoided the Princess's gaze as she followed his movement, her expression hard to read.

'I asked Avella to help me gather an army to defeat the Witch Queen.'

Reid had tried to explain it all to Avella between their hours of fitful sleep last night, tried to convince her of his fate that Kasin had thrust upon him. He knew she would have allies in the mountains that might help turn the tides of a war.

'What in Zadea do you need an army for?' Elisavet said as she edged her way over the seat ever so slightly. The move was so subtle, Reid thought she was simply adjusting her seat. But Avella's expression flickered and she shifted uncomfortably. Reid turned to see Elisavet fixing her deep green eyes on Avella's blue ones, a silent look he didn't quite understand passing between them, but he sensed somehow that battle lines had been drawn.

'Eventually, the witches will march on Thornwell,' Reid went on, hoping to avoid whatever was happening between the two. 'It seems that King Oswald is willing to wait for that to happen before he decides whether to fight back.'

Oh, look at you, dodging drama better than you dodge Orrin's sword, Kasin teased.

You noticed it too, huh?

It's hard to miss.

'Your King is a fool,' Avella said. 'I don't plan on sticking around while the witches destroy your city like they destroyed my tribe and the Northern Realm.'

'My uncle is no fool,' Elisavet hissed at Avella. 'He has kept us safer than the other kingdoms with his wall, and by refusing to partake in this silly war – unlike Artor.'

'King Artor at least tried to save his kingdom and his people,' Reid said quietly.

'So, you're on her side?' Elisavet stabbed her fork into her plate, the porcelain screeching with the impact.

'I'm on the side that Kasin wants me to be on,' Reid replied bluntly as he put another spoonful of melon into his mouth. He was so acutely aware of the tension simmering between Avella and Elisavet, but he had no idea how to handle it.

'I don't like the idea of you going off alone in search of some army,' Elisavet reached to brush Reid's hair out of his eyes. Her touch was soft, lingering longer than necessary.

Out of the corner of his eye, he noticed Avella cringe, her gaze fixed on her plate. She seemed distant, lost in thought. Reid's mind flickered back to the previous night – memories blurred slightly by the haze of alcohol. A pang of guilt ran through him as he recalled failing to mention anything about Elisavet. But was there anything to mention? They weren't together, were they? His skin felt hot as he remembered calling Avella beautiful, remembered how different it had felt being close to her compared to the times he had been close to Elisavet. It felt so ... natural.

'Well, if Avella comes with me, I won't be alone,' Reid replied.

'I don't think your lover would appreciate that,' Avella mused as she moved her food absently around her plate.

Reid looked over at Avella, trying to gauge her reaction as he said, 'Oh, Elisavet and I aren't ... lovers.'

'Oh, aren't we?' Elisavet's voice sharpened, bitterness evident as she went on. 'Is that why you decided to spend the night somewhere out there alone with this … *thing*?'

She gestured pointedly at Avella, her princess etiquette vanishing in her frustration.

'I have a name,' Avella's face flushed as she slammed her fork down.

'It wasn't like that,' Reid began. 'We were in a tough spot. Avella helped save me—'

Elisavet scoffed at him as she stood from the table.

'And why are you so mad?'

'As if you even have to ask! I can see it written all over your face, the way you look at her. You haven't even denied that you slept together!'

'Nothing happened.' Reid put his fork down. 'We got stuck out there together. Was I meant to leave her to fend for herself?'

'Did getting stuck out there mean you had to get drunk on cheap whisky?' Elisavet demanded, her eyes blazing with jealousy. 'I can still smell it all over you.'

I wouldn't say it was cheap.

Reid glowered inwardly as Kasin revelled in his pain.

The weight of Elisavet's accusation hit him like a ton of bricks. He put his fingers to his head and rubbed his temples.

'It was his birthday.' Avella risked a glance at Reid, as if to say, *what is happening right now?*

'Oh, by all means'—Elisavet threw her hands in the air—'forgive me for being vexed that he chose to confide in you, a stranger, about his birthday rather than the woman who has been at his side every day.'

Guilt washed over him anew as he caught Avella's eyes darting away. She seemed to shrink into herself, clearly uncomfortable. Reid knew there was more to their night than just drinking, but he also couldn't deny what Elisavet was saying. He had been allowing the Princess to get close to him, had been letting her think they were more than just friends. Elisavet had been the only constant since he'd become Kasin's Protector, the only source of familiarity. Yet, seeing Avella's reaction to Elisavet made his chest tighten.

'Elisavet—' Reid groaned softly as the Princess slammed her bathroom door shut. The sound of her filling her bath followed shortly after.

The room felt stifling. Reid's mind raced as he tried to navigate his feelings.

'You had better go fix things with your lady,' Avella said as she fiddled with the end of her braid.

'I told you, she's not my lady,' Reid replied as he ran his hands through his hair.

'She sure fusses over you a lot for just being friends.'

'I mean'—Reid stumbled over his words—'we're close, but I've never told her I wanted anything more.' He didn't know what to do. He had never been in this situation before. His hand tapped his smoke tin absently in his pant pocket.

'More than what, exactly?' Avella asked as she looked up from her plate. Reid locked eyes with her, the half-siren, half-fae girl that mesmerised him. Her meaning was clear – had what happened between them last night meant anything, either?

He had no idea what last night had meant, the drunken kisses, the truths, the warmth as they fell asleep. He had no idea because it was all new to him; it differed from what he *allowed* Elisavet to have, of that he was certain.

'What I had with Elisavet ... what she thought we were'—he fumbled over the words—'I never wanted it to be more than just friendship, even if our actions sometimes blurred those lines.' he finished.

'Mmm,' Avella murmured, unconvinced.

Reid struggled to find the right words to bridge the distance forming between them.

'I need some clean clothes,' Avella said, 'and you need a bath.'

'Avella,' Reid began as he stood with her, 'last night—'

'Was just blurred lines,' Avella finished, her voice cold and clipped as she turned away. 'Can you have someone send me some clean clothes, please?'

'Sure,' Reid said, defeated as she started toward her room, not waiting for his response.

'I'll come with you,' she said suddenly as she reached her door, 'to find an army or to fight Isadora alone, whatever you decide. Not for you, but for my people.'

Reid nodded silently and watched as she disappeared into her room, the door closing behind her with a soft click. The tightness in his throat seemed to ease slightly. His mind flickered to Elisavet, and he wondered if she was alright. He knew he had likely said the wrong things – to both of them. The memory of their accusing stares and the harsh words replayed in his mind.

Finally, with a deep breath, he decided to leave. Knocking on the bathroom door to speak with Elisavet would only stir more confusion. He needed space to think. The sound of his footsteps echoed through the empty hallways of the palace as he moved further away from the room, and the complicated relationships with the two women within.

CHAPTER FIFTY-FOUR

Thornwell, Southern Mortal Realm

+ REID +

As HE WALKED BACK to his room, he mulled over the odd conversation that had just unfolded. The exchange between him and the two women left a sour taste in his mouth. He wanted to explain everything to Avella; about last night, about Elisavet, all of it. He didn't know what it meant precisely, but it wasn't *nothing*, at least not to him.

His thoughts drifted to the times he had been alone with Elisavet. Sure, he had let her hold his hand when they were around others, and they'd stolen kisses in the shadows and heated moments together, but he'd never thought he had given her the impression that he was interested in more. He'd even told her they couldn't be together the first time they'd kissed.

You never said no, though. Kasin spoke to him. *You told her she'd have to wait.*

Even as Kasin said it, Reid knew it was the truth. Elisavet had given herself to him in her own way on more than one occasion. The closeness in the quiet tavern booths, the sneaky alley-way kissing, the heated moments in the gardens hidden by the wall of brambles. Part of him was glad he hadn't answered the door the few times she had knocked in the early hours after midnight. There would have been no denying it if things had progressed as far as the Princess wanted.

Maybe I liked not being alone for once in my life.

There is nothing wrong in enjoying the Princess's company, Kasin said as Reid opened his door and went inside.

No, but I want Avella's company more.

So, tell her that, Kasin replied as Reid headed into the bathroom. He sunk himself into the already warm bath until only his head was above the water.

I don't think she'd believe me – she thinks I'm with Elisavet. Reid's thoughts spiralled as he sank beneath the water, its warm embrace a brief respite from the chaos swirling around him. Avella's mistrust gnawed at him. She was so convinced he didn't want her, had lied to her. He *had* lied to her, by not telling her about Elisavet.

As he resurfaced, the quiet bath seemed to cradle his weary mind. For now, this solitude was his only comfort, a break from the tangled web of misunderstanding and unspoken feelings. Deep down, though, he knew he couldn't stay there forever.

Talk to Elisavet first, Kasin suggested. *Explain to her that you never felt more for her than the brief moments you shared.*

She'll hate me forever, Reid sighed as he scrubbed himself with the scented soap the maid had left for him. The aroma wafted around him, a bittersweet reminder of Avella, how her hair had smelled like the oak trees in the forest, the scent soothing as he breathed in the memory of her asleep on his chest. Every inhale filled his mind with regret and longing, making the steamy bathroom feel like a prison.

They both need to hear your true feelings, Kasin said before he went silent again. The bath was meant to cleanse, but his mind was a tangle of emotions. As he rinsed off the suds, he knew he couldn't avoid the inevitable confrontation much longer.

'We have to stop meeting like this,' Gillian quipped as Reid stepped from the bathroom, clad in just a towel.

'You have to stop letting yourself into my chambers uninvited,' Reid replied, shaking his head as he walked toward his room to dress.

'Perhaps you should consider locking your door,' Gillian called from the lounge, 'or do you prefer to leave it unlocked in case one of your women come to visit? Who were you hoping for this morning – the Princess or the half-breed?'

Reid felt a prickle of irritation at Gillian's words as he stepped into his room. He quickly pulled on his clothes, trying to ignore the jab.

'Her name is Avella.'

'Ah, so the half-breed, then.' Gillian laughed.

Reid scowled as he flopped onto the sofa across from his old master. 'I take it you have a reason for being here?'

'Indeed, the King sent me, in fact,' Gillian replied. 'It would seem that some travellers spoke to the council about a band of witches and demons marching south this morning from the witch's keep.'

Reid sat up swiftly 'I knew it. I knew they would come soon.'

'Not soon, boy,' Gillian said, 'they'll be here by nightfall.'

'Is the King evacuating the city?' Reid asked.

'The King intends to do nothing. He does not think they can get past the wall,' Gillian replied nonchalantly.

'They're witches and demons'—Reid hung his head in his hands—'of course they can get past a stupid wall.'

'So, what, may I ask, do you intend to do about it?' Gillian sat forward in his seat while he waited.

'Me?' Reid asked, 'Why would I be able to do anything?'

'You're Kasin's Protector, aren't you?' Gillian replied dramatically. 'Surely he's concocted some elaborate plan in your head.'

'No,' Reid replied. 'Why would he if this is the first we are hearing of the witches coming?'

'Well, ask him now.' Gillian leaned back and folded his hands behind his head. 'I'm in no rush. I mean, the witches are, but I have all day.'

Reid glowered at him as he waited for Kasin to give him something to reply with. The god was silent a long moment before he replied simply.

Get out of the city, head toward Thames.

'Thames,' Reid repeated out loud.

'Splendid.' Gillian dropped his hands back onto his thighs with a hearty clap. 'I've always loved visiting Orabelle Bay. When do we leave?'

'I've given you one word, and you're ready to go?' Reid looked at Gillian with more disgust than usual.

'Of course,' Gillian replied enthusiastically. 'Do you think I've made it this far in life without being prepared for things like this?'

'No,' Reid admitted. 'I suppose cockroaches live through anything, don't they?'

'So, shall we leave now or in a few hours?' Gillian asked. 'I have some unfinished business I would like to attend to first, if possible.'

'I'm going to speak with the King.' Reid stood. 'If you want to come with me to Thames, you'd better be there.

CHAPTER FIFTY-FIVE

Thornwell, Southern Mortal Realm

+ REID +

REID STOOD AT the front of the room, his posture rigid. The King sat in his usual seat at the head of the table, his face a mask of stern authority, eyes narrowing as he listened to Reid's arguments. Around them, the council members sat quietly, their expressions ranging from curiosity to outright disdain.

'I told you, the witches are coming, and your wall won't be able to deter them this time!' Reid's voice echoed through the chamber, each word carrying the weight of his convictions.

The room filled with the low murmur of whispered conversations, the rustling of robes and the occasional clink of a goblet being set down. The scent of burning incense mingled with the faint aroma of old parchment and polished wood. The King's response was measured, his tone icy and unyielding.

'The wall will stand,' King Oswald assured the councilmen. The high vaulted ceilings amplified his words, making them seem more resolute.

'Your wall will do nothing to prevent the witches and their demons from tearing your city apart.' Avella's words cut through the silence like a blade.

Reid glanced over at Avella, admiration and worry tugging at his chest. She stood firm, her feathers bristling slightly.

'You have no place to speak here, half-breed.'

The snarl came from where Elisavet stood, beside her uncle. Reid knew she had spent most of the day hiding in her bathroom, and for some reason he wasn't truly surprised by it. She had made it very clear that she wasn't happy with Avella being in the palace.

'Avella has seen these demons first hand.' Reid didn't look at Elisavet, though he could feel her eyes piercing him as he spoke. 'She, if anyone, knows what they are like. You need to listen to her.'

The council members exchanged uneasy glances as they waited for King Oswald to respond. The King's expression remained inscrutable, his gaze shifting from Reid to Avella, then finally resting on Gillian.

'What of you, Lord Brione?' The King looked to where Gillian had stood at the back of the room. 'What do you make of all this?'

'I'm afraid, my King'—Gillian ran a hand through his auburn hair— 'that the last time we didn't believe … Kasin's chosen one, the god made it clear what would happen should we make the same mistake again'

'Yes.' The King studied Reid thoughtfully.

'Uncle, we cannot leave the city.' Elisavet moved closer to the King. 'We will be sitting ducks, with no way to defend ourselves.'

There was murmuring amongst the council members as they began voicing their opinions on who was right. Most sided with the King, but a select few seemed to agree with Reid. The rest were uneasy as they waited to hear what the vote would be.

'Uncle, we've done so much to ensure Kasin's Protector remained in our city …' Elisavet eyed the King, desperation beginning to ebb out of her.

'Elisavet, please see reason.' Reid finally turned toward her. 'We have to evacuate – the witches won't show mercy.'

'You don't know what the witches will offer.' Elisavet grit her teeth. 'Why do you care what we do, anyway?'

'Because it's my job and—'

Elisavet snorted. 'Was it your job also to bed some soulless wretch?'

'If you're willing to let your people die out of arrogance, then go right ahead.' Avella declared, the insult seeming to roll off her with ease, her eyes burning. 'Don't say that Reid didn't warn you. Your people should know whom to lay the blame on – if any survive!'

Reid could feel the intensity radiating from Avella as she watched Elisavet take a determined step from the table towards them. He sensed her anger simmering beneath the surface, blue eyes ablaze. Though he knew couldn't entirely blame Elisavet for her feelings, her attitude was only fuelling the tension and distracting from the real issue at hand. The future of their people was at stake, and personal conflicts had no place in the conversation. It was why he had been so hesitant to allow anything to start between the Princess and himself, even if it was just physical.

'Please.' Reid stepped forward, placing himself between the two. 'Kasin wants us to leave.'

'Kasin chose you to fight, to protect us.' One of the council members stood from their seat to the side.

'Yes, why would he want us to leave? This is your duty!' Another shouted, so the entire court could hear him.

'Yes,' Reid admitted, 'Kasin chose me to defeat Isadora. But at the right time.'

He turned as he spoke, speaking to the council members now, more than the King.

'Now is not the time to fight. Now is the time for us to leave, regroup, and seek aid.'

'May I suggest a simple solution?' Gillian finally spoke again.

'I don't see why not.' The King leaned back in his chair. 'Everyone else is throwing their opinion around.'

Gillian half smiled as he made his way into the light, where Reid stood, looking all but defeated.

'If it pleases the court and Kasin,' Gillian began, 'why don't those who wish to, stay, and those that want to leave with us, leave?'

'Because if you all leave, how will we defend ourselves?' Elisavet crossed her arms.

'We don't want to fight.' A servant sat the glass tray she was holding down. 'Pardon my forwardness, but if we have a choice, a lot of us would like to leave.'

The King rested his chin in his hand. 'Lord Brione, your suggestion isn't a bad one.'

'You can't just let Kasin's Protector leave?' Elisavet stared at her uncle in disbelief.

The King rested his gaze on Reid. 'You will not stay? You would truly leave us to perish?'

'I do not want anyone to die,' Reid explained, 'which is why I'm asking everyone to evacuate.'

Reid watched the King mull it over, and for a long moment everyone in the room held their breath waiting for the answer. King Oswald's eyes swept around the room, lingering on each of his councilmen and the servants gathered by the door. Reid noticed a flicker of something – perhaps regret – as his eyes settled briefly on Reid, then Avella, and finally on Elisavet. The future of Thornwell hung on this moment.

'My wall is strong.' The King stood. 'Those that wish to leave may do so. But, those that wish to stay and fight, I stand with you.'

A crushing weight settled itself on Reid's shoulders as the King's decision echoed through the council chambers. His shoulders slumped, the fight draining out of him. He had poured all his will power into trying to convince them all, but now, faced with the King's stubbornness, he felt utterly defeated. The room seemed to close in around him, threatening to undo him.

The people of Thornwell would be left vulnerable, their fate sealed by a decision made out of pride and arrogance. Elisavet's face was rigid, unreadable. A pang of guilt shot through Reid. He had failed her, failed to protect the city he had called home for eighteen years. They would stay, and they would watch their city fall. In this moment, all Reid could do was bow his head and accept the bitter reality of the situation.

'Let's go, Reid,' Avella's hand gently reached out and wrapped around his. Her unexpected touch sent a jolt of electricity through him. 'They've made their choice.'

Reid allowed Avella to lead him away from the table and towards the door, Gillian already there holding it open for them as he spoke quietly with one of the servants. The council members were all silent, waiting for their King to dismiss them. Reid wondered how many would choose to go with them, and how many would stay to face their doom.

He stopped as they neared the door and faced Elisavet, mere feet away from him. He hoped she could read the apology on his face, the pleading in his eyes as tried one more time.

'Kasin chose me to end a war. He didn't choose me to fight this battle.'

'Perhaps'—Elisavet glared at Reid—'your god chose wrong.'

CHAPTER FIFTY-SIX

Thornwell, Southern Mortal Realm

✦ REID ✦

AVELLA AND REID WAITED at the eastern gate with the few people who had chosen to travel with them. Anticipation hung in the air around them, and the desert wind carried the scent of dust and distant hopes. The vast dunes stretched out before them, golden waves rolling under the deepening sky. The sun, a blazing orange orb, was beginning to set, casting long shadows and bathing them in a warm, fading light.

'You need to forget about it.' Avella's voice was cautious as she placed a hand on Reid's shoulder. By *it*, Reid knew she meant Elisavet's last words to him.

Perhaps your god chose wrong.

Five words. Five simple words, and Reid had been fighting an internal battle ever since.

I'm rarely wrong.

Reid struggled to believe the reassurance that swam through his foggy mind.

By the time the last of the stragglers had arrived, the sky had shifted to hues of purples and reds, a beautiful contrast against the pale sand. Each person carried bags of their most valued possessions, carefully selected for the three-day trek to Thames. The instructions Reid made sure Orrin gave to everyone had been clear: pack lightly for quick travel. Most had chosen items they could sell to start anew near the Bay of Orabelle, a chance for a new life, for survival.

'Where is he?' Reid pushed himself off the wall, his body fighting him as he moved away from Avella's presence. The sound of the wind whipping through the dunes quieted as he wandered back inside the gates. His eyes fervently scanned the streets, waiting to see the unmistakable auburn hair or flash of silver clothing he loved to wear.

'We need to go.' Avella came to stand beside him. 'If we don't leave now, who's to say we won't be far enough ahead of the witches?'

He was still in shock that Avella had agreed to travel with him. She had been so set on heading into the forest the night before, so sure that it was what she needed to do. A part of Reid hoped that whatever had transpired between them in the basement, drunk or not, was the reason she was choosing to hang around. Surely she felt it too, the spark that was between them – felt the strange pull that he felt every time she came near, every time she uttered his name or let her eyes wander over him.

'Give him a few more minutes,' Reid replied, allowing his hand to linger incredibly close to hers, their fingers grazing as they stood beside each other.

Gillian wouldn't stay here to die, although Reid wasn't completely sure why he was worried about the man, or why he was waiting for him. The sly bastard had managed to get inside the wall before they closed it, with none of the Inner Ring knowing. Reid was sure he would be able to get out of the city just as fast.

'Lord Reid!' Orrin came tearing into view. He stopped in front of them, doubled over, trying to suck in as much air as possible.

'What's wrong?' Reid asked, 'Where's Gillian?'

'It's the witches,' Orrin breathed. 'Who is Gillian?'

'I meant Lord Brione. Did you see him?' Reid looked past Orrin.

'Lord Brione said to go.' Orrin stood, his hand on his chest as he panted. 'He told me to make sure you left the city. He'll catch up to you.'

'Reid, don't.' Avella laced her fingers through his as he made to head back toward the palace.

'I can help him.' Reid reluctantly slid his hand from hers.

'He went back to his chamber to get something,' Orrin offered. 'I tried to tell him it was useless, but he insisted.'

'Stubborn as always.' Reid muttered under his breath.

Leave, Reid. Kasin affirmed.

'He'll die,' Reid replied. He tapped his head when Avella and Orrin gave him weird looks. 'It's the god.'

"The god" is what I'm referred to as now, is it? Kasin asked.

'Of course not,' Reid replied again. *Stop, you're making them think I'm crazy.*

Just trying to assist you, Kasin chuckled.

'Reid, these people chose to leave because of you.' Avella gestured to the people waiting outside the wall for them. 'They need you to lead them to Thames.'

Reid glanced over his shoulder, the eastern wall standing tall behind him, a formidable barrier that separated them from the unknown. There weren't many of them – maybe fifty in total – all huddled together, their faces etched with fear and worry. Others had left for the south, hoping to seek a new life in The Blue Sands or beyond. To Reid's dismay, most had chosen to stay in their homes. These people before him were leaving behind the comfort of Thornwell, all their belongings shoved into a few meagre bags. And now, they looked to him – a street rat from the Outer Ring – for guidance. The enormity of the responsibility threatened to overwhelm him.

Reid's eyes found Avella's, a silent understanding passing between them. This journey meant something for her too, Reid knew that. It was a path to redemption, a fight for a future that she wasn't able to have with her tribe.

'Alright.' Reid put his hand on Orrin's shoulder. 'Let's go.'

Orrin hefted his own pack onto his shoulder and followed Reid and Avella past the gates, right as an explosion shook the ground beneath them. Smoke rose in the air on the western side of the city.

'We need to move as fast as we can,' Reid called to the group. 'It's about a three-day walk to Thames, so I suggest we get moving.'

'Isn't it dangerous to travel at night?' one of the women asked nervously.

'I won't lie, sometimes it is,' Reid admitted. 'But we will move quickly while it is not so hot.'

'The witches have arrived at the western gate,' Avella added. 'We need to go now.'

'It's okay.' Reid held his hands up as murmurs of panic began running through the group. 'We will be able to get a decent lead on the witches, as long as we leave right now. They have no reason to follow us. It's the city they want.'

Reid hoped that what he was saying was the truth. He wasn't sure if word of the new Protector had spread throughout Emodorea yet. Hopefully, they would be able to travel quickly, putting distance between the city and the group before sunrise. If they could get to Thames, he was sure the people would be safe. He wasn't so sure he could say the same for himself – perhaps ever again.

'Lead the way,' Avella gestured to the open dunes before them. Reid stood tall and took one last long look at the city he had called home for the past eighteen years. In front of him lay an expanse of golden dunes and sweltering heat, leading to their destination in Orabelle Bay. As the final rays of sunlight began to disappear, they started their journey.

I don't suppose you know where we're going? Reid asked Kasin quietly.

The stars will guide you, Kasin said, showing Reid.

'We'll follow the constellation of Kasin.' Reid pointed to the sky.

Made up of twenty-three stars, the constellation of Kasin roughly resembled the shape of a sword. It sat high above the northern horizon, the tip pointing toward the west and the hilt pointing east toward Thames.

Reid steeled himself and stepped forward, his resolve solidified with each step into the unknown. The small band of travellers followed, their footprints quickly swallowed by the shifting sands.

CHAPTER FIFTY-SEVEN

Thornwell, Southern Mortal Realm

+ ISADORA +

DARKNESS HAD BARELY SETTLED over Thornwell when the first wave hit. The flying witches, not many in number, descended upon the city like a swarm of locusts. They seemed to float through the air like feathers, silent and eerie, until they landed with a force that shook the very ground. Their fierce and fearless faces grinned with malice as they tore through the King's guards near the gates as though they were mere paper.

Isadora stood proudly at the gate of the wall. Screams of pain echoed through the desolate streets, piercing the quiet night sky. The witches' initial assault was swift and brutal, a harbinger of the chaos to come. Thornwell's walls, which once stood as a symbol of impenetrable strength, were now vulnerable and fragile against the onslaught.

In the distance, the ground forces began to stir, preparing to join the fray. The berserker-fae – dark, twisted beings with a savage thirst for blood. Isadora had twisted the very essence of the shifter-fae that had been loyal to her to create the beasts that had been terrorising the forest. She had used ancient magic, forbidden spells that had been hidden away, warping their innate abilities, turning their nature shape-shifting powers into something monstrous. The dark spirits of those now long-forgotten corrupting their minds and forcing them to walk between two worlds, one foot with the living and one foot in Wynlara.

The Witch Queen rolled her eyes with disdain at the ruins around her. It was almost annoying how the humans lived. Sure, they had lesser and higher covens, but not one of her sister witches would ever go without. She wrinkled her nose as the stink of the humans they'd found hiding wafted past her. To let their own kind live like this disgusted her. She would order them to bathe upon returning to her castle.

'How much longer will it be?' She picked her fingernails, sharpened finely that morning before they broke camp. A Queen had to look her best while ripping a King's heart out, after all. Of course, he would grovel – she hated when they grovelled. If she didn't kill him, however, what would that say about her threats? Beside her, a group of the newer berserker-fae twitched with anticipation. Shoving against one another as the iron in the air grew heavy.

'Not too long now, my Queen,' Imogen assured from her other side. The side Norella usually stood on. She'd sent her niece north to hunt down the traitorous ones, a task and a test. The Northern woods were a labyrinth of ancient trees and hidden paths, and Norella hadn't returned before they had marched south.

Isadora hadn't wanted to go without her most trusted warrior, but her covens were getting restless. They had been cooped up in the forest for too long, and had begun to thirst for bloodshed. They craved the chaos and carnage that only battle could provide, and who was she, if not a dutiful Queen?

'It is a wooden gate,' Isadora huffed. 'How is it so difficult to best?'

The witches trying to pry the gate open scattered as Isadora strode toward them, Imogen racing to keep up with her. She stretched her hands out in front of her as she spoke in the ancient language.

Flames exploded from her hands.

It seemed as though she sucked away what little light the sun had left behind. The fire latched itself onto the gate like a leech, hungrily devouring the wood, and the flames spread quickly, the orange wave smothering the gate until it was blackened. The witches shuffled back in the face of the searing flames, their eyes reflecting the blaze.

'Zala.' Isadora motioned to the young witch. 'If you will.'

Zala stepped forward with two others. The air stilled as they each sucked in a mouthful of air, holding it momentarily before blowing at the now charred gate. The three streams of air collided, twisting together in a braided wind tunnel before slamming into the wood. The gate shuddered under the strain before collapsing on itself, the thunderous boom echoing around the city. Black smoke rose into the sky above.

Isadora waited as the witches surged into the city. She loved the taste of human blood just as much as any witch, but she would not show herself to be weak to temptation in front of the others. As Queen, Isadora needed her covens to be in awe of her – otherwise, there was the chance of rebellion. Her sister's daughter had already revolted, she didn't need others to follow suit. As the last of her army strode through the gates, Isadora began walking. They would clear a path for her directly to the King.

'The streets are bare,' Imogen reported as the witches and berserkers pushed further into the city. 'They had half the number of guards we had assumed would meet us.'

'Send the berserkers ahead to the castle,' Isadora ordered. 'No one touches the King except me.'

'Perhaps they did not know we were coming?' Zala asked as she joined her cousin and the Queen.

'No,' Isadora mused, 'they knew we were coming.'

'Oswald, Oswald, Oswald.' Isadora twirled her dagger as she stood in front of the King of Thornwell. The metallic scent of blood permeated the air, heavy and unavoidable as the last of the guards fell around her. The covens had made quick work of the human army, or what they considered an army anyway. The berserker-fae had torn through the initial flood of armed men within minutes. A few had fallen in the process, but no one had cared to count. Not yet, anyway.

'Leave the child be,' Oswald said softly as a whimper escaped the young woman that Zala held tightly.

'Zala,' Isadora signalled for the witch to bring the girl over to her. Black curls hung limply around her abnormally pale face. Isadora gripped her chin, tilting it to look at her. 'The Princess, I assume.'

The girl managed a slight nod, tears rimming her green eyes.

'Whatever shall I do with you?' Isadora mused as she turned the girls' face side to side. 'You are a pretty little thing.'

'Let her go,' Oswald pleaded. 'She is of no use to anyone.'

'If she is of no use'—Imogen pulled the King's head back—'then my cousin and I would be delighted to taste her.'

Zala gave a small smile that mimicked the malice in Imogen's voice. The red flecks in their eyes glowed slightly as the bloodlust threatened to consume them.

Isadora seemed amused by the idea.

'N-no,' the Princess stammered, 'please.'

'Your uncle said it himself,' Isadora dropped her chin and walked around behind her, examining her. 'You're of no use to anyone.'

'I-I …' The girl flinched as Zala ran a finger over her delicate throat. 'I know where Reid is going!'

'Who is that?' Imogen questioned playfully. 'Your lover?'

The girl flushed. 'He-he is …' She eyed her uncle. 'He is the—'

'He is no one,' Oswald interjected.

'Well, now.' Isadora turned to the King. 'He must be significant if a coward such as yourself is willing to lie about him.' She turned back to the Princess, smiling sweetly. 'Who is he?'

When she didn't answer immediately, Zala slapped her across the face, the sound echoing around the quiet room. 'Answer your Queen.'

'Elisavet, don't,' Oswald urged his niece. 'She's going to kill us, no matter what you offer her.'

'No, Elisavet,' Isadora purred, letting the name roll off her tongue. 'I might be gracious and let *you* live.'

'He's the chosen one,' Elisavet sputtered out.

'The what?' Imogen asked.

'Elisavet, that's enough,' Oswald ordered.

'The one Kasin has chosen to defeat you.' Elisavet looked to the ground at her uncle's sigh.

'My, what a secret you have been keeping.' Isadora stalked toward Oswald.

'It was not a secret,' Oswald replied. 'I'm sure rumour reached you.'

'Yes,' Isadora thought for a moment before continuing, 'though not in as many words. We heard of someone killing our berserkers, but not of one chosen by Kasin himself. We haven't had a chosen one since my mother was Queen.'

'Where is he, then?' Zala hauled Elisavet to her feet, her nails drawing blood at her throat.

'Elisavet …' King Oswald's voice was strained, her name a delicious plea that set Isadora's pulse racing.

'He's heading to Thames.' Elisavet met her uncle's eyes as they filled with shame.

'Tell me'—Isadora cupped Elisavet's chin once more—'who has Kasin chosen this time? Who is this "Reid"?'

'He is a street rat from the Outer Ring,' Elisavet's voice grew steadier, the Queen's clear interest buoying her.

'A human?' Isadora grinned as the Princess nodded. 'How quaint, we haven't had one of those before. Perhaps this will be interesting.' She kissed Elisavet's brow.

'May we go now?' Elisavet asked.

'We never made such an agreement,' Isadora cooed as she walked back toward the King.

'But you said if I told you where he was—' Elisavet choked as Zala tightened her grip on her throat.

'Oh, I never said anything of the sort.' Isadora stroked the back of the King's head before sinking a rough fist into his hair. Imogen released him and stepped away to join her cousin. 'I said, if I was feeling gracious, that I might let *you* live.'

'Please,' Elisavet whimpered as Isadora ran her nails delicately across King Oswald's throat.

'Elisavet—' Oswald was cut off with a gurgle as Isadora's nails sliced through his neck, blood spraying outward. She released his head and stepped forward over his fallen body.

Elisavet screamed and thrashed as Isadora approached her once more.

'Royal blood always seems to have a finer taste, wouldn't you agree?' She ran her nail across her tongue, the dark red blood running down her chin.

'What shall we do with this one?' Zala asked as she eyed Elisavet's throat.

'Bring her with us,' Isadora ordered. 'We have a god to hunt.'

The Witch Queen strode out of the throne room, her black lace cape leaving a trail of blood in her wake.

'Oh, and girls,' Isadora called over her shoulder as she heard Elisavet cry out in pain. 'Don't be too rough with our new friend. I'd like the Princess alive.

+ END +

PRONUNCIATION GUIDE

CHARACTERS

Alanah – (A-LA-NAH)
Anika – (ANNE-ICK-AH)
Arhias – (AH-RYE-AHS)
Artor – (ART-ORE)
Athena – (A-THEEN-AH)
Avella – (A-VEL-LAH)
Cilla – (SIL-AH)
Elisavet – (ELIE-SAH-VET)
Elsbeth – (ELS-BETH)
Erikah – (EH-RIK-AH)
Gillian – (GIL-EE-AN)
Graciella – (GRAY-SEE-ELLA)
Imogen – (IMM-O-JEN)
Isadora – (IS-A-DOOR-AH)
Jerola – (JE-ROLE-A)
Jessamine – (JESS-AH-MEAN)
Marlo – (MAR-LOW)
Merlian – (MER-LEE-ANNE
Nerophine – (NER-O-FEEN)
Norella – (NO-RELL-AH)
Odessa – (OH-DESS-AH)
Orabelle – (O-RAH-BELL)
Oscar – (OS-CAR)
Oswald – (OS-WALD)
Peita – (PEE-TAH)
Raynor – (RAY-NORE)
Reid – (REED)
Sirennea – (PSY-REN-EE-AH)
Tallon – (TAL-ON)
Zala – (ZAH-LAH)

PLACES

Emodorea – (EMO-DOOR-EEAH)
Navassa – (NAH-VAH-SAH)
Nonnelle – (NON-NELL)
Osteria – (OS-TERRY-AH)
Thames – (TAIMS)
Thornwell – (THORN-WELL)
Tretara – (TREH-TARA)
Winhelm – (WIN-HELM)
Wynlara – (WIN-LAR-AH)

GODS AND GODESSES

Brielle – (BREE-ELLE)
Dagmar – (DAG-MARR)
Kasin – (KAS-IN)
Katinka – (KAH-TINK-AH)
Krah – (KRAAH)
Thora – (THOR-AH)
Typhonis – (TY-FON-ISS)
Zadea – (ZAY-DEE-AH)

FLORA AND FAUNA

Snakyte – (SNACK-ITE)
Scocin – (SCO-SIN)

A Divine Farewell

In the grand throne room of the celestial skies, the Eternals of Emodorea assembled. The room stretched magnificently, with walls shimmering in stardust and a ceiling that mirrored the vast cosmos. Each deity's light contributed to the ethereal glow, creating a kaleidoscope of colours that danced and intertwined across the space. It had been centuries since they had all gathered at once, and yet aeons of familiarity flowed between them.

Thora, the Goddess of the Sky and Air, floated down from the ceiling, her white light blending with the clouds that formed her ethereal body as she took her seat among the others. Her brother, Typhonis, the God of the Moon and Water, stood beside her. He was her twin in every way, except where her body was light and mist-like, his was covered in scales that glistened under the celestial light. His deep, green light was reminiscent of the ocean's depths. He placed a protective hand on her shoulder.

Krah, the God of Death, stood apart from the others, not taking his allocated throne to the left of Kasin, the dark god's red light casting an eerie glow over the brilliant colours of the others. Brooding power emanated from him as he folded his arms. His wife, Dagmar, the Goddess of the Earth and Life, stood proudly by his side as they waited for the meeting to commence, her golden light and warm smile a stark contrast to the God of Death.

Brielle, the Goddess of Magic and the youngest of the Eternals, sat on the edge of her throne, her hands twitching with anxiousness. She was different from the others, with her glittering silver light, ebony hair and grey eyes; she was born from a darkness at the root of Emodorea. Beside her, Katinka, the Goddess of the Sun and Fire, with her bright orange light and even brighter orange hair, completed the assembly. Less patient than the rest, she played with a small flame, juggling it back and forth between her fingers and bouncing her leg restlessly.

Zadea, the Goddess of Knowledge, the undeclared leader of all meetings, stood gracefully in the centre of their ring of thrones. Her soft, purple light illuminated her black hair and sea-green eyes. The only one somewhat void of emotion when it came to decisions, she glanced at Kasin, the God of Protection, whose bright, blue light reflected his warrior-like presence. Their eyes met briefly, a silent understanding passing between them, unspoken words lingering heavily in the air.

Zadea stepped forward, her voice soft yet commanding. 'We have nurtured Emodorea and its races for millennia. The fae, sirens, mermaids, witches, and the humans, have flourished under our guidance. But it is time for them to stand on their own.'

A murmur rippled through the room. Krah's voice was the first to break the silence, a low rumble filled with discontent. 'And what of the souls of the dead? Who will guide them if we leave? Who will make sure that Wynlara continues to take those that have passed on?'

Dagmar placed a calming hand on his arm. 'Life and death are inter-twined, my love. Just like you and I. The humans will honour us with their rituals, and the earth will continue to bloom.'

Kasin's deep voice resonated through the throne room. 'We have given them knowledge, protection, and the elements to thrive. Now, they must learn to use these gifts without our constant presence.'

Thora's voice was like a gentle breeze. 'The Sirens will continue to sing in the skies, and the mermaids will rule the oceans. Our creations are strong and wise. They will endure.'

Beside her, her brother nodded in firm agreement. 'The tides will still follow the moon, and our influence will remain, even if we are not here.'

'And you do not think your precious sirens and mermaids will slaughter each other the moment they know you are not here to punish them?' Krah's eerie voice echoed through the chamber. 'They have already had two wars in the time since their division.'

Both siblings stiffened at the dark god's words, Typhonis' fingers biting into Thora's shoulder as he fought to regain composure. His sister gently placed her soft hand on top, understanding flowing through their shared connection.

'I will continue to oversee the passage of souls, guiding them to their rightful places. Even if it means having a foothold in every afterlife I create. Wynlara will not be abandoned.'

Silence filled the room as the others considered Krah's words.

'Magic will always be a part of Emodorea.' Brielle broke through the silence. 'The witches will keep our legacy alive and strong.' Her silver eyes swirled with flecks of red as her lips tightened. 'They shall not falter on their path.'

Though her words were sure, Brielle's uncertainty was evident in her voice. Katinka's eyes flicked to the young goddess. The elder goddess had taken a shine to Brielle when she was still a witch, training her to wield the Sun and Fire elements. The flame on Katinka's fingertips moved to form a glowing crown of light and sparks atop her brow. 'The sun will rise and set, and fire will burn. Our presence will be felt in every ray of light and every spark.'

Despite the few reassurances, tension hung thick in the air. Zadea turned to Kasin, her eyes searching his. 'Kasin, do you truly believe they are ready?'

Kasin stepped closer, his bright blue light mingling with her soft purple glow. His voice was almost a whisper, almost too quiet for the others to hear, as he spoke only to her. 'Zadea, they have your wisdom and my protection. They are ready. But if you have doubts, we can stay awhile longer.'

Their proximity didn't go unnoticed by the others. Thora exchanged a knowing glance with Typhonis, while Brielle's lips curved into a subtle smile. Krah's eyes, however, darkened, and Dagmar reached numbly for his hand.

Zadea sighed, her resolve wavering as she thought of the countless years they had guided and served Emodorea. 'I trust your judgement, Kasin. But leaving them feels like abandoning our children.'

Kasin gently took her hand, his touch reassuring. 'We are not abandoning them. We are giving them the chance to grow.'

With a final, long look down at Emodorea, the Eternals turned their gaze to the cosmos. In silent agreement, they channelled their divine energies, and a new world began to take shape. The throne room filled with brilliant light as they embarked on their next grand adventure, leaving Emodorea to its own devices, yet forever imprinted with their essence. As they departed, Zadea and Kasin lingered for a moment longer, their hands still entwined, a silent promise of their enduring bond.

ACKNOWLEDGMENTS

I began weaving stories as a child, around the age of six or seven, but it wasn't until I was ten or eleven that I truly started writing them down. One of my early school teachers, whom I was fortunate to have for three consecutive years in primary school, introduced me to the epic fantasy books that I cherish today. Their influence profoundly shaped my writing style, genre, and skills. Though they have since passed and will never read this book or receive my gratitude, I will forever be thankful for their impact on my life and my writing journey.

This book series began as a childhood tale called Avalon, where I wrote about myself and three of my best friends as the main characters, as kids often do. As I grew older, the story evolved, but the core idea lingered in my mind, demanding to be written and written well. Now, at 30, I remain friends with just one of those original three. One of the friendships in this book is a tribute to that enduring bond – but I'll leave it to you to guess which one.

First and foremost, I must thank my husband, Chris. Without your unwavering support and hard work, I wouldn't have had the opportunity to study and write as much as I did to bring this first book to life. I am forever grateful for your patience in listening to my endless ramblings, assisting with map layouts, and ensuring my distances and timeframes were spot on. Thank you for enduring the late nights and breakdowns with me.

Secondly, to Danikka, the best editor and friend anyone could ask for. You were the first person I ever trusted with my writing, and your belief in my talent gave me the confidence to share my story with the world. The journey of creating this first book was smooth and wonderful, thanks to you. I look forward to crafting more incredible works together with you and the team at Authors Own.

Thank you to the friends I made in The Secret Writers Guild, a group of talented and amazing writers who welcomed me with open arms. Despite our different time zones and my occasional absence online, I am deeply grateful for all the help and encouragement over the years. Your support has been invaluable in keeping me inspired to write.

Finally, to all my friends and family who supported me in countless ways throughout this journey – thank you. Whether you were beta reading, listening to my ideas, or simply offering words of encouragement, you made this dream feel real and achievable. Your unwavering support means the world to me.

ABOUT THE AUTHOR

Kristie Harris is an epic fantasy author from Queensland, Australia. The spark for the Chronicles of Emodorea first appeared when Kristie was 12, and as the characters grew in her mind, she decided to finally write the story she wanted to read. An avid student, she has a Bachelor of Arts (Creative Writing) and is currently studying a Bachelor of Innovation with Honours. Away from her desk she loves reading, PC gaming, watching anime, and spending time with her husband and kids.

Website: www.talesandtrinkets.com.au
Instagram: www.instagram.com/kmharris.author